Anne Baker trained as a nurse at Birkenhead General Hospital, but after her marriage went to live in Libya and then in Nigeria. She eventually returned to her native Birkenhead where she worked as a Health Visitor for over ten years. She now lives with her husband on a ninety-acre sheep farm in North Wales. Anne Baker's other bestselling Merseyside sagas are all available from Headline and have been highly praised:

'A stirring tale of romance and passion, poverty and ambition' *Liverpool Echo*

'Highly observant writing style . . . a compelling book that you just don't want to put down' *Southport Visiter*

'A gentle tale with all the right ingredients for a heartwarming novel' *Huddersfield Daily Examiner*

'A delightful tale of love and family' *Woman's Realm*

'A truly compelling and sentimental story and rich in language and descriptive prose' *Newcastle Upon Tyne Evening Chronicle*

Liverpool Lies

Anne Baker

HEADLINE

First published in 2000
by HEADLINE BOOK PUBLISHING

First published in paperback in 2000
by HEADLINE BOOK PUBLISHING

10 9 8 7 6 5 4 3 2 1

ISBN 0 7472 6436 8

Printed and bound in France by
Brodard & Taupin

Typeset by CBS, Martlesham Heath, Ipswich, Suffolk

HEADLINE BOOK PUBLISHING
A division of Hodder Headline
338 Euston Road
London NW1 3BH

www.headline.co.uk
www.hodderheadline.com

Liverpool Lies

Chapter One

May, 1941

Charlotte Brinsley turned over in bed, pulling the bedclothes high around her head.

'Lottie, come on. You've got to wake up!'

'Go away,' she gasped. 'Leave me alone.'

She felt fuzzy with sleep and craved more. The Blitz was at its height. Last night had been terrible; the bombers had kept coming over, wave after wave. She'd been working flat out. It couldn't be time to get up yet.

'Lottie . . .' It was her sister Connie's voice. 'Wake up.' She felt the blankets being dragged from her. 'Something awful has happened.'

She forced her eyes open. Her bedroom in the nurses' home swam round her. Her sister's face, anguished and tearstained, was a foot from her own. It brought a stab of fear that woke her fully.

'What is it?' She knew it must be something dreadful for Connie to look like that.

'Crimea Terrace – it was hit last night. A direct hit.'

Lottie could no longer breathe. There was a tight band round her chest. She sat up slowly. This was what they'd both dreaded above all else. Their home bombed, their family . . .

'Are they hurt? Badly?' Her sister's dark eyes stared back at her in distress. 'Dadda? Is he all right? Mam? Jimmy?' Connie kept shaking her head. 'Oh, my God! How d'you know? Are you sure?'

'They've been dug out.'

Lottie knew their family went down to the cellar during raids, thinking it as good as any air-raid shelter. Well, Dadda couldn't get down but everybody else did.

Connie's eyes were glazed with grief. 'They've all been killed. Mam, Dadda and Jimmy.'

'All?' Lottie felt for her sister and pulled her close. Clung to her. She'd heard of this catastrophe happening to others. But now her own family . . .

'How d'you know? Who told you?'

'Police message. Matron told me.'

'What about our Cliff?'

He was the elder of their two brothers. Since he'd turned fourteen he was often out fire-watching during raids.

'I don't know. I've heard nothing about him.' Connie burst into tears. 'He could be all right. I do hope so.'

Lottie leapt out of bed, feeling as though her whole world had collapsed. Her alarm clock told her it was nine-thirty and that she'd had four hours' sleep. She snatched up her dressing gown and strode down the corridor to the bathroom. She was supposed to be on day duty but now, with the air raids, there was an added rota on which nurses were woken in the night when the normally reduced night staff couldn't cope. It fell heavily on those who'd had experience of casualty and theatre work and Lottie had had both.

There had been heavy air raids on the last ten nights, and the day staff had been called out on seven of them when casualties came flooding in. Lottie had worked all yesterday on the ward and had come off duty at eight. She'd fallen into bed and been asleep before nine, only to be woken yet again by the chilling rise and fall of the sirens.

Only half awake, she'd slid into her dressing gown, pushed her feet into shoes, grabbed for her clothes and an old blanket and raced down to the shelters. Scores of other girls were doing the same. As she waited in the crush above the shelter steps, she'd heard the throbbing engines of enemy bombers and seen parachute flares floating in the sky, lighting up the city.

Despite the restless tossing all round her, the nervous whispers and coughs, she'd been asleep in moments. It was midnight when she'd been woken up to help in Casualty. They'd been desperately busy attending to those injured in the bombing.

She'd known her own family was in the same danger; they were all equally so. She'd never allowed herself to think about that, and in any case there wasn't time to think once the bombs started falling. Ambulances kept arriving disgorging patients with dreadful injuries. She'd had to keep her mind on what she was doing.

Last night, Liverpool had had a bad time. She'd heard the *crump crump* of falling bombs and felt the foundations of Walton Hospital shake more than once. Since the beginning of the month there had been little respite. Lottie knew that fires started two nights ago were still blazing. The smell of smoke and burning was acrid in the atmosphere. She'd found the only way to keep panic at bay was to believe it wouldn't touch her or those she loved. Now that it had, she felt icy cold with shock and was beginning to shake.

When she got back to her room Connie was lying across her bed. She was officially on night duty. In many ways that was better because she could bank on being allowed to sleep all day. Lottie started to pull on her clothes, and reached for a pair of slacks.

'Are you sure? That it's them, I mean? There couldn't be a mistake?'

Connie mopped at her eyes. 'It was a police message, how could there be? Mam and Jimmy were crushed, suffocated. Dadda – well, it would have been different for him.'

Dadda had been sleeping in the parlour for two years before the war started, because he could no longer get up and down stairs. At the beginning of the war, Mam had had the electric light put in the cellar, so they could use it as a shelter. It had been black and creepy down there and difficult to see their way down without it.

Lottie had helped to carry down two old beds as well as some easy chairs. But the cellar stairs were even steeper and narrower than those going up to the bedrooms. Cliff had carried Dadda down on his shoulders when the raids first started but after that Dadda had refused to let him do it. He'd said he'd rather stay on his couch in the parlour and if his end came so be it.

That was where Dadda would have been, in the parlour by himself. Lottie clenched her teeth hard as she thought of him being blown to pieces. Mam would have taken Jimmy down the cellar. They'd have been together on one of the beds. Little Jimmy was only nine and he was terrified of raids. Mam always put her arms round him and pulled him close when the bombs started to fall, trying to comfort him. She and Connie sometimes used the other bed, if they happened to be home when a raid started.

Lottie swallowed hard. She felt sick. 'Where – where are they now?'

'Been taken to a makeshift morgue, the church hall in Bodmin Street. There've been so many killed recently. Matron says we can have compassionate leave to see . . . to see to things.'

Lottie felt as though she'd received a kick in the stomach. The all clear had gone just after two but it had been five in the morning when she'd come back here to sleep. She'd had special dispensation to stay in bed until lunch time instead of getting up to go on duty at seven-thirty.

She reached for her navy blazer. 'Shall we go now? We have to be sure it's them.'

'It is, Lottie. I think they've been officially identified – the neighbours, I suppose. We wouldn't have been informed like this if—'

'I have to see for myself. Come on, I'm nearly ready.'

That brought Connie rolling off the bed to stand beside her. She peered over Lottie's shoulder into the dressing-table mirror.

'Don't I look terrible?'

Connie's dark brown eyes were red-rimmed and puffy, her face white and waxy as a candle. Lottie stared at her. Although they were sisters they weren't alike. Connie was both taller and broader; bigger boned. She looked stronger and more mature – well, she should, seeing she was twenty-four already. Lottie had had her twenty-first birthday last month. By comparison, she thought she looked a slip of a girl.

Both sisters had brown hair, though Lottie's was a few shades darker than Connie's. She ran a hasty comb through it. She'd had it cut short with a fringe, and left it to nature to bend where it would, whereas Connie worked hard on hers.

She watched her sister pull her white cap free of the clips that held it in place, and start to unpin her rolled-up hair. It fell to her shoulders in long springy curls that bounced when she walked. Connie had pretty hair.

'I can't be bothered changing.' She snatched off her crumpled and bloodstained apron. Usually the night staff put on clean aprons before going in to dinner. 'I'll come in my uniform. I won't be a minute, I'm going to my room for my gabardine.'

'Then you'll have to put your hair up again too. I'll be down in the kitchen.'

Lottie's mouth was dry, and she craved a cup of tea. She went to see if there was some made, but the kettle was cold and the teapot washed out. It would waste time to make some now. Instead, she drank a glassful of cold water from the tap and shivered. She desperately needed to know for sure.

Lottie knew that buses were rarely able to run to a timetable after a bad raid, because the roads were left full of craters and debris. The sisters tagged on to the queue waiting at the bus stop. Up ahead someone said they'd heard that the bus station had been damaged and some of the buses burned out. Just as they were about to give up and start walking, one came. Everybody crowded on; they had to stand but it was better than walking.

All the way there, Lottie told herself they'd find the bodies were not those of their family, that there'd been some mistake. Easy to make mistakes like that in the aftermath of a bombing. She prayed she would be proved right.

She felt numb as they tiptoed into the hall. Connie's grip was stopping the blood going to her fingers; she could feel her heaving with distress. The bodies were laid out in rows, each covered with a sheet. The number was truly appalling. There were priests of several denominations offering comfort.

Now as she looked down on the faces of her loved ones, laid out on the floor with so many others, Lottie knew her prayer had been fruitless. Mam was here and Jimmy, covered in that dust that always came from gutted buildings.

'Dadda? Where's Dadda?' Connie sounded full of hope. 'Perhaps he's all right.'

'No.' Lottie swallowed and gripped Connie harder. 'No, not if Mam and Jimmy caught it. He'd be up in the parlour. It'd be worse for him.'

They were shown a body bag then, labelled Herbert Edward Brinsley, with their address and other information about Dadda. Hot scalding tears ran down Lottie's face for the first time.

She wept for poor Dadda, who'd been gassed in the Great War and had been unable to do much ever since. War had ruined the last twenty years of his life and now another war had killed him.

She wept for Mam, who'd held the family together. As the district midwife, she'd been the breadwinner. Mam who'd persuaded them both to train as nurses.

'You won't be sorry if you do,' she'd told them. 'It brings its own rewards and you'll never starve. There's always work for nurses.'

Lottie had been close to her little brother Jimmy and grieved particularly for him. Because he was only nine years old, they'd all expected him to be safe. The war would surely be over before he was old enough to be called up. Now his body was crumpled and broken and dead. She clung to Connie, horrified at what she was seeing.

'Where is Cliff?' Connie wept. A search was made through the lists for his name.

'Not here, thank God.'

They'd all been more fearful for Cliff. He was nearly fifteen; in a little over three years he'd be called up to join the forces.

'He'll be devastated. We've got to find him,' Lottie sobbed.

The vestry had been set up as a temporary office. A registrar of births, marriages and deaths was in attendance and so was a firm of undertakers. The girls sat there for a long time, giving particulars and arranging for the funerals.

Wood for making coffins was in short supply; it seemed they were now being made from a mixture of plasterboard, papier mâché and even stout cardboard. They chose the cheapest available because they didn't know how they were going to find the money to pay for it all. They were told that burial grants were available and they filled up the forms they were offered, but even so they were worried about the cost.

Then, feeling sick and disorientated, Lottie found herself out on the pavement in the morning sunshine. It seemed inconceivable that nothing had changed out here. Housewives lining up outside a grocer's shop told them the queue was for chocolate biscuits. A postman whistled as he rode by on his bicycle and a toddler whose pushchair was filled with poultry meal was yelling that he didn't want to walk.

'We've got to find Cliff,' Lottie said. 'He's only a kid.' She felt responsible for him now. 'He'll be feeling awful if he knows.' She felt a rush of anger that the Germans should do this to her family.

'He'll be at home,' Connie said.

'It's gone – blown to bits, but where else can he be? Anyway, I'd like to see it.'

'It'll be awful.' Connie's face was full of dread.

'We've got to look for him. Besides . . .'

Lottie couldn't stay away. She had to see what had happened to Crimea Terrace before the whole place was flattened to make it safe.

'Come on. We're used to seeing bombed buildings and rubble-filled streets. There's plenty of them everywhere.'

But Lottie had to admit this was different. The landmarks were changed so she hardly recognised that which had been so familiar. Connie was hanging on to her, hardly able to look.

'Oh, my God,' Lottie breathed. The devastation in Crimea Terrace was appalling. Part of the roof and some of the upper floors were swinging unsupported, and furniture, fireplaces, woodwork and bricks had fallen to ground level. There was a turmoil of furniture that was almost unrecognisable, mostly in bits. When last she'd seen it, she'd thought the house shabby and much in need of refurbishment.

'We'll do it up when the war's over,' Mam had said many times. 'No point now, even if we could get the paint.'

They'd had broken windows and falling plaster in previous raids, but now the main timbers were swinging loose, and broken slates and glass lay everywhere. The smell of the Blitz was horrible, a mixture of leaking gas, charred wood and cordite with the whiff of fractured sewers. She'd smelled it on casualties being brought in. Here it was strong enough to make her put her hand over her nose.

They'd been brought up in the small house that had stood here since Queen Victoria's reign. Theirs had been the last one in a terrace of twelve, and now only the end wall was standing. Their family had been sheltering in the cellar but that hadn't saved them.

Three nights ago, Lottie had been in the cellar here with her family. She and Connie always spent their days off at home, sleeping there the night before. Lottie's hand went across her mouth as she remembered.

'I changed my day off this week,' she gasped. The thought was hitting her with the force of an explosion. 'Oh, my God! If I hadn't . . . I'd have been here last night.'

Another nurse working on the same ward had wanted today off to meet her boyfriend who was coming home unexpectedly. Lottie hadn't been keen to change. She didn't like taking her day off at the beginning of a week; it meant she could find herself working for almost two weeks without a break. She thought she'd been doing her colleague a big favour.

Goose pimples were running up her arms. If she hadn't been persuaded, she too would have died here last night. It seemed impossible that death could hang on chance like that. Life had never seemed so precarious, so fraught with danger.

'How awful!' Connie's dark eyes were pools of horror. Lottie felt sick. She sat down on a large coping stone that had ended up on the pavement.

Her home had been an anchor to her. A place of retreat from the busy hospital. She'd felt cared for and cherished there, safe and protected. Suddenly she felt very vulnerable.

Through a shimmer of tears, she saw a toy that she'd bought for Jimmy for his last birthday. He'd treasured that red fire engine.

'I'd like to have that.'

She pointed it out to Connie who tried to reach it, struggling through the rubble, but a policeman waved her back because of the danger. An elderly man in ARP uniform retrieved it. Like everything else it was covered with dust, and the red paintwork was scratched, but otherwise it was unharmed. Lottie wanted it as a keepsake.

'There's my wardrobe,' Connie called excitedly to the man. 'Please, please . . .' It was tipped on its side, the mirror on the front was broken and one end had been stove in, but it was still in one piece. He kicked away enough debris to open the door and carried the contents over to them.

Her clothes had been partially protected inside the wardrobe, but everything that survived an air raid got its share of thick grey dust. Pulverised cement and plaster added to dirt and dust that had accumulated under floorboards was expelled with force over everything else. Connie shook off as much as she could, and burst into tears again at being reunited with her best winter hat and coat.

Lottie could see Civil Defence workers still digging into the cellars further up the terrace. She'd known the neighbours who had lived there, they'd been part of her childhood. She clenched her fists in anger that they should all die like this. Old Mr Roper had lived alone at number ten; they were bringing him out now on a stretcher. Connie was hiding her face in her coat, hardly able to watch. An ambulance was waiting and further up the street a WRVS van was dispensing tea.

'There's our Cliff.' Lottie shrieked with joy as she caught sight of his thin lanky figure. She tore up the pavement jumping debris to reach him, glass crunching beneath her feet.

11

He'd been helping to dig Mr Roper out and looked only marginally more alive than the crumpled body on the stretcher. His brown hair was turned to grey by a coating of that awful thick dust. His normally clear skin was grey with it too, though a tear had washed a single furrow down his cheek. Connie was right behind her.

'Are we glad to see you,' she panted. 'We were so afraid you'd been hurt too.'

He relinquished his end of the stretcher to an air raid warden and his sisters each latched on to one of his arms.

'Mam and Dadda,' Lottie said. 'Do you know?' She could see from his face that he did.

'Isn't it dreadful?' he blurted out. 'Little Jimmy too. I had to identify . . .'

'You identified them? Did you see Dadda?'

He pulled a face. 'What was left of him. Ghastly.'

'You poor kid, you're all in. Have you been at it all night long? Working here, digging people out?'

His eyes, usually alert and full of mischief, were red-rimmed pools of despair. Connie put her arms round him. 'You hadn't anywhere else to go?'

Lottie felt another shockwave run through her. Cliff had been made homeless. They all were, really, but she and Connie had their rooms at the hospital. Cliff had nowhere to go. Who would look after him now?

Feeling at a loss, Lottie looked round. Mrs Smith who'd lived next door had always been ready to give a hand but her house had gone too. Probably she was under one of those sheets in the church hall. Lottie could feel herself shaking.

It was a relief to recognise the face of someone she knew

quite well. Mrs Cooper who lived behind them in Sebastopol Terrace was bustling up.

The last time Lottie had seen her, she'd been seated at their kitchen table, a stout figure topped with iron-grey hair. She'd been complaining to her mother about the boys.

'I've seen your Cliff out by himself at all hours,' she said. 'After the siren's gone too. He needs more discipline.'

'He'd be fire-watching,' Mam had returned. 'Civil Defence duties. He's nearly fifteen, you know.'

'Little Jimmy isn't. I saw him out on his bike after dark last night. I know it's hard for you, Marion, when you have to work, but they both need a firmer hand. Jimmy will be as wild as his brother in another year or two.'

Mrs Cooper was sharp-tongued but good-natured. For the past three years, her son Sandy, an officer in the Merchant Navy, had been taking Lottie to the pictures and to dances. Now plump arms tried to stretch round all three of them.

'You poor things, losing your home like this. You must be devastated.'

Connie burst into tears again. 'Our Cliff's got nowhere to go.'

'Come on round to my house, all of you. Our front windows have gone but we're still standing. What a night it's been.' Sebastopol Terrace was two roads further up the hill.

'You can stay with me, Cliff. Have our Sandy's room. If you'll behave yourself.'

'Course I will.'

'He's not wild or anything,' Lottie protested.

'We'd be very grateful.' Connie was drying her eyes. 'Lottie and me, we're all right, but Cliff . . . Can't have him in the nurses' home.'

13

'Wouldn't want to go.' Cliff straightened up. He looked shattered.

'Don't worry, you can stay with me. Our Sandy would want that, him being so keen on you, Lottie.'

Lottie told her how Cliff had been helping dig people out all night.

'Cliff lad, you've been a right hero and you nothing but a stripling. Come on, you need a bath and then you'll want to put your head down and sleep this off. Lottie, have you heard from Sandy? He'll be writing to you as often as he can.'

'I had a letter from him the other day. He was in Ireland.'

'Ugh – I hate to think of him crossing the Atlantic.'

'He'll be in a convoy.'

'Yes, but the U-boats . . .' She sighed. 'I've been expecting him to write saying you two are getting married. I'd be right pleased if he did. When's it to be, then?'

'He hasn't mentioned marriage to me.' Lottie smiled for the first time that day. 'Not yet, but when I write back I'll tell him you're looking forward to having me as a daughter-in-law.'

'Eh, you're just like your mam. Always joking even now when you've lost your home.'

'It's not only our home,' Connie gulped.

'It's losing our family,' Lottie added.

'Yes. Your mam was a real saint. She'd do anything for anybody. You had a happy home. Look, I managed to salvage a few things for you first thing this morning.'

'My school books?' Cliff asked. 'Did you find those? I looked . . . I'd done my geography homework, too. I have to hand it in today.'

'No, lad. Not your books.'

14

They'd reached Sebastopol Terrace. Agnes Cooper led them in through the back yard of Number 4, and put the tin bath hanging on the yard wall inside the wash house.

'There you are, lad. I'll bring you a kettle of hot water and some towels. You'll feel better when you wash some of that dust off.'

'I'll give him a hand,' Connie said, running cold water into a bucket from the outside tap. 'You'll need your hair washing, Cliff. It's grey with that awful stuff.'

Lottie helped him off with his jacket. She hardly recognised his school blazer, it was so torn and impregnated with thick grey dust too. She was afraid it was ruined, like his trousers. She noticed his fingernails were broken and his hands covered with cuts and deep scratches.

'How did you do all this?'

'There was nothing to dig with.' He was almost in tears now. 'Had to get down to Mam . . . fast like, as fast as I could. I thought they might still be breathing . . . but it was no good.'

Lottie shuddered. She thought of Cliff as her little brother. Like her, he looked younger than he was. Not yet fifteen and he'd dug Mam and Jimmy out with his bare hands. Some of the neighbours too, by all accounts. No wonder he was physically and emotionally worn out.

They got him clean and Mrs Cooper found a pair of flannelette pyjamas and some slippers for him. Smelling strongly of TCP, the only antiseptic she could find, which Connie had applied liberally to his cuts and grazes, he let himself be led into the warm kitchen to sit beside the range.

'I've got a pot of tea made. I expect you girls could do with a cup too.'

Lottie was so tired she was beginning to feel dizzy. It was

a relief to sit down in a room that was undamaged and sip at the cup of hot strong tea.

'I can hardly believe it,' Connie groaned. 'The house, the family, all gone.'

'It feels lonely doesn't it? I feel so alone,' Cliff had drained his cup.

Mrs Cooper refilled it. 'Shall I make you a sandwich?'

'Yes, please.'

Connie's face was bleak. 'Out of a family of six, there's just us three left.'

'I'll get a job,' Cliff said. 'I'll earn my own living. I'm old enough.'

Lottie cut in: 'You'll stay on at school, our Cliff. It's what Mam wanted for you.'

He'd won a scholarship to the grammar school and his future looked bright – if only the war would end before he reached the age of eighteen and was called up.

'You can go to school from here,' Mrs Cooper told him. 'Aren't you sitting your Matric next year?'

'S'posed to be.'

'You will be,' Connie said. 'And you'll be staying on to do your Higher.'

'But now . . .?'

'You've got two big sisters,' Lottie told him.

Cliff raised eyes that were heavy with sleep. 'There's Uncle Steve too,' he said. 'We mustn't forget Uncle Steve.'

Chapter Two

Shortly afterwards, Agnes Cooper led Cliff upstairs to Sandy's bedroom. While she was alone with Connie, Lottie said: 'We'll have to make sure our Cliff's all right. Keep an eye on him.'

'Yes, of course. He's not really wild.'

'It's just that Dadda never knew where he was. He was always out.'

'He couldn't control him.'

'But he'll do what Mrs Cooper wants.'

'It's asking a lot,' Connie said. 'A big responsibility for her to take on.'

'I don't like leaving him here by himself. Not now, after what's happened.'

She could see Connie didn't either. 'He hardly knows the Coopers. Not like you.'

'But we've got to. He knows that.'

When Mrs Cooper came down to the kitchen again, she said: 'He couldn't keep his eyes open. Poor Cliff. He did very well to keep going all night. He'll be out for the count now.'

Lottie said: 'We'd be very grateful if you'd let him lodge with you. There's nowhere else.'

'Of course. I've said he can stay here, haven't I?'

'He's only a kid but he won't give you any trouble.'

'And we know he'd be fine here, with you.'

'I'll do my best for him, love. You know that, but there's things you'll have to do. I'll have to have a ration book for him.'

'I'd forgotten the rations. His book would have been in the kitchen drawer . . .'

'You'll have to go down to the Food Office and ask them for another. There's one in Cobham Street next to the library. I hear there's no problem when people are bombed out and lose everything. They'll replace it.'

'We'll do that this morning,' Connie said. 'We'll go straight round when we leave here.'

'We'll pay you for looking after him,' Lottie added.

'It's all right, I could manage . . .'

'It's not fair that you should.'

She'd already discussed with Connie what the funerals were going to cost. It was more than they could afford, but Connie was earning over ten pounds a month with all found as a staff nurse. She could be too very soon, if she passed her finals.

'Would a pound a week be all right?'

'Eh, that would be grand, more than enough. Fifteen shillings. I don't want to make a profit. Not out of the likes of you.'

'We could manage that, thank you. Every month, we'll give you a couple of pounds each from our salary.'

Mrs Cooper looked from her to Connie. 'Your mam would be proud of you. All of you. Sticking together like this.'

'We have to now.'

'Eh, she was a lovely woman. She's brought you up just grand.'

Lottie knew their family hadn't been a normal one. How

18

could it be, when Dadda was incapacitated and Mam had to go to work?

'There's another thing. Have you been down to let her boss know? She'll be wondering why your mam hasn't turned up for work this morning.'

That made Lottie screw up inside. 'We haven't got round to things like that. Not yet.'

'You should. There'll be a bit of money coming for you. Your mam's worked part of this month, hasn't she?'

'So she has. Didn't think of that either. Our Cliff's going to need new school uniform. New everything, come to that.'

'We'd better get on and do it.' Connie stood up and started gathering up her belongings.

Mrs Cooper seemed loath to let them go.

'I've salvaged part of your mother's best tea service. It's in the parlour. Come and see the mess in here. There was glass everywhere. George is coming home early to board this window up.' George was her husband.

She showed them a cardboard box half filled with cups and saucers. 'Not a chip out of these cups. Do you want to take them with you?'

'There's only four.' Lottie could feel a lump the size of a tennis ball in her throat. There had been six in the china cabinet.

Connie stirred. 'We've nowhere to put them. Can't carry anything more, either.'

'Don't worry, I'll look after them till you want them. I'll miss your mother too. Always had a cheery word for everyone, she did. There's more stuff that's hardly damaged. I could see that new piece of carpet you had in the front room but there was too much rubble on it for me to lift, but they'll get everything out before they make the place safe. Can't leave the roof hanging like that. I'll get a cart round there, shall I? George will see to it.'

'That's very kind, but what would we do with it now?'

'If you can't use it there's plenty who can. It can go to the sale room. Bring you a few shillings. You might as well have what you can – it'll be little enough.'

Lottie felt too tired to think about such things. 'Thank you,' she said. 'I've told Cliff we'll be back to see him tonight. We'll all feel better when we've had some sleep.'

They walked to the Food Office, and saw other recent bomb sites near by. They weren't the only ones applying for a replacement ration book. They were issued with an emergency card for Cliff to cover the next two weeks.

'A replacement book will come through the post to his new address,' they were told.

'Can I get extra clothing coupons?' Lottie wanted to know. Clothes were to go on ration for the first time next month. 'I kept a lot of my clothes at home and I've lost them all.'

'Afraid not. You're not entitled to anything extra unless your registered address is bomb-damaged. That's the rule. Your address is given as Walton Hospital, not Crimea Terrace.'

'Just my luck,' Lottie said as they went out into the street again.

'You won't have any money to buy clothes anyway,' Connie consoled her. 'Certainly not more than your ration.'

Lottie insisted on hanging about at the bus stop in the hope that one would turn up to take them back to the hospital. 'We've so much to carry. We're loaded down with your stuff.'

She was wearing Connie's best hat. Like most of Connie's

things it was too big for Lottie and it was too eye-catching for her taste, all artificial flowers on natural straw.

'It's the best way to get it back without crushing it,' Connie had told her. She couldn't wear it herself because she was in uniform and had to wear the regulation gabardine cap.

Mrs Cooper had given them two brown paper carrier bags. Lottie carried one full of shoes, handbags and blouses, and had Connie's best dress draped over her arm.

'We might as well give up and walk,' Connie said, though she was equally burdened. 'If we walk, we can call in the district midwives' place on the way and tell them about Mam. If we don't, we'll have to do it tomorrow.'

'Couldn't we phone?'

Lottie was persuaded to walk, though she felt dead beat and it was an effort to put one foot in front of the other now. Connie still seemed to have plenty of energy.

'When I think of Mam being killed – it's so unfair. She did so much good. She lived for other people.'

Lottie thought of her mother. She'd never known anyone so utterly unselfish and totally honest. Although nobody worked harder, she always seemed to have plenty of time to stop and talk. She had a placid look, almost like a Madonna.

'Don't even think bad things, Lottie,' she used to say.

'She was such a contented person,' Connie murmured. 'She rejoiced in other people's luck. She gave unstintingly to Dadda.'

'And to us.'

'She said that was the way to be happy. "Do the best you can for others, never do anybody down, then you can look the world in the face."'

'She had so many friends.'

Lottie felt her mother had known half the population of Liverpool. Neighbours had come asking for her advice at all hours; about crying babies, sick children, even husbands with back pain. They'd rarely seen a doctor first, but Lottie had never heard Mam refuse to see a sufferer. Mam had collected baby clothes from the more affluent of her patients to hand on to mothers who needed them and she'd always known where a cheap cot or pram might be bought second-hand.

'And what harm did Dadda ever do anybody?' Connie sniffed.

Lottie remembered her father, struggling for breath at the slightest exertion. She'd fetched and carried for him from an early age. She could see him now in her mind's eye, sitting in a chair by the fire peeling potatoes for their dinner. He'd ask her to fetch the saucepan for him, clear away the peelings and wash the potatoes. It was all to help Mam, so the dinner would be ready for her when she came home from work.

She and Connie had often talked about the life Mam led. It seemed impossibly hard, full of work and sacrifice and very little else. Certainly very little money to spend on herself. Lottie had said as much to her once.

She'd smiled and said: 'Your dadda made great sacrifices for all of us. He was gassed in the trenches fighting for his country. That's what ruined his health – ruined his life, too. There's so much he can't do now.'

'Mam, you've sacrificed a lot too. You have to do so much for him. And he can't work.'

'I knew what I was taking on. I nursed him in hospital – that's how we met. It doesn't seem a sacrifice if it's for someone you love, Lottie. It's what I want to do. Doesn't Dadda deserve all the love and help he can get?'

'What Mam would like best,' Connie was blinking back her tears again, 'is for us to live our lives more as she did. We should try to be more like her.'

'I've made up my mind what I'm going to do.' Lottie knew she sounded far fiercer than her mother ever had. 'As soon as I'm qualified I'm going to join up and be an army nurse. I want to see this war brought to an end as soon as possible. I want to do all I can to help.'

'They won't want you.' Connie sounded superior. 'No use applying until you've had at least two years' experience after you've qualified. They only want nurses who know what they're doing.'

Lottie hoisted Connie's dress higher on her arm. 'Then I'll join up as soon as they'll take me.' They'd covered another hundred yards before she said: 'They'd take you now.'

Connie yawned. 'I'm not joining the army. Here we are, this is the clinic Mam worked from. Sister Ogilvie, wasn't it? Her boss?'

They'd heard Mam speak of her and knew she hadn't been fond of her. They found themselves facing a very formidable lady.

Connie told her who they were. 'Our parents and young brother were killed in last night's raid.'

'I'm very sorry to hear that.' For a moment, the frost left Sister Ogilvie's eyes and she showed a glimmer of sympathy.

'We wanted to let you know as soon as we could,' Connie went on. 'You'd have been expecting our mother to come to work this morning.'

'No, she doesn't work on Wednesdays.'

'Yes she does,' Lottie contradicted. 'She works every day and often does a night or two a month as well.'

'Mrs Brinsley, you said? Marion Brinsley of Crimea Terrace?'

'Yes.'

The starch in her apron crackled as she reached for her record books.

'She works part time only. Sixteen hours a week. I asked her to do more but her husband – your father – was an invalid, I believe? She wasn't able to.'

Lottie couldn't believe what she was hearing. She was thoroughly awake now. Connie was still trying to tell Sister Ogilvie she was making a mistake but she wouldn't have it.

'Do you have a death certificate for her?'

Connie took the three from her pocket and peeled off the right one.

'Good. We'll work out her final salary and pay it to her estate.'

'There won't be anything like that,' Lottie said awkwardly. 'Any other money, I mean.'

'Then perhaps if you bring your identity card, and sign for it, we can pay it over to you as next of kin.' She took their address. 'I'll be in touch. Very sorry to hear about Nurse Brinsley. She was highly thought of here.'

Lottie could hardly wait to get outside before she burst out: 'What does she mean, part time? Mam worked all the hours God sent. Didn't she regularly work a few nights every month as well?'

'Two or three nights at a time. And it was every fortnight.' Connie was frowning.

'Then why . . .?'

'She showed me the records in her book. Mam was being paid for only sixteen hours a week.'

'That's impossible. She was always out at work.'

'Surely she couldn't have kept us all on what she earned part time? The whole family?'

'Dadda had a small pension from the army.'

'Next to nothing. No, we'd have starved. What Mam earned would hardly have paid the rent and the coal. I don't understand it. It can't be true.'

'But you say that's what was down in the records,' Lottie said slowly. 'Sixteen hours.'

'It was no good arguing when I could see it written down in black and white. I turned back the page. It looked as though Mam had only ever worked sixteen hours a week. What's bothering me is where did she go if she wasn't working? I mean, she was never in.'

Lottie shook her head. 'Even when we were small, she was never at home.'

'I don't understand it.'

'Nor do I. Why did she tell everybody she was working when she wasn't? And why leave Dadda to do everything if she didn't have to? She told us she hated leaving us all.'

'She must have had another job.'

'If she did, she never mentioned it.'

'She could have taken private cases.'

'She never spoke of doing that.'

'What bothers me,' Connie said, 'is that we thought we knew Mam well, but things might not have been as we supposed.'

'It doesn't make any sense.'

'At least we've done everything we have to now.'

'Except get in touch with Uncle Steve.'

'Oh, him,' Connie said dismissively.

* * *

Lottie followed her sister out of the hospital dining room where they'd eaten spam with cabbage and mashed potatoes followed by rice pudding and prunes. They crossed to the nurses' home and went upstairs to Connie's room.

She had a wireless of her own and was proud of it. She'd saved up for months and their parents had given her money at Christmas to put towards it. She switched it on now to hear Alvar Lidell reading the one o'clock news. Lottie threw herself on Connie's bed to listen. He was telling the country that Liverpool had had very heavy raids for the last ten nights.

'Much property has been destroyed. Some areas of the city have been without electricity and telephones over the last few days and ships have been sunk in the river.'

Connie said: 'It doesn't sound so bad when he reads it out like that. He's so smooth.'

'It's all being played down. There's no mention of roads being blocked with rubble and buses burned out.'

'He did say public transport was disrupted.'

'It's in a chaotic state. The Luftwaffe's been coming over night after night since the beginning of May. We get bombed with high explosives, incendiaries and land mines. Everything's disrupted and it's caused terrible loss of life, quite apart from our family.' Lottie couldn't stop. 'And he's made no mention of the fires that have been raging along the docks for days or of the large number of homeless who were directed to a rest centre which received a direct hit only hours later.'

Connie sighed. 'I heard those stories too from the casualties coming in. Just think of being bombed twice in one night.'

Lottie felt a growing anger. 'It doesn't bear thinking about.'

26

Connie carried on stowing the clothes she'd salvaged into her cupboard. 'It's safeguarding the country's morale, that's why it isn't on the news.'

Lottie turned on her. 'It's all right for you, you've still got all your clothes. And you're not exactly homeless.'

Connie sat down on the bottom of her bed. 'Neither are you.'

They'd seen plenty who were, sitting on dusty chairs salvaged from their homes, their belongings rolled up beside them, waiting to have rest centre accommodation found for them. 'But our Cliff is.'

Lottie sighed. 'At least he's not in a rest centre. He'll be all right with the Coopers. We've got to look on the bright side.'

'There is no bright side,' Connie wailed. 'We've lost our parents and our little brother – oh, and just about everything else. And there's so many things we have to see to.'

'We still have each other,' Lottie said. 'And I'm very glad of that.' She meant it. Having Connie gave her somebody to cling to. She'd understood what Cliff meant when he said he felt so alone. Even though she considered herself grown up, having parents and a home were a prop and a support, the very underpinnings of life as she'd known it. Now all that had suddenly gone. Lottie felt she was floundering and Connie seemed to be floundering more than she was.

'You're right, we have each other.' She came to lie down beside Lottie. 'We're tired now. We'll feel better when we've had a sleep.'

Lottie had not felt fully awake for most of the morning. She'd been fuzzy and in a state half removed from reality. Now when she could sleep, she felt wide awake.

'There's just Uncle Steve to tell. He'll want to know.'

Connie grunted: 'How do we do that, Lottie?'

'I've been wondering that myself. We don't have his address.'

'I certainly don't. You know him better than I do.'

'Don't say things like that. This is no time to be . . .' She'd always thought Connie unaccountably prickly about Uncle Steve.

He always provided generous gifts for Christmas. He took them to pantomimes and lavished treats on them for birthdays.

'It's true you know him better. He makes a big fuss of you.'

'No more fuss than he makes of Cliff and Jimmy.'

'Don't let's start that again. You all see more of him than I do. Where does he live? Do you know?'

Lottie tried to think. 'Not exactly.'

'He never came to see us at home and he never took us to his house, did he?'

'He lives on the Wirral, I remember Mam saying that. And that he was her brother and he and Dadda didn't get on.'

'Dadda stayed at home when Uncle Steve took us out.'

'He was never well enough to come to theatres and things. He'd have been struggling for breath in a crowd. He wouldn't have enjoyed it.'

Lottie looked at the gold watch she wore. It had been a twenty-first birthday gift from Uncle Steve only last month. An expensive watch with a seconds hand with which she could time pulses on the ward. And he'd taken them out to a restaurant for dinner.

Mother liked them all to write thank you notes afterwards. They'd always had to do that. Lottie had asked for his address, but Mam had said she'd see Uncle Steve got her note.

'He didn't give me a gold watch for my twenty-first,' Connie complained.

'He gave you something. And you had a birthday treat.'

'He took us all for a trip in his car.'

'You chose where we went.'

'It was as much a treat for Mam and you lot, as it was for me.'

'It's a treat for you when it's Cliff's birthday or mine.'

'He forgot all about my twenty-fourth.'

'No, you had that handbag. The brown leather one.'

'I think he forgot. I'm sure Mam bought that for me. She started to say something about choosing it and then tried to cover up. And he didn't take us out.'

'Mam said he was away on holiday. She took us to the Empire and we saw George Formby. For heaven's sake, Connie.'

Lottie was tired of hearing her sister complain that Uncle Steve left her out. She'd been on about that for years.

'He was always taking photographs of us all. There were as many of you as there were of the rest of us.'

They'd been all over the house in handsome frames. Now they were all gone. Lottie heard a gentle snore and realised Connie had fallen asleep.

How silly, she thought, to go on about Uncle Steve like this. Any mention of him always made Connie irritable, whereas she'd thought him great fun and so had her brothers. He was always in such a good mood and ready to indulge them in any way he could. Much more than Dadda ever did.

'It's because your Dadda can't do it,' Mam had explained.

'Uncle Steve tries to compensate. He wants us all to enjoy life and be happy.'

The fact remained, however, that neither of them knew his address. It would be no good asking Cliff, he wasn't likely to know either, which meant they couldn't get in touch with him. Mam probably had it written down in her address book but that had gone for good now.

Lottie got up slowly and went down to her own room. There was no comfort in sharing Connie's single bed now she was ready to sleep. She set her alarm for half past six. They could have supper before going to see Cliff. She felt sorry for him, and they had to take his emergency ration card to Mrs Cooper. It was awful having to leave him there at a time like this.

When Lottie's alarm went off, it didn't seem such a good idea to get up and go out. She felt more like staying where she was and going back to sleep until tomorrow morning. She knew she wouldn't be asked to work tonight however hard pushed they were on Casualty, but when the sirens sounded they all had to get up and go to the shelter in the grounds. That was a strict rule they all had to obey.

It was the thought of Cliff feeling lonely and grieving for their parents that made her get dressed. Still heavy-eyed with sleep she went up to Connie's room. She was up and dressed and combing her hair. They went to the hospital dining room for supper first.

It was a long walk to Sebastopol Terrace, and when they got there Mrs Cooper told them Cliff hadn't stirred since he'd gone to bed.

'Went up to see but he was flat out. Thought it better to

leave him. You go up and look now, Lottie. I've saved some dinner for him if he wants it.'

Lottie opened the bedroom door quietly and looked down at her brother. He had brown hair, a lighter brown than hers and somewhat straighter; he was more like her than Connie. Tonight he looked so young and vulnerable it made her want to protect him from the heavy knocks life was throwing at him. He was breathing deeply and evenly and was at peace. It seemed pointless to wake him. She went downstairs to report.

Connie said: 'Sleep is probably what he needs most. Leave him be.'

'I'll have to wake him when the siren goes. There's room for him in our shelter, don't worry about that, and I'll not let him go fire-watching tonight.'

'You'll make sure he goes to school in the morning?' Connie asked.

'I will that.'

'We might as well go, then.'

'Before you do, come and see what's in our back yard.'

Lottie recognised the copper pot that had held Mam's aspidistra. It was a little dented and the plant had gone. Seeing the detritus of her home brought another lump to her throat. There was Mam's armchair, its new coating of dust making it shabbier than ever; there were a couple of small tables and some dining chairs. Over the line was the carpet square that Mam had bought recently for their parlour. That too was impregnated with grey dust.

'I give it a couple of bangs every time I come out,' Agnes told her. 'I'll get it better before it goes to the sale room.'

Connie, too, wanted to escape. 'You're very kind to go to

all this trouble for us. We'll be off. We want to be back before the siren goes.'

'It's going earlier and earlier. I hope we aren't in for another bad night.'

Lottie put her arm through her sister's and hurried her down the street.

'We needn't have come,' Connie said. 'Tomorrow would have been all right for the ration card.'

'I didn't want Cliff to feel we'd abandoned him.'

'This all looks so different . . .'

The bulk of Crimea Terrace had gone. Workmen were just packing up now that daylight was fading. The roof had disappeared altogether. Slates had been collected in huge piles. The end wall was down. Their house had virtually been wiped off the map.

Lottie's eye was caught by a lone figure standing with his toes against the building line. He wore a grey suit with a smart trilby covering most of his silver hair, but his head was bent, his whole body personifying grief.

'That's Uncle Steve,' she exclaimed in surprise.

Loosening her arm from Connie's she ran to him. Close to, he seemed to have aged in the short time since she'd seen him. The sight of his face shocked her. He was in tears. Such tears – his face was wet with them, and he wasn't bothering to wipe them away. Agonised grey eyes looked into hers.

'Charlotte? It is you?'

'Yes, yes.' His arms went round her in a hug of relief.

Hope trembled in his voice. 'Your mother, she's all right?'

'No, I'm sorry. No, a direct hit. She was killed. And Dadda. They didn't stand a chance.'

She saw his face fall. 'Oh, God!'

Connie said: 'We wanted to tell you but didn't know how to get in touch.'

That made him freeze, and then his body was racked with sobs.

'Last night was very bad. I was afraid – when she didn't turn up this morning – that something like this . . . Marion was always so reliable. Always there when she'd said she'd be.'

Lottie's mind registered that this explained where Mam went on Wednesdays, and no doubt all the other times when they thought she was out working.

It was Connie who asked: 'Did Mam work for you?'

Lottie saw the confusion on his face. 'Yes.' He stepped forward to kiss Connie's cheek. Lottie noticed he did it with less warmth than he'd shown her. It made her feel confused too.

'Mam didn't tell us. We thought she was out visiting her midwifery cases – working.'

'She was, much of the time.'

'What did she do for you?' Lottie wanted to know.

'The boys? They're all right?' The look in his eyes told her he was praying they were.

'Cliff is. Jimmy was at home – I'm afraid no.'

'Jimmy gone too?' He looked devastated. Lottie tried to put a comforting arm round him. For a man he was short and slightly built, but he was too tall for her. Her arm went round his waist.

'It's awful, isn't it?' Connie said. 'Unbelievable that this time yesterday everything was normal.'

'Jimmy! Poor little Jimmy.' Uncle Steve collapsed on the same coping stone that Lottie had sat on that morning. His head was in his hands. 'I can't believe . . .'

He was clearly very shocked. Lottie hadn't realised how close the bond was between him and her mother. Connie was telling him about Cliff, that he'd dug Mam and Jimmy out of the cellar, that they'd arranged for him to lodge with a neighbour. They walked him round to Sebastopol Terrace and showed him the house.

'He's asleep now. We've just come from here. No point in waking him.'

Uncle Steve looked up at the terraced house of smoke-blackened brick.

'We'll find something better.'

'It's the best place.' Lottie told him Mam had been friendly with Agnes Cooper.

'Agnes Cooper? Yes, I believe I've heard her mention the name.'

Connie told him about Lottie's friendship with Sandy Cooper.

'We've known the family a long time,' Lottie said. 'Cliff had less contact than me and Mam, but he'll be well looked after there.'

'Perhaps for the short term.'

Lottie was no longer at ease. 'We ought to be getting back to the hospital. The siren went about nine last night and the buses aren't running. We had to walk here. I don't like being caught out in a raid.'

'I can drop you off. Only got the van, though.' He nodded towards a vehicle parked some distance away. Lottie couldn't believe he was apologising for having only that to transport them.

'The van will be fine. Thank you. Much better than

walking.' As they got closer, she could read the lettering on the side. *Lancelyn's Loaf, Liverpool's Best Bread.*

'You work for Lancelyn's?' She vaguely remembered hearing he worked in a bakery. Lancelyn's bread was sold all over the district. It was a very well known Merseyside firm.

He nodded towards the van. 'It belongs to my business.'

'Your business?' Connie asked. 'Your own? Lancelyn's?'

'Yes.'

'Mam never said.'

Mam had been keeping a lot of things from them. Things were not as they'd supposed. Lottie knew Mam's maiden name wasn't Lancelyn. It had been – yes, Tennant, that was it.

As Uncle Steve drew up at the hospital gates, she said: 'I thought your name was Tennant.'

'No, where did you get that idea? I'm Steven Lancelyn.'

'I don't understand. How is it then . . .?'

'I'm sorry. Such a terrible shock, hardly know what I've been saying. I'm very upset. Some other time.'

His eyes were glassy, his lips set in a stiff straight line. He looked barely in control of his emotions.

Chapter Three

'What d'you make of that?' Connie demanded as he drove away from the hospital gates.

Darkness had fallen but it promised to be another bright moonlit night. Lottie hung on to Connie's arm as they walked up the path to the nurses' home.

'Nothing is as we supposed.' Lottie's stomach was churning. 'Mam was working for Uncle Steve?'

'Why didn't she tell us? Why pretend she had a full-time job as a district midwife? It doesn't make sense.'

Lottie pulled her to a stop. 'It does if . . .'

'If what?'

'If Uncle Steve was her lover, not her brother.'

'Don't be daft. Mam wasn't like that. Anyway, she's too old. She wouldn't be interested.'

'She said he was her brother – but I don't think that's true. The name's wrong. And he was embarrassed, didn't want to tell us anything.'

They let themselves into the home. Lottie went to her sister's room.

'Why didn't Mam tell us he owned Lancelyn's bread? Everybody's heard of it.'

'We always had Lancelyn's bread at home,' Connie said. 'Mam used to bring it. You'd think she'd be proud it belonged to her brother.'

'If he was her brother.'

'He was very upset . . .'

'We're all upset.' Lottie felt like crying. 'And this isn't making me feel any better.'

'The neighbours thought Mam was wonderful. Nothing was too much trouble. She was never too tired to care.'

Lottie shook her head. 'I wonder. I mean, did we know what she really was like? What we saw – well, it was all a sham. A show she put on. To hide—'

'Lottie – she's just been killed. That's a terrible thing to say. Even to think.'

She knew it was, and got up quickly. 'I'm going to bed.'

'The siren will go in a few minutes. We could go straight down to the shelter and bag a good spot.'

'I'm going to have a hot bath and go to bed. Good night.'

'Perhaps things will look different in the morning.'

Lottie didn't see how they could.

Everybody expected the heavy raids to continue; there was no reason to suppose they would stop before the war was won. The first bombs had fallen on Liverpool at the end of July 1940. The bombing had continued, sometimes heavy and sometimes spasmodic, through the rest of that year and throughout the spring of this, but the first nights of May had brought their heaviest bombardment ever.

By the tenth, when Crimea Terrace was hit, it seemed the Luftwaffe was gaining the upper hand; that the people in the city wouldn't be able to stand much more.

Lottie was woken the next morning by the noise of the day staff getting ready to go on duty. It surprised her to find the air raid siren hadn't wailed its warning during the night. She wasn't going to get up this morning until she'd had her sleep out. She lay curled up, neither asleep nor awake, thinking about her family.

She hadn't known them all inside out and back to front as she'd thought. Family relationships were very strange things. It wasn't the closeness of the blood relationship that counted. It was loving the people and sharing their lives, understanding their problems and their hopes. She could sympathise with Dadda because she'd seen him struggle to get his breath, struggle to get a hot meal on the table for them all. And most of all because he'd put his arms round her so often as a child. He'd been a source of comfort and support to her all her life. That's what really counted.

It was ten o'clock when Connie came in with a cup of tea for her.

'I feel terrible,' she said, sitting on the end of Lottie's bed. 'The funeral hanging over us and now all this strange business of Uncle Steve and Mam.'

All that was in Lottie's mind too, as well as the loss of Dadda and Jimmy. 'Life seemed so normal before.'

'Could Mam have hidden what she was doing? For years on end?'

'If she did, she was even better at organising things than we thought. Must have been.'

'She was living a lie. All pretence. It wasn't real.'

'All this is supposition,' Lottie said. 'We have to find out for certain, one way or the other.'

'How are we going to do that?'

'Ask him. Ask Uncle Steve.'

'What, outright? We can't just say, was our mother your mistress!'

Lottie retorted: 'I can.'

'You do it then. What if we're wrong? If we are, I'd be ashamed. For him to know we'd been thinking such things about Mam.'

'We can't be wrong,' Lottie insisted. 'Something's been going on that we knew nothing about.'

'What are you going to do this morning?'

Lottie closed her eyes and swallowed hard. She wished she could go home to see how Dadda was. It was what she'd often done on a morning off. If he was having a good day, she took him out. If not, perhaps they'd play chess. This last year he'd had an oxygen cylinder in the parlour to help him breathe and he'd grown a little afraid of being away from it.

She said: 'Revise. I've got to make a start. My finals are coming up next month.'

'You'll never be able to get down to it now. Don't you feel all adrift? Get the funeral over and you'll be able to concentrate. Why don't we find the address of Lancelyn's bread factory and take a look at it? It'll be in the phone book.'

Lottie jumped at it. 'Why don't we? A little detective work on Uncle Steve, eh? Yes, there's a lot more I'd like to know about him.'

The phone book told them there were two Lancelyn factories making bread; one in Birkenhead and the other in Old Swan which wasn't very far away.

'Let's go to Old Swan,' Connie suggested.

'Yes, let's.' Lottie was out of bed and getting dressed.

They were lucky enough to catch a bus that took them to the gates. They stared up at the huge building in wonder. Lottie didn't know what she'd expected, but it wasn't this.

'It's an enormous place.'

'Surely he doesn't own all this?' Connie's eyes were wide with surprise. 'He must be a rich man.'

'That makes it all right then? For Mam to do what she did?'

'No, of course not. It smells heavenly, doesn't it? Baking bread. You can smell it out here in the street.'

'For a mile around too, I should think.'

'It's making me feel hungry,' Connie said.

As they watched, vans kept going through the gates and round the back; there was a steady stream of them coming out too. There were large vans and smaller ones, all painted cream; the logo Lancelyn's Loaf, Liverpool's Best Bread written on the side of each one. They walked to the end of the building and from there they could see a loading bay with bread being loaded into the vans. There were workmen about but no sign of Uncle Steve.

Lottie said: 'We want to get this straightened out, don't we? Why don't we go inside and ask to see Uncle Steve now? Get to the bottom of it.'

Connie was kicking the kerb. 'Dare we?'

'Of course we dare. Come on.'

Lottie thought Connie was dragging her feet, pushing her ahead to get the embarrassing questions asked before she showed her face. It was just like Connie to back off when something had to be done. Lottie felt her heart pounding, but she was quite prepared to do the asking. She needed to know.

Inside, Steve Lancelyn dragged himself upstairs to the office floor. The corridor off which the offices opened was a gallery from which he could look down on the factory floor below.

He went slowly past half-empty offices. The one that had been the accountant's was occupied by a junior accounts clerk. That which had once housed the production manager was no longer used. He passed the larger rooms for clerks and typists, not that he had many of those left either. The narrow slit of a room where they made tea was the only place that seemed busy. His own office was at the end of the row. He paused outside it to get his breath and look down on the clanking machinery and white-clad bakers attending it. He was keeping the place going, all was well.

He mopped at his forehead. However short of fuel the country might be, he always received a generous consignment. Temperature and humidity had to be carefully controlled within the bakery to ensure the yeast remained active.

The heat was getting to him today. This morning, two people had already asked him if he was all right. He felt terrible and couldn't think, couldn't work, couldn't do anything.

He had to be on his own for a few minutes to pull himself together. He slammed the door of his office as he went in and collapsed at his desk. He'd always looked upon this as his sanctuary, a place of calm away from the noise and bustle of the factory floor.

He closed his eyes in misery. God, how he missed her! Why, why, why, did Crimea Terrace have to receive a direct hit? If the bomb had fallen just a few yards away; if it had killed Herbert and just injured Marion and little Jimmy – injured them ever so slightly, not enough to give them any pain. Then things could have been very different.

He felt swamped with memories. It eased the pain to let his mind fill with thoughts of Marion. Let it fill – that was a silly way to put it. He hadn't been able to get her out of his mind. Not since it had happened.

He'd always thought her the most beautiful woman he'd ever seen, with her bright red hair and womanly body. The heavy breasts, narrow waist and long slim legs. But it wasn't just her looks. Marion had a warmth about her. She'd been interested in everybody and everything; brimming with vigour and enthusiasm. Even asleep in bed, she tossed about and often flung her arms round him. He couldn't imagine her stilled for ever.

He'd been able to unload his worries about the business on her. He talked to her incessantly about the difficulties caused by the shortages of ingredients and of fuel for his delivery vans. She'd eased him into all the changes the government were insisting on.

He'd been cutting down on his fancy breads since the war started; he'd had to because he hadn't been able to get the ultra-fine flour he needed, that had come mainly from America. The bloomer had had to go, and the French stick.

He used to make a huge number of buns and teacakes and Sally Lunns. He still made a few when he could get the dried fruit, dried milk powder and fat they needed.

It had come as a shock to find there was to be a national loaf. It seemed like bureaucracy gone mad for government to dictate a national recipe for bread. His father, who had owned a small bakery in Heswall and baked bread for the village at the turn of the century, would have turned in his grave if he'd been forced by law to add chalk to his bread.

'It's a sensible move,' Marion had retorted. 'I'm all in favour. The ration of dairy produce doesn't give the population enough calcium in their diet. To put it in bread will prevent a general deficiency. Think of it as calcium. That's what you're putting in.'

'It'll make it taste funny. Nobody will eat it.'

'We've got to eat it, there's nothing else. I don't think it will alter the taste.'

It didn't much, but home-grown wheat wasn't being ground as finely as it used to be; much more of the husk was left on to provide a greater bulk of flour. The government laid down rules about that too. The national loaf was neither white nor brown, but rather greyish in colour, and could be gritty and lumpy in texture. Heaven only knew why it turned out like that but it did, and his customers had to get used to it.

He made it in two shapes, cob or tin, but it was exactly the same mixture. The only consolation was that all bakeries were in the same boat. Like everything else in wartime, the national loaf sold well. People had to eat.

Marion had felt guilty about what she was doing, he knew that. He'd been consumed with guilt, still was. Their secret drew them closer. They couldn't talk about how they lived to anybody else. It had put them outside normal society. He'd lived for her, tried to show her how much he appreciated what she'd given up to be with him. But it had had to be like that.

It bothered him that she'd had to leave the children with Herbert. He'd wanted the best for them too.

'Herbert loves the children,' she'd smiled, though he knew she'd ached at what she was doing. 'He'd be lost without them.'

'But leaving them with an invalid? What can he do for them?' It would be almost impossible for him to do anything.

'They make his life.' He'd thought her sad that they were not making hers. 'They'll grow up fast. Does them no harm to have a little responsibility early in life.'

They'd talked about their plans for the children many times. He thought about them a good deal and wished he could see more of them. They could do nothing while Herbert was alive, so they'd waited, while the children grew up.

Never had he foreseen this. Herbert had seemed barely alive for years, and now suddenly he was dead, but so was his Marion and what was he to tell the children? How was he to tell them? He was afraid the story would alienate them and he mustn't do that. He wanted them on his side.

He wished he could think it through and make a decision, but he couldn't. His head was a torrent of heaving emotions.

He thought he heard a tap on his door. He almost called out to them to go away. It came again, louder. A clerk put his head round.

'Two young ladies asking to see you, sir. They say you know them. The Misses Brinsley.'

Steve's head swam as he stood up. Oh no, he wasn't ready. What could he say?

The next moment, Charlotte was pecking him on the cheek. It was what she usually did when they met. Her kiss lacked its usual warmth. Connie kept her distance. He tried to smile at her but her dark eyes looked nervously away. They seemed ill at ease too.

He had to give some explanation now. It was clear to them both that their mother hadn't been working all the hours she'd said she was. Not as a midwife. He found another chair so they could both sit down. Rang for some tea. Tried to appear his usual self.

'How nice of you to come and see me. I wanted to ask you to, Cliff as well, so I could show you round.'

45

He knew that wasn't why they'd come. He was afraid it was to ask about his relationship with their mother. Yet he wanted this out in the open. The trouble was, it had been a secret so long, something that must never be mentioned, he found it hard to talk about it now. Particularly to them.

He'd never seen Charlotte so tense. She looked as if she was screwing herself up to do something difficult, something that was important to her, though she was talking about Cliff.

'He needs to settle down. He's sitting his Matric next year.'

Steve tried to fix his mind on Cliff. 'Poor lad, this couldn't have come at a worse time for him. Having to get down to study now.'

'We're both in the same boat,' Charlotte said. 'My finals are coming up next month.'

He'd forgotten that. He hadn't had so much contact with Charlotte. She was older and the sort who always coped with everything. It didn't seem the right thing to say to her now. Instead, he said: 'I've been thinking. Boarding school would probably be the best thing for Cliff. I'll see if I can get him a sixth form place for September.'

'Boarding school?' Connie looked astounded. 'Nobody from Crimea Terrace goes to boarding school! We all felt he was doing very well to get to the grammar.'

He'd wanted his children to have a reasonable education. He'd missed out on that, but he'd wanted it for them. He'd persuaded Marion to make sure Charlotte and Cliff were entered for the scholarship exam. Fortunately, they'd both passed. If they hadn't, he'd have wanted to pay for them, but that would have meant awkward explanations for Marion about where the money was coming from.

He knew Connie was very conscious that her general

education had fallen somewhat shorter than theirs. Marion had said she kept bringing it up. She'd reminded Connie that as she'd managed to pass the entrance test to get into nursing school it didn't seem to have done her any harm.

Steve caught Charlotte's anxious look and came back to the present. 'Cliff's lost his home and his mother. He's bound to feel . . . Boarding school is the best answer under the circumstances. It'll get him right away in a different environment.'

Charlotte said coldly: 'We arranged for him to lodge with Mrs Cooper – for as long as there's need.'

'What about paying her?'

'We're going to give her a couple of pounds each out of our pay each month.'

He said: 'You can leave any payments to me. I'll see to that.'

'Thank you,' Connie said stiffly. 'It's a weight off our minds, with the cost of the funerals and everything.'

He dropped his head in his hands. 'I'm sorry, I haven't been thinking straight. I should have known they'd have to be paid for. I'll see to those too.'

They thanked him with formality, hardly knowing what to say to such generosity.

Steve thought he saw Connie nudge her sister, and guessed she was urging her to put something else to him. Charlotte wouldn't look at him now. He saw her take a deep breath.

'Uncle Steve, were you Mam's brother?'

The tea arrived at that moment. It gave him time to think, but he was no closer to handling this properly when they were alone again.

He heard himself say: 'You're both grown up and Herbert,

47

poor devil, is dead, so you might as well know the truth.'

He saw them exchange looks of alarm. He was afraid this wasn't the right way to go about it.

'I was not your mother's brother. Neither was she working for me in the usual sense, though she helped me a lot with the business.'

He thought of Marion, ached for her and for what he was about to tell her children. Connie was like her in appearance except that she had a 'don't dare touch me' look about her. Charlotte had more of her mother's manner.

He looked her square in the face. 'I loved your mother,' he said simply and sincerely. That gave it a certain dignity. He wasn't going to belittle what Marion had given him. He saw Connie swing her foot towards her sister.

'Tell us,' Charlotte urged. 'We want to know. This has come as another shock, on top . . .'

'I know. Your mother and I . . . We'd have liked to tell you, but with Herbert alive, we couldn't. It was loyalty that tied your mother to him. She told me many times that he wouldn't be able to cope without her. She wouldn't leave him, so this was the only way.'

Charlotte was gathering confidence. She had eyes the colour of tawny wine, and now they bore into his. 'Are you telling us she was your mistress?'

That was a word he'd hoped to avoid. It nearly floored him. 'I didn't think of her as that. She was just the woman I've loved for most of my life.'

'Most of your life?'

Connie was staring at him in horror. 'This has been going on for a long time, hasn't it? How long?'

'Years and years, I can't remember.' Why was he being so

damned coy about that? He should have . . .

She burst out: 'Where was she when she wasn't with us? Here at your works, with you?'

'No, I bought a house nearby, in the next street. Close enough for me to slip in and out several times a day to see her.'

Charlotte looked astounded. 'Mam had two homes then?'

'I suppose you could say that, yes.'

He caught Connie's stricken look. 'And what did she do there all day?'

'She usually cooked a lunch for us. Shopped for it.'

Connie's mouth opened wider. 'Just for you two?'

He tried not to cringe. He was thinking of Herbert left with all four of the children. He was afraid the girls were too.

'I'll take you round to see it . . .'

There was no mistaking Connie's look of loathing this time.

'No, thank you. We need to get back.'

'Some other time.' Charlotte was on her feet, backing towards the door.

He'd upset them and it was the last thing he'd wanted. 'Tomorrow then? I'll take you there tomorrow.'

'I don't think we can face any more just yet.' Charlotte's usual friendliness was gone. 'It's all hurtful, upsetting. Horrible.'

'After the funeral,' Connie told him.

'We'll go to that together,' he said. 'I'll pick you up at the gates on Wednesday. Two o'clock.'

Charlotte nodded, looking grim. 'Thank you.'

When the door closed behind them, he sank back in his chair and closed his eyes in misery. He hadn't told them one half of what he should. They were shocked already. They couldn't have taken more, but he wished he'd got it off his chest.

Connie strode blindly downstairs.

Lottie was trying to keep up with her. She said: 'It's no good getting agitated about it. We wanted to know and now we do. At least it stops us wondering.'

'Agitated? I'm furious. It isn't possible! Can't be.'

'It is.' Lottie took her by the arm, hurrying her out into the street. It had started to rain.

'How are we going to tell Cliff about Mam and him?'

'Tell him the truth. We've all had a basin full of keeping things under wraps.'

Connie said: 'I wouldn't know where to start. He's only a kid. He thought a lot of Mam.'

'We all did. Anyway, he's sure to ask. He'll be just as curious as we were. Come on, hurry up, we're going to get soaked.'

'Everybody admired Mam. Looked up to her because she worked so hard. All the time it was a tissue of lies; she was another man's mistress. We were all living on his money. Mam didn't work for it. She was sitting around in her second home, preparing lunch for him instead of looking after us.'

Connie was choking with anger. From a tot she'd had to run herself ragged helping Dadda about the house.

'It's up to you to look after Lottie,' Mam had told her many times. 'Dadda can't run round after her so I'm making you responsible for your sister.'

As the eldest, she'd had to look after all of them in turn, she'd had to mop floors, set the table and run to the shops. She'd been a drudge all her childhood. There'd been jobs she'd had to do in the house that had stopped her going out to play with her friends. Mam had battened on her. In fact, Mam had battened on them all.

Connie couldn't stop. 'All the time we thought she was at work, she was relaxing with her lover, enjoying herself.'

'Not all the time,' Lottie put in. They'd reached the bus stop. 'We're in luck, here's a bus coming.'

'No doubt Mam enjoyed every comfort with him. Day in and day out. She was indulging herself while I had to do her work for her.'

'We all pulled our weight, Connie.'

'It means Mam didn't care about us or Dadda.'

'I wouldn't say that.'

'I was looking after the house and all you lot and getting meals ready for when she came home. I'm absolutely brassed off to find that all the time Mam was indulging in her private pleasures.' Connie snorted with rage and glared out of the window as the bus slowly passed scenes of tremendous devastation. 'I feel she used me. Put on me.'

Yet Mam was the last person she'd thought capable of being another man's mistress. She hadn't dressed to attract attention. Quite the reverse – if anything she'd dressed too plainly. Connie had thought she looked rather drab.

Mam had had red hair, but over the years it had faded and become laced with grey. She'd worn it taken back severely under her midwife's cap. It had sat on her collar in a tight hard roll.

Connie had seen it swinging loose at night, curling over as though it couldn't wait to be wound back and pinned in place. But Mam must have been quite pretty when she was young. Connie could see her now in her mind's eye. Her face had

51

been pleasant enough, though it could have been much improved with the use of cosmetics. Like Lottie, Mam had believed soap and water was enough.

Connie really couldn't see why any man should want to make her his mistress. Certainly not a rich man like Steven Lancelyn. He could have had anybody.

Not that she'd ever liked him. She hadn't been taken in by the presents he'd showered on them. Not like Lottie and Cliff. Connie felt put out all day.

When it was time for Cliff to come out of school, Lottie wanted to go to Sebastopol Terrace to see him.

'Better not say too much about Mam and Uncle Steve,' Connie warned. 'We don't want to upset him.'

'We'll tell him he's going to boarding school though. Uncle Steve will think it odd if we don't.'

They found Cliff hadn't been to school after all.

'I thought it better not to rush him back,' Mrs Cooper told them. 'It's been a shock for him. He needs to stay quiet for a while. Soon enough after the funeral.'

Cliff looked pale and tired. He seemed switched off and hardly able to believe he might be going to boarding school. That worried Lottie. Mrs Cooper made a pot of tea and gave them bread and marge with plum jam.

'Don't you eat too much,' she told Cliff. 'There'll be a meat tea at six.' That was when her husband came home from work.

'He's taking it hard,' she whispered as she saw them out. 'But he's bound to, having dug his mam out. He'll feel better when the funeral's over.'

'We all will,' Connie agreed.

Chapter Four

The day of the funeral was warm and sunny. Not at all the sort of weather for a funeral. Lottie was dreading it; it was like a wall standing between her and normal life. She and Connie sat about in their dressing gowns for half the morning trying not to think about it.

She knew her sister was as downcast and jumpy as she was but Connie's way of dealing with the misery was to talk at length about what they should wear.

'It doesn't matter,' Lottie told her half a dozen times. 'I shall wear my navy blazer, it's all I've got anyway.' It helped that she had no choice.

'But which skirt will you wear with it? You've only got that red one. You can't wear that. I'll lend you my navy one. Come on, try it on.'

Connie wouldn't let her rest, she had to do it there and then. The skirt was loose round her waist and hips and kept twisting round. It was also too long and made her feel a frump. Connie had half the contents of her wardrobe draped over the end of her bed.

'It'll be warm this afternoon. I think I'll wear this black and white dress.' She was keen on clothes and made many of them herself.

'You'll look very smart.' Lottie thought Connie's outfits

more suited to a wedding than to a funeral.

'But what about a hat?' Connie rummaged in her clothes cupboard until she found a white straw hat with lots of velvet pansies round the brim.

'If I take them off, it'll look just right.' She eyed Lottie's dark head. 'I've got that navy beret you could wear.'

'I don't need a hat.' She didn't care what she wore. What she looked like would make no difference to how she felt.

At two o'clock they walked down to the hospital gates to meet Uncle Steve, who had promised to pick them up in his car. Lottie had enjoyed his company in the past, but he'd told them lies, hidden the truth, and she didn't feel as friendly as she had.

He came on time, looking as though he hadn't slept for a week. His dark suit and black tie were smart. She'd always thought him a handsome man compared to Dadda. He had a full head of thick silver hair and he'd laughed a lot when he'd taken them out for birthday treats. Now he looked woebegone, ill even.

His car was large and comfortable and they'd ridden in it before. He drove first to Sebastopol Terrace to pick up Cliff and Mrs Cooper. She had told them in her kind fashion: 'I'll find a suit for Cliff. Our Sandy's got things in his wardrobe he's grown out of.'

The suit Cliff was wearing was not a good fit. He was thin and wiry and Sandy fairly well built.

Connie whispered: 'He looks like a refugee in that.'

'So do I in this,' Lottie returned. She'd worn the navy beret because Connie thought a hat essential.

Cliff moved slowly like a zombie. He had a bandage round

the knuckles on his right hand, but the other grazes on his hands were healing.

Lottie had not been to a funeral before and didn't know what to expect, but it wasn't that they'd virtually have the church to themselves. At the last minute, Sister Ogilvie led in a group of midwives and district nurses in full uniform.

The sight of the three plain coffins ranged side by side at the front brought a lump to Lottie's throat. Jimmy's looked pathetically small. She tried to think of her parents and her little brother as they'd been in life. They'd not been an ordinary family, but she thought they'd been happy together.

It was a brief ceremony taken by the curate. Just a few stock phrases in praise of people he hadn't known, who were departing to a better world. All rather hurried, almost as though they were on a conveyor belt. A reminder that there were many more waiting to be buried as a result of the Blitz.

Then out in the sunny churchyard to the grave. Lottie shivered even though the sun was warm on her back, as she watched first Dadda's coffin, then Mam's and finally little Jimmy's being lowered into the earth. The mourners were gathering for the next funeral as they trooped out of the churchyard.

They stood in an awkward group blocking the pavement. Connie had been sobbing openly and Cliff's eyes were wet. Lottie was struggling to hold back her tears and couldn't help but notice that both Cliff and Uncle Steve had large white handkerchiefs screwed up in their hands on which they kept blowing their noses. This was a perfectly horrible afternoon for them all. She wanted it over and done with.

Cliff's face was paper white and he looked totally switched

off. She saw Uncle Steve put a comforting arm round his shaking shoulders.

'Come on, m'son. We're lonely and lost without your mam. I know just how you feel. I can't take her place but I'll do my best for you.'

The word 'son' riveted Lottie's attention. Had he said 'my son?' It hadn't occurred to her until now that Uncle Steve could be Cliff's real father. Connie's dark eyes met hers, and she knew Connie was thinking the same.

'You're not alone, son, you've still got me and your sisters.'

Uncle Steve was looking even worse than Cliff; his eyes were tormented and his skin looked grey. He was suffering, Lottie could see it in the lines on his face and the dejected look about his mouth. He was knotting with grief just as they were.

He said: 'We might feel better if we had a cup of tea. There's a Kardomah café just down the road. Shall we go there?'

He included Mrs Cooper in this invitation, but she wanted to go home to prepare her husband's tea so they left her at the bus stop.

Uncle Steve was urging Cliff down the road with an arm round his shoulders. Lottie couldn't take her eyes from them as she walked behind, clinging to Connie. Once inside the café, Uncle Steve led them to a table in the window. He blew his nose again and surreptitiously wiped his eyes. She couldn't help but feel sorry for him.

Connie choked out: 'I need to make myself presentable first,' and set off in the direction of the ladies' cloakroom.

Lottie watched her go. 'Me too. We won't be long.'

Connie was splashing cold water on her face when she went in. Her eyes were puffy and her nose red. She said with half-suppressed rage: 'Did you hear what he called our Cliff? My son! I think he really meant it.'

Lottie thought it too horrible to contemplate. 'He said "son" but lots of people say that to young lads. Agnes Cooper does all the time.'

'My son, is what he said,' Connie insisted.

'Could have been just a slip of the tongue.'

'It slipped out all right. But what if it's true? He's taking over all responsibility for him. He's willing to pay for him to go to boarding school.'

'He did sound fatherly,' Lottie had to admit. 'But why didn't he tell us the other day? When we were asking.'

Connie turned on her, her face twisting with irritation. 'You thought you'd got to the bottom of everything, but you haven't.'

Lottie said slowly: 'If Cliff is his son, then what about Jimmy? He could be too.'

'That's horrible, disgusting. I can't believe it. He's some sort of satyr. He's so old, too, and who would have thought Mam was like that? Ask him, Lottie. Let's clear it up this time.'

They went back to the table hand in hand. Lottie felt the ground was being cut away from under her feet; she needed to cling to Connie.

Cliff was sitting with hunched shoulders staring out of the window. 'I want us all to stay together. I don't want to be sent away by myself. Not far away.'

'We've talked about a Liverpool school, Cliff. But you'd be safer in the country.' Uncle Steve's large hand was covering Cliff's. 'Most boarding schools have been evacuated to safer areas anyway.'

'But I don't need to board. I can live at—'

'Not on your own,' Uncle Steve cut in quickly. 'Not yet, you're too young. I've written to one or two schools. We'll have to wait to find out if they've a place for you. I'll let you know as soon as there's definite news.'

Lottie held her breath. It sounded as though they'd discussed this several times; as if Cliff was on closer terms with Uncle Steve than they were.

'Cliff will be all right in Sebastopol Terrace,' she said firmly. 'With the Coopers. It's the best place for him now. We've arranged it, it's all fixed.'

Uncle Steve's grey eyes came to rest on her. 'Cliff will stay with Mrs Cooper until the end of this school term and he's sat his exams. He can walk to school from there.'

'He can lodge there for as long as he needs to. There's no need for him to change schools. You don't want to move, do you, Cliff?'

'I don't really know what I want.' He pushed his straight brown hair back from his forehead.

'Boarding school would be better after that,' Uncle Steve went on. 'Different surroundings. It takes the place of home and parents for all the boys. Cliff won't have to see the bomb site that's Crimea Terrace every day. I've already had a word with Mrs Cooper – she understands and is quite agreeable.'

Lottie was full of resentment. 'Cliff? What do you want?'

She and Connie had made what they thought were satisfactory plans for their brother and now Uncle Steve was changing everything without consulting them.

Cliff was blinking in distress. 'I think perhaps Uncle Steve . . .'

The waitress brought their tea at that moment. Scones had

been ordered for them as well.

'A pathetic funeral.' Uncle Steve changed the subject. 'Cheap, fast, not the way I'd have wished to say goodbye to your mother.'

'We thought it was all we could afford,' Lottie said pointedly, helping herself to a scone and spreading it with the nondescript red jam. There was a long uncomfortable silence; she couldn't look at the others.

Connie reached for the tea pot and started to fill their cups.

'Uncle Steve.' Lottie had to know for certain. 'Is Cliff your son?'

She saw him start, saw the rush of water to his eyes again.

'You called him "my son". Is that what he is?'

Cliff was stirring his tea, the spoon going endlessly round and round. He was staring at his cup, asking no questions.

'Yes,' Steve said at last. 'I wish there was some other way to tell you.'

To hear it said openly like that made Lottie draw in a long slow breath. It would be unbelievable if it wasn't for the solid wall of guilt and embarrassment he was projecting.

'And Jimmy?' she pressed.

He was nodding apologetically. It almost made Lottie feel sorry for him.

'Cliff's fifteen soon. All those years?' She found it hard to believe. It had been going on all the time she'd been growing up.

'Longer than that,' he sighed again. 'I'm your father too, Charlotte. You were named after my mother. Charlotte Mary.'

She hadn't even thought of that! It caught her unawares. Bile was rising in her throat. Uncle Steve was her father! Mr Steven Lancelyn of Lancelyn's bread?

They'd all stopped eating. Connie said: 'This is awful.'

He was speaking again, sounding a long way away.

'Sorry to give you a shock like this, Charlotte. But it's only right you should know now. You've lost your mother and part of your family, but you still have a father. I want you to know you still have a father.'

Connie felt on fire. She'd been right all along. Unbelievable though it was, Uncle Steve had been Mam's lover and of the four of them, she was the only one he hadn't fathered. She should have trusted her instincts and not believed Mam.

She knew she remembered more about their parents than Lottie and Cliff. After all, she was three years older. One long ago Christmas, Uncle Steve had been going to take them to see Mother Goose at the Empire. All that day, Lottie and Cliff talked about nothing else. They were excited and unruly, brimming with anticipation. Dadda had been resigned.

Connie had never enjoyed these outings as much as the others. When Uncle Steve put his arms round the four of them, she felt that in some way he'd have preferred to exclude her. She'd even mentioned it to Mam, who had assured her she was imagining it. It made her prickly and envious of Lottie. Everybody seemed to like Lottie better. She resented Uncle Steve, while the other three seemed to see him as their own private Santa Claus. They spoke of him in glowing tones, they loved him.

She never had done, and she was sure Dadda never had either. They'd got it right. Looking at Steve Lancelyn's thick white hair, she hated him now. Without him they would have been a normal family. Mam would have been home more of the time. Mam wouldn't have had to leave the others in her care. Connie had hated looking after them; they never did what she told them, they were not her responsibility.

But she was forgetting Dadda couldn't work. Nothing would have made them a normal family.

Lottie felt physically sick. The afternoon was turning into a nightmare. She wanted to get away from Uncle Steve and knew Connie felt the same. He kept talking.

'There's a lot I need to explain. I'd like you to be part of my life. We had such hopes for our children, Marion and I. I bought a house for her – in her name, I mean. In Brightland Street. Onc never knows what's going to happen in this life and I wanted her to have some security. Come and see it. Shall we all go now?'

Lottie felt herself cringe. She had to get away from him. 'No . . .'

'No, we're all too upset today. Let's leave it for a day or two.'

'When can you come?'

It was Connie who agreed that Sunday afternoon would be the best time. 'We don't have to go back to work until Monday.'

'All right. I'll pick you up at the hospital gates after lunch.'

He looked at Cliff who was still switched off. 'Will you keep me company this evening? Or would you rather go back to Sebastopol Terrace for a meat tea? None of us could stay with you. We can't expect Mrs Cooper to feed the whole family on your rations.'

Cliff wouldn't look at his sisters. 'I'm not hungry now. I'd rather come with you.'

Lottie was cross with him. She didn't want Cliff to visit

this house without her and Connie. She wished they hadn't refused to go, but was too full of resentment to tell Uncle Steve she'd changed her mind.

To make matters worse, he was trying to be kind and friendly. He insisted on running them back to the hospital. Lottie would have preferred to walk. She hated saying goodbye to Cliff and leaving them together.

When they reached the nurses' home, dance music was blaring out of the sitting room. She wasn't in the mood for that. She wasn't in a good mood at all.

'Come up to my room,' she said to Connie.

'I knew,' Connie fumed from two steps behind her on the stairs. 'I always felt left out. I kept telling you he made more fuss of you lot. I'm not his child.'

'The only one of us four!' Lottie marvelled.

'I always thought he looked at Mam with more than a brother's eye.'

'No you didn't! You've just thought of that now.'

Once in her room, Lottie felt like a caged tiger. She kept pacing the four steps to the window and the four steps back to the door. Connie had thrown herself full length on her bed.

'My father! How can I think of him as that? He can't just step into Dadda's shoes.'

'Can you believe it of Mam? We all thought her an angel.'

'She was always telling us about her patients, little anecdotes. You'd have thought they were her whole life.'

Connie shook her head. 'It was just a cover. That job was just a cover. All the time she was carrying on with him. A lover. For years and years.'

'I bet he seduced her.'

'Of course he did – he took advantage of her. And he's

rich! Mam was so careful with money. Made us careful too, as though she didn't think there'd be enough till the end of the month.'

'Part of her cover,' Lottie said. 'She couldn't let us see she had plenty. It was his money we were living on.'

Connie shook her head. 'Yes, he must have given her money. He's very upset.'

'So he should be. He's been a husband to her. More of a husband than Dadda by the sound of things.'

'Did Dadda know, do you think?' Connie looked horrified at the thought.

Lottie considered that. 'No, I think Dadda believed he was Mam's brother too. He spoke of him as though he did. I hope he did.'

'She wouldn't leave Dadda. That's what Uncle Steve said. That's the one good thing in her favour.'

Lottie felt overcome. 'It doesn't seem right. I'd have sworn that Mam loved Dadda. She seemed devoted to him; always at us to be good and not cause him any trouble, always reminding us to be kind to him. And all the time she had a lover!'

'I'd have thought her far too old for that.' Connie pulled a face. 'I mean she'd have been forty-nine next birthday.'

'But only twenty-seven when I was born.'

'I just can't see her having a lover. And going to the lengths she did to spend so much time with him. Mother and sex! It's unbelievable.'

'Poor Dadda,' Lottie said. 'This going on behind his back for all those years. I always felt sorry for him. Now, I want to cry for the life he had.'

'Fighting for his country did that to him.'

'Dadda was a true hero.'

'I'm disgusted with Uncle Steve – and I'm not going to call him that any more. He's no relation.'

'No relation to you, Connie. He says he's my father.'

Connie caught at her arm. 'We aren't real sisters! Only half . . .'

It was a frightening thought. Everything they'd believed in was turning out to be false.

Lottie said: 'We won't let that make any difference. Full sisters or half sisters. We've always been friends, haven't we?'

'Sort of friends.' Sometimes they'd fought like cat and dog. 'No wonder we don't look alike. I always thought that was strange.'

'We aren't alike in any way.'

'Yet you and Cliff are. And Jimmy – there's a family resemblance there.'

'Are we like . . . him, Uncle Steve?'

Connie was staring into her face. 'Yes, I can see a likeness. He's slight and . . .'

'Dadda was slight.'

'Dadda was ill. A chronic invalid. He'd have looked different if he'd kept his health.'

Lottie said: 'I wish our house hadn't been bombed. Then we wouldn't know any of this. I feel as though the whole world's turned upside down.'

That night, Lottie curled up in bed screwing the blankets round her as tight as she could. To think of Steven Lancelyn as her father brought a rush of repugnance. How then must she think of Dadda? As far as she was concerned, he was her father and she wanted no other. She wept again for Dadda.

Family relationships were not as straightforward as people tried to make out. Dadda had always been part of her life, more a part of it than Mam. When he struggled for breath she'd suffered too, wanting to ease things for him.

As a toddler, he'd been both mother and father to her. He'd looked after her while Mam was out. And once Connie started school, there'd been just the two of them together all day.

'Now be a good girl for Dadda,' Mam had said every morning before she set out. 'Remember he can't run round after you. You must help him. He'll tell me tonight whether you've behaved yourself.'

Lottie had known that if Dadda gave a good report of her she'd be rewarded with a caramel or a fruit drop after dinner. If he did not, it would be withheld while the rest of the family enjoyed them. She'd struggle all day to receive that treat.

Connie used to take herself to school, but it was only two streets away. Lottie could see it from her bedroom window and she and Dadda could hear the children when they were let out at playtime. She liked to go upstairs and try to pick Connie out among the ever-moving throng in the school yard. Dadda was nervous for her.

'Be careful on the stairs, Lottie. I can't pick you up if you fall.' Lottie was always ultra-careful; she'd never fallen there.

When she was very young, Connie had seemed like a second mother to her. Being three years older made a big difference. Mam would say: 'See you do what Connie tells you. She'll look after you.'

Connie had been primed for authority. She'd developed just the right tone of voice to call upstairs: 'Lottie, what are you doing up there by yourself? I hope you aren't making a mess. Come down so Dadda can see you.'

Lottie had thought Connie would make a tyrant of a ward sister when the time came, but somehow nowadays she seemed to be losing her dictatorial manner. She didn't push herself forward any more.

Dadda hadn't been too ill in those early days. He'd been able to read little stories to them without losing his breath. On Saturdays and Sundays if Mam was at work he'd look after all four of them. He'd play Ludo and Snakes and Ladders and Tiddlywinks with them and organise card games. They were all expert at card games.

She'd seen him nurse Cliff and Jimmy as babies too, and bring them up through the toddler stage. Poor Dadda, she could see him now in her mind's eye, looking limp and ill, with a concave chest. His skin always had a greyish-yellow tinge, and what there was of his thin, wispy hair was a darker grey. His eyes too were grey and there was resignation in them. Always he was wheezing and struggling to get his breath. He said he felt as though he was suffocating.

Life had dealt him some very bad cards, but he was accepting of it. To Lottie, he seemed to have the attitude of a dog who lies on his back with his legs in the air. An attitude of complete submission to all the ills life could throw at him. He'd grown worse as the years had gone on. She knew now she was a nurse that it was emphysema and he never would get better.

But though he was submissive he had a lively mind. Lottie couldn't forget that he'd taught her to read and write before she started school. He'd taught her some rudimentary arithmetic too. He did the same for Cliff and Jimmy; it had given them all a good start.

Lottie had thought hers a very caring family. When Dadda

no longer had enough breath to walk around on the ground floor, Mam had had an old Windsor armchair adapted for him. She had a carpenter cut a little off the legs and extra big castors added, so he could roll about on that. It had taken much less effort for dadda to give a push with his foot than to get up and walk.

He soon became adept at scooting from the fireside to the table and then out to the kitchen to see to things out there. Dadda learned to twirl it round and would do it to make them laugh.

Lottie had made a cushion in her sewing lessons at school. It was covered in lime green cotton, and all the time she'd been sewing it she'd thought how nice it would look against the green velvet of the sofa in the parlour.

But Connie had put her down. 'Your sewing isn't up to much, and it's a vile colour. It clashes with the green velvet. Mam won't want it. It isn't big enough or thick enough to give any comfort. It's rather a mean cushion.'

Lottie was disappointed until Dadda put it on the seat of his chair.

'Just the job, Lottie. I'm much more comfortable now.' She was proud that he used it every day.

Uncle Steve never came to the house but he managed to affect their lives there. Every summer, he took them to Ainsdale beach and bought them buckets and spades to dig in the sand. Afterwards they used them to carry in coal from the shed in the back yard, because a full coal scuttle was too heavy for them to manage.

One Christmas before the war, several years before, he gave them a wireless.

'Why is it called a wireless?' Cliff wanted to know. 'It's got wires coming out of it.'

'That's just the aerial,' Dadda told them.

The wires went up to the picture rail and then all round the room. Mam said the sound that came out of it had a good tone. It was a big box covered in black leatherette with gleaming chromium fittings round the speakers. It stood on the end of their sideboard and transformed their lives.

Dadda could tune in the programmes better than anybody else. He was fond of military bands and soon had Cliff marching up and down with a very straight back and Mam's umbrella in place of a rifle.

'Playing at soldiers,' he called it. Now, looking back, Lottie hoped it didn't foreshadow Cliff's future.

Connie had taught her to waltz and quickstep to dance music from the wireless. They took the dining chairs away from the table to make space on the living room floor. Lottie had loved that.

They'd played musical bumps with Jimmy, all dropping to sit on the lino when Dadda turned the wireless off. It had been great fun. When Dadda no longer had the breath to read to them, they listened to stories and plays on the wireless too.

Lottie couldn't stop thinking about Dadda. He'd helped her with her school homework. When she'd found it difficult to answer questions on *A Midsummer Night's Dream*, he'd read the play through and told her Shakespeare was wasted on the young. He'd been able to explain it to her and she'd called him her private tutor after that.

'I enjoyed it,' he'd told her. 'I'm getting an education at last.'

Dadda had loved to read. It was just about the only thing he could do with ease. Lottie often changed his library books for him. He told her that of all the family she chose the books that appealed to him most. She came to understand that his tastes were so wide she could hardly choose a subject he wouldn't like. He loved to read about war, particularly the Great War. He liked biography and most sorts of non-fiction, but he also read novels avidly, whodunits and crime.

At the hospital, she saved the reading matter that patients were throwing out. Dadda was grateful for anything. He read all the Sunday papers on Monday or Tuesday. He liked Lilliput and Reader's Digest and Picture Post. She pushed Connie and her friends into saving magazines for him too.

She'd been working at the hospital for six months when she learned from a patient who was wheelchair-bound that he hired it from the Red Cross. Lottie thought a proper wheelchair would be more comfortable for Dadda, and she'd be able to take him out in it.

Dadda had been housebound for almost ten years because he couldn't walk more than a few steps without getting breathless. To see him fighting for breath frightened them all. He spent a lot of time at the parlour window staring out into the street.

With this in mind, Lottie had taken a good look round the house. The front door opened straight out of the parlour, and there were two steps down to the street, quite big ones. But she reckoned the kitchen was wide enough for her to manoeuvre a wheelchair through and then there was just one shallow step down to the back yard. From there it was level into the street. She was a bit concerned that after all this time Dadda might not want to go out so she said nothing to him or her family. She just hired a wheelchair for a week and took it home. His face lit up when he saw it. He was thrilled.

'It's my day off tomorrow,' Lottie told him. 'I'll take you out in it.'

As she carefully negotiated it down the street for the first time he was excited.

'Just look at that, Lottie,' he kept saying as they passed shop windows. 'Isn't it wonderful to be out in the fresh air?'

She pushed him round their nearest Woolworth store and he was able to queue for his own stick of shaving soap. She found it hard to believe that something so ordinary to her could provide him with such joy.

After that, she'd taken him occasionally to the Dog and Gun, a recently built roadhouse designed to attract motorists. It was some distance away, but the only pub where she could push the wheelchair through the door without having to negotiate steps.

They had to go at eleven in the morning, soon after it opened, because the smell of cigarettes got on his chest. Lottie wondered why he could enjoy the smell of beer while tobacco smoke made him gasp and cough.

To see the look on Dadda's face the first time he looked round the pub lounge was a treat. It was all imitation black beams and copper kettles.

'It has to be the lounge for you,' she told him, moving a stool so she could push his chair to a glass-topped table. 'I could see wreaths of blue smoke still clinging to the ceiling in the public bar.'

'Ladies aren't allowed in the public bar,' he wheezed. 'So it has to be the lounge for you too.' When he had his breath back, he said: 'Really, I shouldn't let you come in here. Young ladies shouldn't frequent pubs.'

'I'll be safe enough with my dadda,' she smiled.

'I hope I'm not leading you astray.'

She always bought half a pint of bitter for him and a lemonade for herself.

'I've been before. That's how I knew there were no steps.'

'What?' He was quite shocked. 'Who's brought you in here?'

'Sandy Cooper.'

'Good lord! And I thought he was a nice lad.'

'He is. Things change, Dadda. These days I'm not the only girl to come to places like this.'

'You are at the moment,' he pointed out.

'And you're the only man. We're too early for the crowds.'

Back at home, Dadda said: 'You've given me a new lease of life, Lottie. I've seen nothing but these four walls for years and now suddenly I can get out in the world again.'

He enjoyed the wheelchair so much that Mam paid for it to be kept on permanent rent. Cliff started taking him out too when he wasn't at school. Everybody took him when they went shopping. Dadda loved it. He'd return sharing his wheelchair with bags of potatoes and other groceries. Even Connie pushed him to the park on fine afternoons.

Lottie had felt closer to Dadda than anybody else. They'd shared so much. It had been wonderful to watch his face light up like a child's at sights everybody else took for granted. She'd thought of him as her father for twenty-one years and she couldn't change now. She still felt raw that she'd lost him. He'd left a great gaping hole in her life. Uncle Steve couldn't just step into his shoes.

Chapter Five

Steven Lancelyn had spent the last few nights in the house in Brightland Street. He knew he was wallowing in grief by coming here and it was the wrong thing to do. He would have liked the strength to stay away, to get on with his life and his work, but he hadn't. He couldn't banish Marion from his mind.

Here in this house he felt close to her. She'd chosen most of the furniture and the decorations; her personality was stamped on the place. He still felt the door could open at any minute and she'd come in smiling as she had so often in the past.

Last night he'd tossed and turned for hours. He could no longer sleep in the bed they used to share. This morning, he'd got up feeling old and discouraged. He was sixty-two, due to retire in another three years. He'd made himself some tea. He could almost imagine Marion sleeping on upstairs, though that was not what she'd ever done.

He walked to the factory in the cool of a summer morning. Inside, the moist heat enveloped him but he was used to heat, and it comforted his stiffness and all his vague arthritic aches and pains.

He felt better here surrounded by his busy white-clad employees. He stood by the prove box watching the dough now fully risen in the tins being carried on the belt to the latest travelling ovens he'd installed just before the war started. The same belt took the tins through the ovens taking around half an hour. By the time the bread rolled out at the other end it was beautifully brown and thoroughly cooked. There was no guess work here as there'd been in the old days. The temperature of the oven was set always to the exact degree and the process timed to the last second.

The scent of bread was intense here, so powerful that it impregnated the clothes they wore. The loaves were cooling on racks. He'd bought a slicing machine of constantly moving knives, but it had been idle this last year or so. He couldn't slice the national wartime loaf. Wax paper for wrapping it was no longer obtainable.

He picked out a loaf at random and sliced it in half. The crumb was an unattractive greyish colour, slightly mottled with darker specs. He'd heard that the amount of wheat in the flour was to be cut again. His bread would get darker.

By now he was hungry, and he ate a whole slice without butter or marmalade. It was still warm and it tasted as good as any loaf made to the national recipe could. Now he had something in his stomach, he felt he'd had his breakfast.

He climbed the stairs to his office. Miss Langford, his secretary, was near retirement age too. She'd left a pile of mail on his desk. He tried to concentrate; most of these letters needed an answer. He felt tired. He was often exhausted by the long hours he worked, but he couldn't contemplate early retirement, not with the present workforce. These days, all the young men were in uniform or working in munitions factories. He had to provide most of the daily bread consumed on Merseyside with the help of youngsters just out of school and old men past retirement age. And now he didn't even have Marion's help.

She'd been part of his life for the last twenty-two years. Ever since he'd advertised for a nurse to set up and run a first aid post in his factory.

He'd felt the tug of attraction from the moment she'd walked into his office. She'd told him a little of her circumstances, that she needed regular hours of work so she could care for her little daughter and invalid husband. He felt sorry for her, a young woman with so many family responsibilities.

She didn't have the right experience or qualifications to run a factory first aid post. She was a midwife, but he gave her the job anyway. He wanted to help her and he wanted to see more of her and that seemed the obvious way. He'd paid her over the odds. It was the only time he'd ever put the needs of an employee above the needs of his business.

Not that her lack of experience had mattered. The needs of a first aid post were well documented and Marion had coped well. He'd hardly changed what she'd set up to this day. It didn't take him long to realise he was spending a lot of time in his first aid post.

'More time than you spend in your own office,' Marion had laughed. 'People are noticing.'

He'd had to move fast. A few days later he was negotiating for the house in Brightland Street; that had seemed a very daring thing to do. It shocked him when, within weeks, Marion was pregnant and he'd had to advertise for another nurse to take her place. That had been a weight on his conscience, yet he'd gone on and it had happened again and again.

Steve got up with a sigh and went over to the window. He would have liked to take Charlotte into the business when she left school but Marion had been against it.

'She doesn't know you own Lancelyn's bread. I might just have mentioned at home that you worked there, but don't you see? It would make it harder for us if she came. It would be impossible to hide that I'm around so much.'

It was one of the difficulties of a liaison like theirs that it had to be kept hidden from so many. Marion had wanted to keep him and her family apart as long as Herbert was alive. He could understand that. Marion was a caring person. She cared about everyone, and she owed loyalty to Herbert.

Connie was already training to be a nurse, Charlotte had wanted to follow her and that was that. By then he'd had sons, and public opinion considered them better than daughters for running a business. He'd been delighted when Cliff was born, and he'd always had great hopes for him – he'd had great hopes for Jimmy too but now he had only one son. It was only right that Cliff should have the best chances in life he could provide.

Cliff was a lad after his own heart. He felt closer to him than he did to Lottie or Jimmy. There was a liveliness about him; he had his mother's enthusiasm for everything and that included bread-making.

He'd talked to Marion many times about taking Cliff into his business. He'd asked her to broach the subject with him, just as a possibility. He thought it best to leave such things to her.

Cliff had shown interest. Steve had done his best to fan the flame and now he had reason to hope that when he'd finished his schooling he'd come and learn the business. Steve was impatient for it. Without Marion he needed Cliff, but three more years at school would be in the boy's interest.

Education was more important than it had been in his day.

Everything had changed now. Herbert couldn't be hurt any more and he still had Cliff. That was the main reason he'd decided to tell Charlotte and Connie what had been going on. Not that he could have kept it hidden. Too much had leaked out since Marion had been killed. No amount of subterfuge on his part could have covered it.

Staring down into the yard where the vans were being loaded with fresh bread, he had another idea. Charlotte might like to come and work for him now she knew the truth. No reason why she shouldn't; there'd be work enough in the business for both his children. It was what he craved now above everything else.

Marion had been everything to him while she was alive; she'd had to come first, but he'd always wanted to see more of their children, to know them better. She'd said Charlotte picked up things very quickly.

When Marion was killed, he'd thought the house in Brightland Street would be superfluous, but it needn't be. Their children could use it. Charlotte could live in it. What could be more appropriate? When Cliff came to work for him too, there would be a home waiting for him. If he could persuade Charlotte to forsake nursing now, Cliff could live there with her instead of going to boarding school.

Steve felt the first ray of hope for the future. Their children were the future – he must think of them. They had nobody else to look after their interests. It would be up to him.

He'd have liked to discuss all this with Marion, see what she thought about it. She always knew the best way to go about things. He hadn't gone the right way about telling Charlotte. He didn't know how he was going to cope with showing the house to her and Connie. He'd ask Mrs Cooper to keep Cliff out of the way while he did. He needed to concentrate on the girls. He wanted them on his side but he was afraid he'd upset them more if he wasn't careful.

He was overcome again by the magnitude of his loss, and felt like crying. He didn't think he could manage without Marion.

On Sunday afternoon, as they walked down to the main gates of the hospital, Connie said to her sister: 'You aren't nearly so keen on Uncle Steve as you were. You and the boys, you used to think the sun shone out of his eyes.'

'Cliff still does, but I don't like all the lies . . .'

'You wouldn't listen to me. I was right all along.'

'Okay, Connie, you were right about him. But he's got a lot more to explain. We might as well hear the full story.'

'And see the house. He hinted it would be ours now. Think of that, Lottie – we'd own a house between us.'

'I don't want to see where Mam spent her time,' Lottie retorted. 'The less I know about the place the better. I want to put all this behind me. I want to remember Mam as we thought she was.'

'But to own a house. Think of the security of owning a share of a house. Of course you want to see it.'

'I don't.'

'He's here waiting for us. Don't be tetchy with him.'

'Of course I won't.' She let Connie sit beside Uncle Steve in the front. She could stay quiet on the back seat without giving offence. He looked more his normal self.

'Right, we're going to Brightland Street. Do you know it?'

A silly question, Lottie thought. Of course they didn't, he

and Mam hadn't wanted them to know.

She asked: 'Aren't we going to collect Cliff first?'

'No, he's already seen the house the other day. He didn't want to wait.'

'I should have thought he'd want to come again. Just to be with us.'

'No, he said he has other things to do.'

'What else is there to do on a Sunday afternoon?'

Lottie was afraid Uncle Steve had been talking Cliff round to his way of thinking. She should never have given him the opportunity of taking Cliff to this house on his own. She wanted to know what he'd said to her brother.

'I took him round the factory too. Explained the whole set-up to him. He was interested.'

She was taken aback. 'Is he all right?'

'He's much better. Seems to be accepting . . . Cliff's strong, he's got both feet on the ground. He'll be all right.'

He was turning his head towards Connie. Lottie knew what she'd be thinking, that they both knew their brother better than he did. Uncle Steve couldn't tell them anything they didn't know about Cliff. He pulled up in a street of terraced houses.

Connie asked: 'This is it?'

'It was what your mother wanted. She chose it. It's very close to the factory, just a few steps from the end of the road, in fact you can see it.'

From the outside, Number 6 Brightland Street didn't look very different from the houses in Crimea Terrace. It had an extra storey so it would be bigger inside and it had a bit of polish about it; a well holystoned doorstep, ultra-clean nets at the windows. Uncle Steve kept talking; he seemed no more at ease in their company than they were in his.

'Four bedrooms though we never did very much with two of them. We had a new kitchen built out in the yard at the back to give us a bit more room, and a new bathroom built above that.'

Connie was on her best behaviour, asking polite questions. Lottie knew she'd expected something better and was disappointed. She followed them inside. Here it was much smarter than their own place had been. Fresh paint everywhere, plain white walls and comfortable furniture gave it a middle-class veneer.

Lottie looked round feeling a little sick. This was Mam's love nest. This had been as familiar to her as the house in Crimea Terrace. There were paintings on the walls, and spread everywhere were photographs of them as babies and young children, some in silver frames.

When Connie commented on this, Steve brought out several albums of pictures he'd taken of them on their birthday treats. Lottie knew her sister must be feeling the same nostalgia for their childhood.

There were books and magazines about, as though Mam had had leisure to read here. There were so many things that had belonged to Mam, which seemed to point to a personality Lottie didn't recognise.

They trooped up the carpeted stairs behind Uncle Steve to look at the bedrooms. Lottie felt worse. Mam had said she was working nights but instead she'd slept in this bed. With him. There were fluffy slippers by the bed, a frilly dressing gown hung behind the door and the big wardrobe was full of clothes they'd never seen her wear. Everything smarter and newer than what she wore at home.

'Feel free to take anything you want,' he told them.

'No, thank you,' Lottie said firmly, though Connie stopped to finger the satin dressing gown. Uncle Steve had put the kettle on before they'd come upstairs.

'It'll be boiling now.' He led them back down to the hall and asked Connie to make a pot of tea. He took Lottie into the living room.

'I've a few things to explain to you,' he told her. 'Sit down.'

She felt acutely uncomfortable, for he was gazing at her intently and seemed to want something from her. She didn't like it and looked away.

'As I told you. This house is in your mother's name. I gave her a little money too; she had a bank account and some shares.' He opened a drawer and took out a sheaf of papers. 'Her bank statements and share certificates.'

He put them in front of her, and she stared at them stony-faced.

'Don't you want to know how much it comes to?'

She shook her head. It seemed none of her business.

'Marion made a will. Her money and this house were to be divided between our three children; you, Cliff and Jimmy.'

She felt goose pimples run up her arms. Connie had pushed open the living room door to bring in the tea tray in time to hear that. Lottie could see her cheeks flushing bright pink. Her brown eyes shone with a mixture of disappointment and resentment. She felt a rush of protective sympathy for her sister and had to ask: 'What about Connie?'

This was turning her right against Uncle Steve. Connie had always felt he pushed her out. She hadn't been imagining it after all. No doubt he'd dictated the terms of Mam's will. Probably insisted that she make one.

Everything of Mam's had been bought with his money; it seemed obvious that he still thought of it as his. Connie was not his child and he hadn't wanted her to benefit from it. Uncle Steve exuded guilt but he looked Connie in the face.

'Marion didn't forget you. She's left you her jewellery.'

'She had no jewellery,' Lottie retorted. 'Only her watch and wedding ring.'

He was shaking his head with patience that was too obvious.

'I gave her a few pieces. They're here, upstairs. Come and see them. A fur coat too. When I gave it to your mother, I remember her trying it on in front of her mirror and saying, "Connie would love this."'

Lottie knew Connie had expected to have a share of this house and she knew how badly she'd wanted it. More than any of them, Connie valued money and property. A share would have given her the security she craved. A fur coat and jewellery would hardly compensate. Connie must be feeling hurt . . . no, this would be cutting her like a knife. To know Mam had left her out. It wasn't fair.

She knew too that Uncle Steve must see the smouldering resentment coming from both of them. He couldn't get them back upstairs fast enough. He flung open the wardrobe doors and brought out two posh fur coats, laying them across the silk coverlet of the bed.

'These were your mother's. This one's almost new.'

It was unbelievable. At home Mam always wore a grey tweed coat or a long scruffy mac. Lottie couldn't even imagine Mam in a fur coat. It seemed she'd had two lives – two very different lives – and had managed to keep one of them hidden from the whole family. She'd made them believe she was self-sacrificing and hard-working and all the time she'd been here with all these luxuries.

Lottie couldn't believe the change in her sister. Connie was trying them on, first the Persian lamb, then the musquash. She was purring over them.

'They look good on you,' Lottie told her as Connie twirled in front of the full length mirror. Uncle Steve agreed.

Lottie felt cold inside. Mam had had wonderful bracelets and necklaces and Chanel No. 5 perfume. Mam, who'd always seemed plainly dressed, even a little drab, had had all these luxuries, and kept them secret.

Connie was placated, pleased with her new possessions. Mam's clothes would fit her and her only, but they didn't equate to a share in this house and the money she'd left.

Uncle Steve's eyes came up to meet Lottie's again.

'This house with all that's in it, her money and her shares will now be divided between you and Cliff.'

'I don't want any of it.' Lottie didn't know how Mam could have loved this man. Not only was he devious but he wasn't being fair. 'It's really your money not Mam's. You keep it.'

'Don't be silly,' he said, but without aggression. 'These things are not mine to keep. According to the law of the land, they belonged to your mother and she's willed them to you and Cliff. They'll shortly become legally yours, whether you like it or not. There's no need for you to worry about anything. I'll apply for probate and see to it.'

Steve Lancelyn knew this wasn't working out as he'd expected. Over cups of tea in Marion's little sitting room, he'd tried to outline his plans to the girls. He'd felt reasonably sure of Charlotte's affection. She'd always shown it in the past. It was Connie who'd stood off, holding herself aloof. But she'd seemed to accept him when he'd offered her Marion's furs.

He should have left it there, taken things more slowly. He should never have gone on talking as he had. He'd made matters worse. Upset Charlotte.

'Having children is important to me. Having three children to whom I was unable to acknowledge my paternity – I hated that. I hated you having a name that wasn't mine. I wanted to share in your growing up, believe me. I wanted a bigger hand in it, but I couldn't have that without letting Herbert know the true position. It was part of the bargain I made with your mother, that you shouldn't know. The other thing I feel passionately about is my business and it's always been my dearest wish to hand it on to my children. It's been a huge disappointment . . . that here I am, not far off retirement age, and so far none of you have come to work in it. Not one of you has started to learn the first thing about it. I think Cliff would like to.'

Charlotte interrupted. 'Has he said so?'

'No, I haven't asked him. I'm not giving him the choice. At his age, school's important, it's better that he stays there for now. But eventually, I believe he'll want to work for me. I very much hope so. I need help. Charlotte, now you know you're my daughter, how do you feel about it? You could keep the business going until Cliff's old enough. Help him. I'd see you got a good grounding in each process. I'd teach you to manage it, the accounts too, everything. I'd like to see you taking some of the responsibility off my shoulders. Leaving me more time . . .'

If he'd been Hitler himself, Charlotte couldn't have looked

at him with greater wariness and dislike.

'Work for you?' He was left in no doubt she was astounded, shocked even at his suggestion. 'Whatever for?'

'I need someone I can rely on. Trust. It's a good business, I've spent my life building it up. I don't want it to go downhill. It would be a waste of all the effort I've put into it. I want my children to benefit from what I've done. I want you—'

'I'm a nurse. I'm about to sit my finals. Next month in fact.'

'Well, of course you must do that first.'

She was looking at him stony-faced. 'There's a war on. Nursing is a reserved occupation.'

'I could put up a good case to have you working for me.'

'I don't want you to,' she protested. 'Uncle Steve—'

'I'm your father.'

'Yes, I know.' She shook back her short dark hair as though that were of no concern to her. 'I make my own plans. I've decided to join the QAs, be an army nurse as soon as they'll have me. I need more experience of hospital work, not of making bread. I want to do my bit for the war effort.'

'People have to eat. Bread is essential.'

'I don't want to change horses in midstream. My way is to join the army, and that's what I'm going to do.'

Connie was wary of him again. He could see that in her big dark eyes. He understood how she felt; she was excluded from much of what he was offering Charlotte. She wasn't his daughter.

For the first time, he wished he hadn't persuaded Marion to exclude Connie. He hardly knew any of them. He'd had to turn his back on his children because of the circumstances but he hadn't wanted to. To have heirs for his business had always been a fundamental need. Perhaps he shouldn't blame Charlotte for not seeing things his way now.

Connie seemed more easily swayed to his way of thinking. He should have been more generous to her. But there had been three of his own blood and what was to be divided would seem little enough when cut into three.

Connie looked more like their mother than the others. She had Marion's womanly figure, the heavy bosom, slim waist and wide hips. Perhaps she was more like her mother in other ways. More caring, more understanding of the needs of others. She was Marion's daughter if not his, and he felt drawn to her now.

He got up abruptly and opened the fitted cupboard in the hall. He'd had a small safe installed here. He hadn't wanted Marion to have this house, he'd wanted her to have something better, but nowhere else could have been so convenient.

He found what he was looking for and opened Marion's jewellery box on the mahogany dining table. He showed Connie the emerald and diamond ring and saw her eyes light up just as her mother's had.

'That was Mam's?' Charlotte's voice was harsh. 'I never saw her wear it. She never wore anything but a wedding ring.'

'She wore it when she was here. These too.' He showed them the opal ring, the pearls, and the brooches.

'They're fabulous.' No mistaking that Connie was gratified.

'You might as well take them now,' he told her.

'Take them? She can't keep those in the nurses' home. They could be pinched.'

'They're insured. I'll keep that up for you, Connie.'

'No, it wouldn't be safe.' Charlotte was adamant. 'Girls

who get engaged wear their rings threaded on gold chains round their necks. Under their uniform, of course. Nobody would leave stuff like that lying about in their room.'

'They wouldn't,' Connie agreed. She was trying on a heavy gold bracelet with obvious approval. He'd given that to Marion for her fortieth birthday. Those days when they'd been so happy were gone for ever. He wanted Connie to take these things away where he wouldn't have to be reminded. He wouldn't come to this house so often.

Chapter Six

Their compassionate leave over, Lottie found the days that followed dragged painfully and her nights were anything but restful. She had nightmares in which Connie and Cliff were in mortal danger. Horrible dreams in which she felt herself falling, making her fearful for her own life. It was always a free fall through space, from which she'd wake up sweating before she hit the ground.

She grieved for Dadda. He was never out of her mind, and sometimes she dreamed of the old days when she'd spent so much time with him. These were softer dreams, disturbing in a different way.

She'd be transported back to the time when she was eight years old with Dadda at Crimea Terrace. It was the school holidays, and Connie was outside in the street playing hopscotch with Flora Jones. She could hear them laughing.

'Lottie, I want you to go to the shop.' Dadda was puffing and fighting for breath. 'We need a pound of carrots and a pound of onions. We'll make a stew for dinner. Can you remember that or shall I write it down?'

'Carrots and onions, I can remember.'

'Find a bag for them.'

She felt trustworthy as she unhooked the shopping bag from behind the kitchen door, and folded her fingers over the silver sixpence Dadda put in her hand.

'Look after the change, there's a good girl.'

To be in charge of housekeeping money made her feel almost grown up. She strutted across the hopscotch squares Connie had drawn on the pavement, pretending not to notice they were there, giving Connie's stone a barely visible kick to nudge it into the gutter.

'Look what you're doing,' Connie shouted angrily. 'You're spoiling my game. I won't let you play with us.'

'Don't want to.' If Connie was with a friend, Lottie was never allowed to join in. 'I'm going to the shop for Dadda.' She put on an air of importance.

Dakin's was a little general shop at the end of the street. It sold sweets as well as groceries, aniseed balls, gob-stoppers and pear drops. Lottie loved to go there to spend any halfpennies that came her way. Her favourite was the sherbet fountain, a paper tube of sherbet with a sucking straw made of liquorice.

When she went in, an elderly woman from Sebastopol Terrace was being served by Miss Dakin the proprietor. She had a mole at the side of her mouth with three long black whiskers that twisted and twirled when she spoke. Lottie found it hard to keep her eyes away from them. Also waiting to be served was Joe Bradley, from her class at school.

Lottie waited patiently; grown-ups didn't hurry to serve children. Miss Dakin was gossiping with her customer, Joe Bradley was shuffling his boots and eyeing the sweets with an acquisitive eye. She didn't like him; he was a bit of a bully.

At last it was his turn to be served. He handed over his shopping bag and asked for five pounds of potatoes. While Miss Dakin turned away to get them, Lottie saw him take a gob-stopper and slide it into his pocket. There was a rattle of scales from the back of the shop, and his hand went out again and hooked a bar of chocolate into his pocket.

'And a loaf, a large tin,' he said when Miss Dakin turned round and handed over his bag.

'Help yourself from there. Anything else?'

Lottie felt rooted to the spot. Joe was helping himself to sweets. She knew by his furtive manner he had no intention of paying for them and she couldn't believe how easy it was. For the first time ever, she wasn't looking at Miss Dakin's whiskers. He gave her a wink as he turned, and left the shop unchallenged.

She moved closer to the counter to hand over her bag for onions and carrots and Miss Dakin turned her back to get them. Lottie sniffed appreciatively. The scent of aniseed balls was deliciously strong. Bars of chocolate, packets of chewing gum and so many lovely sweets were set out temptingly in boxes along the front of the counter.

She did what she'd seen Joe demonstrate. While Miss Dakin's back was turned, she slid a sherbet fountain into her pocket.

She smiled up, watching the whiskers dance as she handed over her sixpence in payment, and then whisked out of the shop with the bell clanging triumphantly behind her.

She bounded up the pavement towards home feeling exultant. The sherbet fountain came out, and she bit off the liquorice end and sucked deeply. Sherbet exploded delightfully in her mouth. Connie had stopped hopping to stare.

'Dadda's given you a halfpenny for going to the shop! It's not fair. He never gives me anything.'

Lottie swallowed and had her first misgivings about what

she'd done. She lowered her shopping to the pavement.

'Have a suck,' she said, offering it to her sister.

Connie did but it didn't stop her following Lottie into the house.

'It's not fair,' she complained to Dadda. 'You've given our Lottie a halfpenny to spend. What about me?'

Lottie watched Dadda's smile fade. Connie and her friend Flora Jones were sent outside again. She was made to sit opposite Dadda at the kitchen table and hand over the change.

'I think we need to have a little talk,' he said. That made Lottie squirm.

He was puffing, unable to get his breath. It was a moment before he could go on. 'I didn't say you could buy sweets. That was housekeeping money.'

The change she'd brought back was spread out on the table before him.

'I wish I could give you treats, Lottie. I'd love to be able to give you halfpennies to spend, but it can't be done, not every time you go to the shop.'

He was moving the halfpennies up and down, wanting to know exactly how much the carrots and onions had cost. She told him. Miss Dakin always explained that to her.

'Then you haven't spent the housekeeping money? How did you come by the sherbet?'

Her cheeks were burning. 'Took it.'

'When she wasn't looking?' She knew by Dadda's face that this was a worse crime. 'That's stealing, Lottie. You mustn't do that.'

Slowly, she choked out the tale of how Joe Bradley had done it and taken a chocolate bar that cost twopence.

'That's no excuse. If Joe Bradley put his hand in the fire

you wouldn't do the same, would you?'

The tears were scalding her eyes. 'Miss Dakin has so many sweets . . .'

'That's no excuse either. They are hers, not yours. You can't just help yourself to other people's goods because you want them. How would you like it, if somebody came in and took your doll?'

'I'm sorry.'

The width of the table separated her from Dadda's sorrowful eyes. She got down from the chair to go to him. She wanted the comfort of his arms round her, to let her know she was forgiven.

'No, Lottie, you stay there until we've had this out. So what are we going to do about it, eh?'

The half-eaten sherbet fountain was on the table between them. Lottie couldn't look at it. She wished she'd never touched it. She didn't think she'd ever enjoy another.

'Come on, nobody likes little girls who steal. What are you going to do? To put things right?'

The tick of the grandfather clock filled the silence. 'Come on, you'll have to do something, won't you?'

'Say I'm sorry?'

'Yes – that's a good place to start. What else?'

'Take it back to her?'

'She can't sell it to anybody else now. You've eaten half of it. Will she want it, do you think?'

Lottie shook her head in dumb misery. Dadda pulled himself to his feet and gasped, 'Find – a paper bag for it, Lottie. In the kitchen – drawer.'

Glad to be allowed to move, she rushed to the kitchen. Dadda solemnly put the remains of her sherbet in the bag and propped it on the mantelpiece. When she turned round she found there was a halfpenny on the table in front of where she'd been sitting.

'There you are. That's our housekeeping money. We can't afford sherbet fountains but you've already spent it.'

Lottie tried to swallow and couldn't.

'I want you to take that to Miss Dakin and tell her what you did. I want you to say you're sorry and won't do it again.'

The horror of doing that seemed overwhelming. 'Dadda! I can't.'

'Now you listen to me. You think Miss Dakin has lots of everything but she hasn't. She has to sell all those things in the shop to earn her living. She's as poor as we are and she has an invalid mother to look after. So come on. Pick up that halfpenny and let's get it done.'

Lottie stepped back defiantly. 'Joe Bradley won't be taking his chocolate back, will he? Or paying for it. It was Chocolate Cream.'

'Probably not. But I want my little Lottie to grow up honest. Children have to learn what's right and what's wrong. He might grow up to be a thief and go to prison. You knew it was wrong to take the sherbet, didn't you?'

She could see her own legs in irons. They were so heavy she could hardly move them. She felt shocked. 'Will they send me to prison?'

For the first time Dadda smiled, but she knew he was finding it hard to get his breath too.

'To be honest – I don't think a little girl like you would be sent – to prison for stealing sweets.'

'Then I don't—'

'You must do as I say. Pay Miss Dakin for what you took.'

'Dadda,' she wailed. 'I don't want to tell her I stole it.'

She tried to put her arms round him, but he peeled them off and set her away from him. He'd never done such a thing before.

'You have to do it, Lottie. That halfpenny means as much to her as it does to us. Come on, I'll come with you, if you like.'

Lottie knew Dadda hadn't been out of the house in ages. That he said he'd come with her drove home the importance he attached to this. Reluctantly, her fingers felt for the coin.

'I'll go by myself,' she said with as much dignity as she could muster.

'Carry that chair outside for me.'

Lottie picked up the old kitchen chair and put it out on the pavement. Connie and her friend were still playing hopscotch there. Dadda liked to sit outside on fine days, people stopped to talk to him. But today wasn't all that fine.

'Go on, Lottie.'

She dragged her feet, going ever more slowly. She knew why Dadda had come out, it was to make sure she did what he asked. She turned round every few steps to see if he was watching her. He could see the shop from where he was; he'd know whether she went in or not.

Her heart was thumping. How could she admit she was a thief? She was ashamed of what she'd done. She could see now that there were no customers in the shop and was glad of that. The bell clanged louder than ever as she went in. She heard Miss Dakin's slippers shuffle in from the living room behind the shop.

Lottie put the halfpenny down on the counter and retreated, standing with her back to the door.

'I'm sorry, Miss Dakin.'

'Did you forget something, Lottie?'

'No.' Her mouth felt dry. Her heart was pumping like an engine. She stood breathing as heavily as Dadda and couldn't say anything.

'Your dadda's given you a halfpenny to spend.' Miss Dakin picked it up and put it in the till. 'Well, what are you going to buy?'

'I took it. A sherbet fountain. When you weren't looking. I'm sorry.'

Then she burst into tears and fled. The clanging doorbell seemed like a peal of laughter. Dadda was holding his arms out to her and she threw herself on him, though Mam said she mustn't because that made it even harder for him to breathe.

'There, there, Lottie. It's all right now.' He was hugging her and kissing her wet face.

It was all she could do to gulp out: 'What will Miss Dakin think of me?'

'She'll think you're lovely, just as I do,' Dadda said.

Later, when the stew was giving off lovely smells and she was setting the table ready for when Mam came home, Dadda reached up for the paper bag that contained the remains of the sherbet fountain.

'You'd better take this,' he told her. 'Mam might ask what it's doing here.'

Lottie didn't want to touch it. She flung it straight into the fire and watched it burn up with a strange blue flame.

In the first hazy moments of wakening, Lottie felt that Dadda was close, that he was still with her. A little more wakeful, and she realised it was only a dream and that Dadda was dead. All the same, it brought the warm feeling that Dadda was watching over her, near at hand, caring for her as he always had.

Everybody was surprised to find the nights were passing without the chilling wail of the air raid warning. They were having a break from the bombing and slowly Liverpool was getting back to normal.

Though she dreamed, Lottie had had time to catch up on her sleep and knew it was time to start revising. She got out her books and tried to put her grief and her problems out of her mind. Life at the hospital went on unchanged and that helped. She and Connie went to see Cliff regularly. He was full of Uncle Steve's plans.

'Isn't he the bee's knees? Isn't it nice to find he wants to help us like this? A relief.'

Lottie was pleased to see him more his normal self, and didn't want to upset him by saying she didn't agree. She and Connie still thought Steve had been high-handed in the way he'd turned round all the arrangements they'd made. Cliff seemed to want to go to boarding school now.

'I'd like to try it. To stay on for my Higher would solve everything for me. Uncle Steve's heard from a school that's been evacuated to Llandudno. He's taking me to see it.'

Lottie wanted to shut Uncle Steve out of her life but she could see he'd won Cliff over.

Agnes Cooper had been as good as her word and had arranged for furniture and fittings that were still usable to be salvaged from the wreckage of Crimea Terrace and sent to a sale room.

'They've been sold,' she told Lottie the next time she went

round to Sebastopol Terrace to see Cliff. 'Twenty-six pounds they made altogether.'

'That works out at eight pounds thirteen and fourpence each,' Lottie said to Cliff. 'I shall spend mine on clothes.'

'You should see the new clothes I've got. All ready for the new school. Only half the stuff they had on their list, though. My coupons ran out.' He smiled at her. 'They'll take me if I do well in my end of year exams.' He was revising hard for them now.

Mrs Cooper said: 'Cliff's delighted with the new school your uncle's chosen.' She seemed relieved she wouldn't need to lodge him for the next three years.

As Cliff's fifteenth birthday was drawing close Lottie said: 'I expect Uncle Steve's giving you the usual birthday treat?'

'Yes.'

'Have you decided what it's to be this year?'

'A trip to Southport. If the weather's good enough, it'll be a picnic on the beach at Ainsdale and a swim, so bring your costume. Then dinner at the Prince of Wales Hotel. If it's raining then it'll be lunch at the Prince of Wales followed by a theatre matinee.'

'Just like the old days,' Lottie said, and then wished she hadn't. Mam wouldn't be with them.

'Father's coming here first, then we'll pick you up at the hospital gates.'

Lottie stiffened. 'Father? Can you call him that?'

'He said he was my father and that he'd like me to.' Cliff looked so young, so anxious and full of concern. 'What do you think?'

'It's up to you, Cliff.' It was one more instance of Uncle Steve taking over.

'I couldn't call him Dadda. Of course not. But to call him Father – that's different.'

That didn't please Lottie one bit. She couldn't understand how Cliff could relate to him so well, when she couldn't forgive him for making Mam live such a life of lies.

Even harder for Lottie to understand was that Connie seemed to have changed her mind completely about Uncle Steve. The ring he'd given her was flashing green fire on her finger. She'd taken that and a gold chain so she could wear it round her neck while she was on duty. The rest of Mam's jewellery had been put back in the safe in Brightland Street.

Connie now seemed to accept that she'd never own a share in the house. Yet she still thought highly of it. She said: 'It's very nice, Lottie. You could live there.'

'It was Mam's love nest. I don't want to make a home of it.'

'Why not? We all need a home and we've lost the other. You won't have to live in the hospital once you pass your finals. You could make a home for Cliff. I wouldn't mind living there.'

'No.' Lottie didn't want that to happen. She knew Connie couldn't do it if she was against it. She had the power to refuse her that.

'What do you want to do with it then?'

'I don't know. Nothing really.'

'You should think about it. Talk to Cliff. What's the point of leaving it locked up?'

'Cliff will be there for his holidays. It's what he wants. Apart from that, Uncle Steve can use it himself.'

Chapter Seven

Lottie supposed she and Connie were closer than most sisters but she had her reservations. Connie had a bossy side. She'd say: 'Sometimes I feel more like your mother than your sister. I've had to do so much for you. Tell you what to do . . .'

'I wish you wouldn't.' How many times had she wished that?

'Somebody has to. I've almost brought you up.'

'Nonsense.'

'Who do you think made sure you'd cleaned your teeth and washed your face before you went to school? I was doing that for you when I was eight. Mam was never around to do it.'

'You never stopped nagging me. "Comb your hair, Lottie, it looks a mess." "Hurry up, you'll make us all late for school." "Eat up your cabbage." Always, it was eat up your cabbage.'

'You never did anything unless I kept on at you.'

'That's nagging.'

'You needed it. Mam nagged at me to nag you. You know she did. I got my share of nagging too.'

'Connie, you know you've got a selfish streak. You're no angel. You used to shut yourself away upstairs and leave me to see to the dinner while you sewed dresses for yourself.'

101

'When you were old enough. It was only fair for you to take a turn.'

'When I was ten?'

'Fourteen, more like, when I was doing that. I'd made up my mind I'd have to be a bit selfish or I'd end up having a life like Mam's.'

'I'm beginning to think she had a pretty good time.'

'Like we thought hers was, then. She was making me do all the work she should have done herself. I had to have some pleasure. I wanted to have fun and enjoy myself like everybody else.'

And just when Lottie had come to the conclusion that Connie was totally self-centred, she heard her talking to Mam.

'I'd like to make a frock for our Lottie. She could do with a new one. Poor thing, she's got nothing decent to wear.'

A few shillings were forthcoming, and Connie took her to the local shops to choose the pink and white striped material. There was the fun of choosing the style and Connie fussing round her with pins making sure it would fit. Connie was good at dressmaking. Mam had a sewing machine, old but still working well. Connie had taken it over and thought of it as her own.

'You can get put on if you do too much,' Connie told her now. She made it only too obvious that she felt she had been. 'All that cleaning I did. I was a drudge before I was ten years old.'

Once Connie had settled in at the hospital she hadn't come home much except for her days off.

Lottie had started her nurse training the year before war broke out and was due to sit her final exams very soon.

'I've got to get down to revising,' she said to Connie. 'If I fail, it'll be even longer before I can join Queen Alexandra's Royal Army Nursing Corps.'

Connie laughed at her. 'I keep telling you, you won't like it! You'll be ordered about left right and centre. You hate being told to do anything. Tell you to do one thing, and you do the opposite out of cussedness. No, the army won't be your cup of tea. Bet you'll spend half the time in jankers.'

'I won't then. You seem to think you're more suited to it. You should join up too.' Connie had been qualified for two years and was working as a staff nurse. 'They'd be glad to have you right away.'

'I'm doing enough. Nursing is a reserved occupation. No need.'

'You'd be more help in the QAs.'

'The hospitals here have to be run too.'

'I thought you were ready for a move?'

'I am. I'm fed up here. I might try a hospital in a safer area. I'm terrified of air raids. I can't stand many more.'

'We're not getting any more.'

'Not for the moment, while the Luftwaffe's concentrating on other cities, but there's nothing to stop them unloading their bombs here again. Now Cliff's going to boarding school there doesn't seem much point in staying.'

'I'm here,' Lottie wailed. 'I don't want to be left by myself.'

'You'd be off to join the army if you could. You wouldn't worry about leaving me on my own, would you?'

Since their parents had been killed, Lottie had clung to Connie. She felt she needed her more than she ever had before. She thought her sister felt the same. Nowadays, they tried to get the same days off so they could be together. Connie liked to go round the big shops in town, take afternoon tea in upmarket tea shops instead of the hospital dining room. Sometimes they went to the pictures together but usually Connie wanted to spend her evenings off with her current boyfriend.

At the moment, she was going out with a fireman by the name of Reg Stanhope but she wasn't in love with him. Lottie knew her sister was keen to get married. At twenty-four, she felt it was time she met up with the right man.

Lottie knew exactly the sort of man Connie was seeking. He'd have perfect health and be as strong as an ox. His character would be much as they'd thought Mam's had been before her fall from grace. He'd be self-sacrificing and want to do everything he could to make Connie happy. He'd be a professional person, keen on his job and good company – fun to be with. Reg Stanhope wasn't measuring up to this. Connie was now admitting he wouldn't do as a husband. He was too self-centred for one thing.

It was generally thought amongst their friends that the worst fate that could befall any nurse was to remain a spinster and end up as a fussy fault-finding ward sister.

Lottie discounted all that, but anyway, she had a boyfriend in Sandy Cooper. She'd known him all her life; they'd gone to school together. He'd been taking her to the pictures and to dances for the last three or four years but she didn't feel the same urgency to get married. Neither did he, for that matter. He was only in Liverpool intermittently and then he wanted to have all the fun he could. It suited her that he was away at the moment – she'd be able to spend most of her off duty time poring over her books.

But because Connie felt the need so strongly, she'd done

her best to help her. When Lottie had been working on Casualty on night duty, she'd met up with a policeman called Mark Belling who frequently brought in drunks who'd injured themselves or been hurt in a fight.

He'd invited her to the pictures to see Dorothy Lamour, Bing Crosby and Bob Hope in *The Road to Singapore*. She'd gone with him but he wasn't her cup of tea. However, she thought Connie might like him so she'd introduced them. Connie had thought him Mr Right for a time, and had gone as far as getting engaged before she changed her mind.

Much the same thing happened with Colin Barton who worked in the hospital laboratory. He'd been out with half the nurses in the hospital, including Lottie, and seemed to be actively looking for a wife. She'd brought him and Connie together but after a couple of months that affair had broken up too.

Lottie was afraid her sister was going to be very hard to please.

Connie lay on her bed staring up at her bedroom ceiling. She hadn't the energy for anything these days; she wasn't herself at all. Lottie was on duty, or she'd be here organising her to do something or other.

None of the family was exactly happy. How could they be when they'd lost so much? But Lottie and Cliff seemed to be coping better than she was. Lottie always did. When things went wrong, she found it easier to pick herself up and start again. Connie felt she was being left behind. Lottie was like quicksilver, able to think and move more quickly than she could.

Connie wanted an easy life. Perhaps that was the problem.

Lottie was ready and willing to fight wars on behalf of others, but she wasn't. She wanted to get married and have children, but it wasn't happening for her. Here she was heading towards twenty-five without ever meeting a man who would make the sort of husband she was looking for.

Lottie attracted men in droves. Connie couldn't quite see why. In a way, she was like Mam. She did nothing to make herself attractive to them. She wore flat-heeled shoes all the time because she said they were comfortable. She had her hair cut short because she said it was easier to manage. All she did was wash it and comb it round her face – she never thought of putting in a curler. And she was as long and thin as a prop for the washing line, though she did have quite a pretty face.

It was coated with freckles, which she hated and railed against, but some thought them attractive. They were all over her nose and across her cheeks. Her eyes were her best feature, wide apart and tawny brown.

Connie turned over and viewed the collection of cosmetics ranged across her dressing table. She had creams for night and day, lotions, foundations and powders and dozens of lipsticks. In a drawer, she had setting lotions for her hair and curlers of every shape and size. She had a collection of nail varnishes in bright reds too, but nurses were not allowed to wear nail varnish on duty so she painted only her toenails, except for special occasions.

They weren't allowed to wear any make-up on the wards but most, like her, wore a touch of foundation and some face powder to stop their noses shining. She wore Tangee lipstick too. It was a clear orange in the tube but on the lips it enhanced the natural pink colouring by about one shade. Lottie wore it when she went out, never anything else. She said she didn't want to look painted, and whatever she put on came off as soon as she had a drink or ate something.

Connie sighed. She really worked hard at making herself presentable and what good was it doing her?

Lottie felt out of sorts. It was Cliff's birthday, and it brought with it a feeling of impending doom. Three more years and he'd be called up. The war had to end before then. It had to.

It was turning out to be a wet morning. At ten o'clock, Lottie huddled close against Connie to share her umbrella as they scurried down to the hospital gates as arranged. She was wearing a new blue dress under her blazer.

'They're here waiting,' Connie said. 'Thank goodness.'

Uncle Steve sounded cheerful as they climbed on to the back seat of his car.

'All this rain. What a shame, today of all days.'

Cliff was excited. Lottie thought he'd recovered from what had happened more quickly than either she or Connie, and marvelled at it. He couldn't stop talking of the microscope Father had given him for his birthday.

'It isn't new,' Steve told them as he drove. 'I bought it at a sale room. It isn't possible to buy new things any more, but it's a good one.' Cliff wanted to carry on with biology for his Higher.

'I've been thinking, since we can't go to the beach, why don't you come to my factory? I know you've all been once but that was a cursory visit. I'd like to show you round properly. I want you all to understand the business. Learn how it functions.'

Cliff seemed keen to go and today they all had to fall in

with his wishes. Lottie thought it was traitorous of Connie to be so full of enthusiasm.

'We'd love to,' she beamed at Uncle Steve.

Lottie wanted to resist, but she was aware Uncle Steve was trying to win her round too. Whatever Cliff thought, she was never going to call him Father.

'We've never even seen your Birkenhead factory,' Connie added.

Steve said: 'If we're to be in Southport for lunch, we'll have to leave that for another day.'

The car rolled through the gates of the factory at Old Swan, making Lottie sit up straight in order not to miss anything. Once inside the bakery doors, the damp heat seemed almost tropical. In the cloakroom, Uncle Steve provided them with white Wellington boots, white caps to cover their hair and white coats like the ones doctors wore in the hospital.

'We have to be as hygienic as possible,' he explained. 'There are strict regulations where food is concerned.' Lottie was intrigued in spite of herself and kept her eyes and ears open. He led them first to the flour rooms.

'We received a delivery of flour yesterday. Thank goodness – we were getting dangerously low.' Lottie thought he had an enormous amount waiting to be used.

'It's bulky, Charlotte, and we use a prodigious amount when we work full out like this. If we ran out, we'd have to stop baking and that would be a disaster.'

'Liverpool would go hungry,' Connie said. 'There'd be very little bread.'

'Disaster for this business too. We have to keep our flour stocks up because we can't use it straight away. It has to come up to the right temperature in these rooms, otherwise it would upset the yeast. Then it's sifted through these fine screens and drawn into this hopper over the mixing machine. Everything's measured automatically, the flour, water, yeast and malt.'

Lottie watched the machine's mechanical arms mix the dough. They followed the conveyor belt to the fermentation room where the dough was left to rise in long troughs.

'It takes two to four hours and increases in bulk almost four times,' Uncle Steve told them as he led them to another bay in the bakery. 'Then it comes this way to another machine where more ingredients are added and mixed thoroughly.'

'Then to the ovens?' Connie wanted to know.

'No,' Cliff told her. 'Back to the fermentation room to rise again. Then on by conveyor belt to be rolled and kneaded by another machine.'

Lottie stood watching it. 'You know a lot about it, Cliff.'

She saw Cliff and Uncle Steve exchange glances.

'Cliff's interested.' Uncle Steve smiled at her as he led them on. 'This machine is called a divider. It cuts the dough to the exact weight.'

'And this is the rounder,' Cliff added. 'It makes the dough into balls. After that, it's squeezed and rolled some more before being made into the familiar loaf shape or put into tins.'

'As you can see, everything possible has been automated. We need fewer workers and they don't have to be skilled bakers.'

Steve was talking directly to Lottie, as though he still hoped to persuade her to come and work here. She could see he was proud of his business. 'The process is much the same as making bread at home.' The scent of baking was heavenly.

'You make it seem simple and easy,' Connie said. 'But it doesn't taste like bread made in a small old-fashioned bakery. Not so good.'

'There's a war on. You saw the sort of flour we have, rough grey stuff, that's all there is, and by law I have to put additives in. And it's a daunting task to get enough labour, and almost impossible to keep it.'

Lottie was looking round with wonder. The workforce seemed to be mainly women. The few men were either elderly or very young. All turned to nod or smile at Uncle Steve, showing deference almost as if he was royalty. She could see he was a popular boss.

'There wouldn't be enough bread to go round if Britain had to rely on small bakeries doing everything by hand,' he said. 'And even they have to bake the national loaf. You may think our bread doesn't taste as good but it stays fresh longer. That means less waste. This sort of bakery comes into its own in wartime, Connie. There've been big advances in my lifetime.'

Cliff said proudly: 'Father knows all there is to know about bread.'

'I should do. I was brought up to it.' They finished the tour by looking at the ovens and then went to the canteen for a cup of tea.

Steve started to reminisce. 'I started work in my father's bakery when I was thirteen. He taught me the basics and I've been making bread ever since. It was nothing like this. A small bakery making bread of many different sorts just for the village. Cakes and pies too. We had a shop as well in those days, where we sold all we baked. Bread tasted really good then. We started at five o'clock every morning. We don't have to do that here. We could work factory hours, from eight in the morning until five-thirty, but because of the war and the need to turn out as much as we can, we work regular overtime.'

Lottie said: 'You must have worked very long hours in the old days, what with the shop as well.'

'My father did especially, but it was his own business and he was making a success of it. He didn't mind how many hours he put in – he enjoyed it. It gave him a good living and he wanted to hand it on to me and give me an even better living. I wish he was here now to see what I've made of my inheritance. Each generation does better than the one before; that's the nature of things. I want to hand this on to my heirs. I want to see you make an even better living from it.' His eyes sparkled; he was full of enthusiasm. 'I want to see you build it up even more. How do you feel about that, Cliff?'

Lottie smouldered. There was no doubt that Cliff was interested.

'Now you're trying to talk Cliff into coming here to work for you.'

'Well, you've refused. Not yet, Cliff, obviously, but if you start here before you get your call-up papers . . . before you're turned eighteen, there should be no problem about keeping you.'

'You're offering me a lot,' Cliff said slowly. 'I realise that. I'm grateful.'

Uncle Steve turned back to her. 'That's what you want, isn't it, Charlotte? You don't want him to go in the forces and fight? You don't want him to risk his life?'

'No, of course not. You'd be safer here, Cliff. That makes sense.'

'One day, Cliff, you'll own a share of this factory. I want

you to think carefully about it. Would you like to work here? Make this business grow even bigger?'

Lottie recognised that Uncle Steve was hoping she'd help to persuade Cliff.

'Perhaps.' Cliff was guarded and couldn't look any of them in the eye. 'If the war's over by then . . .'

'Even if it isn't,' Uncle Steve said.

'Particularly if it isn't,' Lottie added.

'If it isn't – then I think I ought to join the forces. Same as Lottie thinks. I want to pull my weight.'

That made Lottie shiver, brought back the pall of dread.

'It's three years off yet,' Connie said. 'The war will surely be finished by then.'

On the day Lottie learned she'd passed her finals she felt lifted out of her low spirits for the first time since the bombing. Today she was being swept along on the crest of a wave. She'd done what she'd set out to do and could now call herself State Registered.

There was a great deal of whooping for joy amongst the other girls in her group, and she did some herself. She was having elevenses with them in the dining room when amid the laughter and the clatter of cups, Connie slid silently into the seat next to her.

'I've passed,' Lottie crowed.

'I knew you would. Congratulations.'

She knew by her sister's face that something was wrong. 'What's the matter?'

'I've broken it off with Reg. We had a bit of a row last night.' Reg was the fireman.

'Plenty more fish in the sea,' Lottie told her. 'You said

112

ages ago he was self-centred and was never going to make the grade.'

'Yes.' Her sigh was martyred. 'I'm just fed up generally. I'm going to look for another job. Move right out of Liverpool.'

'No,' Lottie protested. 'I want you here with me.'

'There's too much to remind me . . . Besides, all the girls I trained with have gone.'

'Why don't you train as a midwife? Do what most of them have done. You could do that without moving from this hospital.'

'No. Don't want to end up like Mam. Working long hours, being pushed on nights.'

'She wasn't being pushed to work on nights.'

'No, I was forgetting. Anyway, I don't want my life to be like we thought hers was.'

'It won't be.'

'He asked me to marry him, Lottie. I said no.'

'Reg, you mean?'

Connie nodded miserably.

'Well, you'd already made up your mind he wouldn't make a good husband, so what's the problem?'

'He wanted us to get married straight away. He'd seen a couple of rooms he thought would do for us.'

'So?'

'I can't stand the thought of penny pinching for the rest of my life. I want a reasonable standard of living. Reg doesn't earn all that much.'

Lottie was buoyed up with her own success, and didn't feel this warranted any depression.

'Not good enough for you. As I said, plenty more fish in the sea.'

'It's all right for you, but I'm nearly twenty-five. I can see myself ending up on the shelf.'

Lottie laughed. 'Nonsense, you've loads of time.'

Connie started to study the adverts in the nursing press. Within a few months, she'd found herself a job as a staff nurse at Clatterbridge Hospital on the Wirral.

'It's out in the country,' she told Lottie. 'Fields all round it, but there's a good bus service into Birkenhead. It'll be much safer if the raids start up again.'

'It's not that far from the docks. Or the big factories making soap and margarine. If the bombers are aiming for them, it's no distance at all.'

'It looks safer. Why don't you come too, Lottie? I'm on a men's medical ward and there's a vacancy for a staff nurse in theatre. Wouldn't you like that?'

Lottie thought about it for a long time. She needed post-graduate experience before she could join the army, and she'd widen it if she moved hospitals, especially to a theatre post. Besides, she didn't want to be parted from Connie. On her next day off she decided to go over to see her and have a look round.

The bus took her through the suburbs of Birkenhead. Connie was right, the hospital was surrounded by fields and woods. She liked what she saw.

In the late afternoon, Connie took her to see the theatre sister. They'd just finished the day's list and were clearing up. Lottie was impressed with the theatres and thought she could get on with the staff. She filled up an application form then and there.

'You'll get the job,' Connie assured her. 'It's not easy to get trained staff these days.'

Lottie did, and settled in very quickly. She enjoyed the work and the camaraderie of the other nurses. She didn't forget her intention to join the army, but she became immersed in her new surroundings and her new job and was content.

When Sandy Cooper docked in Liverpool, Lottie did her best to arrange her days off so that she could spend as much time as possible with him. He wasn't pleased she'd moved so far away.

'Not nearly so convenient,' he told her. 'It takes so much time to come over to see you.' But he took her to see George Formby in person at the Empire, followed by a meal in China Town.

It was so late by then he had to take her back to Sebastopol Terrace for the night. Lottie had a day off the next day and had a lovely lazy morning followed by a hectic afternoon and evening that finished with dinner at the Bowler Hat.

She had to work the following two days while he was in port but he came over to see her and they managed to fit in visits to the cinema and to pubs. Lottie felt she had a wild time while he was home. It always took her a day or two to catch up on her sleep when his ship had sailed.

Connie had a rapid turnover of men friends and seemed as far away as ever from settling down. There were no more raids but the war dragged on; there seemed to be no end to it.

With Cliff away at school, Lottie was surprised to find that Uncle Steve kept inviting her and Connie over to Old Swan. If they could get the same day off, they went over to have lunch with him in the factory canteen. He liked to talk about Cliff, and they knew he kept in close touch with him.

'He's settled down in his new school and loves it.' He'd

been delighted to tell them that. He had keys to the house in Brightland Street cut for them and encouraged them to go.

'You could stay there when you have a night off,' he told them. 'You used to do that when you could go to Crimea Terrace.'

'We went home to see Dadda,' Lottie told him. 'There's not much point in coming to an empty house.'

'I'm often there. I'll stay if you will.'

Lottie shook her head. She didn't want to go to that house. She was still upset about Mam, finding she'd gone behind Dadda's back, and wasn't hard-working and good-living. Uncle Steve had fallen in her opinion too.

When he told her Cliff would be coming home for a few days at half term and would be staying in Brightland Street, Connie persuaded her to change her mind.

'You want to see our Cliff, don't you? Anyway, I like the house. It's comfortable and cosy, and Uncle Steve will be there too. He'll arrange all sorts of outings and treats.'

'It's easy to see he's charmed with Cliff,' Lottie said.

'He'd like to be closer to you, if only you'd let him.'

'And you too, Connie.'

They went over together after finishing work at five o'clock, both having got the next day off. Cliff's train would have arrived at midday. When they got there, the house in Brightland Street was in darkness, although the fire had been lit and the sitting room was warm.

'They know we're coming. The table's set for four.'

'Cliff will be at the factory with Uncle Steve.' Lottie dumped her overnight case at the bottom of the stairs. 'Shall we walk round and find them?'

'Better than waiting here,' Connie agreed.

The nights were drawing in. It was cold and already dark. Because of the blackout, there was no light to be seen anywhere, but as soon as they pushed open the door they could see the factory was still working, though most of the offices above were in darkness. Lottie thought the warmth and the smell of bread were lovely.

They changed into white coats in the cloakroom and went in. Lottie could see a group of figures crowding round a machine, Cliff and Uncle Steve among them.

Cliff flung his arms round them both. He'd grown taller, and even more lanky, but his face shone with pleasure at seeing them.

'I'm glad you've come round.' Uncle Steve smiled. 'I hoped you'd guess where we were. We've a bit of a problem here. Got to do something about it before the morning.'

'What's the matter?'

It seemed the belt conveying the baking tins was slightly out of sync with the machine that dropped the measured amount of dough into them, and though the fitters had tried to solve it, they hadn't yet succeeded.

Half a dozen men were fiddling with it when Lottie saw the girl who worked the switchboard come into the bakery. She wasn't wearing whites and called across from the doorway.

'Phone call for you, Mr Lancelyn. It's your wife, she says she's being trying to catch you all day.'

Lottie heard Connie gasp, and felt herself go rigid as he hurried away with the girl. The words 'your wife' sang in her mind. Cliff's eyes met hers, and she knew he'd taken on their significance too, but straight away he went on fiddling with the machinery.

When Uncle Steve returned a few minutes later looking somewhat sheepish, Cliff suggested a different solution to the problem, which Uncle Steve decided to try.

'We might as well go, then,' he said. 'I've locked up my office.'

As the four of them walked down the street in the cold, Lottie could feel the sweat breaking out on her forehead. She said: 'Uncle Steve, we didn't know you had a wife. Did Mam know?'

She heard him catch his breath. 'Yes, of course.'

'We didn't know. You told us Mam wouldn't leave Dadda. Because he needed her. That that was why you didn't marry.' Connie cleared her throat. 'We didn't know there was another reason.'

He sounded guilty. 'You didn't ask, so I didn't say anything. Iris and I were married eleven years before I met your mother. I couldn't have married her.'

'Oh!' Connie gasped.

'And does she have any children?' Lottie's face was hard.

'Two daughters, Doreen and Rita. They're both older than you lot.'

'A wife and two daughters! Why keep that from us?' Lottie wailed at his hunched shoulders as he strode in front of her. 'You could have told us straight out. When you were telling us about Mam.'

Cliff was feeling for her hand. 'Because you go off the deep end whenever he tries to talk about anything like that.'

It brought her up short again. 'Do I?'

'Yes,' Steve grunted.

'You know you do.' Cliff squeezed her hand.

'Perhaps I do. But a wife and two daughters and I didn't

know of their existence? It comes as a shock, doesn't it, Connie?'

There seemed no end to the things she had to accept. What Steve and Mam had done was not as straightforward as she'd first thought. There were others involved.

He unlocked the front door and ushered them into the little sitting room.

'You'd better tell us about them,' Lottie said as he poked up the fire.

With Charlotte's reproachful eyes on him, Steve Lancelyn couldn't even start. Anything like this tied him up in emotional knots. To talk to his children about what he saw as his sexual extravagance was impossible. And he'd trained himself to say nothing about one side of his family to the other. Marion hadn't wanted to hear a word about Iris.

He poured himself a stiff whisky, found some cider for them. Busied himself lighting the oven to heat the meal his canteen manager had organised for him. Charlotte didn't let him off the hook. She wasn't the sort to have her attention deflected. She pressed him again when they sat at the table to eat supper. He had to start.

'I thought I was doing very well to marry Iris Lowther.'

'When was that?' Charlotte wanted to know. 'I need to get everything straight in my mind.'

'1908. May the tenth if you want the exact date.' He bit into his rabbit pie. 'Iris came from the social class above mine. I'd inherited my father's bakery but it was a one horse band. I couldn't expand on the premises, they were cramped already. We made the bread by hand in the traditional way. It was her father who loaned me the capital I needed, to expand my business into what it is today.'

Talking about it now brought it all back to him.

'Factory bread?' Iris had asked, her beautiful blue eyes rolling heavenwards to show how much she disliked the idea.

'It's good bread even if it is made in a factory, I'm very careful to ensure that. I want people to enjoy it and come back for more. It has to taste better than anything else on the market. And it does.'

The factory had been a dream when he was young. In those early days of marriage, Iris had listened to him. She'd spoken to her father about it and he'd thought it a feasible idea. He was a businessman who'd earned his money from a gravel pit; digging out aggregates for the building trade.

'I liked and admired my father-in-law. He talked over my ideas with me, made suggestions and helped me work out my plans. He helped me build the factory here at Old Swan. An interest-free loan. He couldn't have treated me more generously. "I've an interest in getting you started," he told me. "I want you to prosper. I want Iris to be comfortable, to be able to live well." Iris had brothers who worked the gravel pit. She does get a little money from it now, but he knew it wouldn't be enough for her. I worked hard.'

Those really were the days. To see his dream come true had been one of the highlights of his life. 'It took me six years before I was able to return the money to Ezra Lowther. He refused to take anything extra by way of interest even then, though I could have afforded it. I've always been grateful for what he did for me.

'Iris accepted it as her right. "Why shouldn't he? He doesn't want me to starve, after all."

'She wasn't interested in my bakery. Only in what it could

earn. I almost gave up trying to talk to her about it. She didn't want to hear my worries, or about any new ideas I had. The last time I tried, she said: "What can I do about your bakery? If it's the law that you bake the national loaf, then you'll have to do it. I shan't eat it, it sounds horrible." Iris never wanted anything to do with my business. It wasn't the sort of thing she thought women should be involved in. She'd conveyed this attitude to Doreen and Rita, our daughters . . .'

'How old are they?' Lottie demanded.

'Twenty-eight and twenty-six now. '

'Don't they want to come and work for you? I mean, you're asking us . . .'

'They're like their mother, they won't have anything to do with it. Consider it a man's province. All the time they were growing up, I'd only to mention the factory for them to chorus: "Don't start the bread round again, Dad. Spare us that." I pleaded with both the girls to come and work here. By the time they'd grown up I'd built the second factory in Birkenhead. I wanted to teach them how to run the business.

'I'm not boasting when I say I bake most of the bread eaten on Merseyside. Now, more than anything else, I need help. My skilled staff left to go into the forces in droves. I'm proud of building up this empire. It earns a lot of money but it's not easy for me now. "Not a healthy place for girls to work," Iris said. "Nice girls don't spend their lives in a factory." I lost patience with her and said: "I'm not unhealthy, am I? Why should they be?" "It's different for them. We've brought them up to be young ladies. It wouldn't do. Not for our Doreen."

'I made it clear they'd only be working on the factory floor for a while. Just long enough to learn what it's all about. The war's given women opportunities they didn't have before.

Women are doing men's jobs and I was in need of staff I could trust. Still am. Doreen really put me down. She said: "I know with a war on I've got to work, but I'd rather do anything than work in your factory."'

'What does she do?' Connie asked.

'Neither of them were career minded. They took courses in typing and shorthand because I wanted them to be trained for something. Iris spends her days playing golf and bridge. The golf club and the bridge club provide her with a social life that largely excludes me. If there's a dance or a dinner for which she needs a partner, then I'm expected to be in attendance. Neither of the girls wanted to do more than join the tennis club and go to the parties and dances their mother could arrange. Doreen's married now with two young children. Her husband's serving with the Eighth Army in North Africa. She spends more time at home with Iris than in her own house. She thinks looking after two small children on her own is very hard work.'

'And the other one – Rita?'

'She hasn't yet married. She's been conscripted into the WRAF where she's driving Air Commodores around. She says she's enjoying herself, that the social life is better than at home.'

Connie said: 'So your first family was a disappointment to you? Apart from your father-in-law.'

'He died many years ago. Yes, you could say that. I don't have a lot in common with her brothers.'

'But your wife, most of all?'

Charlotte's tawny eyes were searching into his. Surely that must be obvious? He'd never have turned to Marion otherwise.

'Yes, Iris most of all.' She wanted to hear him admit that. He tried to explain.

'She didn't feel strongly about anything. Except perhaps her daughters when they were small. She was a good mother, I have to say that for her, but she'd always had help in the house. After the first year or so of marriage, she had a live-in cook-general and a maid too.'

The war had put an end to all that. There had been a crisis when each of their domestic staff left. It was difficult to persuade anyone to take their place when there were plenty of jobs in factories at twice the money.

'Iris does her own housework now – with the help of a daily woman who comes to do the rough three times a week. She never stops complaining about the war. It's giving her insurmountable problems.'

Connie couldn't get over what Steve Lancelyn had told them. Up in the bedroom at Brightland Street which she shared with Lottie, they whispered into the early hours. They were both consumed by curiosity about his other family.

'I've two half sisters I've never even seen,' Lottie marvelled. 'Can you believe it? What a family ours is.'

'Like Mam, he had two separate families. What complicated, convoluted lives they had.'

'We didn't ask if they knew about us. I don't suppose they do; he's very secretive about everything. He wouldn't have told us about them if we hadn't found out.'

Steve went to work early the next morning. They were to spend the day with Cliff.

'It hasn't been easy for Father,' was his only comment. He didn't want to talk about it. Connie couldn't see how he was able to accept all this with greater ease than she or Lottie.

He wanted to go round the Walker Art Gallery. They went into town on the bus. Connie enjoyed the art gallery, but she couldn't get Steve's revelations out of her mind.

It was rather a constrained half term. Steve took them to the Empire that evening. It was vaudeville and the audience rocked with laughter. Connie didn't find it all that funny.

Chapter Eight

The following week Connie was promoted to ward sister and given a men's orthopaedic ward to run.

'Congratulations.' Lottie gave her a hug. 'You deserve it.'

'Waited a long time for it.'

She was pleased, of course she was. It was what she wanted, but she'd be twenty-five in a few months. More than promotion, she wanted a husband.

Being in charge of the ward wasn't always easy. Mondays and Thursdays were operating days and they were always hard and sometimes produced a crisis, but she felt she could cope and began to enjoy it.

The weeks were passing quickly. It was over six months since Crimea Terrace had been bombed, and there hadn't been a raid on Liverpool since. She and Lottie continued to visit the bread factory and were always welcomed.

Steve said: 'Cliff will be home for the Christmas holidays next week. He'll want to see you two. Do come over as much as you can.'

'Of course.'

'I don't suppose it'll be much of a Christmas.' 1941 was the third Christmas of the war. 'We can't forget what we've lost, but we'll do our best. I'd like you to spend Christmas Day with us.'

'I won't be able to,' Connie said straight away. 'None of us on the wards can have Christmas Day off and there's no off duty either. We spend the day seeing that the patients have a good time, those that are too ill to go home.'

'That's hard on you.'

'No, we only do essential jobs. We go round all the wards singing carols and we're getting up a show too. Anyway, we have our Christmas dinner a few days later.'

'I might be able to come,' Lottie said. 'They keep a skeleton staff in theatre for emergencies but all routine surgery stops.'

'Do come, if you can. It'll be lonely for Cliff if there's just the two of us here.'

Lottie was afraid it would be a Christmas of shortages. The shops seemed almost empty. She didn't know what she could give as presents. She knew Connie was sewing something for her but she had no talent in that direction. She managed to find some bath cubes for Connie, and she queued to buy razor blades for Uncle Steve.

She went to visit Agnes Cooper and afterwards called in at the corner shop to see if she could get some writing paper. Now that Crimea Terrace had been flattened, it had a more prominent position. Miss Dakin had grown stout and the three whiskers on her mole were longer than ever. She was pleased to see Lottie and hear her news. They talked of the Blitz and the customers she'd lost.

She had no writing paper but two small boxes of Black Magic chocolates were produced from under the counter. That pleased Lottie, who had enough sweet coupons for them and now had a few gifts for her family.

On Christmas Eve, there was a works party in the factory

and both she and Cliff were invited. The canteen had been decorated with holly and paper streamers. As the staff had shed their white coats and caps, Lottie hardly recognised anybody. It surprised her to find Cliff more at home amongst them than she was. Everybody seemed to know him and came over to speak to him and ask about his new school.

'How come you know everybody?' she asked him.

He looked a little put out. 'I've been coming here quite a bit.'

'You've been away since September. I've been more often.'

He got up to fetch a plate of sandwiches from one of the tables and offered it to her.

'Lots of good food,' he said, tucking in himself. 'You've put on a good spread for us, Mrs Caldwell.'

That surprised Lottie too. She hadn't known who was responsible for the catering, which mostly consisted of titbits spread on their own bread and buns.

Back in the Brightland Street house afterwards, she found Cliff had put up coloured streamers in the sitting room.

'Pre-war stuff.' Uncle Steve chuckled. 'Good job you remembered where they were kept.'

Lottie was helping Cliff to finish decorating the Christmas tree. She hadn't known of the existence of Christmas decorations here.

'How did you know, Cliff?'

'I've been here more than you. Haven't I, Father?'

'Yes. Perhaps we should tell her.'

Uncle Steve had built up the fire until it roared up the chimney, and now he brought out a bag of chestnuts and set some to roast on the fire bars. He poured three glasses of port and handed one to Lottie.

She sipped it but didn't like it much. Cliff pulled a face at her to show he didn't either.

She said: 'Tell me what?'

It couldn't be that Cliff had been here last Christmas. They'd all been at home in Crimea Terrace then. She'd seen him there, when she and Connie had gone home after the night staff had come on at eight o'clock. Cliff was over six years younger than her. She thought of him as someone she had to take care of.

She said: 'Come on, little brother. You can't keep things from me. I was worried about you but you're more resilient than me and Connie. We're both amazed you're coping so well. You've been able to put everything behind you, and get on with your life. You're so relaxed and at home here. And at the factory.'

Neither he nor Steve said anything. The silence seemed loaded. Then Cliff looked up at her, his face serious.

'It was easier for me, Lottie. Easier for me to accept because I knew beforehand.'

'Knew what? Not about Mam?'

He exchanged looks with Uncle Steve and seemed suddenly older than his years. 'About this house, about Father, everything.'

'What?' Lottie stared at him, astounded. 'When did you know?'

'Ages ago, since the beginning of the war.'

She couldn't believe it. 'But how?'

Steve was smiling with fatherly pride at his son. 'You know what young lads are . . . Full of curiosity. Got to get to the bottom of everything. Tell her, Cliff.'

Cliff looked almost embarrassed now. 'It was like this. You

and Connie were at the hospital most of the time and that left Jimmy and me with Dadda.'

Steve put in: 'Jimmy was only eight and Marion knew he was scared stiff when there was a raid.'

'I slept like a log and Dadda was having sleeping pills so we could both sleep through the siren. Anyway, Dadda couldn't take Jimmy down to the cellar and he wouldn't go alone, so Mam wanted to be with us once the siren went.'

Steve looked at him fondly. 'He soon figured out that his mother came home if there was a raid whether she'd said she'd be working or not.'

Lottie looked from one to the other. 'But how did you find out, Cliff?'

'One night I was playing at Tommy Halter's house when the siren went. His mother told me to run home before the bombs started to fall, but I didn't rush. There was nobody about, everybody had run to the shelters. It was pitch dark in the streets but there were searchlights threading through the sky, lighting up the barrage balloons. It was kind of spooky, but exciting. I came to the end of the road and watched them for a bit. Then I saw Mam being brought home in Uncle Steve's car. We all knew she went to work on her bike, didn't we? We saw her push it out of the back yard every morning. I recognised the car even in the blackout, and I wanted to speak to him. We didn't see him all that often. Mam grabbed me and pulled me to our front door and he drove off pretty fast. I knew she was put out that I'd seen him; she asked me not to tell Dadda because they didn't get on and Dadda didn't like her seeing him.

'Well, that set me wondering. You know Dadda, I didn't think he'd be cross if Mam saw her brother. He wasn't that sort. The siren had gone early that night. Dadda and Jimmy were playing some game, Ludo or something. Mam kept talking nineteen to the dozen about nothing, just so I couldn't get a word in and put my foot in it. I sensed I'd caught her doing something wrong. So when we three went down the cellar I started asking questions. She wouldn't tell me anything and that just made me more curious.'

The room was filling with the scent of roasted chestnuts. Steve removed those that were cooked and set more on the bars. 'He followed his mother here, that's how he found out.'

'It was in the school holidays and I was at a loose end. When Mam set off on her bike one morning, I followed her on mine. She came here to this house. I thought at first she was visiting one of her patients because she was in her uniform and she'd said she was going to work. But she took her bike round the back into the yard, when I knew she normally left it in front with the pedal propped up against the kerb. All the same, I gave up and turned for home.'

'Then how . . . ?'

'The bread factory interested me too. I was hanging about outside, watching vans go in to load, when I saw Uncle Steve walk down and let himself into this house with a key. I knew I'd cracked it then. I knocked on the door.'

He laughed. 'That put the cat amongst the pigeons, I can tell you. You should have seen Mam's face when she opened it and saw me. "What are you doing here?" she screamed. "What are you?" I yelled back.'

'The bombing made things very difficult for us,' Steve put in. He started to peel one of the hot chestnuts and encouraged them to do the same.

'So what did Mam say?' Lottie wanted to know.

'They had to let me into the secret.' He grinned at Steve. 'Didn't you, Father?'

Lottie said: 'I can't believe it. You were only a kid. You couldn't have understood how things were.'

'He had his wits about him even then,' Steve put in.

'I'd seen Clark Gable and Madeleine Carroll. I thought I knew about love affairs.'

'You were just a child. Connie and me – we were trying to look after you.'

'I used to come here quite a bit. I was looking at adult behaviour then. Always watching. Worried at finding such a secret. Worried about Mam embroiled in it all. Fretting about the impact on Dadda and you. Mam and Uncle Steve suddenly started treating me as an adult. They had to, or I'd have gone running back with the story to you and Dadda. The panic I set up in their minds was a revelation to me. I grew up in a hurry, forgot childhood things.'

'Gracious,' Lottie said, sucking the finger she'd burned on the chestnut.

'The rest of you didn't notice. There was a war on. I'd always liked Uncle Steve but this shocked me. To have another house was like fantasy land, something out of a story book. Yet it was here, solid and furnished and comfortable. Mam seemed so different here. It gave me another life too and I loved that. She didn't want me here, but I came. They couldn't keep me away. I used to come every afternoon after school instead of going home. I told Dadda I was round at Tommy Halter's. School holidays and weekends, I was here with Mam all day.'

'I solved the problem,' Steve said, 'by taking him to the factory.'

'I loved that too. It was a real treat to go inside and see the bread being made. I pretended to myself I was grown up and at work. More fantasy. I knew Uncle Steve was going back to see Mam and leaving me there. That's how they achieved their privacy, and how I came to feel at home there. That's how I can accept Father.' He nodded in Steve's direction. 'I've had longer to think about it. I saw him and Mam together many times, and I understood why. With Dadda and everything.'

Lottie was amazed. 'But you never said a word about it at home. We didn't know all this existed.'

'That was the deal. It was a secret and they made me promise to keep it.'

She lay back in the armchair. 'You knew all the time! You might have told me and Connie.'

'Mam said no. She was afraid you'd be upset. You were anyway.'

'Perhaps.'

'Of course you were. Mam said you were too idealistic. Too fond of Dadda. It would be better if you didn't know. And since you weren't living at home it was easy to keep it from you.'

'We couldn't let Jimmy know,' Steve explained. 'He was too young. He'd have given the game away, even if that wasn't his intention.'

'That was why it had to be kept secret.' Cliff was smiling at her. 'The point of it all, was that Dadda wouldn't have to know. He thought a lot of Mam.'

Lottie picked at the chestnuts and tried to accept that Cliff had never needed much help from her or Connie. He'd grown up without them noticing. He'd kept a secret like that for nearly a year!

Uncle Steve said quietly: 'I wasn't sorry Cliff found out. I saw much more of him after that. It gave me back my son. We got to know each other.'

His soft grey eyes were watching her. 'I'd have liked to see more of the rest of you.'

Lottie said: 'We've got to know each other now.'

'Well enough to call me Father too?'

'Connie does already,' Cliff put in. 'Even though he isn't her father. He really wants to be a father to you.'

'If you're not ready for it yet, Charlotte, if you can't, just call me Steve. Let's drop the uncle tag, eh?'

'I'll try,' she choked. Cliff pleading with her to accept Uncle Steve! What a turn-up that was.

'If you and Connie can do it . . .' She turned to Steve. 'You've been kind to us all. Searched us out to be kind. Tried to support us.'

'It's what a father does,' he said gently.

'Yes.' Lottie tried to smile at him. 'All right. Father then.' She understood now about him and Mam. She had to accept things as they were. 'But only if you stop calling me Charlotte. It's a bit too formal.'

'Lottie then?'

'That's more me.'

All the same, what she'd learned put a whole new slant on the way her family had lived. She did feel shocked, and she couldn't wait to tell Connie.

'Cliff's not a little boy any more,' Connie said sadly. 'We mustn't think of him as that. He grew up without us noticing. Everything's changing.'

Lottie felt she needed a change too. She'd grown used to working in theatre. It was her responsibility to set up the trolleys for many of the operations performed and to make sure everything was sterile. She assisted the surgeons at some of the operations.

She'd found it exciting at first but lately she'd begun to miss the patients. She hadn't lost sight of her goal; she knew she needed wide experience. So when she heard that there was a vacancy for a staff nurse in Casualty, she asked if she could move there.

The New Year came and the months rolled on. She settled down in her new job and enjoyed it, but she preferred working on a ward. She decided she'd stay where she was for six or nine months and then when a ward vacancy came up she'd ask to be moved again.

When Cliff was home from school she and Connie always went to stay in the Brightland Street house if they could get the time off. They continued to visit Father in the Old Swan factory and he'd taken them once or twice round the Birkenhead factory too. They were beginning to understand the extent of his business and to know the people who worked for him. They knew he relied very much on Geoffrey Montague who had managed the Birkenhead factory for many years.

It was all part and parcel of her life. Lottie felt she was accepting the situation, but it could still deliver an occasional shock.

Cliff had been home for his summer holidays for a month, and it was the third time they'd been over to spend the night with him at Brightland Street. She could feel the emotional tension in the air as soon as they arrived. Cliff was on edge; her father seemed jumpy.

Over the macaroni cheese they were having for supper,

Cliff suddenly announced: 'We're taking steps to have my name changed to Lancelyn.'

He looked her in the eye and managed a smile. 'By deed poll. I'm telling you now well beforehand, so you can't say we're keeping it secret.'

Lottie had difficulty swallowing what was in her mouth. Brinsley was the name on their birth certificates. Their father's name was given as Herbert Brinsley. To change it seemed like publicly denying their relationship to him. That would be hurtful – if Dadda knew.

Their father put down his knife and fork and tried to explain.

'I was caught in a net of my own making when you were born, Lottie. In order to maintain the story, your birth had to be registered in Herbert's name. When I had to agree to that again when the boys were born, I felt as though I was giving away my most precious possessions.'

Nobody moved. 'It's what Father wants,' Cliff said into the silence. 'It's my rightful name, after all.'

'It makes him officially my son.'

'I won't do it,' Lottie said angrily. 'It's no good trying to talk me into doing that too, because I won't.'

There was another fraught silence. Connie broke it. 'At least this needn't concern me. I'm glad Brinsley—'

Lottie burst out: 'You're right, it needn't!'

Her father seemed too relaxed. 'It's all right, Lottie. Even if you did change your name, you'll probably get married sooner or later and have to change it again.'

'Different for me,' Cliff smiled.

The year went on. 1942 was a year of bitter fighting but in

135

North Africa and on the Russian front, the tide of war changed in favour of the Allies. But throughout 1942 German U-boats in the Atlantic lay in wait for Allied convoy ships and sank them in ever-increasing numbers. In Britain, as fewer supplies got through, it made it a year of privation for civilians. Rations had to be reduced.

One dark Sunday afternoon towards the end of that year, Connie was admitting patients who were to have an operation the following morning. One man, the second to arrive, drew her attention when he came to sit beside her desk in the office. His round brown eyes wouldn't leave hers as she took his medical history, and got him to sign the necessary forms.

She took longer over it than usual. He was chatting about the progress of the war, about a programme he'd heard on the wireless, anything and everything. By the time she handed him over to her staff nurse, a small queue had built up outside her office.

Connie had never seen the men she nursed as anything other than patients. Most of them were elderly anyway. Mam had married one of her patients and look at the life she'd had with him. Connie had always preferred to find her boyfriends elsewhere, but Waldo Padley was different.

When she'd written up all her patients' files, she went back to study his. Waldo, admitted with a 'sports injury', was almost two years older than her, which was good. He was just a factory worker, building Spitfires, but he seemed more sophisticated than that implied, and his fingernails were clean. She felt drawn to him. She told herself he'd probably been drafted into his job. She'd heard they were drafting miners back to the mines and that soon almost any man could find himself hewing coal.

Every time Connie walked past his bed he tried to inveigle her into conversation, keeping her beside him as long as he could. He was showing such obvious interest in her that she couldn't help but be interested in him. He had soft short honey brown hair and was very good-looking and wore the smartest pyjamas in the ward, unbuttoned at the top to show part of a smooth brown chest. If all went well, he would be on her ward for ten days.

On Monday, he made no fuss about being prepared for theatre. She would have liked to have gone down with him to see the operation performed. He did ask her to, but that was the job of a second or third year nurse, not the ward sister. She allotted the job to the most competent nurse on her staff.

Everything went according to plan. She was there when he came round. He was a good patient, giving no trouble and making good progress. He was popular with all the nurses, outgoing by nature and chatting to them all, but his round brown eyes watched for her coming and going about the ward. He chatted to her more than to the nurses. She began to wonder what he'd do when the time came for him to be discharged. Would he ask if she'd meet him outside? She hoped so, but feared it might be the last she saw of him.

Connie had a day off on Friday and knew Lottie had too. She wanted her sister to go over to Old Swan with her. The day before, she rang Steve to let him know they were coming. He always made a fuss of them, gave them lunch. Sometimes they spent the afternoon in Brightland Street and he took them out in the evening.

'He's not in today,' his secretary told her. 'He had an accident last night. He always stops off on his way home to buy the latest edition of the *Echo*. It seems he was crossing the road in the blackout and was hit by a car. He was taken to the General Hospital in Birkenhead.'

Connie felt herself cringe. She was fonder of Steve than she used to be. 'Is he badly hurt?'

'Mr Montague's been in to see him, says he's badly bruised and shocked. He's got two cracked ribs and a broken wrist. He'll be there for another day or two.'

'Could be worse, I suppose,' Lottie said when she told her. 'We could go and see him in the General. Cheer him up.'

'He's on Private Block so we can go in any time.'

'What can we take him?'

'Do we need to take anything?'

'Yes,' Lottie insisted. 'He's always giving us things. We don't want to look mean. Have you got any sweet coupons left? We could try to get some chocolate.'

For the visit, Connie wore her mother's musquash coat and felt both warm and smart.

'You don't look anything special in that blue utility coat,' she told Lottie, though she looked prettier than ever and never cared one jot about what she wore.

It seemed strange to go from one hospital to another. The General was down near the docks in the centre of town.

Father didn't look at all well. He smiled when he saw them and tried to pull himself up the bed, but it made him wince with pain. His face and arms were covered with grazes, not all of them superficial.

'Makes me look worse than I am,' he told them. He was pleased they'd come, pleased with the chocolate and Lottie had a fund of stories that she brought out to amuse him.

'Don't make me laugh too much,' he pleaded. 'It hurts.'

'It hardly seems like a hospital at all,' Connie told him, looking round the room. Occasionally, other visitors could be heard coming and going in the corridor, but they couldn't see them.

Afternoon tea was being brought round. Being Private Block it was served with some style. It came on a tray, complete with tray cloth, teapot and hot water jug.

'Shall I bring extra cups and saucers?' the junior nurse asked Steve. 'Would your visitors like to have a cup of tea with you?'

'Gosh,' Connie said. 'You wouldn't get this on an ordinary ward.'

Lottie was biting into a cake which her father said he couldn't eat when the nurse returned with the extra cups.

She said: 'Your wife's arrived, Mr Lancelyn.' She looked at them. 'And your other daughter. They're just having a word with Sister.'

Connie saw the colour drain from Steve's face and felt the sudden rush of tension. 'What do you want us to do?'

The door was opening and two women came in before anybody could move. Lottie was staring at them thunderstruck with her mouth full. The atmosphere in the room seemed to hit boiling point.

'You said you might come in this evening,' Steve said faintly. 'Hello, Iris.'

She was tall and gaunt and terribly old. Her face was wrinkled. She must be years older than Mam. She pushed past Connie to the bedside. Kissed him briskly on the cheek. Started to unfasten her smart burgundy-coloured coat. She kept her felt hat on; it had burgundy feathers pushed in the band. Grey wispy curls showed round her thin suspicious face.

'Rita's going out tonight. She wanted to come earlier, didn't you, dear?'

'Hello, Dad. How are you?'

Connie couldn't breathe. Rita was more like Lottie than she was, the same slim lanky build. The WRAF uniform suited her, but she wasn't as pretty as Lottie and her mouth turned down at the corners giving her a dissatisfied air.

Connie pulled herself to her feet. 'We were just going.'

'Who are your friends? Do introduce us.' Iris was eyeing Lottie.

'I'm Charlotte,' she said. 'And this is Constance, my sister.'

'You work in the factory?'

'No.' Steve had recovered, though his cheeks were now scarlet. 'My other family. I told you about them.'

Iris's gasp was very audible. Lottie got up and offered her hand. 'I'm sure you've been as curious about us as we've been about you.'

Iris ignored her and said coldly: 'I'm afraid we haven't given you much thought. Have we, Rita?'

Connie could see her assessing Mam's musquash coat as she put it on.

Lottie began to fill the cups. 'Poor Father, you're still waiting for your tea.'

Connie couldn't stand the thought of staying to drink tea. It would peg them here for another ten minutes. 'Let's go, Lottie.'

But Lottie was handing their cups to Iris and Rita.

'Sugar? No? I've eaten the cake, sorry about that. The nurse might bring more if you ask her nicely.'

Connie thought they both looked sour. She was itching to get away.

'Goodbye, Father. Hope you feel better soon. We'll be in touch.' She kissed his cheek.

Lottie made a point of calling him Father too and showing affection.

'Thank you for coming.'

Connie stood fidgeting with the door knob. They should be thinking of him. He was the patient. This wasn't making his day. His eyes met hers.

'Come over to Old Swan to see me on your next day off.'

'Don't rush back to work, Father.'

'I have to. Goodbye, Connie.'

Connie found herself walking out to the bus stop with Lottie who couldn't stop giggling.

'Aren't they awful?'

'We should have stayed and found out more about them.'

'What made us take to our heels like that?'

'We wanted to spare Father's feelings. I've never seen him look so totally embarrassed. Well, not for a long time.'

'Doesn't she look old?'

'And bad-tempered.'

'I was so curious about them. Imagined them to be . . . well, not like that.'

'We can understand why he liked Mam now, can't we?'

'He loved Mam.'

For once, Steve Lancelyn was glad to see the girls go. He felt as though he'd been run over by a tank. He hadn't the energy for what he knew was coming and he mustn't lose his temper. That never got them anywhere.

Iris looked outraged and ready for battle. 'You don't realise what an embarrassment all this is to me. You said it was over;

that your mistress had been killed.' She snorted with indignation. 'Though it took you long enough to tell me. I must have been the last to hear.'

Steve told himself to stay cool. 'I was upset, Iris. I couldn't talk about it for a long time. Yes, Marion was killed in the Blitz, together with my younger son.'

'I thought that would put an end to all this nonsense. You don't realise what it does to me.'

'Do stop shouting at each other,' Rita protested. 'You're upsetting Mummy. Taking advantage of her. It isn't fair.'

'I'm not the one doing the shouting.' Steve ached every time he moved. Even his face felt sore when he spoke. 'You had a right to know how things stood, and I told you.'

'I was glad when she was killed. Your mistress disposed of, out of your life and mine. I was delighted. I thought that would remove the embarrassment once and for all.'

Steve felt sick. That turned him off completely. To say outright she was glad Marion was dead! And for such a reason.

'We are your family. What will people think?'

'You have to think of poor Mummy. What she's had to put up with.'

Steve said nothing.

'I expected the whole sorry business to be over. Now I find we're to be plagued by her offspring.'

'You knew about the children. I made no secret of that.'

'You did, for at least ten years. I don't want to know your illegitimate children. I don't want them paraded in front of me. And particularly not in front of Rita. I'm your wife, for goodness' sake.'

'Iris, do stop. Rita's a big girl now, there's no reason to keep it a secret from her. She might as well know we haven't had much of a marriage. You're my wife, but only in name. My other children mean a lot to me.'

'You didn't tell me you had two daughters.'

'Only one, Charlotte. Connie is Marion's elder daughter.'

Iris sneered. 'So she had another family too? She wronged her husband in the way you wronged me? You shouldn't have those girls here. It puts me and Rita in a difficult position. What'll the staff think? We shouldn't have to put up with this.'

'I didn't know they were coming. They tried to ring me at work and heard I was in here. They said they'd come to cheer me up. And they did for a while, until you came.'

'But you encourage them. You shouldn't have them over at the factory all the time. They're all over you because you have money. If you hadn't, I dare say they wouldn't come near you.'

'Iris, you are the one interested in my money. You and Rita and Doreen. That's all you are interested in – what I can give you.'

'I am your wife . . .'

'I know, and I'll not forget my obligations – my financial obligations – to you and the girls. My real interests lie elsewhere as you know. You never wanted to hear about the factory or help in any way. I suggest that in future you go your way and let me go mine.'

'What does that mean? You're going to leave home altogether? I don't want that.'

'I know you don't. Please leave me alone now – I'm not up to having arguments like this. Not at the moment. I need to rest. I'd like a bit of peace.'

Steve closed his eyes and put his head back against the

pillows. He told himself it was silly to get worked up like this. It was yet another version of the argument they'd had over and over again.

Iris was buttoning up her coat. 'Come on, Rita. This is getting us nowhere.'

The door slammed behind them. He was glad they'd gone, leaving the tea cold in the cups. He couldn't rest, not after that. His mind was on fire. It was agony to get out of bed but he struggled to the window. Below him in the yard in front of the hospital a few cars were parked. He saw Iris and Rita hurrying over to her Morris. She had no petrol ration and shouldn't be driving around the way she did. To keep her happy he'd had to arrange for her to collect petrol from the Birkenhead factory. She drove on the allowance they had for deliveries. Rita got into the driving seat. Iris would be too flustered after that episode.

He'd leave her to her own devices. Pack his things as soon as he felt better. He'd have done it long ago if she hadn't implored him to stay, so that her friends and neighbours could see she had a husband in tow.

To be honest, other things had conspired to keep him there. It was convenient to call in the Birkenhead factory before going over to Old Swan in the mornings. It kept him in touch with Geoffrey Montague and what was happening there.

Rationing meant he had to give an address and register with shops in the district, but now he'd go down to the Food Office and have that changed. He'd only been able to stay in Brightland Street as much as he had because of the factory canteen.

He often stayed a night or two there. Always when Cliff or the girls were there. Just as he had when Marion was alive.

She'd had to go back to Crimea Terrace and he'd usually come home to Birkenhead. In future he wouldn't. He'd stay at Brightland Street. If and when Cliff and Lottie wanted to make more use of the house themselves, he'd find himself a flat somewhere. Perhaps take a room in a hotel on a permanent basis. That would solve the domestic problem at the same time.

He'd sever his links with Iris after this.

Chapter Nine

1943

It was April and Lottie was expecting a phone call from Sandy any day now, to say his ship had docked and he had shore leave. Connie kept asking when they were going to get married.

Lottie wasn't sure they were heading towards marriage. Sandy spoke of wanting to see the end of the war first. She too felt she had other things to do before she settled down. Sandy was a close friend of long standing and she was looking forward to going out with him and having a bit of fun.

One afternoon, she swept into the home with a group of her colleagues, having come straight from the dining room after tea. The phone rang as they were passing it and one of them picked it up.

'For you, Lottie.'

She felt a rush of anticipation as she took the receiver, almost sure that it would be Sandy. She was off duty now. She'd said she'd go to the pictures with some other nurses but she could easily drop out of that. It was Mrs Cooper. Lottie knew immediately this wasn't good news.

'A terrible thing. Our Sandy's gone down with his ship. It was torpedoed in mid-Atlantic.' Lottie could hear the tears in her voice. 'I've been so afraid of this. All last year . . .'

The home was quiet now. Lottie dragged herself up to her room and lay down on her bed. She'd heard plenty in the news about Atlantic convoys being attacked, of ships being torpedoed and sunk. She'd talked to Sandy about it on his last leave, but she'd refused to believe it would happen to him. She'd already lost so many of her loved ones, it didn't seem possible she'd lose somebody else she cared about. It would be like lightning striking twice in the same place.

But it had happened. It made the war seem even more dreadful and the end was nowhere in sight. She wept angry tears for Sandy, whom she'd known for most of her life. It hardened her resolve. She had to do her utmost to stop this slaughter.

After half an hour, she got up, washed her face and changed. Then she went over to Liverpool to see his family. She didn't know what to say to comfort them. Nothing would, but she did her best. Agnes Cooper looked terrible.

'Sandy was all we had,' she sobbed.

On her way back to the bus stop, she stared at what had been Crimea Terrace. The building had been flattened and the cellars filled in. The brick-strewn earth was now covered with rosebay willowherb, a thick green growth where once there'd been buildings. Soon it would be in flower and a sea of pale pink.

She was tired when she got back to her room at Clatterbridge. It had been a long slow journey although buses and trains were running to a timetable again. It had given her time to think. She went straight to sleep.

The next day, she took out all the information she'd accumulated about Queen Alexandra's Royal Army Nursing

Corps and sent off for the application forms. She didn't quite have two years' post-graduate experience but she wasn't far off. Connie was aghast when she told her.

'Don't do it. What if you didn't like it? Besides, I want us to stay together.' She had a morning off too and had brought her knitting to the sitting room.

Lottie urged: 'Join up with me.'

'No fear, I'm happy here. I thought you were too.'

'I am . . . but Sandy Cooper going down with his ship, that's shaken me . . . and we lost our mam and . . .'

'That was two years ago. I thought you'd got over it.'

'I have and I haven't – you know what it's like. It was always my intention . . . and now with Sandy too. I have to do all I can. Come with me. Other people are being killed, thousands of them.'

'Lottie! I don't want to be killed. I haven't got what it takes. I want to stay a long way away from the fighting. Anyway, I'm doing my bit here.'

'I'll go by myself then,' she retorted. 'It's something I've got to do. My way of getting revenge on Hitler. Daft, isn't it?'

Within a very short time Lottie was attached to a military hospital near Chester for her basic training. By the time she'd spent a day or two there she wasn't at all sure she'd done the right thing. She was one of a large intake and they seemed to spend a lot of time hanging around, waiting to be issued with uniform and equipment.

There was a never-ending stream of instructions that had nothing to do with nursing. They were not free to leave the premises even if they were off duty, except when they had a special pass. There were lectures to attend every morning and they had little to do with nursing either. The wards seemed alien. The patients were all young men wearing uniform pyjamas. Not all were suffering from injuries received in battle though many were. There were plenty of more familiar illnesses like appendicitis and stomach ulcers.

She'd thought the ward sisters in civilian hospitals were disciplinarians, but they had nothing on the sisters here, where they were the only women. The ward work was carried out by RAMC nursing orderlies. There was a much more masculine atmosphere.

She had to queue up with other nurses in the same intake to receive inoculations, and, worst of all, she had to learn to march. Every afternoon, outside in a concrete yard, they had square-bashing. It always seemed to be raining and Lottie felt she'd never learn to keep in step. It seemed far removed from anything she was used to, or anything that would help speed up the end of the war.

But on the rare occasions when she was allowed to leave the hospital, she was near enough to go back to Clatterbridge to see Connie. The bus journey took only an hour. She felt at home there and knew many of the staff. Now she no longer had a room of her own, she had to share Connie's single bed if she stayed the night.

She saw this as an unsettling interim before she could get down to the job in earnest and be of use. An uncomfortable time of change that she wasn't enjoying.

Connie thought she'd found the man she was looking for in Waldo Padley. He had a smile that would turn anybody's heart. He wasn't the professional man she sought but he spoke of his ambitions. He wasn't planning on being poor for much longer. He was working hard and saving hard so he could buy a nice house and live in comfort. Connie approved of that. She was quite pleased to tell Lottie about him, brag about him even. She wanted her sister to meet him. She hadn't needed Lottie's help to attract Waldo.

Lottie was full of her own problems now she was in the army, and was in no hurry to meet him.

'You'd like me to come and admire him?' she'd asked.

'I want your opinion, you ass.'

'This is the one? Mr Right?'

Connie had really thought so at first. He seemed keen and he showered her with gifts. Chocolate, perfume – and the other day he even gave her an orange! It was years since she'd tasted one; very few were imported these days and they were reserved for children under five. She loved his gifts, but the orange worried her.

'How did you manage to get this?' she asked him.

He said his friend had a young daughter who didn't like them. It didn't sound a likely story. She was afraid Waldo was on the make, not as honest as he should be, and that was a disquieting thought. Lottie kept telling her that one good thing about the war was that it had made everybody pull in the same direction. Everything was shared equally now, differences in class and status forgotten. Connie had the feeling that Waldo wanted more than his fair share of the goodies available.

Also, he was forever pestering her to sleep with him and she didn't like that. He kept inviting her to see his flat. He'd recently moved there from lodgings and seemed pleased with it. She was afraid that what he really wanted to do was to inveigle her into his bed. He kept saying: 'If you really loved me, you would.'

Connie thought she loved him but she didn't trust him enough. She'd heard of too many girls who were deserted when they fell pregnant. She wasn't prepared to risk that happening to her. It wasn't part of the easy life she sought.

Anyway, his flat had proved a real turn-off. She knew he wasn't rich, but she was looking for a man who could afford to keep her in modest comfort. The basement flat was dark and growing black mould because it was damp. It was an untidy mess.

Waldo shared a bathroom up on the first floor. It was a long trek up cold, thinly carpeted stairs to a dank and none too clean bathroom with a stained tub and a geyser into which a shilling had to be fed to gain hot water. He had sole use of a lavatory out in the back yard.

Connie was glad to get back to her room in the nurses' home. At least it was centrally heated and cleaned for her. Perhaps the Brightland Street house had trained her eye to a standard that was too high, but she wasn't going to live in a dump like that.

It was the same old story. She'd more or less written Waldo off. Would have done, except that she liked having somebody to take her out on her evenings off. And Waldo was very presentable and great company.

Lottie knew all about Waldo Padley. Connie had been talking about him for weeks. She went to see her sister one evening when she had a twenty-four-hour pass and found her room empty. Lottie went to the sitting room and chatted to the nurses who were off duty. It seemed homely compared to her new billet. When Connie came back she was settling down to sleep in her bed.

'You said you'd be staying in tonight.'

'Waldo asked me out. We went to the Ritz to see Greer Garson in *Mrs Miniver*.'

'Ah, your new man – how did it go?'

'Fine. A good film.'

'A patient, you said? I thought you were dead against going out with a patient? Afraid you'd end up like Mam, nursing him for the rest of your life.'

'Don't talk daft. A slipped cartilage is quite different. He thinks he caused it by kicking a football too hard. He's healthy.'

'Don't tell me you go to watch him play? Stand around in a cold field . . .'

'The season's over, Lottie. It's summer now.'

'Oh, then that's a pleasure saved up for next winter?'

'I doubt it.' Connie got into bed and pushed her to the far edge. 'He says he hardly plays, it was just one of those things. Come and meet him next time. You'll like him. I'll get him to bring a friend to make up a foursome.'

'Is it serious?' It was what she always asked Connie when she met up with someone new.

'Could be.' That was what she always answered.

The foursome was arranged for the next time Lottie had a twenty-four-hour pass. It was a warm summer evening. She was wearing her new grey army uniform with scarlet flashes, which felt hot and heavy, and the bus was late dropping her outside Clatterbridge Hospital.

Connie was done up to the nines and looked cool and glamorous in a green flowery summer dress. She always took a lot of trouble with her make-up when she was going out and her dark curls swung round her shoulders.

'I wish I'd worn a dress,' Lottie said, feeling hot and frumpish beside Connie's elegance. 'Can I borrow something of yours?'

'If you can find something to fit.' Connie was often rude about her lack of shape. She said she was flat-chested and beanpole thin. 'Hurry up, we don't want to be late.'

Lottie selected a white blouse, a dirndl skirt and a pair of sandals. Throwing off her uniform, she rinsed her face and helped herself to her sister's make-up. Connie used only Elizabeth Arden, not the hotch-potch of bits Lottie seemed to collect. Only the best was good enough for Connie.

She glanced in the mirror to check on her appearance. With her short straight hair and slight build she looked much younger than her sister.

'You ought to make more of yourself,' Connie said, her hand on the door knob. 'You've got a nice face really . . .' Although her hair was dark, Lottie had fair skin. 'If only you'd do something about those freckles. There's more than ever.'

'I've been out in the sun. All the marching they make me do. What can I do about them?'

Connie studied them for a moment. 'Can't you bleach them off?'

'Bleach? I wouldn't want to try.' Tonight her cheeks were rosy. She looked the picture of health.

'What's the matter with your fringe? It's sticking up.'

'We're not supposed to wear our hair over our faces. I have to pin it back under my cap.'

'Wet it and comb it down. It looks a mess.'

Lottie went to the washbowl and tried it. 'Have you got a safety pin to take in the waistband of this skirt? I don't want it to fall down. Right, I'm ready.' It had taken her six minutes flat.

'Come on, then.' Connie was impatient. 'We'll have to run for the bus.'

They caught it by the skin of their teeth and within minutes were getting off outside a pub. Connie had been against pubs when Lottie had started to go. Not ladylike, she'd said, and then during the raids nobody went. It was foolhardy to be caught in a crowd. Now, like most others, Connie had decided it was the place to go for a bit of fun.

They paused in the doorway, looking round the lounge. There was a good buzz of conversation from the preponderance of servicemen present. Lottie saw two men at a corner table stand up. She followed Connie over to be introduced.

'This is Walter Padley.' Connie was full of smiles for him. 'Known as Waldo.'

Lottie's hand was gripped and pumped twice. For a man he was short, hardly taller than Lottie herself, but he was rounded and cuddly-looking. He reminded her of a teddy bear she used to take to bed with her when she was a toddler. He had the same honey-coloured hair, soft and silky, but Waldo's was curlier; the same cherubic face and round brown eyes. They fastened on hers as they sat down round the small table.

She was hardly conscious of Jim Turner, who said: 'What would you girls like to drink? I'm afraid there's only beer or orange squash.'

'Every pub gets its quota of beer.' Waldo's smile seemed just for her. 'And it's usually been watered down.'

Lottie knew that wine and spirits were almost unobtainable

these days and Scotland's whisky production went to America to help pay for armaments.

'Beer will do nicely,' she said. She felt an immediate rapport with Waldo.

'I'm very envious,' he told her. 'That you've been able to join the QAs to do your bit. I tried to get in the air force but failed my medical.'

That made Lottie glance at her sister. Perhaps he wasn't as healthy as he seemed?

'It's upsetting to be stuck in Civvy Street in times like these. Makes me feel useless. As though I'm incapable.'

But it turned out he was doing essential work in an aircraft factory at Hooton and fire-watching several times a week.

Lottie noticed he was adept at dividing his attention between her and Connie, as though he didn't want either to feel he neglected them. He did most of the talking but it wasn't what he said that captivated her, it was the way he affected her feelings. She'd never known anybody who could do this to her. His gaze melted her; she couldn't drag her eyes from his.

He asked how she intended to spend the next day, which she also had free.

'Connie's working all day. I'll go back to Chester, have a look round the city. I've hardly seen anything of it yet.'

Jim Turner was pleasant enough, chatting non-stop to Connie. Singing broke out in the public bar; they could hear them roar and thump, 'Roll out the Barrel' and 'Run Rabbit, Run'.

Shortly after ten o'clock the pub ran out of beer, the singing petered out and the customers began to melt away. They went too, walking through the village to try two other pubs, but all seemed to have run dry and were very quiet.

'Might as well give up for the night and go home,' Connie shrugged. The men saw them on to a bus going back to Clatterbridge and waved goodbye.

'What do you think of him?' Connie wanted to know as she paid their fares.

'I like him. I like him very much.'

'You looked riveted. Hope you aren't falling for him.'

Lottie smiled. 'You're always talking of falling in love and thinking of getting married. I'm going away, Connie. I've other things on my mind.' She knew that in a few weeks she'd get a posting which could be to anywhere. 'Yes, he's good company. How old is he?'

'Twenty-eight.' Connie turned to look at her. 'You are interested in him!'

'If things were different – perhaps.' He'd had so much warmth and personality she felt he'd quite bowled her over. 'But he's your friend. Have you made up your mind he's right for you?'

In the semi-darkness of the bus, Connie smiled at her primly. 'I'm not sure yet. I mean, a job in an aircraft factory ... that's a bit off-putting.'

'I hear they're getting a pound a day now.'

'I'd like him better if he had a job with a bit more status. Jim works in a bank.'

Lottie smiled. 'He's not good enough for you?'

'It's not that.' Connie's voice was sharp. 'But you have to think of such things before you commit yourself to marriage.'

Waldo had been taking a deep swig of beer when he saw Connie leading Lottie across the bar towards him. She'd spoken of her sister with such affection.

'You must meet her,' she'd said. The bond between them was very plain to see now. He stood up.

'Here they are,' he said to his friend Jim.

'Wow – a bit of all right, both of them.'

There was a veneer of glamour about Connie. Waldo could smell her perfume from yards away and see the plum-coloured lipstick and pancake make-up. She had a womanly figure with plenty of bosom and a narrow waist. The younger one was more natural and sylphlike by comparison. She had shorter hair, more plainly styled. They were not much alike to look at.

'How much younger than Connie are you?' he asked when they'd sat down. He was wondering if she was old enough to be drinking here. He didn't want to get involved with jail bait.

'Three years.'

He'd have guessed nearer five, possibly even six, but her manner was confident and outgoing. They had the same dark eyes, but Lottie's were set wide apart. They fastened on his.

'Waldo.' She rolled his name across her tongue. 'An unusual name.'

'It's Walter really. I hate that. Been in my family for generations. High time it was dropped. Walter Donald.'

'Donald's fine. I like that.'

'I don't want to be associated with Donald Duck. I combined them both to make Waldo. Got a bit more style, don't you think?'

'Does it sound a bit Germanic?'

'No,' Connie protested, 'it doesn't. Lottie's anti-German with a vengeance.'

'Aren't we all?'

'Course we are,' he put in. 'They're the enemy.'

'She's more anti than anybody else,' Connie insisted.

'Well, they killed our family. You can't expect otherwise.' Lottie had looked at him and smiled. 'Anyway, you look very English.'

She had a very wide smile and perfect teeth. Long eyelashes that cast shadows on her cheeks. Everything about her was drawing him to her.

'Lottie.' It was his turn to roll her name round his tongue.

'Charlotte really, but I don't like being called that. Too formal.'

'I love the name Charlotte.'

'Call me Lottie.' She was laughing. She laughed more than her big sister; there was more sparkle about her. She had plenty to say and he let her talk. He felt unaccountably smitten.

Waldo got up and went to the bar to get in another round of beers. Well, to get beer for himself and Jim. The girls were just toying with their glasses. Neither was a drinker. He needed to think. The little sister excited him. Just to look at her made him tingle, but how did he transfer his attentions from one to the other without offending? If he didn't play this right they would both be mad at him.

He'd seen the bond between them and knew it was strong. He'd listened to Lottie's tale of joining the QAs because she wanted to help the war effort. There was a transparent honesty about her. He admired caring people who put the good of the masses before their own, but he wasn't like that.

He'd always worked on the principle that nobody else put Waldo Padley's interests first. Therefore, if he wanted something, he had to go all out for it himself. He knew straight away that he'd never be able to talk to Lottie about the things he thought important, or admit to the things he did. Actually, there were things he couldn't talk about to anybody. Things that had to be kept quiet.

If she was prepared to risk life and limb, he was not. Lord no. No one in their right mind wanted to be killed at twenty-eight. Neither did he want to be maimed for the rest of his life. He'd taken reasonable steps to avoid service in the armed forces but he daren't tell anyone that. Especially not Lottie. He wanted to make money and he wouldn't do that by becoming a private soldier in another world war. His father had been killed in the Great War and he and his six siblings had been brought up in great poverty. Two of them had died of TB before reaching adult life. He was the youngest of the family, and his four brothers were called up before him. All were prepared to fight for England, the country that had done so little for them. Waldo didn't see why he should do the same.

His own call-up papers had arrived shortly before the war started; by then few doubted it was coming. When he'd been told to report for his medical exam he'd gone well prepared with a false history of illness. He'd spent weeks talking to his brothers about what to expect and had then studied books both in the local library and in bookshops.

He'd spun the doctor some real whoppers. He'd been lucky enough to go for his medical with a chesty cough. It was the back end of a head cold that had gone down to his chest, but he'd let it be known it was a permanent affliction.

He told the doctor that he'd had rheumatic fever as a child and had been on total bed rest for months. For good measure, he'd added that he'd hurt his back carrying sacks of coal and that he was often in pain. He'd talked at length about his father dying at thirty without mentioning the last war. About his mother who was also in her coffin by the age of forty-five. And he'd laid it on thick about his two sisters dying in childhood.

He'd had a poor diet as a child and at twenty-three he'd had a lean and hungry look. To enhance that, he'd starved himself for a few weeks beforehand to lose even more weight. He'd put it all back since, in fact rather more than he should. As Connie had put it, he was well rounded and rather chubby.

He'd been found unfit for military duties and directed into an aircraft factory. It didn't take him long to figure out that not only was it safer but he was being paid much better for his services.

At the beginning of the war, a private soldier was paid three shillings a day, with a bit more if he was married. But war workers like him were earning a pound a day. He thought he'd fallen on his feet for once.

His was a carpentry job, and the girls glued the fabric to the wooden frames he helped to make. The hours were prodigiously long. He found it monotonous work and spent much time ruminating about the difference between the interests of the individual and those of the country.

He soon decided he wasn't being paid enough if he wanted to save up to buy a house. He'd had a hard upbringing and knew what it was to go without the necessities of life. It was a state of affairs he didn't mean to continue.

He admired those who were more selfless. He respected what Lottie was doing, but it was not for him. He knew better than to think he could talk her out of it. He'd tried to make his brothers see sense, have some thought for their own future. He'd talked to each of them in turn but none had changed his

161

mind. It was a principle by which they lived. They wanted to be heroes and wouldn't compromise for their own advantage. Two of them had lost their lives at El Alamein.

Lottie slept like a top that night. She and Connie had figured out how best to sleep two in a single bed. They pulled it about six inches away from the wall, so she could have a little overhang without falling out.

But nobody could sleep through the racket at half past six when the staff had their morning call. On the floor below doors were banging, lavatories flushing and footsteps and voices echoing through the building.

They'd both drifted back to sleep when half an hour later the ward sisters were called. The maid knocked politely and came in to flick on the light. She heard Connie's grunt of acknowledgement. The noise level on this corridor was much less. After ten minutes' more snooze time, Connie heaved herself off the bed and started to get ready for breakfast.

Lottie intended to have a lie-in, now that she could spread herself across the whole bed. The noise died down and she drowsed on for a couple of hours. When she came round again bright sunshine was streaming through the curtains. She pulled herself up the bed and thought about taking a bath.

She heard the payphone at the end of the corridor ring for a long time. Then shuffling steps came to the door, there was a timid knock and one of the cleaners put her head round.

'Are you Lottie Brinsley?'

'Yes.'

'Somebody wants you on the phone.'

'Me?' Lottie was surprised. Nobody knew she was here

except Connie. She grabbed her sister's dressing gown and ran along the corridor.

'Good morning. Hello?' At the sound of Waldo's voice, she was tingling all over. He sounded buoyant, on top of the morning. 'Thought I'd give you a buzz. You're still going to Chester? What time did you plan to leave?'

Lottie hadn't made any plan. She liked to drift on her day off.

'Would eleven o'clock suit you? I've managed to borrow a car. I'll drive you back.'

'Really? That's kind.' What she really meant was that it was wonderful.

'Eleven then? Outside the main gate?'

'You can drive in. Take the left turn. You'll see the nurses' home.'

'Fine. I'll do that. See you then.'

Chapter Ten

Lottie looked at her watch. It was just after ten in the morning and the home was as quiet as the grave. She wanted to whoop for joy. She went to the kitchen and made tea and toast, but she felt so thrilled to be seeing Waldo again she couldn't eat.

She took her time getting ready, for once she wanted to look her best. Her mind was on his teddy bear hair and charming innocent smile. She had to wear her uniform, she had no other clothes with her, but these days everybody was in uniform, so it wouldn't matter.

She made Connie's bed and tidied the room. That had to be done because Home Sister would inspect it later, and there'd be trouble if it didn't pass muster.

Waldo was early. From the window she saw a small Morris pull up in front. One glance to make sure it was him and she went careering downstairs. By the time she reached the front door he was out of the car, as if seeking confirmation he'd come to the right place. He saw her and came rushing towards her with a look of pure pleasure on his face. She felt his arms go round her in a big bear hug.

'Lovely to see you again.'

He was holding her so tight she couldn't breathe.

'It was only last night. You make it sound as though it's been years.'

'I lay awake thinking about you. I was afraid you'd be spirited off to Timbuktu and I'd never see you again.'

Lottie laughed. 'What a welcome you give me.' He was ushering her towards the car. 'And I can't believe you're taking me for a drive.'

'Only the best for you.'

'But how do you do it?'

Petrol had been rationed since the beginning of the war. To start with, private motorists had been allowed to drive up to a hundred and fifty miles per month but in March last year the basic petrol ration had been abolished. Motorists now had to claim it was essential for health or to get to work.

Lottie had read in the papers that people driving alone in cars could be stopped by police and questioned about the reason for their journey and the source of their petrol. She was all in favour of this. Tankers carrying petrol were being sunk in the Atlantic. Sandy Cooper had lost his life that way. It was wrong that men's lives should be put in danger so that others might drive for pleasure.

'I'm doing an errand for a friend.' Waldo beamed at her. 'He owns this car and has an allowance as an essential user. There are documents he wants dropped off and things I must collect for him. If I don't do it, he'd have to.'

They set off. For Lottie it was usually an enormous treat to see the green fields and woods roll past, but today she couldn't take her eyes off Waldo.

He drew her senses. She felt an unaccountable urge to put out her hand to touch him. She wanted to cuddle up to him in a way she never had to any other man. The intensity of her feelings surprised her. She felt a different person, more alive, ready for anything.

'Don't you have to work today?'

It was Wednesday, and she was wondering if he'd stayed off to see her. She knew all factories engaged on war work operated very long hours. It was essential that they did.

'We work shifts now. The factory goes on producing day and night, but we all have a bit of time off.'

Lottie relaxed. She understood shift systems, since she worked that way too.

He parked the car and, after taking out the two large packets he wanted to deliver, walked her through the city, pointing out places of interest. He knew Chester well and she did not. She thought him very knowledgeable about the fine medieval black and white buildings and the history of the place.

Lottie waited outside a building in Hunter Street that announced it housed the District Chamber of Trade and the City Chamber of Commerce.

'I'll need to come back later. There'll be something for me to collect,' he said. 'How about walking the city walls? It'll give us an appetite for lunch.'

He pointed out the bridges and the ancient gates. She saw the castle and the race course, the river and the canal. They had a lunch of pie and salad in a tiny café.

'It's going to stay fine this afternoon. How about a skiff on the river? Would you like that?'

Lottie loved it. He rowed well and tried to teach her. She wasn't very good at it.

'You'll need more lessons,' he said gravely. 'We'll have to do this again.'

At the end of the afternoon she felt full of sunshine and fresh air. Waldo collected some large packages for his friend and then suggested a drink and some supper.

'Will that be all right? Those packages aren't urgent?' She wondered what they might contain. They seemed very light.

'Not desperately urgent.' Waldo smiled easily. They had a leisurely meal before he drove her out to the military hospital. He pulled up before he reached the gates, and drew her into his arms to kiss her.

Lottie whispered: 'You've given me a wonderful day. Thank you.'

'Can we do it again? I'd like to.' His fingers were stroking her hair.

'Will it be possible?'

'Maybe not the car, but I'll make it possible. Just tell me when.'

'I'm not sure. They don't give us much notice.' She'd really enjoyed herself but she was beginning to feel a little guilty. 'What about Connie?'

He leaned back to look at her. 'What about her?'

'I thought you were her boyfriend.'

There was a silence. He was serious now. 'So did I, until I met you.'

'How is she going to feel about this?'

He said gently: 'I don't think she'll be too bothered. Did she say anything to you? About me?'

'Yes – that she wasn't sure . . .'

'Well then? She must have seen the way things were going. I couldn't take my eyes off you.'

Lottie nodded, that was true enough, but . . .

'Connie never wants to say straight out. She'd have to be quite certain.' But she was keen to get married and looking hard for a husband, leaving no stone unturned. 'She seems to like you very much. I don't think she was ready to brush you off.' Not yet anyway.

Waldo's teddy bear eyes stared at her through a long silence. 'Look, Connie and I are never going to get it off the ground. You and I – well, we're flying already.' There was another silence. 'Aren't we?'

'Yes.' How could she deny that? He excited her. It made him take her in his arms and kiss her again.

He whispered: 'I think I'm falling in love with you.'

That made her body run with heat. Lottie felt exactly the same about him.

Lottie admitted to herself that Waldo had knocked her sideways and left her unable to think of anything but him.

She couldn't telephone him, he had no phone, but he said he'd keep in touch. He rang her every day; she'd told him the best time to catch her in the mess.

He said: 'I knew from the moment I saw you that I'd grow to love you.'

For Lottie it fanned the flames. What she felt for Waldo was like a fever that burned ever more hotly. She longed to see him again. The days spent waiting for another pass seemed to go on and on. When at last it came, she met him in Chester in the early evening sunshine.

'I want you to come and see my flat,' he told her. 'I've put a meal in the oven. It'll be ready by the time we get there.'

'In Birkenhead?'

'Yes, Oxton.'

'I oughtn't to be eating your rations.'

'I want you to. Anyway, it'll be spoiled if you don't come.'

'I want to. I'd love to see where you live.'

'It isn't much of a place. One day I hope to have somewhere better.'

'When the war's over.' Lottie smiled. It was a refrain she was always hearing. With so many houses lost in the bombing it was very hard to find anywhere to live. It was a long, two-bus journey, and they had to wait for a connection. For Lottie the time flew.

'This is it,' he said as they walked along the road. 'In this house here.'

It was a shabby Victorian villa. The grey plaster on the outside walls was flaking off, the black paint was peeling off the massive front door. Waldo showed her down slippery moss-covered steps to a little yard and led her into his kitchen. He had the basement flat. It was untidy, the sink was full of dishes, but heavenly scents were coming from the ancient gas cooker. He looked inside.

'It's a casserole with baked potatoes.'

'Lovely,' she said. 'I'm hungry.'

'Ten minutes. Go into the living room. I've got sherry or beer.'

She opened the door. It smelled of damp in here. A small table was already set with a print cloth. A large wireless dominated the tiny room. He put a glass of sherry in her hand and came to sit beside her on the sagging sofa.

'I've spent all my life searching for a girl like you, and when I find you, the first thing you tell me is that you're going away. Whatever made you sign up? You didn't have to.'

She told him how the Germans had maimed Dadda in the Great War and how a bomb had killed him and the rest of her family in this one.

He frowned. 'Connie told me, but she isn't rushing off to fight.'

'Connie sees things differently.' She told him about Sandy and the torpedo that had sunk his ship. 'Is it silly, to think what I do will help?'

'Yes. Connie's got it right.'

'If we all thought that way, nobody would do anything. We'd all sit back and wait. It would drag on and on.'

'There's always somebody else who will.'

Lottie sighed. 'I'm one of those. I felt I had to. I'd do anything to help end this war.'

Waldo busied himself getting the food on the table. She was impressed; the casserole was made with beef and lots of vegetables.

'You're a good cook.'

'A bachelor has to be.'

She giggled. 'You've got a typical bachelor pad here.'

'Shabby and cramped. I'm ashamed of the place.' He pulled a face. 'Ashamed to bring you here. I mean you're an officer . . .'

Lottie smiled. 'Your kitchen looks much the same as the one in the house where I grew up.' Theirs had always been clean and tidy, though. 'We were poor. As I said, Dadda couldn't work, couldn't even do much about the house.'

'My family had a bad time in the depression too.'

'We never went hungry but there wasn't much money to splash around. We didn't have holidays or parties. My mother had a job.'

She stopped. She wasn't quite ready yet to tell him about Mam's lies or that she had another father.

'Connie told me,' he murmured, but she didn't know how

much. What Mam had done was still affecting them both, two years after she'd died. 'Your mother was a nurse like you, wasn't she?'

'The other way round. Connie and I became nurses like her. Mam saw it as an insurance policy – we'd never need to be out of work, never have to go hungry.'

He was serious. 'I knew what it was to go to bed with an empty belly. It was no joke. It's made me . . . ambitious, I suppose. I have to keep a bit in the bank, just in case. One day, I'm going to have a nice house, one I can be proud of. And I'm not always going to be a factory hand. I'm going to get a business of my own.'

'What sort of a business?'

'I'd like a garage but perhaps it'll be a shop of some sort. Almost anything that would make me my own boss. There was a piece in the newspaper yesterday that said a quarter of all retail businesses not selling food had closed down in the last year. Everything's so scarce they can't find anything to sell. But after the war things will be different. The shelves will be stacked again and there might be a shortage of shops. I want to get in on the ground floor and get one now. That's the only way I'll ever be able to earn a good income. I didn't go to a posh school.'

Cliff was going to a posh school. And that was because of what Mam had done. But Cliff was better off, wasn't he? He was happy there, and Lottie wanted him to have a good job afterwards. She had to stop thinking like this.

They went back to the sofa and Lottie cuddled up against him. He kissed her.

'Will you stay here with me? Stay all night?'

She raised her head a little. 'Sleep with you, you mean?'

This time, she hadn't told Connie she had a twenty-four-hour pass. That would have meant telling her she was going out with Waldo. Lottie had expected to spend the evening with him in Chester. She could go back to sleep in her own bed. She hadn't been too concerned about going all the way to Oxton. She knew she could push herself in with Connie if she wanted to spend the night with her, as long as she was there before eleven when they locked the doors of the home.

He said gravely: 'I've put clean sheets on my bed and it's a three-quarter size.'

Lottie smiled. What she had with Waldo was a very physical passion. What was the point of waiting? If they sent her off to some foreign battlefield she might never come back.

'Say you will,' he pleaded.

She wanted to, her mother had done just this, but she was sure Connie would be horrified. If Mam could do it with all the responsibilities of a family, there was no reason why she shouldn't. Mam was dead, her life cut off in mid-flow, and that could happen to her too. Waldo wouldn't be the first. Sandy had persuaded her by saying they might never have the chance to make love again and he'd been right about that. She had to grab what pleasures she could when they were offered.

Lottie heard Waldo's alarm going off at six o'clock the next morning.

He groaned and turned over. 'I don't want to leave you. Can't think of turning out to work. Too awful.'

'You have to.'

He pulled a face. 'I suppose so.'

'Course you do. You want this war won, don't you?'

He was lying still, his soft brown eyes staring at her dreamily.

'I want to marry you, Lottie.' His voice was gentle. 'I want it more than I've ever wanted anything. How about it?'

For Lottie, it felt as though something had burst into life within her. Nobody had proposed to her before. That Waldo wanted to commit himself so quickly endeared him to her even more.

'But I'll have to go away. Quite soon . . .'

'That's why we have to do it.' His voice had urgency. 'Total commitment. I want to bind you to me. Otherwise you'll forget all about me when you go away. Will you?'

'Just like that? We'll not have time.'

Lottie knew lots of girls who had got married. They'd been courted by a boyfriend for a year or two before making up their minds. Then they'd become engaged for another year or so in order to save up and make all the preparations.

'I don't need time. I've thought of nothing else since I set eyes on you. We could get a special licence.'

Lottie could see her life stretching ahead. Always, Waldo would be there waiting for her, loving her. She couldn't believe how much she wanted it. But natural wariness held her back.

'I need to think about it.' She knew she hadn't much time to think.

He shook his head. 'My gut reaction is that I want this very much.'

Lottie felt the same, but what she said was: 'My gut reaction is you're going to be late for work. You've got to get to Hooton.'

Waldo sighed and swung his legs out of bed. 'Stay where you are. I'll bring you some tea.'

But Lottie was getting up too. 'I'll make it. You'll not have time to wait on me.'

When the time came for him to go, it was hard to tear herself out of his arms and away from his kisses.

'Think about it, Lottie. It's the best thing for us. The only thing. I couldn't bear to lose you.'

She went back to bed and thought about it. Hugging the excitement and the thrill of it to her. That Waldo wanted marriage so badly was very appealing. It proved he loved her. Nobody else had ever been prepared to go this far with her. Sandy had talked about it vaguely but he'd made no commitment. Just implied they might get round to marriage eventually, when the war was over. This was very different.

Lottie stayed in his flat for most of the day. It was Waldo's home and she liked being here even if he couldn't be with her. She made his bed and cleaned up for him, and had a sandwich at lunch time, telling herself being married to him would be a bit like this. But it was a big step to take.

She told herself that falling in love with him had come at completely the wrong time for her. She'd just joined up, and within the next few weeks she was expecting to be posted to the other end of the country. Out of the country perhaps. She'd no control over where she went. It was no good wanting to stay here to be near Waldo.

How she wished she'd waited another month before joining up. Or that she'd met Waldo a month earlier. Connie had been talking about him for some time. But it was no good wishing or being sorry about what she'd already done.

She still wanted to do all she could to fight this war, though right now she wanted Waldo more. It was gone six in the evening when he came home again and she had to be back before midnight.

They went out to a café he knew and Lottie told him she'd marry him if they could both manage to get time off together. They spent the evening discussing their plans. Waldo went all the way out to Chester on the bus with her because he couldn't bear to be parted from her a minute sooner than was absolutely necessary.

For Waldo it was second nature to go after what he wanted and he very much wanted Lottie. It was love at first sight for him and he could think of nothing else. Lottie completely eclipsed Connie. He'd never experienced feelings for another as intensely as this.

He didn't care to what lengths he went, he meant to have her. He'd absented himself from work to spend the day with her. He borrowed a car and set up some pantomime to make her think there was a genuine reason to drive her to Chester. He'd glossed over the affair he'd had with her sister and got away with it all. Lottie seemed as taken with him as he was with her.

He was living in a bubble of excitement, very much in love, head over heels. When they were apart he felt bereft. There was no one like her. He couldn't imagine himself being happy with any other woman. He had to bind her to him.

That within so short a time she'd agreed to marry him increased his ardour. This was what they both wanted. Why wait with a war on? They could both be killed. Well, she could. The raids were over by now, so he'd be all right. He'd looked after his own interests.

Lottie needed somebody to look after hers and he was going

to do it. She wouldn't – all she thought about was helping other people. He was going to earn enough to keep them both in comfort. They were going to have a good life when this was all over.

The following week Lottie had another twenty-four-hour pass and Waldo managed to get the same day off. She was spending every minute she could with him now and hardly giving Connie a thought. He rang her every evening and when on Friday she was called to the phone she expected to hear his voice.

'Are you all right, Lottie?' It was Connie. 'I've been wondering – how are you getting on? Are they locking you in or something?'

'No. Sorry. It must seem as though I'm ignoring you.'

'You've met lots of new friends, I suppose. It's a whole new life.'

'I've been out with Waldo once or twice.' Lottie knew she mustn't keep hiding that from her.

'Waldo?' Connie's voice hardened. 'What d'you mean, once or twice?'

'Well, whenever I've been able to get out.'

There was a silence. Then Connie said: 'I was wondering what had happened to him too.'

'We're head over heels, Con. I've never felt like this about anybody before.'

'With Waldo?' She sounded shocked.

'I did ask you. I mean, I asked how you felt about him. You said you hadn't made up your mind.'

'It hasn't taken you long to make up yours. I wish I'd never introduced you.'

'Don't be like that, Connie. I always introduced you to my

friends. You went out with Mark whatsit and that fellow who worked in the lab. It happens that way sometimes.'

'You didn't care about them, Lottie.'

She took a deep breath. She'd worried about how Connie would take it. This was worse than she'd imagined.

'You didn't tell me you cared about Waldo. If you'd said stay clear, I would have done. You must have seen the way things were going that first night?'

'I was glad you liked him.'

'He said there was nothing between you.'

'What?' Her undisguised anger came clearly down the line.

'I mean, just that you were friends, nothing more.'

The phone crashed down at the other end and Lottie felt a rush of guilt. She went back to her room and threw herself on her bed, cross with herself for upsetting Connie. Worried, too, because she hadn't got round to saying he'd proposed and she was going to marry him.

Connie had always been jealous of her. Connie imagined everything came more easily to her, particularly boyfriends. Connie couldn't imagine anyone fancying her with her short straight hair and scrubbed skin.

Lottie liked to think of herself as a responsible person but had she acted responsibly over this? She should have been more careful. She'd been well aware that Waldo was Connie's boyfriend and she'd taken him from her.

She told Waldo when he rang up. His voice was full of sympathy but he didn't understand just how close she and Connie had been.

She said: 'I wish you'd tell me exactly how things were between you and Connie.'

'That's all finished, Lottie. Now I've met you I'll never look at another woman.'

He sounded awkward. She wished she could be with him to explain. It was much more difficult this way.

'That's not why I ask. Connie's upset about you and me getting together. I don't want to be nosy, but—'

'It was all quite casual.'

It didn't sound as though Connie thought it had been casual. 'You took her out quite a lot.'

'To the pictures and for a drink. I never suggested anything permanent. Neither did she. We weren't committed to each other in any way.'

'But you kissed her and hugged her and . . .' She didn't want to suggest he'd made love to her sister. 'You must have done. She referred to you as her boyfriend.'

'The odd kiss, yes. In my fancy free days, I used to kiss every pretty girl I could. Honestly, Lottie, compared to what I feel for you, my affair with Connie was non-existent.'

'Ring her up, Waldo, and try to soothe her.'

'What can I say?'

'Explain things. That we couldn't help ourselves, we were swept off our feet.'

'Have you been?' he asked.

'You know I have!'

Lottie had been anxious about Connie's feelings all along. She hated to think of her being upset.

She hadn't had time to see her and talk it through properly. It was because her movements were restricted, she needed a pass to go out, making her feel as though she was gated. This would finish with her basic training, but by then she'd be very lucky indeed if she was near enough to see either of them in her time off.

Another inner voice told her she could have left a note in Connie's room to say Waldo was taking her to Chester. She could have telephoned and had a long chat the next day. At least they'd both have known how things stood straight away. It did look as though both she and Waldo had tried to keep Connie in the dark.

Lottie remembered then that she hadn't been to see Steve since she'd been in Chester. She'd phoned him after the first few days to let him know how she'd found things, but since then nothing. She dialled the factory in Old Swan to speak to him.

'How are you, Lottie?' He sounded pleased to hear from her, eager and friendly. 'I've been wondering how you're getting on there.'

She told him about Waldo. That they were going to get married.

'Give him my congratulations. He's a lucky man. What should I say to you? I'm pleased you've met somebody you want to marry – pity about the war and that you're going away. This could be a long engagement.'

'No, Father. We're going to be married quite soon. Just as soon as I can get some time off.'

'Lottie! There's no hurry, is there? Better if you waited. You hardly know him.'

'Connie knew him before I did.'

He sounded quite put out. 'Don't rush into it. Take your time. It's important that you do.'

She said to him what she'd said to Connie. 'We're head over heels in love. We don't want to wait.'

Chapter Eleven

The following week Lottie's posting came through – she was to go to the Royal Herbert Hospital in Woolwich. London. Not too far to come home occasionally – it could have been worse. She had another six days of basic training to do and then forty-eight hours' leave. That would be the last time she'd be able to spend with Waldo for the foreseeable future.

She couldn't wait for him to ring her again. It was so important that he'd be able to get the same days off.

'I'll get them if it's the last thing I do,' he chuckled.

Now the time was so close she was beginning to think it was a crazy idea to get married like this, but he wouldn't hear of waiting.

'I've made enquiries about a special licence. We'll be able to do it. In this life you've got to go all out for what you want. Otherwise, you'll be left with nothing. You aren't going to back out on me now?'

'No.'

Lottie knew that now she was in the army she needed permission from her commanding officer to get married. She'd only signed up a matter of weeks ago, but it was long enough to find out that the army wouldn't move quickly on things like this. There wasn't time to go through all the formalities. She was a mature woman of almost twenty-three; she should be able to make up her own mind about such things. She discussed it with Waldo on the phone.

'Just do it,' he advised. 'Ask permission afterwards. They might say no.'

She'd already come to the same conclusion.

He said: 'I've got some forms to fill up for the special licence. I've given your occupation as nurse. Said nothing about you being in the QAs. Mustn't give them anything to ask questions about. They needn't know. They want your address too. Shall I put down mine again? Say you're living with me?'

'Or Clatterbridge Hospital. Who's going to check up when I left?'

'It'll be legal, anyway. That's all we want.'

No difficulty seemed so great that Waldo couldn't overcome it.

Lottie rang her sister to invite her to the wedding.

'You're marrying Waldo Padley?' Her voice crackled with shock and amazement. 'You've only known him five minutes. You must be mad.'

'Madly in love. I want you to be there, Connie. The register office on Saturday. Try and get your day off then.'

'I don't want to come,' she retorted. 'You've taken leave of your senses. You know nothing about him.'

'Do you know any more?' Connie had spoken of him as not being good enough for her.

'I don't want to know any more about him.'

'Don't ring off.' Lottie had the feeling she was about to crash the receiver down again.

'I've no more to say.'

'At least wish us well.'

'For heaven's sake, Lottie. What's the rush? I'm not sure he's right for you.'

Lottie had no doubt at all on that score. 'He is.'

'Far better if you did what you set out to do. Go off and help win the war. Marriage would be better left until it's over.'

'Wait until the war's over! I'm sick of hearing that. I'm tired of waiting too. I want this, Connie. Want it badly.'

'You're mad. You could change your mind about him.'

'I won't.'

'See sense. You can't stay here with him now, anyway.'

'More's the pity . . .'

She was about to say how much she regretted joining up when the phone crashed down again. It brought a lump to her throat that Connie wouldn't talk to her.

The days were flashing past, bringing her wedding closer at breakneck speed. Lottie felt she hadn't time to catch her breath.

She made up her mind about what to wear. She had quite a smart lavender-coloured summer dress and a hat that went very well with it. She'd bought both shortly after the bombing depleted her wardrobe. She'd worn them when she'd gone out with her father, but they still looked almost new. She couldn't get out to buy anything else, and she couldn't afford to splurge her clothing coupons on a dress she might wear only once.

She worried about Connie and rang her again to tell her the wedding was fixed for midday on Saturday.

'I can't come, Lottie.'

'I need you there,' she wailed.

'I've had my day off for this week. It isn't possible.'

'But—'

'Why did you make it twelve o'clock? You know that's too late for a morning off and too early for an afternoon. I might have managed if it had been at ten or two.'

'You could ask for special—'

'It's a bit last minute for anything like that. Anyway, I need to be here – it's my staff nurse's day off. I've got an evening.'

'Perhaps we could fix something for the evening, then? I want to see you on my wedding day. We've always been close.'

'You've got Waldo now. He was my friend, Lottie. You pinched him from me.' Her voice was sharp with complaint.

It made Lottie draw in her breath. 'I'm sorry if it looks like that. Do come. We aren't going away – no time for a honeymoon or that. I'll have a word with him . . .'

'I don't want to come.'

She tried to persuade her but Connie said: 'I don't want to talk about it. I don't want to know any more about your affairs. Count me out.' The phone clicked with finality as she put it down.

Lottie had half expected it, but it upset her to quarrel with her sister, particularly as the quarrel had been over Waldo. It troubled her that Connie wouldn't come. She felt a chasm opening up between them.

Connie's hand hadn't left the phone before she was choking with dismay. She should never have hung up again on Lottie. She'd been too tart, too prickly, and shown her just how resentful she felt.

It hadn't surprised her to find Lottie approved of Waldo. He had good looks and plenty of charm. Lottie didn't know what he was really like; to find that out took time. Connie had known him longer. She thought him underhand and not above engaging in black market fiddles. He could spin stories that were all lies.

It had shocked her when she understood how serious Lottie was about him. Lottie had asked on the bus ride home that first night if she was serious about Waldo, and she'd been off hand. She wondered now, if she'd told Lottie of her misgivings about him, whether Lottie would have backed off. It brought guilt that she hadn't.

All the same, that they were to be married within a month was a calamitous kick to her self-esteem. Connie had been going out with Waldo for eight months and he hadn't got round to proposing anything definite.

That Lottie didn't think he was dishonest, that she had faith in him, and could overlook the fact that he didn't earn much and lived in a terrible flat, made Connie doubt her own judgement. Perhaps she was too fussy?

But no, she wasn't wrong about Waldo. He'd dropped her like a hot brick and that hurt. It made her resentful, bitter. And worse, it turned her against Lottie and nothing should do that.

Lottie rang her father and invited him and Cliff to her wedding.

'I don't approve of all this rush,' he told her. 'But you're of age – I can't stop it. Of course I'll come to your wedding. If this man is going to be your husband, I want to meet him and get to know him. Let me know when and where. But I'm not sure that Cliff will be able to come. They like plenty of notice at his school for special leave.'

She sat down and wrote to Cliff as soon as she'd put the phone down. She wanted him to know and understand what was happening.

She'd known Waldo for four weeks and two days on their wedding day. She felt in a fever of love by then and was absolutely certain it was the right thing to do.

With her basic training behind her, she picked up her bags and went straight to his flat in Oxton. Waldo was waiting for her. He'd managed to get a bottle of wine and some lamb chops for supper. They didn't want to go out. It was enough to be together.

The next day, Lottie dressed herself carefully in her lavender dress and they went together to the register office. Father was there. He and Waldo's friend Jim Turner were to act as witnesses. Nobody else was present. The four of them walked over to the Ritz cinema afterwards and had lunch in the restaurant. Then Waldo took her home to his flat.

'No point in wasting time travelling somewhere else,' he told her with a wry smile. 'I just want to be with you. It doesn't matter where.'

They were so happy at that moment. They spent most of the time with their arms round each other, much of it in bed. The hours were passing quickly and her leave seemed pitifully short. As the time to part drew closer, Lottie felt her spirits sinking. She couldn't bear to look at her luggage stacked in the corner of the bedroom. She'd brought it all here with her, together with the warrant for travelling down to London.

Waldo sat up in bed. 'I'll hate being left here by myself. Do you have to go now you're married? Look, I kept this newspaper to show you. It says it's just unmarried women between the ages of twenty-one and fifty-one who are conscripted.'

'I wasn't conscripted,' she said sadly. 'I volunteered for this.'

'If only you hadn't.'

'I wish I hadn't now.' She'd been wishing that since she'd met Waldo. 'The only logical way out for me . . . well, it's to have a baby.'

'I shall hope for that then.' Waldo smiled. 'I've done my very best.'

Just then it was what she wanted to happen too. She'd be able to come back to him quite soon. Waldo looked the picture of misery standing on the platform as her train pulled out. She stood leaning out of the window until she could no longer see him. Then, feeling desolate, she sat down and took out the book she'd brought to read. She couldn't see the print because tears kept misting up her eyes.

She twisted her wedding ring round her finger, the thought of taking it off was unbearable. She decided she'd continue to wear it. Nobody would know her in Woolwich. She'd keep the name of Brinsley for the time being, though she would dearly have loved to change it to Padley. It seemed the easiest way to cope with the sudden change in her circumstances.

By the time she reached Woolwich, she felt as though she'd been pulled up by the roots. Being parted from Waldo was painful.

As soon as she'd reported in, gone through the formalities and eaten supper, she opened her case on her bed to take out her writing paper. First she wrote to Waldo, telling him about her journey, which had been reasonably quick, and giving him the telephone number on which he could reach her. She asked him to ring at nine-thirty in the evenings, so she could hover near the phone.

Then she wrote to her sister.

Dear Connie,

I'm sorry I've upset you, truly I am. I couldn't help myself with Waldo, nor he with me. It was love at first sight and like a fever. We couldn't think of anybody else though we should both have thought of your feelings. I'm terribly sorry it happened this way. I wish anybody but you had introduced us. You're the last person in the world I want to hurt, honest.

I wouldn't have gone out with Waldo if you'd said straight out you were interested in him. You said he was just a factory worker and not good enough for you. I don't care what he does, Connie. I've lost all reason when it comes to Waldo. I just want him.

There's another thing. You know how he went on about being turned down on medical grounds when he volunteered for the air force? I wanted to know more about that – well, you would have done too. He didn't want to talk about it but I finally got out of him that he'd had rheumatic fever as a child. He'd been very ill and kept in bed for months. You know as well as I do that if the doctors failed him, it must be because his heart has been affected by that.

He might look strong but clearly he isn't, and I hate to think of how well he'll be as he grows older. It doesn't bode well for the future. It seems I could be following in Mam's footsteps after all, but like her, it didn't put me off. Nothing could put me off Waldo, I love him so much I'd do anything for him. But you would have been put off by that, wouldn't you? Your first stipulation has always been that, to interest you, a man must be in prime health. So I don't think you'd have married him anyway.

I'm not just trying to make excuses for what I did, it is the truth.

And oh, Connie, how I wish I hadn't volunteered. I want to be back with you and Waldo. I feel homesick already, and the news of the war is awful. Please please write to me and tell me I'm forgiven. I couldn't bear to lose touch with you.

Love from Lottie.

She had a letter from Waldo the following day and carried it around in her pocket until she could go to her room and be alone to savour it.

My darling,

I want you to know how happy I am that you are my wife. But how I miss you – though you've only been gone an hour. The time I spent with you is very precious. Knowing you, this last month, has made it the most wonderful I've ever lived through.

Parting from you is awful. It's hard to accept that you have to go away. I wish – oh, how I wish that you hadn't signed up.

You are a much more public-spirited person than I am. Much better in every way. Sometimes I wish you were not so willing to give your all to winning the war. I admire you for it, but I'm selfish, Lottie, and I want you to myself and here with me. I shall dream of you every night. Of the time when the war will be won and we can be together for always.

I long to speak to you, hear your voice again. Let me know a phone number on which I can reach you. Write to me, my darling. Write to me. I feel cut off from life itself when I'm cut off from you.

Your loving husband Waldo.

Lottie felt torn in two that she couldn't be with him. She was in one place and her mind and heart were in another. It made settling down in her new job much more difficult. She didn't feel on top of it as quickly as when she'd changed hospitals before.

It was almost another month before she knew she wouldn't be having a baby just yet. There was to be no escape that way.

'That's my hopes dashed.' Waldo was disconsolate when she told him on the telephone. 'I was banking on it.'

Lottie knew she had been too.

He said: 'I'd give anything to have you back here with me.'

'Don't say that! It makes me feel worse when you do. I mustn't even think of it.' She had to see her future here, she mustn't forget why she'd volunteered. Everybody was tired of war. The news wasn't good; it looked as though it would drag on for ever.

Connie didn't reply to her letter, but she had friendly letters from Cliff, and staid letters from her father, both full of their own concerns. Waldo telephoned and also wrote often, though he didn't tell her the things she wanted to know. She spent hours wondering what he was doing and how life was treating him. When he telephoned she seemed to be firing questions at him.

The one good thing was that she'd made two friends at the Royal Herbert. Emily Hall came from Warrington and June Dandridge from Newcastle. Both were nursing sisters and both were blonde but they were unalike in every other way. June was willowy and tall while Emily was a petite five foot two.

Although she was so dainty Emily had a powerful voice and was always singing the popular tunes, like 'Roll out the Barrel' and 'Run Rabbit, Run'.

June was quiet and more serious. She liked to read what they thought of as highbrow books. She was likely to tell Emily to put a sock in it in the middle of 'Lily Marlene', but there was never any antagonism between them.

They too felt cut off from their friends and family and were homesick. To leave the hospital when they were off duty was much easier now. With one or the other or as a threesome according to their duties, they went to the shops and theatres in the West End. Slowly, very slowly, the routine became familiar. The months began to pass and Lottie felt more settled.

Connie was shocked to receive Lottie's letter. She too had heard Waldo's story about having rheumatic fever as a child and being very ill. She wondered how much truth there was in it. It was beginning to look as though Waldo was a draft dodger.

She was sorry she'd quarrelled with Lottie and felt ashamed of throwing such a tantrum and refusing to attend her wedding. She felt guilty because she'd received a letter of apology from her that she hadn't answered. She couldn't bring herself to admit that she'd felt hurt and jealous.

She was full of guilt too because she hadn't told Lottie what she suspected about Waldo and was full of foreboding about the future of the marriage.

With Lottie away, Connie continued to go over to Old Swan to see Steve. He always seemed interested in what she was doing. He maintained contact, ringing her up, inviting her over. Her antipathy had gone now she knew him better. Steve was generous, willing to share the middle-class life she hungered for.

She knew Cliff wrote to him more regularly than he did to her. Steve invited her to go with him on the train to Llandudno to see Cliff, and arranged it for her day off. Connie wanted to see the school. Afterwards, they took Cliff out for a walk along the prom in the watery sunshine, followed by afternoon tea in a hotel. They talked at length about Lottie and her marriage.

'What's this Waldo like?' Cliff wanted to know. 'You knew him, didn't you? You introduced him to Lottie?'

It made Connie feel guiltier than ever. She kept quiet about her fears. It wouldn't help to air them now to the family. It was too late to do anything about them. She must hope all would be well.

She couldn't help but notice how Steve and Cliff responded to each other; they seemed close. They discussed the bakery business, and Cliff seemed very knowledgeable. She wasn't surprised; Steve was always taking them to the factory to explain things. When Cliff stayed in Brightland Street she knew he spent most of the day there.

When she was left alone with Cliff for a few moments, she asked him if he'd made up his mind to work in the business.

'I'd love to – eventually.' He smiled. 'Nothing I'd like better; it's an ideal opening for me. A wonderful opportunity. I feel very fortunate.'

'It's what Father wants.'

'I know. With Mam gone, he feels he has to do more for us.'

On the train going back that evening, Connie had a window

seat. She turned away from the flying landscape to find Steve studying her.

'Connie, how would you like to come and work for me?'

'Me?'

'I've been round everybody else. Lottie and Cliff.'

'I know, but what could I do? Run your first aid post?'

'No, that's running well.' He smiled wryly. 'I'm desperate for help. Too much to do. I need an assistant, someone to run round after me, making sure everything's done.'

'You have a secretary . . .'

'It wouldn't matter that you can't type. Miss Langford does that, but she's got too much to do already. I can't ask her to do more. I could teach you to run the business.'

'I don't know . . .'

'I've come out today for a rest, to get away from it for a while. It's getting on top of me. I have too many balls to keep up in the air.'

'I'm in a reserved occupation.'

'I know. This would be too. The population has to be fed.' He was pleading with her now, his eyes not leaving her face. 'Taking you out of nursing might be a problem . . . but providing I can get permission, you could come right away. I can claim you're family and needed to work in the family business.'

'I'm not really family, not like Cliff and Lottie.'

'You're Marion's daughter,' he said. 'That makes you special to me. Means a lot. I think of you as family.'

Connie warmed to him. She was tempted and played around with the idea for a week, turning it over in her mind. The thought of living permanently in the Brightland Street house appealed to her. Steve was offering a better salary than she earned now, but something held her back.

It wouldn't be easy to change to such a different job. She knew nothing about making bread or factory work and she'd have to make a huge effort to cope. What if she didn't like it? Once working for Steve, it would be a job for life; he wouldn't want her to give it up. In the end, she decided against it. She had to think of what she wanted, and that was to get married and have a family. In the meantime, nursing was what she knew. She'd stick to that. It would be easier.

Lottie had been down in London for several months now and Connie missed her company. She knew she had a hang-up about what she'd done to her sister. She was still coming to terms with the fact that if she'd spoken up right away, Lottie might not have married Waldo.

When she went over to Old Swan to see Steve or Cliff they kept bringing up the subject. They were not happy that she'd married in such haste and were full of curiosity about her husband. Connie didn't like being questioned about him; it made her feel more guilty than ever. She'd meant to tell them nothing but somehow she managed to convey general disapproval of Waldo.

'You don't like him, do you?' Cliff probed. 'Why not?'

Connie told them then she thought he was a wide boy on the make. Always on the look-out to feather his nest. Once started, she couldn't stop.

'You should have told our Lottie,' Cliff told her. 'Before she tied the knot. Warned her. Why didn't you?'

She tossed her long swinging curls. 'She wouldn't have listened to me. She'd have thought I was jealous.'

'She's made a big mistake if this is true.' Steve seemed

worried. 'Why would she think you're jealous?'

Connie couldn't bring herself to tell them. Lottie had leapt at the chance to marry Waldo, and it had made Connie wonder whether she'd been mistaken, whether she'd lost the opportunity to acquire a good husband.

She found it helped to talk about Waldo. It was balm to her self-esteem. Waldo wasn't worth having. Perhaps she'd been lucky to avoid tying herself to him. If he was caught, and there were reports in the newspapers all the time of black marketeers being taken to court, then Lottie might not be so pleased with her choice.

She couldn't forgive him. He'd dropped her the moment he set eyes on Lottie. Without explanation or apology, he'd just cut her off, left her waiting for his next phone call. As far as she was concerned, nothing was too bad for Waldo Padley. She didn't care if he was caught. It would serve him right if he was.

During Cliff's half term, Steve took them both to the Birkenhead factory. They were going to have lunch with Geoffrey Montague in the canteen there.

'My son's home on leave,' he said. 'Seven days. I'll give him a ring and suggest he comes in to join us. I think he finds it a little dull at home.'

He was late arriving and Mr Montague had already led the way into the canteen. 'Here he comes now,' he said.

Connie looked up and saw a tall man of nearly six feet. His dark eyes fastened on her as he weaved between the tables towards them. He had a neat pencil moustache.

'My son, Clovis,' his father said, beaming across at him. 'He's serving in the RAF at Mildenhall.' The only empty seat was beside Connie.

'Clovis?' she said. 'That's an unusual name.'

'A family name. My mother's French. Her choice.'

'I like it.'

Steve said: 'Geoffrey fought in France in the Great War and fell in love with Yvette, one of the girls from Armentières the soldiers sang about. He married her and brought her to England. Isn't that so, Geoffrey?'

'And I'm their only child.' Clovis smiled at his father.

He told Connie he'd been brought up entirely in England, though holidays had been spent in France before war broke out again.

Connie felt quite dazzled by him and was disappointed when he left without asking if he could see her again.

By the time Christmas 1943 came round, the fifth Christmas of the war, the whole population was exhausted by the continual struggle. Everybody's paper streamers were looking tired and dog-eared, and shortages were more acute. Connie had to work all day on Christmas Day as usual, and had thought Cliff would be in for a very quiet Christmas with just Steve for company.

'We've been invited to the Montagues' for Christmas dinner,' Steve told her. Connie had all but forgotten Clovis Montague in the intervening months but now she wished she was going with them. 'Can you come to the works party on Christmas Eve?'

Connie gave herself an evening off duty so that she could. Cliff would start his holiday three days before, and she wanted to take over the presents she had for them.

She went straight to the works and could hear the gramophone playing in the canteen. It was Bing Crosby singing 'White Christmas'. The first thing she saw was the enormous tree decked out with empty matchboxes wrapped in coloured paper.

Then Cliff came rushing up. Steve was beaming at her. It was as though Christmas had given everybody a new lease of life. They were laughing as though they hadn't a care in the world.

Connie didn't notice Clovis Montague until he came across the room and reached for her hand.

'I was hoping you'd be here,' he said. 'I should have asked for your phone number last time. Wished I had afterwards. When I got back to Mildenhall I couldn't stop thinking about you.'

Connie was thrilled. He told her he had another seven days' leave over Christmas and he wanted to see her again. The whole Montague family had come to the party, and he introduced her to his mother. She spoke fluent English but had not lost her French accent.

'Clovis begs me to invite you to share our Christmas dinner. Your brother Cliff is coming, and Steve.'

Connie explained why she couldn't.

'The next day then?' Clovis suggested. 'Boxing Day? Just a quiet meal, Maman?'

'It will be just leftovers by then,' she smiled. 'But do come.'

Connie had never enjoyed a party more. Clovis was clinging to her like elastic. She had to go back to Clatterbridge that night and had meant to leave in time to catch the last bus from Woodside, which went at ten-thirty. Clovis persuaded her to leave early so he could see her back to the hospital. To be alone with him was what she really wanted.

Connie worked through Christmas Day but Clovis was

never far from her thoughts. She was looking forward very much to having supper at his house on Boxing Day. She'd taken to wearing her mother's clothes. Most fitted her without alteration and Mam had had smart dresses that were just right for the occasion. She'd wear Mam's musquash coat on top and some of her jewellery.

Clovis met her at the hospital gates and took her to his home by bus.

'Dad says I can borrow his car to bring you back tonight. So we don't have to worry about buses.'

'A rare treat for me,' Connie told him. He was in uniform, and she was proud to hold on to his arm.

The Montagues lived in Oxton, in a big detached Victorian villa with large high rooms. Connie was impressed and looked around with avid interest.

'Are you warm enough?' his father asked. 'We've lit a fire in the dining room again today, but mostly these days we can't. Not enough coal.'

'It's lovely and warm.' Connie approved of the huge mahogany sideboard set with silver and loved the way the table had been laid with a crisp white cloth, silver and sparkling crystal.

At the end of the meal, she said: 'You said it would be leftovers, but that can't have been.' She'd eaten and enjoyed three courses, each more elaborate than anything Mam and Dadda had ever produced in Crimea Terrace.

'Yvette's ingenious at concocting delicacies from very little,' her husband said.

Yvette smiled at the compliment. 'I've had to be since the war started. I just wish I could get some decent coffee.'

'Maman doesn't like our tea,' Clovis said.

'I have to like it. There's no coffee.'

'I bought you some today. Queued for it.'

'Not real coffee. Just – how do you say? Just substitutes. One made from chicory, the other from acorns. Neither tastes much like coffee.'

'The chicory one isn't bad,' Clovis told her. 'You just have to get used to it.'

Connie saw a good deal of Clovis during his leave. The more she saw of him, the more certain she became that he was the man she'd been looking for. He really was Mr Right. She'd met up with him at last.

Clovis Montague was in prime health. He came from a good middle-class home; she even liked his parents. He was good-looking if not exactly handsome. He told her he loved her and was very attentive.

He could make her tingle; she was really in love this time. On the last day of his leave, he asked her if she would marry him. Connie was thrilled and delighted; at last things were happening for her.

Chapter Twelve

1944

Early in the New Year, Lottie was granted seven days' leave.
She couldn't believe her good fortune. Seven whole days to
spend with Waldo. They'd never had so much time together.
She couldn't wait to get to a phone to tell him.

'A delayed honeymoon,' he laughed. 'Absolutely wizard.'

Lottie caught the train up to Liverpool. It was two hours
fifteen minutes late but he was still waiting on the platform
when it pulled in after midnight.

To see his chubby figure and round face again was
wonderful. She struggled towards him through the crowd
surging off the train, and saw his brown eyes light up when he
caught sight of her. His arms went round her in a hug of
welcome.

'Let's get you home,' he said. 'You must be tired out.'

She was, but the adrenalin was running; she was back
with Waldo. They crossed the river to Birkenhead on the
underground. It was the last train to run that night. From
Hamilton Square they walked down to a shack near the
ferries from which a taxi service ran. There was a queue
waiting.

He caught at her arm. 'There's a bus! I think it's going our way.' It was about to pull away from the stop and in the blackout it wasn't easy to see its route. Waldo set off at a run to hold it up.

'We're in luck, it's just what we want,' he said, ushering her inside.

Lottie felt really tired by the time Waldo was unlocking the door to his flat. He kicked the door closed behind him and took her into his arms again. She was so happy to be home with him.

'We'll go to bed. A cup of tea first? Something to eat?'

'Tea would be lovely.' Lottie yawned. 'Just tea.'

'I'll make it while you get undressed.'

She'd just crawled between the sheets when he brought in two cups. He put them down on the bedside table and took a little package out of the drawer beneath.

'A present for you, Lottie.' He put it in front of her on the eiderdown, his eyes full of the joy of giving. She knew it was an important gift.

She unwrapped the gold paper carefully to find a small leather case. Lottie looked up at him and smiled. 'It's a ring.' Inside was a magnificent sapphire surrounded with diamonds. 'It's beautiful.'

He lifted it out and slid it on her finger above her wedding ring.

'Didn't have time to see to such things before we were married, but now . . . I don't want you to miss out because of that.'

Lottie was touched. 'It's absolutely lovely.' The sapphire was pale blue and the diamonds flashed in the dim light. 'Enormous. It must have cost a fortune. You didn't have to, Waldo. You want to save for a business.'

'I'm doing that, but I wanted to give you something worth having.'

'Waldo, you've already given me everything. But I really love this, thank you. It looks very impressive.'

'Don't take it off. I want you to wear it tonight.'

Waldo was throwing off his clothes to join her in bed. With his arms round her, Lottie no longer felt tired. She was being swept along on a tide of love. Passion such as this was what she'd missed all these months. This was why she'd married Waldo.

At breakfast the next morning, she feasted her eyes on her husband. He was in high spirits.

'I asked for a week's holiday so I could be with you. Told my boss I just had to have it.'

'Wonderful. Lucky to get it at such short notice.'

'We'll spend one day in Liverpool, have lunch out and go to a theatre. Another in Chester. I'll have you all to myself for seven whole days.'

Lottie hesitated. 'I must see my family. Cliff if I can. Father and Connie definitely. I have to make my peace with Connie.'

He pulled a face. 'I hate sharing you with anyone.'

'I must . . . I sent them cards to say I was coming. Connie might never speak to me again if I don't ring her and arrange to meet. Shall I ask her round here one evening? Perhaps Father too?'

She saw a shadow cross his face. 'Why don't we take them out for a meal? I'm not proud of this place.'

Lottie said: 'This would be my home if I hadn't volunteered for the QAs. I'd be living here. Connie will be curious about it. She'll think it odd if we don't ask her round.'

Waldo said nothing. He was frowning at his fingernails when she looked up. Then he said awkwardly: 'No she won't. She's seen it.' It was his manner that alerted her, more than his words.

'Just the once,' he went on. 'Had a few friends in one night. For my birthday. Jim Turner and some others.' He was smiling again.

Lottie was suddenly afraid his affair with Connie might have amounted to more than he was admitting. She remembered Connie's reaction to the news that she'd been seeing Waldo.

She said: 'Then there's no reason for her not to come again.'

'If that's what you want.' She could tell he didn't like the idea. 'Your father . . .'

'We can call at the factory to see him if you'd rather. It's what he'd expect.'

'I'll have a better place before you're demobbed. That's a promise. This is just a bachelor pad, not at all suitable for entertaining. The living room's so cramped.'

His flat was cold now winter had come and it smelled of damp, but she could see he'd made an effort to tidy it up.

'Get your business first. That's what you want most.'

'I'll have them both before you come home for good. I'm working on it now.'

'Bachelor pad or not, you're well organised in the larder.' Waldo had insisted they have egg and bacon for breakfast.

'I've been saving up my food points for your visit.'

'You didn't need to. I've brought an emergency ration card. They're handed out with the leave passes.'

'We'll be able to feast, then.' He was smiling. 'I've laid in lots. I don't want you to go hungry.'

'I never go hungry. Living in hospital has some advantages.'

Waldo frowned. 'It's not that I go hungry, but I rarely feel satisfied. And the food's monotonous. I crave for something different, don't you?'

Lottie didn't spend much time thinking about food. She had a good appetite and never missed a hospital meal, but she was mostly content with what was on offer.

'Don't you fancy something special? Oysters or salmon or dressed crab or something?'

She laughed. 'I can't remember ever having oysters. Or salmon, come to that. We had dressed crab when Father took us out. Roast chicken's my favourite – we used to have it at Christmas before the war.'

Waldo smiled at her. 'Luxury foods are not rationed because there's not enough to go round everybody. Very expensive, though, so I don't usually buy them, but you told me you liked chicken and I've ordered one for Wednesday.'

'Goodness! That'll be lovely.'

'I hope it'll be a big one.'

'Perhaps we should ask Connie for that night? She'll be impressed.'

'It's steak for tomorrow. It's in the meat safe.'

They were in the kitchen washing up by this time. Lottie viewed the generous piece of steak with surprise. 'Is this the ration for one? It's much more than I imagined it would be.'

'I gave my butcher my coupons last week and held the meat over to this.' Waldo's round brown eyes smiled into hers.

Lottie loved to cook; it was a rare treat for her to do it. She phoned Connie who agreed to come round to the flat on Wednesday evening. She seemed pleased to be asked.

On Monday, Lottie took Waldo over to Old Swan to see her father. They'd met only briefly before, on her wedding day. She thought Father seemed a little suspicious of him. He asked a lot of pointed questions about Waldo's job; what exactly he did, the hours he worked, and how conditions at Hooton compared with those in his own factory. Lottie half expected her father to offer him a job after that, but he didn't. He asked him about his ambitions for the future.

'So you can take care of my daughter,' he told him.

Waldo for once was saying very little and didn't look as though he was enjoying it.

'Have you seen Connie yet?' Father asked her.

'No, only spoken on the phone. She's coming over for a meal on Wednesday. She says she's fine.'

He said slowly, 'She is,' and smiled.

'You look as though you're going to tell me something. About Connie?'

'Better if I leave it to her.'

'Go on. She's changed her mind, she's going to come and work for you?'

'No. She'll tell you. You'll have to be patient.'

Over lunch in the works canteen, he said: 'You must try to see Cliff. Ring the school from my office and ask the headmaster if you can take him out to tea. Saturday's a good day for that. It would be a nice trip out to Llandudno for you, and Cliff would love to see you.'

'I'll do that,' Lottie said. 'I'd love to see him – and his school.' Waldo smiled wanly at her over his plate of milk pudding.

On Wednesday evening, she was in the basement kitchen cooking the meal when she saw her sister's four-inch high heels walk along the pavement in front of the window. Lottie had the door open by the time she was coming down the moss-covered steps.

'Hello, Connie. Come on in.' She threw her arms round her. She'd made up her mind to ignore their differences. After all, months had gone by. Connie had written to her quite recently, a careful note on small-size paper that said very little.

Connie's smile was wide. 'Wonderful to see you again.' She pecked her on the cheek. They'd never been a family that kissed much, but after all these months a token kiss was needed.

Connie didn't look entirely at ease. Lottie didn't feel at ease herself. It was difficult when they hadn't seen each other for several months and had parted on bad terms. It had taken a long time for them to exchange letters and Connie hadn't got round to telling her she was forgiven. It was bound to be difficult now they'd come face to face.

'You look like a film star,' Lottie told her and really she did. Connie's dark curls were fluffed out round her face. She was undoing the buttons on the military style coat that was high fashion as far as fashion was perceived in wartime.

'Utility wear.' Connie's smiled wavered. 'Not bad as far as it goes. Not much choice, though.'

'I think utility clothes are good,' Lottie said. 'I've had to get a new winter coat and dress too. They took up all my clothing coupons.'

'Still, you wear uniform most of the time, don't you?'

It was easy, Lottie thought, to talk about things that hardly mattered. It showed good intention, but somehow it didn't diminish the gulf that had opened up between them. Waldo came from the living room.

'How are you, Connie?'

Lottie noticed there was no token kiss for him.

'Hello.' Her tone was less than friendly and caused an awkward pause.

'You look very well,' he told her. 'Let me take your coat.' Connie liked fussy clothes. She was wearing a frilly pink blouse and a skirt that was ornately swathed.

'Come through and sit down,' Waldo said. 'We've got a bottle of wine.' Lottie was pleased to see he was on his best behaviour. They all were.

She whispered to her sister: 'Am I forgiven?'

'Of course. Anyway, it doesn't matter any more. I've met someone else.' Connie's dark eyes surveyed them both triumphantly.

'Oh! You've got engaged?' Lottie whooped, as Connie fluttered her fingers and a sparkle caught her eye. She felt relief mushrooming inside her. Connie hadn't said she'd met somebody better, but that was the implication.

'Yes.' She held her left hand out so both could admire her ring. It was unusual: a row of three small rubies with a tiny chip of diamond at each end, all set into a wide gold band. 'It's Victorian.'

'Lovely, very pretty,' Lottie said. It was, but she didn't want Connie to compare it with the one Waldo had just given her. Fortunately, it was a little large for her finger and it kept turning round so the stones settled against her palm and could not be seen.

'Who is he? Tell us about him,' Lottie urged. She'd go to the bedroom and take her ring off at the first opportunity.

Connie was smiling. 'You know Mr Montague, manager of the Birkenhead factory? It's his son.'

'Father introduced you?'

'It's how we met. He's in the RAF, a navigator.' Connie beamed with pride. 'He's lovely.'

'Oh, Con, I'm so pleased.' Lottie forgot the awkward start and gave her a real bear hug. 'I'm so happy for you.'

'He's stationed down at Mildenhall, which isn't good. I'd rather he was at home in Birkenhead. He wants us to be married so I can go down there and be near him.'

'I'm delighted it's happening for you too, Connie.'

'High time. I'm twenty-six.'

'Just about the right age,' Waldo beamed. 'I'm twenty-eight.'

'Tell us about him,' Lottie said for a second time. 'I want to hear every detail. After all, he's going to be my brother-in-law.'

'Well, he's tall, nearly six foot. Slim with brownish hair, dark eyes and a moustache.'

'I can't picture him from that!'

Connie drew out a photograph from her handbag. Lottie surveyed it eagerly. 'He's a Flying Officer.'

Connie's smile was self-satisfied. 'Yes. Trust you to know his rank from his uniform.'

'It's one of the things you pick up in the army,' Lottie told her. 'Lovely to see you so happy.'

'Ought to be champagne,' Waldo said, pouring the wine. 'A Flying Officer, eh?'

'She'll be better off with him than she would have been with me,' he whispered to Lottie later when he went to the kitchen to carry in the chicken to carve. 'This should let me off the hook.'

He didn't say as much to Connie, who seemed to bristle

when Waldo went near her and never spoke directly to him. She made it plain that whatever he'd done to her, she hadn't forgiven him.

The chicken was cooked to a turn but the gravy was a bit lumpy and the sprouts were overdone. Lottie felt she was out of practice. They all burned their tongues on the jam roly-poly she'd made to follow. Connie was over polite, praising the dinner too much.

'An uncomfortable evening,' Waldo said as they walked home from seeing her to the bus. 'Stilted. She spoiled it for us. She's taken against me.'

On Saturday, they took the train to Llandudno. It was cold but the day was bright with sun. The school had taken over two big hotels, one of which was on the sea front.

Cliff had a grin from ear to ear as he came running down the stairs to meet her. He was excited and pleased to see her again. He offered Waldo his hand and said all the right things about wanting to meet her husband.

He showed them round the school and afterwards they walked along the promenade, arm in arm. Lottie felt buffeted by the strong wind, which whipped up the waves, giving them white tips though the sea was bright blue.

He took them to the tea room most frequented by the boys from school and their parents. It was all dark wood and cretonne curtains, and the tea came in little silver pots. They had toasted teacakes and a Victoria sponge.

Cliff was a little stiff in his manner, wary of Waldo, not quite his usual friendly self. But Lottie could see he loved his school and was happy there. She noticed his hands. The cuts and grazes had long since healed but he'd been left with scars.

On the train going home, Waldo said: 'I like it better when

we're on our own. All I want is you, Lottie. With so little time, I almost resent having to share you with other people.'

Lottie could understand that, but she was glad she'd seen all her family and that they seemed happy. She needed to see them from time to time; it helped her think of them as they were, not as they had been, and stopped them drifting away from her. She wanted to stay close to them.

Waldo took her to dances and pubs and restaurants, and bombarded her with gifts of perfume and chocolate and even nylon stockings. He talked of a dreamy future when the war was won, the house they'd have, the car and the babies too.

Lottie went back to the Royal Herbert feeling refreshed and happier but it was an anticlimax to be without Waldo again. Parting was no easier the second time but at least she knew what she was going back to. She found it very difficult to settle down again.

Waldo had put his mind to augmenting his wages long before he'd met Lottie, but marriage motivated him anew. He'd started in a small way right at the beginning of the war.

At that time, people with long memories and money to spare bought up goods and stored them: tinned and dried foods, sugar and jams, anything that would keep. The acute shortages of the Great War only twenty years earlier pointed out the sense of doing that. Waldo couldn't remember those times, but he remembered his mother holding forth about them.

He used his wages to stock up on almost everything. Socks, women's stockings, gloves, handbags, vests, bedding, buying everything in the best quality he could find. The goods had been stacked up against the walls in his lodgings. He'd had to find a flat of his own to get more space to store his stock.

He'd been lucky; his flat came with a wash-house next to the outside toilet that was ideal for storing things.

The war was five months old before rationing was introduced. By that time the rich had been going from shop to shop buying all they could and the poor wanted a fair share. Shopkeepers were putting things under the counter for their regular customers.

Rationing had started gently at the beginning of 1940. At first, it was just bacon, ham, butter and sugar. The sugar ration was found to be woefully inadequate by most. By March, each person was entitled to a meat ration of a shilling a week. In July it was tea, followed by cheese, cooking fats, sweets and jams.

Waldo started selling his stock at prices that were much higher than those at which he'd bought. He was able to get more. There were occasionally surpluses at grocer's and butcher's shops: the rations of people who were killed in raids or who had gone to the country to avoid them. This food was available to others at a price.

With Lottie once more in London, Waldo wanted to expand his activities. He could do with a phone of his own, to save him having to walk down to the phone box, but his most urgent need was a means of transport. Using buses took up a lot of time and the amount he could carry was limited. It would be a huge luxury to have a car, but then there was the problem of getting petrol for it.

As he went about his monotonous tasks in the factory he spent the time trying to think of a way round that. It came to him eventually.

Waldo found a small business for sale, a greengrocery round that came complete with a delivery van and a lease on an old stable in a back street. Until recent years, a horse and cart had been used instead of the van. He found the stable very useful for storing much of his stock.

The business was cheap because these days it was making little profit for its owner. Many items such as bananas and oranges were no longer available, and because customers were doing the patriotic thing and digging up their back gardens to grow their own cabbages and lettuces they no longer needed to buy what the van could carry. Often front gardens were put down to potatoes too, and even those that weren't grew lettuces between the roses.

Greengrocery suited Waldo because it wasn't on ration. He didn't want to be bothered with all those coupons that other retailers had to collect. He stocked potatoes and such stand-bys as parsnips, turnips and carrots as cover for the very different goods he kept out of sight. It allowed him to register for a petrol allowance and he enlarged the round considerably.

He was very careful about his customers. He had a good memory for faces and the first time a customer came to his van they were only allowed to buy unrationed vegetables. He kept to customers he knew and those that came recommended. He'd heard that most black marketeers were caught when they sold to a Board of Trade inspector mistaking him for a genuine customer.

Waldo knew farmers' wives who had butter, eggs and occasionally meat and vegetables to spare, and at the same time wanted to buy sugar, tea and other luxuries.

He picked up from shops who had surpluses and sold to housewives in the more affluent suburbs. He soon learned who these were. He very quickly added such luxury items as trickled in: wine and gin, oranges, grapes at a pound a bunch.

Some home-produced luxuries were never rationed because they were seasonal, such as game.

Waldo learned where to find such things as fountain pens, combs, toilet paper, razor blades, boot polish and toothpaste. They were never rationed but were rarely available in the shops.

He knew there were countless fiddles on a personal basis. The only difference was that he was organised to earn the most he could. It was a sellers' market. Any of these scarce items that he could put on his van sold like hot cakes.

He started by doing his greengrocery rounds in the evenings, taking the occasional day off work to do more. He felt he was working up a good little business. It quickly brought him in more than his wages.

His factory hours were eight till five-thirty and often he was required to work overtime. He didn't work shifts as he'd told Lottie. He had a bad record for absenteeism and now started taking more time off to do regular rounds during the day. He told his foreman his bad back was playing up, and when he was asked for a doctor's note to support his absences he had to make time to visit his doctor. He did his homework before going, managed to put on a convincing show for him and got his note.

Waldo wanted to give up working in the factory altogether, but because it was war work and he'd been conscripted into it he couldn't just give in his notice. He stayed away more and more. Persuaded his doctor to give him long term sick notes – after all, there was no way of proving he did not have the back ache he complained of. Eventually, he was called in to the factory for a medical exam. He'd had time to study men with bad backs by then. He walked awkwardly, held himself stiffly and complained the job was too heavy for him and made his back worse. He said he needed a job where he could sit down.

Waldo got what he wanted. It came as a huge relief when he was found to be capable of sedentary work only. Now he could spend his day working for himself. He could expand his activities. He knew he had to be careful – that most of what he was doing was against the law.

The government had appointed enforcement officers to see that rationing regulations were strictly kept. These were officially called inspectors, though the man in the street called them snoopers. They were agents of the Board of Trade and there were huge numbers of them. Heavy sentences were inflicted by the courts on their evidence. Waldo knew that if he was caught he could have all his goods confiscated, and be liable to heavy fines and even imprisonment.

When a major black marketeer was caught and brought to court everybody rejoiced, but when people were taken to court for minor breaches of food regulations they did not. Almost everybody transgressed them in some way or other.

Waldo took great pains to cover his tracks. He believed in keeping his mouth shut. He spoke to no one about what he was doing, not even to Jim, whom he paid to do certain jobs for him.

He knew how important it was to keep a firm check on his tongue. He disciplined himself to think of things as either mentionable or unmentionable and he drew a mental line between the two. He never spoke to anyone about his black market activities except the customer who was buying or the person who sold to him, and then he limited what he said to what was needed.

Nothing was put down on paper that could be kept in his head, and what had to be written down was done in such a way that it would make no sense to anyone else. All black market goods had to be paid for with cash on the nail.

He was extra careful about what he told Lottie. She wasn't the sort who would approve of a business like his. He told her he'd bought the greengrocery round for when the war was over. He'd picked it up cheaply and could expand it then. He told her he was looking for a garage for the same reason. He didn't tell her that the ration of petrol he received to run his van wasn't nearly adequate for his needs. Getting more was his biggest headache now.

Waldo saw lots of genuine business opportunities and was very tempted to buy them now while they were cheap. Minds were set on winning the war not on running businesses. Many were folding up because the shortages made them uneconomic. He even thought of acquiring a nursing home for Lottie. Nobody wanted property in case the bombing started again. He saw the war as a wonderful opportunity for people like him who could take advantage of it.

Waldo bought a better wireless from a neighbour who'd fallen on hard times, and enjoyed listening to it. He heard that for those who couldn't afford to pay his prices there were such things as whale meat, dried eggs and reconstituted potatoes. It was also said that people were keeping in good health and the poor were eating better than they had before the war.

Chapter Thirteen

February, 1944

Shortly after her return to Woolwich, Lottie was posted to a mobile hospital unit. She was delighted to find her friends June and Emily were going with her.

For the present, the unit was in settled winter quarters on the south coast. The wards were accommodated in a large old house, and the grounds were filled with Nissen huts, in one of which she was billeted. Brighton was their nearest town but there was no public transport so they were rarely able to go. Even worse was the added distance between her and Waldo.

The unit spent a good deal of time practising packing and unpacking equipment and moving their patients about. When they were truly mobile, everything would be done under canvas. They had their own transport, electric power, field telephone system, water supply, canteen facilities and signals unit. They had tents of all sizes, some that could be used for wards, for an operating theatre, even an X-ray department; a dispensary and a small laboratory. They carried innumerable beds and all the equipment they needed.

In February they moved out of their winter quarters and drove across southern England, continually setting up and dismantling their hospital. A level field was all they really needed. High hedges for privacy, good road access and shelter from the worst of the weather were considered a bonus. There was a lot of surmising about where they would eventually be sent.

Lottie began to enjoy it. She felt they were pulling together as a team. Because they moved continually, they were unable to maintain contact with outside friends. It made the group draw closer together. There was a great feeling of camaraderie, all wanting to do the job as well as they could. All were united in the idea that the better treatment they were able to give the troops the more efficient the fighting force would be. They supported each other.

There was a lot of friendly flirting going on.

'This is as good as a marriage bureau,' June laughed. 'We girls are outnumbered fifty to one – what more could we ask? You jumped too soon, Lottie.'

Lottie didn't think so. To those who tried to flirt with her, and there were several, she responded that she was already married. 'Happily married.'

She made it clear that she wanted to be friends but was not prepared to go further. Most respected her wishes; several of the men were married too and welcomed her restraint.

One, Sergeant Rex Foster, the pharmacist in charge of the hospital dispensary, showed some dismay: 'Married? Oh no! I'm too late then?'

'Yes,' Lottie told him.

'What a shame!'

She knew that when their paths crossed, his deep blue eyes would search her out and follow her.

When she wrote to Waldo she told him about most of

the people in the unit, but for some reason she didn't mention Rex. He was slim and tall, and told her he was twenty-four. With his pale straw-coloured hair and fair skin, the other men teased him, saying he only needed to shave once a week.

'Don't you all wish you had that advantage?' he laughed.

Rex was good at his job and made up ointments and medicines to treat the minor ailments of his colleagues. Lottie didn't want to admit it even to herself but she found him attractive.

As with everything else she found hard to handle, she refused to think about him. When she caught herself doing so, she pulled herself up and forced her mind on to something quite different. She told herself over and over that, attractive as Rex might be, alongside Waldo it would be no contest. Waldo could light her up. The only trouble was he was a long way away.

Nothing she said stopped Rex talking to her whenever the opportunity arose. She found him good company.

A few days later, Lottie had a letter from Connie telling her she was about to be married. She was having a white wedding and she invited Lottie to be her matron of honour. There were to be no bridesmaids.

Lottie wanted to go. Connie's absence from her own wedding had upset her. She felt they'd never completely heal the rift if she didn't go. On top of that, she was filled with curiosity about the man Connie had finally decided to marry. She telephoned her sister.

'I've managed to get a forty-eight-hour pass. I'm coming, but I don't know about being matron of honour.

I've nothing I could possibly wear.'

'Don't worry about that. I've got a blue bridesmaid's dress from a friend. I'll alter it to fit you.'

It was a long cold trip in an unheated train but Lottie counted it worth it to be with Connie. It was to be a full church wedding with as much of the traditional pomp and ceremony as Connie could get together.

For Lottie, it would also be a family reunion because both Father and Cliff would be there. Her father was connected with both families; he'd relied on Geoffrey Montague to manage his Birkenhead factory for many years.

Lottie thought Clovis looked French. Although he spoke English like a native, Connie said he was bilingual and that he wore a beret when he was in civvies. He had gentle sympathetic dark eyes and a neat thin moustache, not the usual bushy style affected by many RAF officers. She thought him rather a romantic figure and fully approved of him as a husband for her sister. The reception was held at the Montagues' house. The rooms were big enough to accommodate the fifty guests with ease.

The buffet spread on the dining table was better than any Lottie had ever seen. She didn't think anybody could ask for more. Yvette Montague had produced it almost single-handed. According to Connie, her mother-in-law did a lot of cooking and baking and had offered to teach her the basics. Meals at their house often consisted of several courses, and never less than two.

In return, Connie had offered to teach Yvette to sew. She'd made the elegant navy outfit her mother-in-law was wearing today.

Connie was wearing Yvette's wedding gown of white satin, high-necked and long-sleeved with over-abundant veiling that had yellowed slightly. She looked very pretty and very happy.

Father had had the wedding cake made in the factory and it held pride of place on a silver stand on the table. It had the traditional three tiers, but as it was against the law to use sugar for icing cakes the silver bells and white roses stood directly on the brown mixture.

'I didn't expect it to look so good,' Connie laughed. She'd borrowed a huge cardboard cover printed with a picture of a magnificent fully iced and decorated wedding cake, with lots of silver paper on it to make it sparkle.

'For the photographs,' she explained.

Waldo had managed to get a film for Lottie and he'd loaded it into his camera for her. She took a picture of Clovis and Connie with the knife posed over the cardboard confection. That provided something of a laugh at the time. Then they posed again with the knife over the real thing. Then with a cake each.

It would have been a wonderfully happy family occasion, except that her father reminded her how close Cliff was to getting his call-up papers. He would be eighteen in less than six months' time.

'Lottie, try and persuade him,' he pleaded. 'I want him to come and work for me as soon as his exams are finished in June. He shouldn't wait for the end of the school term. I want to put up a good case for keeping him with me.'

Lottie tried, but Cliff brushed it off. He'd joined the Officer Cadet Corps at school and was going to join up with his friends. It made her dread the future. For her, the best part of the forty-eight hours was the time she spent with Waldo again.

Just before Easter, she had a note from Cliff saying he was coming to Reading for a few days to stay with a school friend and could she possibly meet him? He suggested London because he thought it might be easier for her and he wanted to go up once or twice.

Lottie was excited at the prospect. She hadn't seen much of him since their home had been bombed in May 1941. She worked through the public holiday and was given a twenty-four-hour pass later in the week. She suggested they meet at a pub in the Strand.

Lottie wore a red suit on which she'd recently splurged her clothing coupons. It was rather plain in style as all clothes were these days, with a narrow skirt and military-looking shoulders. Both June and Emily said it was very smart. She went to the door of the lounge, which was full, and stood looking round. At first she couldn't see him.

'Lottie!' She recognised his voice and turned round but only saw him when he came pushing through the crowd towards her. He caught her to him in a great bear hug.

Cliff seemed to change every time she saw him. He was now six inches taller than she was, broad-shouldered and straight-backed, a grown man. His face was sun-tanned, and even his hair was a shade lighter than she remembered.

His Scouse accent had diminished to a slight burr; that was his posh school. He had polish, too. They had plenty to talk about. Lottie tried again to persuade him to go straight into the business when his exams were finished.

'I wish I could. I know how much Father wants it.'

'We all do.'

'He's been very good to me.' Cliff had had fewer hang-ups about Father from the beginning. 'I'd not have had a very good time if it hadn't been for him.'

He'd taken away the financial worries from her and Connie. Lottie was grateful for all he'd done for Cliff.

He said: 'Father would like you to think kindly of him.'

'I do.' He'd shown understanding and unfailing kindness to her. She knew him better now, felt wiser and more forgiving. Waldo had taught her just how powerful love could be. Perhaps she'd grown up, too.

'Write and tell him so then.' Cliff smiled at her. That, Lottie thought, was proof that he'd truly grown to manhood. He was caring for others now. Even caring for Father.

Over the following months, Cliff continued to drop her little notes. She was always glad to get these. They kept her up to date about what he was thinking and doing.

At the end of April, she heard from Connie. 'You'll never believe it,' she wrote, 'but I'm two months pregnant already. I feel very fortunate and Clovis is over the moon. I expect you'll say I should have waited until the war is over and go on working. Perhaps I am selfish to go ahead with what I want.'

Lottie wrote back telling her how happy she was for her, but didn't mention that she'd asked Waldo to use French letters last time she'd been up to see him. Now that she was being trained in this way she felt compelled to stay and see the job through. After all, it would be helping the enemy if she dropped out after all this time and somebody else had to be trained to do the job.

In May, Lottie, together with most of the other personnel staffing the mobile hospital, was given two weeks' leave.

'Probably disembarkation leave,' they told each other.

'Nobody's said so,' Lottie pointed out.

'Well they wouldn't, would they? Not if we're going to the second front. They have to keep quiet about the date it's going to start.'

There had been much talk of a second front over the last year. Everybody knew it wasn't far off now because there were huge build-ups of troops and equipment all along the south coast. Britain was waiting with bated breath for the action to begin.

'Two whole weeks?' Waldo crowed with delight. 'That's tremendous.' The following night he was on the phone again.

'I need a holiday too, Lottie. Haven't had a proper one since this war started. I'll come down to you, or most of the way. We could have a week or ten days walking in the Cotswolds, staying in boarding houses. Would you like that?'

Lottie thought it would be idyllic. She wore her strongest walking shoes and packed a knapsack. Waldo brought maps but it wasn't easy to find out where they were because all signposts and nameplates had been removed at the beginning of the war to make things as difficult as possible for an invading army. They had to find a room for the night before dark but the days were long at this time of year and they managed very well. Even the weather was kind to them.

'I think I've found the business I've been looking for,' Waldo told her. 'A garage.'

He was very enthusiastic and talked of his plans for it all the time.

'You've made me ambitious. I'd rather be with you than anyone else in the world. I want to give you a good life when you come home for good. I want you to be glad you married me.'

'I am now,' she laughed. Waldo was wonderful company, quick-witted with a tremendous sense of humour.

She wanted to spend the last few days of her leave at home to see her family. The Merseyside air seemed smoke-laden and heavy, the place shabby, and there were bomb sites everywhere.

Waldo took her to the garage he was buying. It was open and on a main road, but it seemed to be doing very little business. He walked her past the ancient hand pumps for petrol.

'I know it's a bit shabby now,' he said. 'I'll soon change that. Turn the business round, make it prosperous.'

Lottie marvelled that he could see such promise in the run-down buildings.

'Can't take you inside yet, the sale hasn't been completed. You'll see a big difference next time you come home.'

Connie was still working at Clatterbridge but was talking of giving in her notice in another month or so.

'I won't be going to Mildenhall after all,' she lamented. 'Clovis's squadron has been posted to India. Air cover for the Fourteenth Army. Just my luck.'

'The news is good. He mightn't be there for long.'

'Yes, not all good, though. There's the new flying bombs.'

'Can't come this far north, thank goodness.'

'Have any dropped near you?'

'Not close – they're aiming for London. Where are you

going to live when you leave work?' Lottie asked. 'Are you going to Brightland Street?'

'No, I don't want to push in alongside Steve.'

'He might be glad of your company.'

'Clovis's parents want me to go there. You saw the big old house in Oxton where they live? They've offered the attic floor to me and Clovis.'

Lottie was relieved to hear that. 'That's very kind of them.'

'Almost impossible to get anywhere else. I tried hard. I'd prefer a place of my own, but the bombing destroyed so many houses.'

'You'll be better off with his parents, Connie.'

She sighed. 'That's what Clovis says, but I hardly know them.'

'You soon will.'

Back with her unit again, the practice sessions went on: living in tents and setting up the tented hospital. Lottie settled back into her old routine and it seemed the second front would never come.

From time to time she received letters from her father with news of how his business was faring. Often he wrote about Cliff. Concern for him was one of the things they shared.

He'll be eighteen in July. I get a horrible fluttering in my stomach every time I think of that. Only a few more weeks, and it's only too obvious now that the war will not be over.

He talks of his exams looming over him – he sits his Highers next month – but as far as I'm concerned it's his call-up papers that are looming over me. I'm very fearful for him.

I could put up a good case for having him help me run the bakery. I really need him. I'm certain I could get his call-up deferred, but he refuses to let me try. I would love to keep him here with me. It's what I've always wanted; to be able to hand it on to my son. But he has to know how to run it. Otherwise, it will have to be sold to strangers.

Please add your voice to mine and try once more before it's too late. Write to him and let him know you think it's the right thing for him to do. Bread is important for the war effort too. An army can't march on an empty stomach.

He has the same bee in his bonnet as you – he wants to do his bit to bring victory closer. I admire you both for being so idealistic, but Lottie, think of the danger. Hasn't our family given enough?

I've pleaded with him, but he won't listen. I'm afraid he's as obstinate as you are.

Lottie wanted to cry for Cliff. On this subject she was with her father. She hated to think of him being a member of the fighting forces. She wrote to him, was as persuasive as she could be, urging him to think seriously of Father's offer, but she was afraid it wouldn't change his decision.

Cliff wrote back saying that he and the majority of his classmates in the Officer Cadet Corps were ready for their call-up. He hoped he'd be selected for officer training.

It was what Lottie had expected, but it lay heavy on her mind.

* * *

Ever since the outbreak of war, Waldo had done steady business in high-class shirts for men. He understood clothes and found it easy to keep up with fashions. He'd seen the price of all clothing double.

Before the war, women in trousers were frowned upon, but they soon discovered that trousers were warm and easy to don when the air raid siren sounded and took to them in their thousands. Headscarves likewise became popular when previously they'd been worn only by mill girls.

The government tried to alter the fashion for turn-ups on men's trousers as a means of eking out the supply of cloth. They were no longer allowed, but men weren't prepared to give them up and bought their trousers two inches longer than they needed and had turn-ups made afterwards. When he had the opportunity to buy slacks and working trousers, Waldo bought only those with the longest legs.

Clothes had first been rationed in June 1941. Waldo had seen it as another opportunity for making money. Clothing coupons were soon changing hands at half a crown each. Many of his best customers asked for them. He couldn't get enough to satisfy demand.

He mentioned it to one of his most reliable suppliers, a man with whom he'd had dealings since the beginning of the war. Charlie Best told him of a woman he knew who could supply all the coupons he needed.

'Where do I find her?' Waldo asked. 'Who is she? I'd like to meet her.'

Arrangements were made for Waldo to meet her in a workmen's café in a New Ferry side street. She asked him to be there at one o'clock, when the place would be busy.

Phyllis Rogan was described to him as a 32-year-old blonde with a Veronica Lake peek-a-boo hairstyle. Waldo arrived a few minutes early but one glance told him she was already here. She had the sort of looks that drew attention.

Her eyes were brown and her skin a pale olive tone that didn't look right with her brassy hair, though there were no dark roots showing. He had no doubt that she was a bottle blonde.

'Hello.' He pulled out the other chair at the small table and sat down quickly. He couldn't believe she was only thirty-two. She had that over-ripe look and her skin was slack. She'd been reading a newspaper; now she folded it up.

'I've ordered beef stew, but if you don't fancy that there's chips and sausage and stuff.'

Waldo talked about Charlie Best to break the ice. She told him her husband bought suits from the gentlemen's outfitters he owned in Birkenhead. He had to assume Charlie was buying her coupons. How else would he know she could supply? If he was, that was a recommendation. Charlie knew which way his bread was buttered.

She had a way of winking at him. With one eye partly covered by hair, he wasn't sure at first whether it was a wink or a nervous tic.

He smiled. 'Mrs Rogan . . .'

'Call me Phyllis.' Her eyelashes fluttered. She'd assumed Veronica Lake's sultry glances as well as her hairstyle.

'Right, Phyllis, about this deal we want to do.' He dropped his voice. 'Clothing coupons.'

She whispered. 'I want one and six each.'

'That's too much. How many do you have?'

'As many as you want.'

Her stew arrived with great mounds of mashed potatoes and cabbage. There was plenty of thick brown gravy with lumps of carrot and turnip and even a little meat. It smelled good.

Waldo asked the waitress: 'Is there anything to go with the chips beside sausage?'

'Meat pie or Spam. It's up on the board.'

Waldo's eyes followed the wave of her hand to the menu chalked up on a blackboard.

'I'll have meat pie and chips, please.'

'It comes with tinned peas, okay?'

'Great.' When the girl had gone he turned to Phyllis again. 'I need to know your source. Where do you get them from?'

Her mouth straightened. 'That's not your business.'

'It is. I don't want to get caught with hot goods.'

'You won't be. These are safe.'

'They're numbered; they can be traced back.'

His pie and chips came. He reached for the bottle of brown sauce. When the girl had gone, she said: 'You can have any numbers you like and they'll mean nothing.'

To give himself time to think Waldo speared a piece of pie into his mouth. The pastry was crisp and tasty; the meat inside looked like sausage meat.

'If that's the case, you're telling me they aren't genuine. Counterfeit then?'

'They're absolutely identical. Nobody could tell the difference.'

Waldo had been prepared to offer a shilling for the genuine article. Now he said: 'That puts the price right down.'

'How much?'

'Sixpence.'

'Not enough. Not for the risks I have to take.'

'Tell me about your risks. Who's printing them?' He felt he couldn't be too careful about such things.

'I am.'

'I'll need to see them. Examine them.'

'I've brought a sample.' She patted her expensive leather handbag.

He wanted to compare them with the genuine article, but . . . 'Not in here.'

'Of course not.' She sounded irritable. 'Are you prepared to do business with me? Charlie said you were just the person, but you're very fussy.'

'It's going to pour with rain any minute,' he said, looking out of the window as the waitress came to remove their plates.

'Spotted Dick with custard, or rice pudding with prunes?'

They both opted for Spotted Dick.

Waldo said: 'It has to be safe – for both of us.'

'Well, of course it has, but—'

'Do you have a printing press at home or are you doing them at work?'

'At work.' She sounded reluctant.

'Then I'll need to know who you work for. I mean, whose printing works are you using?'

She tossed her blonde curtain of hair back defiantly. 'What d'you want to know all this for? You aren't telling me a thing about yourself. You haven't even said you'll do a deal.'

'All in good time. I'm just satisfying myself that it's safe. That's the most important thing. Where are these printing works?'

Phyllis spooned up the last of her custard. 'What about what's safe for me?'

'I'll keep my mouth shut come what may. You can rely on that. It's a promise.'

She said slowly: 'The works are at Ellesmere Port. My husband owns them. Now you know everything. Are you interested?'

'Yes, provided the sample's all you claim it is. Very interested.'

'I want a shilling each for them.'

'Sixpence,' he repeated. 'I've got to sell them. For me there are risks with every transaction.'

'Sixpence isn't enough.'

'Does your husband know you're doing this?'

'I don't tell him everything.'

'That means he doesn't?'

'He doesn't.'

A cup of milky tea arrived for each of them. Waldo stirred his thoughtfully. It should be safe enough.

'Is your husband likely to find out? Can you do it without him knowing?'

'I think so.' Her smile was more confident. 'He's gone to Manchester today, hoping to get a big order. We're security printers. We do football tickets, theatre tickets, that sort of thing. I'm in charge today and this is my lunch hour. I do it when he's away and not likely to see me.'

He paid for her meal. 'Come to my van,' he said as they got up to leave. 'I want to see your sample.'

She got into the passenger seat. Her perfume was strong enough to swamp the smell of petrol that was a permanent fixture here. Waldo held the sheet of paper she gave him up to the light. They were better than he'd expected. He took his own clothing coupons from his wallet and laid them alongside her sample on his knee. They looked identical to him. He took out his magnifying glass and looked more closely.

'You've done a good job.'

'I told you, I've got it exactly right. Undetectable from the real thing.'

'Right – sixpence a coupon then?'

'No, I told you. Not worth my while at less than ninepence. I'm providing exactly the right paper, the right type of ink and the expertise at the job.'

Waldo turned the coupons over. It seemed a safe set-up. His supply was assured. Her husband might find out but nothing he did was without risk.

'Okay. Ninepence it is, then.' He put out his hand. She wore several opulent rings that cut into his fingers.

'Agreed.'

She said by way of a confidence: 'My husband is much older than I am. He has a tight fist on the purse strings.'

Waldo wondered whether she'd married him for his money and now found he wasn't allowing her enough of it. He got the impression she wasn't finding married life as pleasant as she'd expected.

'I'll take five hundred for starters.'

She looked at him with renewed interest. 'I've only got two hundred with me.' She had a way of tossing back her bright hair that was quite seductive.

'I'll take the two hundred now, then. The balance as soon as you can.'

He followed her to a very smart SS Jaguar saloon parked further up the hill and got in beside her. He didn't want it to be too obvious they were making a transaction.

'By Jove, I like this,' he told her. 'You do yourself well.'

One day he'd like to own a car like hers.

He paid cash for her coupons. In this sort of deal it was always cash on the nail whether he was buying or selling. Without immediate payment there could never be a deal. Bills were not something they could send out.

'What about the other three hundred?'

'I'll probably print them this afternoon while Cecil is out. I'm not sure if I can get away tomorrow. How about Friday?'

'Next week will be soon enough.' He arranged to meet her in a different café at lunch time on Tuesday.

Waldo kept as many details of his business in his head as he could. It was the safest place for them. The people he bought from did not know his buyers.

He didn't approve of Phyllis doing these things behind her husband's back. He believed everything should be open and above board between married couples. As he drove off to reload his van, he realised Lottie had no idea what he was doing. There was one big difference, though: Lottie would benefit from his endeavours, whereas Phyllis did not intend that her husband should. She was doing this for herself alone.

When he got home that evening he took the precaution of looking up the printing business in a local directory he had. It was owned and run by Cecil Rogan. He felt that what he was doing didn't carry more than the usual risks.

Over the following weeks, Waldo found his venture with Phyllis Rogan profitable. He met her at least once a week in pubs and small cafés to collect the coupons she printed for him.

He began to look forward to having a glass of beer with her or a cheap and stodgy meal. They had a lot in common. They shared the same philosophy, that it would be foolish not to make money while it was so easy. He'd been thinking up new ideas over the last few days.

'Could you print other sorts of coupons?'

'What sort do you have in mind?' Her red-taloned fingers played up his wrist.

'Petrol coupons?'

'I could try,' she said lazily. 'If you make it worth my while.'

'Try it,' he urged. 'You know it'll be worth your while.'

Petrol was the scarcest and most sought after commodity there was. He'd bought himself the garage he'd always wanted. It was run down and shabby and had been on the point of folding up. Small businesses just weren't profitable with the present shortages, but they would be after the war.

The other reason he'd bought the garage was to give him more petrol for his own needs. To have petrol coupons too – that would open up a whole new field for him. Not only would his garage appear to be more profitable than it was, a very useful thing if he wanted to sell it, but he already had the customers coming to him for their petrol ration. He'd got to know many of them and was sure some would be prepared to pay more than the retail price for extra gallons.

'I know you'll pay me,' she said. 'It's not money I'm thinking of. There are other things . . .'

He guessed what she was trying to tell him. Her knowing winks were making it fairly clear. She'd said her husband was eighteen years older than she was; that the war was getting him down, that it was harder to run the business when their skilled staff were being called up. Neither was his health good.

'Where shall we meet next time?' Her brown eyes stared sultrily into his. It had become a perennial question. It wouldn't do to be seen regularly in the same café. They didn't want the owners to start speculating about them. Now Phyllis added: 'Surely it would be safer for me to come to your flat?'

Waldo hesitated. He'd held himself aloof from all his customers and suppliers up till now. Not to make confidants of them, to keep his distance, was one way he safeguarded himself. He shouldn't make a friend of Phyllis. Meeting her weekly, he'd already let her get too close.

Yet in one way she was right. His flat was the safest place. He knew why she wanted to come. Phyllis had a loud laugh and a habit of touching him. It was easy to see she dressed to attract men. She was making him aware that she fancied him.

To start with he hadn't particularly liked what he saw but she was growing on him. There were times now like this when she could make his body run with heat. She was very sexy and it was so long since he'd been with Lottie. Hell, he was desperate for it himself. He couldn't hold out against her on the grounds of safety.

'I'd like you to come,' he told her, though he knew he was breaking one of his golden rules. 'How about next Tuesday? You don't mind coming?'

'I thought you'd never ask.' He gave her his address.

What he'd done worried him until Tuesday. She arrived that evening.

'God, what a dump this is,' she said when he let her in,

and she took in his shabby kitchen. 'You ought to find yourself something better than this.'

Waldo meant to. Certainly he had to, before Lottie came home, but there seemed no chance of that just yet. Not till the war was over. The trouble was he was working too hard; he hadn't the energy for house hunting too.

Phyllis had applied her perfume with a heavier hand than usual. She laid her new petrol coupons out on his table. He took his own ration card from his wallet to compare them.

'You're the tops at forging, Phyl,' he smiled.

'Tops in other things too.' She put her arms round him and pulled his lips down on hers. 'Cecil is away tonight,' she said. 'Gone up to Glasgow.'

The implication was clear. Waldo knew he shouldn't touch her, that it was a dangerous thing to do. He shouldn't get involved. If Phyllis was caught printing petrol coupons she could take him down too. As a lover she'd know too much and could even unwittingly drop him in it, if she were questioned. It multiplied the risks he was taking many times over.

Waldo looked at the generous tapestry bag she'd had over her shoulder and said with an anticipatory smile: 'I hope you've brought your nightie.'

'A nightie? Won't need that,' she grinned. 'But I've brought a bottle of wine. Where do you keep your glasses?'

Waldo felt his tiredness drop from him. It seemed ages since he'd seen Lottie. Speaking to her on the phone was not the same at all. She couldn't expect him to be a monk. Not year in and year out, until the war was over.

He had a wonderful night. Phyllis was well versed in the art of lovemaking. She played a very active role, winding him up as tight as a drum. He learned a lot from her and enjoyed himself immensely.

When he opened his eyes in the morning and saw her face on the pillow beside him, he thought she looked dreadful. Pale and drained without her thick pancake make-up and with her mascara smudged on his sheets. He decided she must be nearer forty than she was prepared to admit.

Phyllis often came to his house after that. What was the point of meeting in cafés? This was safer. She sometimes came by taxi so her car would not be seen outside too often. She came for a couple of hours when she could. Cecil didn't spend many nights away from home.

'You've got to get yourself a decent place, Waldo,' she told him. 'This is a slum. There's woodlice in your kitchen and I don't like going upstairs to the bathroom. Never know who I'll meet on the stairs.'

'Help me find somewhere then,' he said. He really couldn't find time to do more than he was doing.

'You'll have to buy. There's hardly anything to rent. Nothing decent.'

She came now with details of houses on the market, and sometimes brought the local newspapers when they printed their adverts of houses for sale. She enjoyed helping him sort through what was on offer.

He thought she was becoming more daring. She took him to see her own house in Rothermere Drive while her husband was away at the works. It was as impressive as her car. Beautifully furnished throughout. He thought she had good taste, and was prepared to be guided by her after that. He bought a house because she admired it even though he thought it prohibitively expensive.

'It'll seem cheap once the war's over, you know that. Everything will go up.'

Waldo left the furnishing of it more or less to Phyllis. She liked things to be over-fancy. Too many gilt mirrors and frilly curtains. He toned it down as far as he could. He knew Lottie's taste would be plainer. But Phyllis was prepared to go round the second-hand sale rooms and auction houses. She bought only the best available and took infinite pains to get the right effect. He wouldn't have done half so well on his own. He kept telling her that.

All things considerêd he believed meeting Phyllis was one of the best things that had happened to him.

Chapter Fourteen

Lottie found the easiest way to keep in touch with Waldo was to write in diary form about what was happening to her. Some days she wrote a good deal and on others she had no time. When she had several pages she posted them off.

On 6 June, she wrote: 'D-Day at last! My heart stood still when I heard the news on the wireless this morning. We've been waiting for this for so long. It now seems certain we'll be following the troops across to France.'

On 10 June she wrote again: 'Today our convoy is making the journey to where troops and equipment are being concentrated – we aren't told exactly where.

'I've never seen anything like it. The roads are packed solid, there's thousands of troops, vehicles of all shapes and sizes, all the hardware of war and all going the same way. We'll be briefed officially tomorrow, but none of us are in any doubt now that we're on our way to France.

'Morale is tremendous, people waving and cheering as we pass through towns and villages on the way to the coast. Everybody knows we're off to liberate France. They press chocolate and cigarettes and cake upon us. When I think how scarce these things are, I'm amazed at their generosity.'

Lottie and the staff of the mobile hospital were told to be ready to leave for France at midnight. They were to carry all their personal belongings on their backs, including an enamel plate, mug and eating irons. They were all to wear their tin hats and Red Cross arm bands.

She felt more than nervous as she hoisted the heavy weight up on her shoulders. Just to think of where she was going sent adrenalin shooting round her body. It helped that June and Emily as well as the other twelve nurses on the mobile unit were going with her. Being with people she knew helped to steady her nerves; made everything seem more normal.

'Are you scared?' she asked Emily.

'Course not. We knew it was coming and we've been training for it for so long. I'd be disappointed if I couldn't go now, wouldn't you?'

'Yes,' Lottie assured her. 'I'd hate to miss it. I'll be glad to be on the way after all this hanging about.'

That's what all the troops were saying after months and sometimes years of training. But in her case it wasn't entirely true. Lottie felt all jelly inside, but she wasn't going to admit that when June and Emily looked so cool and confident.

Their unit was divided between several different landing craft. Lottie was pleased the nursing sisters were kept in one group. When the time came to board, Lottie felt a white-knuckled bag of nerves. Tanks, vehicles and men were pouring on at a rapid rate. It seemed packed tight with Tommies already. As June led the way to some empty seats, a round of wolf whistles went up. June was tall and willowy.

Somebody shouted: 'What luck! They're sending some popsies with us – just what we need. I bag the blonde in front.'

Emily boarded just in front of Lottie and caused another outbreak of whoops and whistles. Out of uniform, Emily wore her long blonde hair swinging loose about her shoulders. In uniform under her tin hat, it was taken severely back with an elastic band and pinned up, but she had a pretty heart-shaped face and it suited her.

'We're imagining all this, lads.'

'Cor, I fancy that little blonde bit.'

'We're dead already and up in heaven. These are the angels.'

'What about that dark bit? She's not bad either.'

Major Esmeralda Jones was bringing up the rear. She'd been an army nurse all her working life and was in charge of them now.

'Stop this ridiculous commentary,' she bellowed in a voice that brought an instant hush. 'This is not the time and place for nonsense like this.'

A voice in the bows said clearly: 'We won't need our guns, lads. This one will have the Jerries on the run without firing a shot.'

Major Jones, looking severe, sat down heavily, while a few chuckles went up. Lottie tried to hide her smile. The ribaldry made her feel better.

It was still dark when the time to disembark drew close. They were all subdued and silent now. All round her, Lottie could feel a wall of tension that was rising with each minute. She felt half paralysed with fear and suspected most of the others did too. There was debris floating on the black water, amongst it a felt hat of the sort Connie wore, but this one was battered and waterlogged.

Frequent flashes of gunfire could be both seen and heard from the dark shore on which they were about to land. When the ramp went down at the front of the craft, she wanted to hide and return to the safety of England. She was drawn towards it in the crowd. The ramp was well in against the beach but surf washed over the last few feet. They were all jumping that to keep their boots dry. Not easy with the heavy pack on her back. Lottie landed with a small splash but it didn't penetrate her boots. Then she was struggling up the beach in the darkness.

It seemed almost a miracle that the convoy was able to reunite and form up again. In the grey light of dawn, Lottie looked round at the hardware of war going slowly along the rough and crowded road. The sound of gunfire was closer, but she had a sense of elation now that they'd all landed safely in enemy territory. The order came to set up their hospital in a nearby field and prepare to receive their first patients.

They'd never got the tents up so quickly before, the beds set out and made up, the equipment unpacked. A large Red Cross was pegged out in the middle so it could be seen from the air. After the months of preparation it was an emotional moment for them all when they saw those injured in battle begin to flood in.

Within the hour they had more patients than they could cope with, many of them terribly injured and in need of immediate surgery. It was difficult to decide who should be treated first. The theatre with three operating tables worked non-stop setting bones, removing bullets and shrapnel from torn bodies and trying to repair the awful wounds.

Lottie, together with her colleagues, worked round the clock. She gave injections of morphia and penicillin, set up intravenous drips, stitched cuts and dressed wounds the like of which she'd never seen before.

The unit was officially known as a Field Surgical Unit and

would take patients referred on from dressing stations and casualty clearing stations once these were operating. As soon as the beachhead was secured, base hospitals and rest centres would be set up to take those with moderate injuries, and their mobile hospital would move up behind the advancing army.

In the first hours, first aid was administered to all. Those with minor injuries had to be content to wait their turn. Orderlies brought them tea and cigarettes. Eventually they were patched up and sent back to their units to fight again.

The severely injured needed to be flown to hospitals in England. RAF Dakotas were being used as air ambulances. When each fleet of trucks set off to the airstrip, the nursing sisters took it in turns to go with them to see that the patients were made as comfortable as possible.

For them all, it was a totally different world. When there was work to be done they worked non-stop, sometimes for many, many hours. Occasionally there was a lull in the number of casualties coming in and they could all rest. Gunfire could always be heard, and sometimes aircraft strafed the nearby roads.

When Lottie wasn't working she was mostly catching up on her sleep. She felt distanced from Waldo now he could no longer phone her, as though their relationship had been cut off at its height. Her only satisfaction was that there were no more air raids on Merseyside. Waldo and her family there were safe.

In those rare times off when she still had energy to do so, she wrote letters. Mainly they were to Waldo, but during those first days she also wrote to her father.

We are all craving for bread, even the injured Tommies who are well enough to eat. We have hard biscuits instead – ship's biscuits or hard tack. They taste as though they're made of flour and water and have been baked to unbelievable hardness. Like wood. Must have been baked several times over. I'd love a slice of Lancelyn's bread. So would everybody with me, even a slice or two of our national loaf. We are told they'll be setting up field bakeries on the beachhead as soon as it's properly secured and that makes us happy.

Otherwise, I think we eat better than you civilians back home. We can buy cider and calvados from the local population. Usually they turn up at our field hospital selling it. Cigarettes are supplied to the army in prodigal amounts. Almost all the men smoke and are glad of them, but what we all really long for is a hot bath, clean clothes and a comfortable bed well away from gunfire. Sometimes I feel I could spend two days and nights in bed.

We feel detached from everything except the sick and wounded. We hear conflicting anecdotes from them and don't know exactly what our troops are doing; whether they're advancing or being repelled. And we no longer know what's going on back at home.

The job has always drawn us together. Now we are knotted into a tight-knit community. We know who amongst us will lift our spirits if we are down. Who works hardest, who to ask for expertise on any subject and who to depend on in an emergency. It's a privilege to be part of this unit.

Everybody in it looked forward to receiving mail from England. It made them realise the real world was still there. Today Lottie had a letter from Waldo; sometimes she had more than one in the same post.

I've taken out a mortgage on a house in Oxton. I'm quite excited about it. I would have liked you to see it before I took this step, but you can't so I've gone ahead. It's two hundred times better than my flat, so I think you'll like it.

I want to provide somewhere decent for you when you come home. It has three bedrooms and a nice bathroom and we won't have to share it with anybody else. It's a fairly substantial semi and it's had no war damage. I'd have preferred detached but perhaps we can move up to something better later on. I hope you approve. We will be much more comfortable in this.

She wrote back to Waldo by return, telling him she was delighted at the news and asking a thousand questions. She was thrilled that Waldo was succeeding in what he'd set out to do.

The following week brought two more letters for her, one each from her father and Connie.

Father wrote that Cliff had been commissioned as a second lieutenant into the King's Regiment: 'I'm very proud of him, and of you too, but I'm fearful for Cliff's safety. At least you are a little safer in your hospital behind the lines. If only this war would finish quickly. I pray for that first and foremost.'

Connie wrote in much the same terms: 'There was no stopping Cliff, he's as pig-headed as you are. At least he'll be in England for some time yet. He writes of the training courses he's undergoing. Then I fear he'll be sent off to one front or the other to fight. He thinks it will probably be France.'

Lottie couldn't bear to think of Cliff being in the thick of the fighting which was so near. Shortly afterwards, she had a letter from Cliff himself, saying he was expecting to be sent to fight in France within the next few months.

On 25 August, they learned that the Allied armies had liberated Paris and were going to push on towards the German border. The mobile hospital was only twenty miles north of Paris on that day. Lottie felt they were making progress now. The end of the war wouldn't come soon enough to prevent Cliff coming but it couldn't be all that far off.

Once she knew he was in France, she found herself looking hard at the face of every second lieutenant brought in as a patient. It filled her with dread to think of him being here amidst all this fighting. She found herself asking questions of all wearing the emblem of the King's Regiment. She never spoke to anyone who knew him.

Over the hectic months, Lottie had to push anything not connected with the job to the back of her mind. It was the only way she could keep going at that pace. Everything took longer in the tented wards. Their only means of getting hot water was to boil kettles on primus stoves. Surgical instruments and equipment had to be sterilized by boiling them up in fish kettles balanced on two rings.

At the end of October, she opened another letter from Connie.

Dear Lottie,
    You are an aunt. I have a healthy baby boy of six

pounds two ounces. I'm going to call him Jimmy after our brother. Clovis James for the birth certificate.

He arrived a few weeks early which took us all by surprise but it's done him no harm and I'd had more than enough of being pregnant.

I had a normal delivery and everything went well. I just wish Clovis was here to see his son. His parents have been very kind – they are looking after me just as you said they would. I couldn't have managed without them, not with both you and Clovis being overseas and with no hope of seeing either of you until this horrible war is over.

I don't think baby Jimmy is much like our brother to look at. The in-laws say he's the spitting image of his dad. He's lovely – I can't get over how beautiful he is.

Lottie wrote back by return, full of congratulations and enthusiasm for the idea of calling him Jimmy. She thought Connie sounded a bit lonely, but at least the pregnancy and birth were behind her now. She'd soon pick up. At lunch she told everybody on the table about being an aunt. Rex insisted on drinking the health of baby Jimmy in water since they were both on duty.

'We'll do this again in wine, champagne even if we can get it, when we have an evening off.'

In January 1945, Connie was listening to a news bulletin on her wireless as she fed her baby. The Red Army were advancing on Berlin and had liberated four thousand prisoners from a concentration camp at Auschwitz. She was cringing at the atrocities that were being revealed when her mother-in-law called her to the phone downstairs in the hall.

'Connie?' She hardly recognised Steve's voice, it was so thick with anguish. 'The most awful, dreadful news. Cliff . . . You'd better sit down.'

Connie felt as though a heavy black cloud had enveloped her. 'You've not had a telegram?'

'Yes. He's missing, believed killed.'

She knew Cliff had given Steve Lancelyn's name as his next of kin.

'Oh God, Connie, he was only eighteen. What a dreadful waste of a life.'

Connie could hardly speak. 'Missing,' she insisted. 'That's what it says. Missing.'

'And believed killed.'

'They don't know for sure. He could be alive and well.'

'I'm afraid he isn't. Terribly afraid . . . I feel it in my bones.'

'Don't give up hope.'

Connie had been telling herself lightning never struck twice in the same place. Her family had suffered too much already – nothing could possibly happen to Cliff or Lottie.

'Are you still there?'

'Yes, Steve. Look, I'll come in and see you. Are you in Old Swan?'

'No, in Birkenhead. I came over to see Geoffrey. I can't work today.' There were tears in his voice.

'I'll come down,' she told him.

'Can you?'

'Mother-in-law will look after the baby for me. I'm coming straight away.'

All the way there, visions of Cliff filled her mind. It seemed too cruel that he'd been killed only weeks after landing in

France. She felt sick with grief.

The sight of Steve was another shock. His face was wet with tears. She went to him and put her arms round him.

'It seems like the end of the world to me too,' she said. 'Our Cliff . . .'

'It is the end to me. The end of all my hopes, anyway. I wanted him to come here, Connie. I wanted to hand on this business to him. It's been my dream . . .' He looked up at her, full of guilt. 'Am I being punished? To love your mother the way I did, I know it was very wrong. To have two sons seemed a miracle and now they've both been taken away.'

'Not your fault. It's this war.' Connie had been living in dread of hearing something similar had happened to Clovis. His family had hardly been touched by the war; it must surely be their turn soon. 'No need to feel guilty.'

'There is,' he said sadly. 'I feel guilt-ridden. I've done so many people a wrong.'

'Rubbish,' Connie said, wanting to cheer him up. 'You've always been kind to me.'

'I'm glad you think that, but it isn't true.'

Connie thought back. He was right, it wasn't. As a child, she hadn't liked Steve one bit.

'You always welcomed Lottie and the boys with open arms, but not me.'

'And now you're the one who is kindest to me, the only one with whom I can share this awful feeling of loss.'

'I loved Cliff too.'

Steve looked up, his face ravaged with grief. 'You're the one most like Marion. I was jealous of you, Connie.'

'Jealous of me? Why?'

'Your mother showered so much love and attention on you.

251

I didn't think I could persuade her to be part of my life in Brightland Street. It meant leaving you with Herbert, you see, and she didn't want that. But I persuaded her it was the only way. She knew that if she didn't, once you'd learned to speak, you'd say something to your dadda, and she didn't want him to know about me. I convinced her eventually the only safe way was to concoct a front to hide what she was doing. Make up believable details of a working life. Then nobody would ever know.'

'How did it all start? That's what I don't understand.'

Steve had the palms of both hands pressed to his face. He sighed, then started to tell her.

'Marion came to run the first aid post in the Old Swan factory when you were two. She had to work, you know that. From the first, I was very taken with her. Love at first sight, I suppose you'd say. She brought you to Brightland Street once or twice as a toddler. You were beautiful. She used to sit nursing you in her arms for hours at a time. She was like a Madonna, but I craved the affection she was showing you.'

It made Connie feel better to hear this. She'd always felt the odd one out. Nobody's favourite child. The oldest, pressed into service to look after her younger siblings.

She said softly: 'It's normal for a woman to want to look after her own child. I want to do that.'

'I know it is, Connie. I know that now, but I was jealous and twisted. I'd seen Iris shower love on Doreen and then on Rita. They meant everything to her. Much more than I did. They still do. I was pushed out of my own family. I worked to keep them, that was my role. That sums up Iris's need of me.'

He took out his handkerchief and mopped his face.

'Iris always hated the factories and the business. Said it

was not the place for nice girls to work. I blame the break-up of my marriage on that. When your mother fell in love with me, I went out of my way to shut you out of the life we shared. I was determined not to let anything come between me and Marion. Not you, not anything. I didn't stop to think what that would do to you. I'm sorry. Never have been good at relationships. I've always got it wrong.'

'Not with Mam you didn't.'

'No, not with her.'

Connie got up and patted his shoulder. 'I'll get us some tea. We could both do with a cup.'

Lottie lived for the letters she received from home, always craving news of her family. Today, she had letters from both Connie and her father. Both giving her the news that Cliff was missing believed killed. The news horrified her.

He hadn't been in the comparative safety of a hospital as she was, with the Red Cross marking it out. The dread had been there always, but to see the words written down that he was missing, believed killed, and giving the date . . .

Oh, God! It was almost three weeks ago! For all those days she'd been thinking of Cliff as alive and well. She'd had a note from him only last week.

Connie's letter was full of grief. Terrible memories of the time their home was bombed seemed to have resurfaced for her. There wasn't a word about how her baby was getting on: 'I feel totally raw about our Cliff. Still can't quite believe – it seems too cruel. This is a dreadful, dreadful war and there seems no end to it. I'm scared stiff for Clovis too, of course. I do wish it would end.'

Her father had written: 'I do wish I knew what had

happened to Cliff. Not knowing torments me and I very much fear the worst. I'm afraid that of the three children Marion and I had, there's only you left. My heart breaks today; my body too and my will to work. What is the point of it all?'

Lottie went back to work. She had to, her ward was very busy at that moment, but for once her mind wasn't on the job. She wanted Connie to be here with her. They could comfort each other as they had last time. She wanted Waldo, but he was far away too.

It was late when she went off duty that night. She hadn't been able to think clearly. She stumbled into the tent where they ate their meals though she wasn't hungry. She sought out Rex Foster. He was on his feet before she said a word.

'What's happened?' he asked.

She wanted to know how he knew anything untoward had happened. The words wouldn't come. She hadn't told anybody yet.

'It's on your face. Something terrible?'

'Cliff's missing, believed killed. My brother.'

He took her out into the night and put his arms round her. She put her head down on his shoulder and wept. There were hundreds of people crowded into this one field so there was no privacy to be had. People were stopping to ask what had happened. Rex pulled her closer to the perimeter, into the shadows and held her tight.

All round her Lottie could still hear the noises of war. After an hour or so, he walked her to her own tent and handed her over to Emily. Lottie washed her face in cold water and got into her camp bed. By then, Rex had come back with some warm milk and a sandwich for her.

'She'll feel better if she gets something inside her,' she

heard him tell Emily. She did her best to swallow the sandwich.

Lottie felt low. It took real effort to get through all the tasks that had to be done. She couldn't put Cliff out of her mind and felt she was hardly in control of her tented ward. She kept reminding herself he was only missing, that he could be still alive, but the words *believed killed* were burning themselves on her mind. It meant they hadn't found his body. Cliff could have been blown to pieces – like Dadda, only worse. It made her feel sick to even think of that.

She couldn't stop herself talking about Cliff, to Rex and to Emily and June. She recalled their childhood together and recounted anecdotes about him. The first week was dreadful. By the end of the fourth, she told herself she was over the first shock and was pulling herself together.

She was eating her dinner when an orderly brought in a telegram for her. She felt her heart miss a beat when he put the yellow envelope on the table in front of her. These days everybody associated telegrams with bad news.

She stared at it without moving. This could be confirmation that the very worst had happened. Rex moved nearer on the bench till his body touched hers. His arm went round her waist.

'It's from England.'

She swallowed. 'They've heard something.'

'Shall I open it for you?'

She swept it silently towards him, shivering as his fingers picked it up. Afraid this would bring an end to her hopes.

The next minute, his face lit up, telling her just the opposite. He was smiling and laughing all at once.

'It's all right! Just look at this!'

Tears misted her eyes so she couldn't see the text he was

holding in front of her. 'He's a prisoner of war.'

She mopped at her eyes until she could read. 'Red Cross confirm Second Lieutenant Clifford Lancelyn prisoner of war.'

'He's alive, Lottie. I don't suppose it's much fun being a prisoner, but he's alive.'

'He'll be safe now. The war can't last much longer.'

'He's lucky. I heard the Germans are shooting the Allied troops they capture instead of taking them prisoner. It's less trouble and they haven't enough food to feed them. It could be much worse.'

'I know that.' She tried to smile.

'It's the emotional kick, Lottie. Seeing the telegram and fearing the worst. Look, you've got an address here. You could try writing to him.'

'I'll write to Father too.' He'd sent it. 'I'm relieved, of course I am. Thank goodness.'

The thought of Cliff being captured took a bit of getting used to, but it was wonderful to know he was still alive. That night, for the first time in a month, Lottie slept well.

Chapter Fifteen

1945

Lottie had enjoyed camping in the Girl Guides. Camping had been fun during the spring in England, where it had always been possible to get a hot bath and clean clothes. Even in war-torn France it had been bearable in high summer, but now it was winter. The tents were damp and cold, often bitterly cold. They were having to layer on clothes to keep warm. When it rained it was dismal and the hospital field was soon churned into mud.

It hadn't taken Lottie long to find that living permanently in the tent she shared with June and Emily had its drawbacks.

Emily snored and both Lottie and June teased her mercilessly, telling her she sounded like a motor bike revving up, but it didn't stop them sleeping. They could sleep through nearby bombardment. It was a case of never feeling they could get enough sleep.

Everything they did took twice as long as it would in a building. Baths were an impossible luxury when water had to be heated on primus stoves, and it was difficult to keep clean. They had an equally cold toilet tent where they washed their hair with soft green enema soap that fortunately was in plentiful supply, using enamel buckets and jugs.

The arrival of clean laundry was a red letter day, though the underwear provided by the army was not what they wore beneath their uniforms in England. Large equestrian knickers were issued to all females.

'Just like Mother wears,' Emily laughed. 'Our generation's moved on from these.' But they were glad to have them; they were warm and it felt wonderful to be clean.

As their mobile hospital had to stay close behind the advancing troops, every so often they were ordered to pack up and move. Then most of their patients would be dispatched elsewhere and the convoy would set off up the crowded roads. Horse-drawn carts held them up; Lottie saw countless abandoned tanks and vehicles pushed to the roadside. There was noisy gunfire and shelling close at hand. They saw rocket-firing Typhoons. Occasionally, they were shot at by German planes although all their vehicles prominently displayed the Red Cross. Sometimes they moved as little as twelve miles, sometimes up to a hundred. Then the hospital had to be set up all over again.

Much of the work was done by the Pioneer Corps. They were a hotch-potch of nationalities from all walks of life; refugees from Germany and conscientious objectors. They dug the tented latrines and acted as guards to the hospital. The officers could usually speak several languages and could act as interpreters.

Lottie wrote to Waldo.

Today, I was in the middle of eating my dinner when one of the medical orderlies came rushing in to fetch me. He was in a panic because a free fight had broken out between the patients in my tented ward. He said the

Tommies were shouting at a German I'd just admitted, telling him they were going to finish him off. By the time I'd run back, two of my patients had the German on the ground.

I started laying down the law in my best imitation of Connie. I told them we operated here under the auspices of the Red Cross and the Geneva Convention and that we had to treat friend and foe alike. And if they were captured by the Germans they were entitled to the same treatment. I gave them a real blast of ire. Connie is a splendid role model to me at such times. I feel I lack her bossy nature. She'd have made a perfect army nurse. They settled down after that and put the German back in his bed. He doesn't understand a word we say to him and he looked terrified as well as in pain.

Although I laid into those two and told off the rest in the ward for not stopping them, I don't really blame them. I find it hard to forgive the Germans for bombing my home and killing my family. Until I knew Cliff was a prisoner of war, I was anti anything German. I wanted to kick and fight them with my fists. It came as a shock to me to find I was to care for the enemy too. Major Esmeralda Jones told us, we are to treat them exactly the same as our own men or any other Allied troops.

I'm torn in two about it now, of course. I think of Cliff and want him to be treated humanely. The Red Cross said he was uninjured and for that I'm glad. I wouldn't like him to be in the same position as our German and have half a ward set about him.

I obey orders. We all have to. The Germans are treated as laid down, but they have to wait until all the Allied troops have been attended to first. They're always last on the list for operations and dressings and served last at meal times. The treatment I give them is the same but I don't give it with any generosity of spirit. I keep having to tell myself that it's not the fault of the soldiers in the field or the crews of the bombers. It's Hitler and his generals who decide the strategy. And I do hope Cliff is being treated with kindness. Knowing how hard I find it, I'm not hopeful . . .

Frank Sinclair, one of our surgeons, came to do a round then. He'd already seen this German and he thought he had appendicitis but like the rest of us he couldn't speak to him to get any sort of history. 'I'm not a vet,' he muttered at me. 'It's like working blind. I just hope I'm reading the signs right.'

I persuaded one of the officers of the Pioneer Corps to come and act as interpreter. It wasn't too easy – the first one I approached refused, saying he wasn't bound by Red Cross rules and he wasn't going to help any German. Anyway, the German gave a history that confirmed the diagnosis and he duly had his appendix out.

'Just in time,' Frank Sinclair told me a few minutes ago. 'Looked as though it was ready to burst at any moment.'

If I have more than one German in at any one time, I put their beds side by side. None of the Tommies want to be near them.

Several days later Lottie wrote about the German again:

> He's up and feeling better now. He's making tea for the Tommies and helping with bottles and washes. He's trying to repay us for taking his appendix out. According to the interpreter, he thinks he's been treated well. What a time to get appendicitis! He's off to a prisoner of war camp tomorrow.

For Lottie, it was a long hard trek across Europe lasting many many months. When at last the mobile hospital crossed the border into Germany in the wake of the Allied Armies, they were all in high spirits.

'The war will soon be won,' they told each other. 'We'll be going home before much longer.'

Up until then, everything had gone smoothly enough for the mobile hospital. They pulled together and worked well as a team. Lottie counted her colleagues as friends. Then she wrote again to Waldo.

> A terrible thing happened today. We had packed up and were moving up the road when our convoy was dive-bombed. I was asleep in a truck bringing up in the rear when suddenly I woke to hear screaming Messerschmitt engines and gunfire. I saw one of our personnel carriers at the front of our convoy burst into flames. That really brought home to me how dangerous all this is.
>
> The injured were dragged out before I reached it. Nobody was killed but several of our unit were hurt. Mostly it was bullet wounds, but one, the hospital

dispenser, was badly burned too.

We had almost reached our destination. Never have we set up the hospital and started to attend to patients more quickly. The theatre was in use in record time removing bullets and setting shattered bones.

The pharmacist, Sergeant Rex Foster, came to my ward. If one can call a large tent a ward. The bullet went through the fleshy part of his leg, so he was lucky there, he had no bones broken, but he hadn't been able to get out of the vehicle before it went on fire. His burns were dressed. His whole face is covered with bandages and he's in great pain.

We were all very upset about this. We not only work together, we do everything together. We speak to nobody else but the patients and they're constantly changing. There's a great feeling of camaraderie amongst us – we're all friends.

Lottie didn't tell Waldo that she sat beside Rex's bed when she should have gone off duty. She knew he felt very ill that first night.

He whispered: 'I asked Major Sinclair to send me to your ward. I told him I wanted you to look after me.'

Lottie thought he shouldn't have. 'June has specialised in burns treatment. Burns cases usually go to her.'

'That's what he said, but I told him I'd be thinking of you all the time and wouldn't be able to settle anywhere else.

'We all talk of being killed,' he agonised. 'But what's happened to me is much the more likely. Being maimed and disfigured for life has always been the most likely outcome.'

'Don't talk like that,' Lottie told him. 'Who says you'll be disfigured for life? Frank says the burns on your face aren't deep.'

'That's just to pacify me. Stop me worrying.'

'No,' Lottie insisted. 'He's written it in your notes . . . I'll get them. You can read it for yourself.'

Lottie was conscious of his eyes following her up the ward. They read avidly the notes she held in front of him.

'I suppose you think I'm being silly. That only women worry about disfigurement.'

'No. Nobody wants to be scarred, especially on their face.'

'It feels sore.'

'It's bound to. Wait a few days until the bandages come off. We'll know better then.'

When Frank Sinclair decided the time had come to take the bandages off his face, Lottie knew Rex was screwing with tension. She eased off the dressings as gently as she could, taking infinite care not to pull on his skin. She felt a mounting satisfaction as they came off.

'It's wonderful!' She was half laughing. 'I can't believe how clear your skin is. It's healing well – you've been lucky. There's a little redness along your jawline here, but that should fade. Then there'll be nothing to show you were burned.'

She went to fetch a mirror and held it in front of him so he could see for himself.

'There now, what did I tell you? You're as handsome as ever.'

There was no mistaking his look of relief. Lottie felt his fingers grope for hers, and she squeezed them. Then she saw a tear run down his cheek.

'I couldn't bear pity,' he gulped. 'I want to look normal.'

'Of course you do. You will. Perfectly normal. You'll have

no noticeable scars. Well, not on your face.'

He studied his reflection without any sign of satisfaction.

'I've made a fool of myself, haven't I? In front of you.' She could see he was angry with himself. 'To be so concerned for my looks – you'll think me a vain sissy. I want you to like me, you see. Not turn away; be repulsed.'

Lottie felt for his hand again. 'I'd never feel repulsed by you however bad your scars. I already like you, you know that.'

Lottie was very conscious that he'd used the word 'like' instead of 'love' and that she had done likewise.

'Then I cried. In front of you, of all people. When there's nobody I want to impress more.'

'I only saw one tear.' Lottie smiled at him. 'A tear of relief. No need to be ashamed of that.' She too had felt tears prickle her eyes. 'It was an emotional moment. What you dreaded has not happened: you won't have scars on your face. Why shouldn't you show relief?'

He said, not looking at her now: 'Having you with me made it more emotional. For me anyway. I knew from your face you were pleased with what you saw, even before you brought the mirror.'

'I was pleased for you,' she insisted. 'We all are.'

He was pulling a face.

'Oh, Rex, I'm delighted. You know I am.' She kissed his cheek and laughed. 'Frank will be too, and June. They'll be surprised at this. It's better than we dared hope.'

A few days later it was decided to take the dressings off Rex's chest. He was biting his lip in pain though she'd given him the injection of morphine Frank had written up for him half an hour before she started. This time Lottie was shocked when she saw the third degree burns which covered a large area.

She asked one of the orderlies to find Major Sinclair and get him to come when he was free.

She said to Rex: 'I'm afraid you're going to be left with scars here.'

He was gritting his teeth. 'You said you wouldn't be repulsed.'

'I'm not. And it'll get better than this.'

'Raw meat,' he said, shaking his head. 'I'll have to keep my shirt on.'

'You'll probably need skin grafts. I'm going to get June to have a look at you too. She knows more about burns than I do. Let's see what the experts think.'

Frank Sinclair shook his head when he came. 'The sooner you get to a good burns unit in England the better.'

Rex said: 'Can't I stay here a bit longer? All my friends are here. I'm sure I'll do better amongst my friends.'

'No,' said Major Sinclair in his official military manner. 'I'm ordering you back to England. Your leg's doing all right, but your burns need specialist care. There's a flight out tomorrow, and you're going on it. Sorry, old chap, but it's the best thing for you. Isn't it, Lottie? You tell him.'

'The best thing,' she repeated.

'You'll have plenty of company. The plane will be full. We'll put Lottie on ambulance duty, so she can see you all off. How's that?'

When he'd gone, Lottie said: 'Most of us would give our back teeth to be going home.'

'Home?' His smile had gone. 'I told you, didn't I? I lost

my home in the Blitz, my wife and baby daughter too, so I'm not so eager.'

Lottie found herself blinking hard to hold back her own tears. She knew what it was to lose loved ones in the Blitz. They'd spoken of it before; it was a shared experience that had helped to bind her to Rex. She'd have liked to say more words of comfort now but they wouldn't come.

'I managed to put it out of my mind. Had to, while I've been here on this job, but going back . . . It'll be hard seeing the place. I'm dreading . . .'

'But your parents? You can stay with them?'

'Yes, but we'd set up home close to them in Warrington.'

Lottie had a sleepless night. There was no question now of shutting Rex out of her mind.

The next day, she had a lot of very sick patients to see to on the way to the airstrip, but she went to sit by Rex for a few moments.

'Can I write to you?' he whispered. 'Well, I'm going to anyway. What I'm trying to ask is . . . Will you write back? Please . . .'

Lottie said gently: 'Better to make a clean break now. I'm married to someone else, Rex. Writing would just prolong the pain of it.'

'No,' he protested. 'Don't talk of clean breaks. I hate to think of that. I'll write to you anyway. I don't know what I'd have done without you these last few days.'

'You helped me when Cliff went missing. Goodbye, Rex.'

He held on to her hand. 'Au revoir, please. I still haven't bought you that glass of wine I promised.' His eyes pleaded with her.

She bent to kiss his cheek. He pulled her lower and brought her lips down against his.

'Take care,' he whispered. 'Take care of yourself. Don't let this happen to you.'

Lottie turned away, her eyes misty. How could she not feel for him? He was thinking of her not of himself. She was bound to feel drawn to him, yet the future he wanted was not possible. She was sure that once she was with Waldo again, he would shut off all her thoughts of Rex Foster.

But here and now she couldn't forget him. He'd shared the last year with her and been a good friend. Yes, she told herself. A good friend. She didn't want to think he was more than that.

She watched the Dakota lumber heavily down the airstrip and lift off. As she went back to the hospital in the empty ambulance she felt lost without him.

It was a week before the first of his letters arrived.

Dearest Lottie,

I know I have no right to address you so, but dearest is what you are to me.

My news is good but I'm still a bit woozy from the anaesthetic. I've had skin from my thighs grafted on to my chest today.

I feel very safe here in England but wish you were with me. Everybody is very kind but I'm missing you. I can think of nothing but you. Please, please write to me.

Lottie had made up her mind not to. She was convinced that, in the long run, a clean break would be the best thing for both of them. But to ignore his letter after such a plea would be hurtful and the last thing she wanted to do was hurt him. She wrote, giving him all the news of the hospital.

The staff of the mobile unit who were free to do so had always clustered round the wireless to hear the news at one o'clock and six o'clock. These days it was always good news. The Allied Armies were advancing on Berlin. Morale had never been higher.

Two days after Mussolini was shot by Italian partisans, Hitler committed suicide. The end was at last in sight.

When the war was officially declared to be over on 8 May, there was riotous jollity in the mess. Everybody was celebrating.

'We've succeeded!' Frank laughed. 'We've done what we set out to do. We've won!'

All round her, Lottie could see eyes shining with triumph. There was a smile on every face. The struggle was over. Bottles of wine were taken out of hiding places where they'd been hoarded for this moment.

But the hospital was still full of patients who had to be looked after, and operating lists were still heavy. They continued to be busy. Lottie was up on cloud nine when she said to Frank: 'The really great thing is that there won't be more.'

'Don't bank on it. Flu was pandemic after the last war. It killed more people than the war itself. Everybody's tired and run down now. Thousands haven't had enough to eat. It could happen again.'

'Well, we won't have the wounded flooding in from now on, we can bank on that.' Emily laughed.

Lottie's patients kept asking: 'When will we be going home?'

Anticipation kept all of them tingling as they waited for orders to pack up and drive home to England.

As Waldo went on his rounds in his greengrocery van on 8 May, the whole of Britain seemed jubilant. The Union Jack fluttered everywhere and pre-war bunting was being brought out to drape across the streets. Shop windows were dressed overall with anything in red, white and blue.

On every church, the bells were ringing for the first time in nearly six years. Housewives were tearing down blackout curtains because from tonight the street lights would be on again, and as they snapped up Waldo's luxuries they talked of bringing out food they'd stored for years for just this moment. The war was won.

Waldo felt he'd had a good war and he had reason to celebrate. He'd done what he'd set out to do, he'd prospered because of the shortages. He was no longer a poor man. He could afford to live well.

Like everybody else, Waldo had been looking forward to peace as the time when everything in his life would change for the better. Lottie would come home. Married life would resume and there would be no further point in dealing in the black market.

It didn't take him long to realise nothing could be further from the truth. The civilian population would no longer have to endure enemy action, but rationed goods wouldn't suddenly become plentiful. Lottie was still somewhere in Germany with her mobile hospital and he had no idea when she'd be coming home.

As the weeks passed, goods that had been in short supply continued to be so. In fact, things were becoming even more scarce. The truth was that Britain had ignored the need to make and sell goods in the world market. The huge balance of wealth built up over the years had been spent on her fighting forces and on the hardware of war. Now the whole economy was left teetering on the edge of bankruptcy and it seemed that austerity would be with them for ever.

Waldo was pleased that the conditions on which he'd built up his fortunes were going to continue for the foreseeable future. He went on taking advantage of them; here was his chance to become really well heeled.

Over the months, he'd found Phyllis's petrol coupons even more profitable than the clothing variety. He'd grown closer to Phyllis, and was seeing much more of her. She shared his social life as well as being a business associate.

For a long time, Lottie had only reached him through her letters. There was one on the doormat today. She wrote of packing up the mobile hospital and said it would soon be returning to England though it would be some time yet before she could hope to be demobbed. She wanted to see more of him, so she'd applied through the channels for a posting to Chester.

Waldo sat down and started to read the letter through again. If Lottie were based in Chester she'd be here quite a lot. It would add a huge complication to his already complicated life. He couldn't imagine how he'd manage to keep her in ignorance of what he was doing.

It brought him other problems. Phyllis had settled into his life and was part of it. In the kitchen, over some ham sandwiches she'd brought with her, he told her Lottie was on her way home.

'You won't be able to come here like you do now. We'll have to be a lot more careful.'

Phyllis tossed her bright blonde hair back from her face and stared at him aghast. 'You mean you want to drop me?' Her voice was hard and there was jealousy in every line in her body.

'Of course not,' he hurried to assure her, but he'd want her only as a business partner from now on. He was careful not to say that but she understood and resented what was happening. He had more letters from Lottie about their homeward progress.

Although he was expecting it, it came as something of a shock when he lifted the telephone and heard her voice. She spoke with such delight about coming home to see him that he felt a huge surge of guilt at the thought of having had Phyllis so often in her bed.

'It's wonderful to hear your voice,' he said, doing his best to rise to the occasion.

'We're all expecting to get leave. I'll ring you again when I know more.' Her voice crackled with excitement. 'I only stepped back on British soil half an hour ago.'

When Lottie put the phone down Waldo stood where he was for five minutes. He had too much stock hidden about the house. He wasn't ready for this.

Lottie had a letter from her father telling her Cliff was home from concentration camp after five months in captivity. 'He's safe and well, Lottie. He's going to have a rest and a holiday and then he's coming to work in the factory. I'm delighted and relieved. Over the moon that all has turned out well. He sends his love and says he'll write soon.'

The following day, she had a letter from Connie giving her the same news and saying she hoped Clovis would be home very soon. The day after that came the letter from Cliff.

Such a daunting experience to be captured within weeks of getting to the front. For all the good I did, I might just as well have stayed in England. All it did was give you something to worry about. My months in prison were frustrating and boring and I'm delighted to be out. I shall be demobbed with indecent haste. All this hasn't been good for my ego.

I should have done what Father wanted and gone to work in the Old Swan factory straight from school. I'm looking forward to starting there as soon as I can. Father thinks I should have a rest first, as if I hadn't been resting for months. What I really need is some excitement, but I don't know how to go about that in austerity England.

You've done far more towards winning the war than I have. Hope to see you soon.

For Lottie, the end seemed to come quickly. They'd packed up the mobile hospital and driven back to England with the few patients they couldn't discharge. They were told the unit was to be disbanded. It was what they'd all expected but it brought feelings of sadness, if only momentarily. Everybody was happy to be back in England. They were all looking forward to going home and getting on with their own lives.

The following day she was able to ring Waldo and tell him she had a seventy-two-hour pass and that after that, she and

Emily had a posting to Netley Hospital.

'That's Southampton,' she told him. 'I'm glad Emily's coming too, but it's not the most convenient place for either of us. June's going back to Woolwich and we hate to part company with her.'

'I'll meet you in London,' Waldo told her. 'We'll have three nights in a hotel. We've got a lot to celebrate and we aren't going to put it off any longer.'

Lottie would have liked to see her new house, but, as Waldo said, she'd have to spend a good deal of her seventy-two hours travelling up to see it, and soon she'd be demobbed and would be home for good. She agreed to meet him in London.

She said to Emily: 'Rex is at Netley. I think he'll still be in. If you see him . . .'

'Of course I'll see him,' Emily retorted. 'I'll make a point of seeing him. He's a friend.'

'I'd rather go anywhere than Netley. I'm no good for Rex, am I? I put in for Chester.'

'Then you were guaranteed a posting to the opposite end of the country. Have a good leave first.'

Lottie was excited as her train pulled into the station at Waterloo. She caught sight of Waldo straight away, waiting for her as she left the platform. She thought he looked wonderfully attractive. The next moment he swept her into a welcoming hug and she felt his excitement too. He had a faint tan and was smartly dressed in grey flannels and a check hacking jacket. She told him so.

'I've brought my best clothes,' he smiled. 'After all, I'm in London and I'm meeting you after all this time.'

He'd booked them into an expensive central hotel which rather shocked her. She'd heard her colleagues talking of a boarding house in Clapham that was quite good.

'We're celebrating,' he reminded her. 'We've waited a long time for this. Longer than most. Anyway, I've got my own business and it's doing very nicely thank you. We can afford it.'

'Things have changed since we got married?' she teased.

'You could say that.' His smile was self-satisfied. 'We're going to do this in style.' He took her to the theatre and to expensive restaurants.

Lottie was surprised at the freedom with which he spent money, but she relaxed and enjoyed herself. She told herself that the time had come for them to shut out the horrors of war and take up where they'd left off.

She said: 'All I want now is to be demobbed and come home. I wish I could come straight away.'

'It'll happen in due course.' That surprised her. Waldo wasn't patient by nature.

'It'll be quite a while. Those who've been in longest are being demobbed first,' she explained. 'And I didn't join up until 1943. There's no shortage of work because there's a lot of war wounded still in hospital. Those needing further surgery – plastic surgery for one thing. Not to mention all the normal illnesses.'

'Your turn will come.' Waldo was frowning.

'I can't wait to start married life,' Lottie laughed. 'I don't want to wait even one more month. It's been deferred too long.'

'You'll just have to be patient.'

She had an uncomfortable feeling that Waldo didn't feel the same urgency that she did. She didn't feel as close to him as she had.

When the time came to leave him, the parting seemed pointless. She'd done what was needed. The war was won. Now she wanted to get on with her own life. She wanted to spend more time with Cliff and Connie and hold Connie's baby. She needed to be back where she belonged. She couldn't wait to be demobbed. The hardest thing was not knowing when that would be.

Chapter Sixteen

1945–1946

Going back to Southampton on the train, Lottie felt she had a
lot to learn about relationships. She and Waldo had been living
such separate lives, such different lives, they'd grown apart.
She hadn't foreseen such a possibility. She couldn't really
believe it now. She told herself it wouldn't take long to get
things back the way they had been. A week or so in his
company and she'd feel head over heels in love with him
again.

She was tired by the time she reached Netley. She threw
her bags in the room that had been allotted to her and went to
look round. Emily was in the sisters' mess and was delighted
to see her.

'You'll have to go and see Rex Foster,' was almost the
first thing she said.

'You told him I was coming?'

'No, I said as little as possible about you. I know how you
feel.'

'How is he?'

'Making good progress. He'll be discharged soon.'

'Good. That's the best news yet.'

'He never stops talking about you, Lottie. He kept asking

where you'd been posted. I didn't like to say you were coming here. You know how you are about him. But he's really got a thing about you.'

'I know! I hope you told him I had leave and was meeting my husband in London.'

'No, I didn't. He feels undying devotion. Lucky you.'

'It isn't lucky for either of us. I keep telling him I'm happily married but he won't listen. There's no future in it. Nothing for him.'

'How do you manage it? Rex's really nice. Reliable. You seem so suited.'

She retorted: 'I'm suited with Waldo, Emily.'

But even as she said it, she knew she no longer felt so single-minded about Waldo. She daren't allow herself to compare him with Rex.

Lottie had Rex on her mind as she went to bed. She had more in common with him than she did with Waldo. Perhaps she understood him better, but that didn't alter the fact that she was married.

She decided to slip in to see Rex the following morning during her coffee break, telling herself it would be churlish not to. He was lying on top of his bed wearing the regulation dressing gown and reading a newspaper. He didn't see her until she stopped at the foot of his bed. When he looked up, she saw delight and incredulity cross his face.

'Lottie!' He was on his feet quickly. Reaching for her hands. 'Dare I kiss you here?'

'No. Please don't,' she giggled.

'You're coming to work on this ward?' He had a huge smile on his face. He could see by her cap and apron that she was working in the hospital.

'No. It's orthopaedics for me. My ward's at the far end.'

'But the same hospital! You look so pretty, Lottie, so smart in that uniform.'

'Tin hat and fatigues not needed here. I'll get myself a chair.' She pulled it to his bed and sat down. 'You're looking more yourself. I'm so glad.'

Truly she was very fond of Rex. How could she not be when she saw such affection shining in his eyes?

She told him about her leave. About Waldo. To talk of her husband seemed the best way to deal with this. Surely it would turn him off? Surely that was the best thing she could do for him? It was also the best defence for her.

He didn't want to hear about Waldo. She could read Rex like a book and he was hating this. He asked about his friends. She told him where they'd been posted as far as she was able, but he'd heard all this from Emily already. He mourned the fact that the unit was disbanded and he'd been in hospital during the greatest celebration in decades. It wasn't, Lottie thought, a satisfactory visit for either of them.

'You will come and see me again?' he pleaded when she got up to go.

How could she say no? She looked in on him every day, sometimes staying only a few minutes, occasionally lingering an hour or so after the night staff had come on. She took him books to read.

Soon he was saying: 'I'll be going home soon, back to Warrington. Another week or so at the most. I've been told I can get dressed and go out. Try my legs in the big wide world again. Will you come out for a drink with me?'

'They mean just walk round a bit. Get out in the fresh air.'

'I've been practising up and down this ward, fifty times a day.'

'You won't feel like going far. Not straight away. It'll take you time to—'

'I'll ask the switchboard to ring for a taxi. Will you?'

Lottie felt torn in two. 'Perhaps if you ask Emily as well.'

He groaned. 'It's just you I want. You know that. It won't be the same if somebody else is with us. Not even Emily. I won't step out of line, Lottie, do anything you don't want. I promise.'

It wasn't something a married woman should do, but all the same . . . 'All right.'

He knew which pub to take her to. 'I've been talking to the other patients on the ward. This one was recommended.'

They sat quietly in one corner and talked of old times, of mutual friends and relief that the war in the Far East had ended too. Rex was as good as his word. He knew how to handle himself.

When the taxi dropped them back at the hospital, he said: 'I've enjoyed myself immensely. After being in hospital all these months, it's wonderful to see the outside world again. Thank you for coming with me.'

He bent and kissed her cheek. A swift peck that was totally suitable between friends. In her mind that night, Lottie saw Waldo and Rex side by side. She compared them. Rex was kind and gentle, he'd never knowingly do anybody down, he was loyal and steadfast and supportive. She wasn't so sure about Waldo.

A few days later, when she went to see Rex, he told her he was being moved up to Deva Hospital near Chester and would be discharged a day or two later.

'You're pleased, aren't you?' He didn't seem at all excited at the prospect.

'Yes and no.'

'Come on, you'll be pleased to get out of hospital. Pleased to get back to normal.'

'Yes, very pleased about that. You know what I'm not pleased about.'

Lottie wanted to throw her arms round him, give him a reassuring hug, but she kept her elbows firmly tucked in to her sides.

'I'm not pleased about leaving you.' His eyes shone with love and sincerity.

'There's no future for that . . .'

He put a finger across her lips. 'You'll let me have your home address? You'll be leaving here soon and I don't want us to lose touch.'

'Rex, forget about me. I'm no good to you.'

'I wish I could. Don't think I haven't tried. You'll be giving Emily and June your home address? Of course you will. I'm a friend too.'

Lottie was moved by the depth of his feelings. She didn't want to lose touch with him either.

'I'll be discreet. I won't write anything that would upset your husband, I promise.'

'I know, but not yet,' she told him. 'I'll be here for the next few months.'

She was able to talk to Waldo regularly on the phone. She could ring him now as he had a telephone both in the garage and at the house. He told her he'd had a wonderful time in London and that he was very impatient to have her home with him for good.

It made her feel disloyal. She didn't mention Rex in her letters or phone calls. She was afraid Waldo wouldn't understand. She didn't really understand herself.

Rex had been gone for a month when she received his letter.

Dearest Lottie,

I'm home now with my parents who are spoiling me with every kindness. I'm very glad to be here except that I can't look forward to you dropping in to see me at coffee time or before you go off duty. I'm missing you.

Today I've had a letter from Emily, who's over the moon because she's got her demob papers. She comes from here as you know and says she'll come and see me. I'm looking forward to that because she's your friend and that makes me feel a little closer to you.

It won't be long before you're demobbed, and I won't then be able to think of you going up and down your ward at Netley. Please, please, send me your home address. I promise I won't send you love letters or anything to embarrass you or upset your husband. I just want to know where you are, without having to ask Emily.

It's very hard to recover from unrequited love. I've loved you since I first set eyes on you. You know that, but this is the last time I'll be able to tell you. I even feel, deep down, a little response from you, though you do your best not to show it. I can't get you out of my system. I'm afraid I don't try hard. I want you there, and I feel that, despite the logic of all you say, eventually

I'll get what I want so very much.

All my love, Rex.

Rex's letter arrived the day after Emily left for good. Lottie was missing him and knew she'd miss Emily too. It was unsettling to lose her friends. She wished her turn for demob would come. She wrote to Rex and sent her home address. Already she was feeling a little lonely.

Waldo was worried. It had niggled him for ages. He was afraid Lottie would turn against him if she knew how he earned his living. He'd told himself he was doing it for her, but he knew she'd be dead against it. He'd imagined he'd stop before she came home, so she need never know, but now the war was over. She'd be home soon and his black market turnover was greater than ever. It might be possible to hide some things from her but not all. She couldn't help but see that his standard of living had risen spectacularly. He wasn't going to cut that back.

He'd put off telling her by going down to London to see her. He'd said it was to save the time she'd have to spend travelling up to Merseyside; that he wanted to spend every minute he could in her company. It was the truth. He did.

They'd both had a good time. It had saved a lot of awkward questions Lottie would have asked if she'd come home and seen the set-up. To come face to face with her again had been wonderful. He'd enjoyed her company; she was a lot of fun. And she looked so fresh and young compared to Phyllis. Her wideset eyes had been full of anticipation. She was his wife and she captivated his senses. When he compared her smooth scrubbed skin and freckles with

Phyllis's thick make-up he knew which he preferred.

The problem was that Phyllis was much more a part of his life now. He was tied up with her and felt torn between the two of them.

Waldo had always thought of himself as having a well-balanced and easy-going temperament, but the continual need to look over his shoulder was making him edgy as never before. He was beginning to see trouble where none existed, and at the same time he was afraid he was missing the early signs of it. He felt he was becoming obsessional about his safety.

He no longer slept soundly. He had nightmares in which he found himself in prison. He imagined Lottie coming home to find his house had been confiscated. It was useless to tell himself, over his morning toast, that his house couldn't possibly be confiscated, even if the worst possible scenario came to pass. He'd safely laundered his black market earnings by converting them to businesses and property. And now the profits from his businesses were giving his income respectability. It was useless to tell himself he was in a safe position. Waldo was afraid he was becoming a nervous wreck.

He'd had countless scares over the years but so far none had landed him in any serious trouble. He told himself he was lucky, that he'd be all right. He was a survivor.

He'd been stopped several times when out doing a round with his van. He'd been questioned by inspectors from the Ministry of Food, the dreaded enforcement officers. His stock had been searched. He schooled himself to be careful at all times. He never allowed himself to be caught with more than the few pounds in cash on him that such a business would earn. He hid it around the cab. Taped it under the seat, inserted it into the seat itself.

The same with all rationed goods. He kept them well wrapped up and hidden under potatoes or in sacks of sprouts. Everybody could see the sprouts through the mesh. Only one had thought to feel through them and he'd been half-hearted about it and failed to find the bacon.

Waldo told himself the best way to survive being searched and questioned by snoopers was to stay cool and keep his wits about him. He made every effort to appear friendly and open. He tried to cultivate an easy and relaxed manner and not get rattled. Any signs of nervousness would be interpreted as signs of guilt and only prolong the ordeal.

But it was very hard to keep the tension from showing when his van was being searched. With his heart pounding twenty to the dozen and his hands shaking visibly, he'd had to display the contents of the leather satchel in which he kept his takings, and of any box they might point to.

Once he was caught with eight pairs of pheasants, several fresh salmon and a whole lot of rabbits, but such luxury goods were not on ration and they could not take him to court for handling them. He'd started the round with twenty pounds of cheese on the van but they hadn't found what remained of that.

'What are you doing with goods like this?' they wanted to know. 'You're a greengrocer. It says so on your van.'

'Fishmonger and game merchant too. Not easy to earn a living now with just greens. Can't get the bananas and pineapples I used to sell.'

'Where do you get these things from?'

'The wholesale market, of course. In Liverpool.'

'I haven't seen stuff like this there for years. And all this coming to one retailer? One small retailer.'

'I've got to get up at four in the morning to get it,' he'd grinned. 'You'd see it around at that time. You should try it one morning.'

But he'd had to sell the fellow a brace of pheasants at less than their real value, just to prove it was all hunky-dory.

Waldo knew he was sailing close to the wind and that he was being watched. Three inspectors from the Board of Trade came to his garage one day and made a systematic search which they said was routine. They pored over his accounts for hours. Waldo's black market petrol sales were booming, but the petrol coupons he received from Phyllis made it all seem legal. He made up his books with the snoopers in mind. They went away baffled because they'd found nothing amiss.

He told himself he'd be all right if he continued to be careful. He made a point of knowing all the enforcement officers who lived locally and might be expected to take an interest in what he was doing. He knew he must always be alert if any of them came snooping round.

It was becoming harder to keep one jump ahead of them. The problem was that half the population of Birkenhead knew him. Either he bought from them, or he sold to them, and his expertise on acquiring goods was widely known.

To start with, he hadn't seen this as a bad thing – it brought more customers who wanted to trade. Now, he was beginning to fear that the inspectors might get a tip-off about him. He did his best to stay on friendly terms with those he traded with. He couldn't afford to make enemies. Even so, he was afraid he might be dropped in it inadvertently. Every so often one of his suppliers was picked up and investigated further.

Several had been taken to court and one had gone to prison. To think about that really filled him with dread.

Waldo knew his best plan would be to stop all illegal activities, but he couldn't. Now was a wonderful time to make money and it wouldn't last. Soon there would be plenty of everything and the opportunity would be gone for ever. Nobody with business sense could stop now.

Neither could he leave town. He was hiding his black market activities behind legitimate businesses and he couldn't leave them. All his instincts were to acquire more.

Common sense told him to draw his horns in. He was living on his nerves, afraid his luck wouldn't last much longer, but when Lottie came home they'd have a wonderful time. He'd be able to do her proud. She deserved the best, didn't she?

In the new year, Lottie wrote in great excitement that at last she'd been given the date when she'd be demobbed. She was to leave the hospital on 19 February and travel to a dispersal centre in London where she'd stay overnight. The next day, the 20th, she'd be demobbed and would then be free to come home.

Waldo felt a surge of pleasure but it soon ebbed away. This was what he'd been looking forward to, but he'd have to be more careful than ever. The easiest way would be to tell Lottie everything, but he was afraid she'd make a fuss, be horrified. He didn't want anything like that. It would be better if he told her nothing. He didn't want her to despise him.

To keep Lottie in ignorance would mean a huge change in the way he worked. He decided that from now on he'd bring no more black market goods to the house, and he'd start removing the things already stored there.

Waldo was still seeing a lot of Phyllis and she was already touchy about Lottie coming home. Their relationship would have to be restricted once she was back. Phyllis understood that, she'd always known about Lottie, but she didn't like being pushed out. He'd have to handle her gently. Not hurt her more than he had to. Women could turn nasty if they thought they were being pushed out to make room for another. He didn't want Phyllis to seek revenge. That would be awful. She was in a position to wipe out everything for him. He'd have to be very careful.

Phyllis had been coming regularly to his house. It had seemed the ideal arrangement. It was where she always contacted him; it was so easy when they knew nobody else was around. For months, she'd been printing three hundred petrol coupons for him every week.

She usually rang him on Tuesdays in the early evening to find out if he wanted additional coupons for clothing or sweets, and to confirm she had the petrol coupons ready. Every Wednesday, she brought them round to his house in time for a late lunch. Her husband spent the middle of the week seeking new orders, often away from home. She'd said that was the best day for her.

Waldo was always back home in plenty of time to make sure his daily woman was gone. He didn't want her to know Phyllis was a regular visitor at his house. Phyllis was in the habit of bringing sandwiches or Cornish pasties that she'd made herself. When they'd had those, with some beer or a few glasses of wine, she was usually keen to get him up to his bedroom. They usually made an afternoon of it. If her husband was away from home they made a night of it too.

If Phyllis stayed the night, he set his alarm clock so she could be gone well before half past eight the next morning, when Mrs Gully returned.

The weeks were passing quickly. Waldo knew he'd have to alter his arrangements. He'd talked to Phyllis about meeting her in a pub.

'When we really have to,' she'd said with terrible logic. 'No need until she's here.' As far as he was concerned, Lottie's return was getting dangerously close.

'She'll be back next week. On Wednesday.'

'This week will be all right then. Come on, Waldo,' she wheedled. 'One last time. What's the harm?'

The harm was it made him nervous. He was glad it would be the last time Phyllis would come to his house. He was beginning to feel the strain.

'Next week, we'll have to do things differently,' he told her.

'She'll be back on Wednesday? What time? Could we still do lunch?'

'Yes, but not here, Phyl, Lottie doesn't know what time she'll get away. It'll probably be late when she gets here, but I have to have things straight. I don't want her to notice . . . you know. We've got to change everything. Next week, ring me at the garage and we'll eat at a café. What about that place at Woodside? Down by the ferry?'

On Tuesday, Phyllis rang him at the garage as he'd asked. She caught him at a bad time, when he had a customer with him. He needed privacy for this side of his business. He didn't like anybody listening to what he was saying.

Her voice sounded agitated. 'Waldo, I've got to talk to you.'

The man beside him seemed to be all ears. Waldo said:

'Have you got the goods parcelled up for tomorrow?'

'Yes. Do you want any extras?'

He'd impressed upon her that she mustn't be too explicit on the phone. One never knew whether the operator was listening in.

'Not this week. I'm still well stocked.'

She persisted. 'I'd like you to take more.' She'd never tried to press coupons on him before.

'No, I can't pay for any extras tomorrow.'

He could if he wanted them. He preferred to hold cash rather than have more coupons for clothes and sweets than he could move in the coming week. It was safer.

'You can pay later.' That disconcerted him. Their terms had always been cash on the nail.

'No, no thank you.'

She was breathing more heavily than usual; he could hear her.

'Waldo, I've got to see you. Can I come round tonight?' That made his heart jerk and pump faster.

'I'll be out tonight.' He'd got ten tons of coal to move on. It was like gold dust at the moment. Schools and factories were closing because there was none available. 'Tomorrow. You always come on Wednesdays.'

Phyllis said quickly. 'Tomorrow, then. One o'clock, at that café near the ferry,' and put the phone down.

It left him with the feeling that something was wrong. He was worried about Phyllis, but he had to think about Lottie. She'd be home by tomorrow night. He had to get something for dinner. Something special. He had some very nice cheese in his store at the moment; he'd take some home. He wanted to make her feel welcome.

Waldo didn't like moving coal. If it weren't so profitable he wouldn't touch the stuff. He was helping to hump hundredweight sacks about until nearly ten o'clock. He'd have liked to hire someone else to do the job but it was safer to do it himself. He was exhausted by the time he'd finished.

He'd been collecting food all day for Lottie's homecoming. He wanted to call at his store on the way home and get more fruit and vegetables, and the cheese he'd mentally earmarked for tomorrow's dinner. He was planning a celebration meal.

His store was in a back street, a ramshackle building full of nooks and crannies behind a high brick wall. It had been damaged in the Blitz and repaired roughly with sheets of asbestos at one time, and zinc at another. It was cold and draughty, the glass blown out of the windows and the spaces covered with wire netting and iron bars. It was just the place for storing fresh fruit and veg.

He could drive his van through the high wooden gate, which had a large board nailed to it with the previous owner's name. W. W. Smith, Greengrocer and Fruiterer.

For Waldo it couldn't have been better. It was very private for loading and unloading his van. The snoopers had been in twice and failed to find anything they could prosecute him for.

But even better was the old stable that had come with the business. It was right alongside his store but it had a separate entrance to the street. He'd fenced it off so now it wasn't obvious that he owned both. The snoopers hadn't asked about it and he hadn't volunteered any information. He rated the stable as his best hiding place. There was a loft above it where hay had once been stored. He kept a few sacks of potatoes on the ground floor, just in case. The place was half derelict, but worth its weight in gold to him.

Waldo was tired tonight. He parked his van outside the gate to his store and took a cardboard box inside to load up with enough fruit and vegetables to last a few days. He balanced a large bunch of grapes he'd been saving for Lottie on top. He slid the box into the van and then opened up the padlock on the gates to the stable.

He'd hidden several cheeses up in the hayloft. He had bacon there too, and some sugar. He'd had to buy several new dustbins to keep his groceries in, because there were mice about and he wasn't aiming to feed them. The dustbins were lined up behind a pile of old hay, ancient stuff smelling of damp and turning to dust, but it hid the dustbins from view. He always removed the ladder, which was the only way to get up into the loft, and hid it underneath the woodworm-riddled manger.

Waldo thought he'd have to be very unlucky to have his cache found by snoopers, but to be on the safe side he didn't keep anything here for longer than he had to.

Tonight, he went first to the cold water tap in the yard and rinsed his face and hands. He felt filthy from the coal. He took off his coat and shook off some of the coal dust. No point in going home looking like a coalman.

He crept about as he always did, replacing the dustbin lids silently and shielding the beam of his torch as he worked. He went out feeling dead-dog weary, and was replacing the padlock on the double gates when he realised he was not alone. He felt the hairs on the back of his neck stand on end.

'Evening. It's Mr Padley, isn't it?' The side street was dark, but a torch played over him.

Waldo was instantly alert, his heart thumping, his tiredness gone.

'It is, but I can't be selling you potatoes now, it's too late. You'll have to come back in the morning.'

'I don't want to buy potatoes.'

Waldo gave a discreet flash of his own torch. 'Sorry. Thought you were Jack Birch, the builder from round the corner. He was asking about potatoes earlier. Wanted a sack.'

'Edwin Carruthers.' An identity card flashed in front of him. 'Ministry of Food inspector.'

Waldo knew him; he didn't need to introduce himself. He was one of the pair who'd searched his store next door, a couple of months ago.

'Who owns these premises?'

'I do – store my spuds in them.' He was painfully conscious that his coat pockets were stuffed so full of cheese and bacon that it made his overcoat swing as he moved. He pressed his elbows in, hiding the bulges, holding his coat against his body. Then came the dreaded request.

'Would you mind if I had a glance round?'

Waldo minded very much. The thought of taking a snooper in terrified him, but it wouldn't do to refuse. He could go through the place with a fine-tooth comb tomorrow in broad daylight. Better to do it now and hope for the best.

Questions were hammering in his mind as he unlocked the padlock again. What was Edwin Carruthers doing here at this time of night? Had somebody tipped him off? Had he followed him? Did he know about the coal? Waldo was afraid he'd been caught in the act. He could smell the cheese in his pocket. Keep calm, keep calm, he kept telling himself.

To the snooper he said: 'This way. Careful of the potholes, it's a bit rough here.'

That kept the man's torch on the ground in front of him, but not for long. The door creaked as Waldo pushed it open. Inside it was pitch black. The beam went round, shining on the cobwebs festooned from the ceiling.

'Let's have the light on. No blackout regulations now, you know.'

'No electricity. Never had any here, it's an old stable.'

'Oh!' The torch went slowly round the walls, checking that there was no electricity, then over the sacks of potatoes. Waldo's knees felt like marshmallows that were about to buckle under his weight.

'You own the building next door?'

His mouth was dry. Edwin Carruthers knew very well he did. 'Yes.'

'What did you buy this for?'

Waldo's back was rigid with hostility he dared not show. 'It came with the rest of the business. In the old days, the round used to be done by horse and cart. I'd have been glad of a horse many times, I can tell you.'

All the time he was talking the beam was going round. Lighting up the opening to the hayloft. What could he say if Carruthers asked about that? Woodworm in the floor? It wasn't safe to go up?

'Right, Mr Padley, thank you.' Carruthers was turning away.

Thank God, he was going. Waldo felt weak with relief. He'd had a tremendous run of luck, and it had held again.

'Good night to you, Mr Padley.'

Waldo watched him walk away in the darkness. He could

just make out a car parked at the end of the street. The door slammed as Carruthers got in. Waldo groped to his van and fell into the driving seat. When he reached home it was only half past ten, although it seemed ages since he'd finished with the coal. He was cold and shaking. Encounters like that were bad for his nerves. He felt drained, worse than he had for a long time.

His phone started to ring as he was reaching for the whisky bottle. He had to screw up his courage to lift it. Lottie's voice clear and excited came across the wires.

'I'm in London, Waldo. At the dispersal centre. You're out late – I've been trying to get you for the last half-hour.'

'Working,' he grunted. 'I've got things to finish before you come.'

She laughed. 'Can't believe it's my turn at last. I've got to hand in my kit tomorrow. Don't know how long that will take. Got to have a medical too and there's chits to sign and formalities to go through. You know what the army's like.'

He didn't and he didn't feel composed enough to talk to her. 'What train will you catch?'

'I don't know when I'll be able to get away, but I'm coming straight home. How do I find this new house?'

'Couldn't I meet you? No, not unless you tell me which train you'll be on. I'll be at the garage all afternoon. Ring me there if you can. Or just come there. You know where it is. I took you to see it.'

Waldo couldn't take in all she was saying. He assured her he was looking forward to seeing her tomorrow. It was all on top of him now; he wished she wasn't coming for another week.

It was after midnight when he got to bed and then he couldn't sleep. Too many things were worrying him.

Chapter Seventeen

20 February, 1946

When the dark February morning came, Waldo didn't feel like getting up. He crawled out of bed feeling stiff with tension. Mrs Gully, his cleaning woman, arrived before he was dressed. He had no appetite for his bacon and egg. Lottie was coming home today. Just to think of it gave him collywobbles. He arranged for a meal to be ready for her and the sheets on the bed to be changed. He wanted everything to be just right.

As he drove to his store to restock his van, he kept checking in his mirror to see if he was being followed. He drove past the side street once and went round again to convince himself he wasn't being watched. He didn't want that Carruthers fellow bursting in on him again. He felt a nervous wreck all morning as he went about his greengrocery round.

It was a little after one o'clock when he went to Woodside Ferry. He went into the café to meet Phyllis, expecting to see her at one of the tables with her bright blonde head bent over a newspaper. He couldn't believe she hadn't arrived; she was never late. He went back to his van to wait outside, wishing he'd chosen somewhere with its own car park. It was a miserable cold wet afternoon.

It seemed ages before he saw her car slide past his to park

against the kerb in front. She sprang out, dragging two fat carrier bags after her which she brought to his van.

'What's all this?' There was an edge to his voice that he couldn't help.

'Coupons. Coupons for everything, clothes, petrol and sweets.'

'I said no, Phyl. I've only got enough cash for the usual.'

She looked suddenly ten years older and was noticeably on edge.

'I can't keep all that on the van, not all afternoon.'

'Can't you take them back to your store? I want to get rid of them. You can pay me later.'

'Why?' Waldo thought at first Phyllis was playing up, that she was jealous because she was being pushed out by Lottie.

'This is everything I've printed up. I was going to destroy them but you might as well have them.'

His heart began to pound. 'Something's happened?'

'Board of Trade inspectors are coming to check us over. Cecil's worried stiff.'

'Tomorrow?'

'No, the day after.'

'It'll be all right.' Waldo tried to reassure her. 'They check businesses over once in a while. If they've made an appointment that far ahead . . .'

'They didn't want to. They arrived yesterday afternoon wanting to start straight away. Cecil was just about to set off to Sheffield. He had to show them his train ticket. They wanted to know which hotel he'd booked, and who he was going to see. He drove off and left me to it. Had to, if he was to catch his train. There were three of them, and they started opening cupboards, poking about . . .'

Waldo felt cold with foreboding. If they could prove that Phyllis was printing petrol and clothing coupons illicitly, it wouldn't take them very much longer to find out how she disposed of them. Then he'd be in big trouble.

'They kept asking me questions; asking to see the books. I told them Cecil had gone off with the keys to the safe. Much of our ticket production and our books are kept locked up for security reasons. I managed to convince them in the end.'

'You mean it wasn't true?'

'We each have a key.' She shook her head impatiently. 'I had to get rid of them. I had all this with me. I wanted them to come back when Cecil was there. I want him to see to them.'

Waldo swallowed hard. The snoopers seemed to be coming at him from every direction.

'But it's all right now? There's nothing else for them to find? Nothing incriminating? What about the printing plates? Where do you hide those?'

She pushed the heavy curtain of yellow hair off her face and her big brown eyes stared up at him full of fear.

'It would be dire if they found those. Absolute proof . . .' Waldo felt himself come out in a cold sweat. He was tied up with her. He wouldn't be able to talk his way out of this.

He'd tried to impress upon her the need to be careful at all times, but he didn't really know if she was. The petrol coupons she provided allowed him to obtain more petrol to sell through his garage than he was entitled to, which he sold at great profit to himself. If she went down, he could go down with her.

'At home,' she choked out. 'I keep them at home, in the pantry behind my jars of home-made chutney and jam.'

Waldo choked. 'You make jam?'

'When I can get the sugar.'

'Phyllis, I can get you all the sugar you want. You know that.'

'I make jam sometimes. When I'm in the mood. Cecil likes home-made jam.'

Waldo told himself not to panic. 'So there's nothing in the works to worry about? Nothing in your desk?'

'There's money.'

Waldo shivered. 'How much?'

'A lot. I can't put it in the bank, can I? Cecil would ask questions – want to know where I'd got it.'

'Get it out of your desk. Put it behind your chutney. Or hang on – they might want to search your house. Have they had a tip-off or something?'

'How do I know?' she burst out irritably.

'Phyllis, love. Don't let this tear you apart. You've got to keep your wits about you.'

She burst into tears and he knew she'd already lost her cool. 'Cecil suspects . . . He asked me outright if I'd got someone else.'

'You didn't admit—'

'Of course not. He said he couldn't help noticing . . . that I was spending more money than he provided.'

That alarmed Waldo afresh. 'I warned you not to throw it around.'

'I haven't, not really. He saw those earrings I bought myself. He thinks they came from a lover.'

'When the snoopers start asking questions, he could draw other conclusions.'

'He's already thought of that. He asked me outright if I was printing anything I shouldn't. I said no. I had to say no, didn't I?'

'Yes. Just get everything incriminating off your premises. Don't let them find anything. They have to have proof to prosecute you. Real proof, that would stand up in a court of law.'

'I'm so worried.'

'Do you want to eat?' She was shivering; it was a cold day. 'Have you had anything since breakfast?'

'No. Didn't have any breakfast. I couldn't eat.'

'Come on then, we better had.'

Waldo stuffed her carrier bags down behind the seats in his van and locked up. Inside, the café was beginning to empty after the lunch time rush. The waitress came over to their table.

'The liver's finished; so's the beef and dumplings. There's only fish pie left.'

'We'll have that,' Waldo told her.

'What am I going to do?' Phyllis started as soon as she moved off.

'We can't talk here.'

'Help me. You've got to help me.'

He felt conspicuous. Phyllis was really in a state, sniffing into her handkerchief not far from tears.

'Of course I'll help you. Eat up now and let me think.'

Phyllis was looking a bit better now she had something inside her. Waldo paid the bill and led the way back to his van. She got into the passenger seat and he drove away and parked in a quiet street. He didn't like staying in one place for any length of time.

Phyllis said: 'Should I admit to something small? I did a few clothing coupons for Lily Landsmore – that big dress

301

shop in Grange Road. You know it? She promised me a couple of new outfits, but she didn't have the ones I wanted in my size. She said she'd order them but she closed the shop down. Went bankrupt or something. If I tell them about her, and say it was the only time, they'll leave me alone.'

'No, don't admit anything.' Waldo felt desperate. He was afraid that once Phyllis started admitting things she wouldn't know where to stop. She'd be telling them about what she did for him. 'If you say that, you're admitting to forging government documents to obtain goods on ration. They'll know how to worm everything out of you, Phyllis. Once you start you'll be finished.'

'I'm scared.' She patted her eyes with an embroidered handkerchief. 'I could go to prison for this, couldn't I?'

Waldo knew he could too. 'It won't come to that. Don't tell them anything. Nothing at all. You're innocent – that's what you have to get across. It shouldn't be too hard. Leave it to your husband. He'll look innocent enough, won't he?'

Something in Phyllis's face made him stop. 'He isn't doing something he shouldn't?'

'I don't know, do I? Any more than he knows about me. He's frightened, I know that, and it's really putting the wind up me.'

Waldo knew it was doing the same to him. Fear was horribly infectious.

'I'll go straight to the works now. Get my money – and there's some special ink . . .'

He said: 'I've got to get back to the garage. I don't know what time Lottie's coming; she's going to ring me there.'

'I'll bring everything to you for safe-keeping. I can take it away again once this is over.'

'No, Phyllis! I'm running out of hiding places. Don't bring me anything more. I've had to clear a lot from my house – I don't want Lottie to come across something and start asking questions, do I?'

He told her about the snooper he'd had to show round his stable last night. He wasn't sure he'd heard the last of that yet. What if Carruthers decided to come back in daylight?

Phyllis was shaking with distress. 'You're trying to push me off now I'm in trouble. You don't even want to help me.'

'I do,' he protested. 'Don't say that. Of course I'll help you.'

'But what am I going to do? There's a lot of stuff I want to get rid of.'

This couldn't have come at a worse time for him. Lottie coming home when all this trouble was boiling up for Phyllis. Boiling up for him too, possibly.

Waldo sighed. It was no good trying to distance himself from Phyllis now, he should never have got himself in this position. But he couldn't have her incriminating evidence on his premises. Not her printing plates – they were dynamite. Not her money either – too much of that always brought questions. Waldo felt bile rising in his throat at the very thought.

'Phyllis, what if the snoopers have seen us together? They're always watching me. That could be what's put them on to you.'

Her frightened eyes stared up at him. She was having a panic attack. Waldo knew he ought to be soothing her, not stirring her up like this. He needed to be sure she'd keep her mouth shut.

'I'm worried about dropping Cecil in a hole.'

'He's away tonight, you said?'

She sniffed again. 'Yes, in Sheffield. He booked this trip ages ago. That's why the inspection was put off. I don't like being by myself. I wish Lottie wasn't coming home tonight so I could stay with you.'

Waldo too wished she wasn't; it was making things more complicated. He had to go. It was getting dark.

'You'll be all right. Just clear out every bit of evidence from your office. Money too, because they'll ask where you got it from. If you do it now, straight away, I could come over to your place and help you hide it.'

'But I don't want Cecil to find anything.'

'Hide it where it won't be found. Much better if you keep control. Specially of your money.'

'But I don't see—'

'You've got that rockery in your back garden. Take out a couple of those big white rocks and hide the printing plates underneath. If we can make it look as though the stones haven't been disturbed . . .'

'That sounds . . . could be all right,' Phyllis was drying her eyes.

'How long will it take you? To fetch your things?'

'Say a couple of hours – perhaps less.'

'It's almost five now. I'll come over to your house about seven and we'll get this sorted. Two heads are better than one. Unlock the back door for me. We don't want your neighbours to see me arrive.' Waldo was very fussy about that sort of thing. No point in standing on her doorstep and ringing her bell. 'They've all ripped down their blackout curtains now, and with the street lamps on they can see everything. We don't want them telling your husband that men visit you when he's away. And you never know what the snoopers are up to.'

Phyllis sniffed into her handkerchief. 'All right.'

Waldo started the van and drove her back to Woodside so she could pick up her car. Time was flying. He ought to be in the garage waiting for Lottie's call.

'Just make sure you aren't being followed.'

'You're getting paranoid.'

'Have to be, to stay safe.'

He dropped her at the top of the hill and watched her walk down through the gloom of a wintry afternoon, her yellow hair bouncing on her shoulders easily visible in the gathering darkness. She got into her car and drove off. He waited for another five minutes to make sure no other car pulled out after her. From here he could see and wouldn't be noticed. He didn't think anybody was following her and felt a bit easier in his mind.

Waldo was heading towards his garage when he remembered the carrier bags of coupons Phyllis had dumped on him. He made a quick detour into a side street to stop and sort them out. He needed his torch.

He took out the carrier bags to look at them. He'd never had so many coupons in his possession at any one time. There were sheets and sheets of them, for clothes, petrol and sweets. He'd have to split them up, hide them in several different places. This amount would immediately mean prison if he were caught with them. He'd be classed as a big dealer.

He'd take the petrol coupons he'd asked for into the garage. He needed to cut the sheets of coupons into random numbers and crumple them slightly before leaking them in measured amounts into the drawer under the till where the legitimate coupons were kept.

As for the rest? He'd have to hide them somewhere. In his own garden? Or should he take them straight to his store now? He lit a cigarette and tried to think about it. He inserted some inside the passenger seat in his van, where he'd made a hole in the cover for this purpose. He put more in the stiff envelope taped to the bottom of his toolbox. He was left with plenty more.

He looked at his watch and was shocked to find it was nearly six. Where had the afternoon gone? Lottie could be here by now. It wouldn't do to keep her waiting.

He took off for his garage, driving fast. It looked better now he could show proper lights. He drove straight across the forecourt and round the back. He knew Lottie hadn't arrived, because there was no light showing in his office. He'd be able to hide a few more of Phyllis's coupons in there.

Old Bill Waters was tinkering around inside the engine of an old car.

'Any phone calls?' Waldo asked. He knew Bill never answered the phone. He was a bit deaf and said he couldn't hear anything over the wires.

'Nope.'

'What about the lads?' Waldo employed two fifteen-year-olds too.

'Went home at five. You didn't want them to stay?'

'No. Did they answer the phone?'

'Eh, I don't know.'

Waldo crashed the office light on and collapsed at his desk. The lads would have left a message tucked into his blotter. There was nothing. He felt exhausted, but no matter how tired he was he had to keep Phyllis sweet. That was important.

He wished he had some idea of when Lottie would arrive. He willed her to ring him now but the phone stayed silent. She could be anywhere between here and London or she could walk in across the forecourt at any moment. Every movement out there, every time a car drove in for petrol, he was up at the window to see if it was her.

He'd told Phyllis he'd go round to her house and he'd have to. He tried to formulate a story to tell Lottie if she came and he had to leave her. Nothing convincing occurred to him; his nerves were raw. He was beginning to worry about what had happened to Lottie, and he couldn't settle to do anything. At seven o'clock there was still no sign of her.

Before setting off to see Phyllis, he asked Bill to stay on. Bill wasn't pleased; the garage usually closed long before this.

The rain had eased off a little. To be on the safe side, he parked his van some distance from Phyllis's house and walked the rest of the way. He couldn't get used to having the street lamps on again after all the years of the blackout. He'd just turned in to Rothermere Drive when a large car overtook him, slowed down and turned through the front gate of what he thought was Phyllis's house.

Waldo felt himself break out into a sweat. He started to jog. He had to make sure. The headlights had been switched off by the time he reached the gate. A stiff and portly figure was pushing a key into the lock on the front door.

He swore under his breath and walked past. When he heard the door shut he retraced his steps. That could only have been Phyllis's husband coming back unexpectedly. Thank goodness he hadn't been ten minutes earlier! He didn't want to think of the shock Phyllis was having as her husband walked in.

He hoped she'd be able to cope, and that she hadn't got the things she wanted to hide spread out on the dining room table. She'd been in a dithering panic when she'd left him. This could blow the whole thing sky high, but there was nothing he could do about it now. It was up to her. At least it was her husband and not some snooper.

He went back to his van. He could feel himself shivering. With this on top . . . God only knew what tomorrow would bring. He'd see Phyllis tomorrow and try to keep her on an even keel.

In the meantime, he had to think of Lottie. He looked at his watch as he passed under a street lamp. Surely she'd be here by now? He had to get back to the garage.

Lottie hadn't expected to catch the midday train. She'd rushed to Euston Station and found it still waiting at the platform. It should have pulled out over an hour earlier, but if it had she'd have missed it. Trains hardly ever ran on time these days.

She'd meant to ring Waldo to let him know what time she'd arrive but there wasn't time. She'd barely squeezed herself on board when she heard the guard blow his whistle. A cheer went up along the train corridor, sending sparks fizzing down her spine.

At last she was on her way home. She'd been looking forward to this moment for ages. Living for it. There was a feeling of energy and high spirits all round her. Many of the passengers, like her, were demob happy.

Twenty miles or so down the line, the train stopped in the middle of nowhere. A groan went up. Along the corridor, Lottie could see people trying to make themselves comfortable. There was little to see outside; rain was running down the windows obscuring the view of drenched fields. She folded her mackintosh on to her suitcase, and wondered whether it would bear her weight if she sat on it. She was about to lower herself gingerly down when the train gave an almighty jerk and started off again, throwing her against the man standing beside her. The impact knocked his cigarette out of his hand.

'Sorry,' she gasped as she saw his foot move to crush it out on the floor.

'Hardly your fault.' He was smiling, offering his packet of Players.

'No thanks, I don't.'

She watched as he lit another for himself. His brown hair was cut severely short round the back.

'Have you just been demobbed too?'

He nodded. Serious blue eyes surveyed her.

'What were you in?'

'Eighth Army. Tanks. Saw a lot of the Sahara and Italy. How about you?'

She told him and he whistled through his teeth. 'A front line nurse?'

She nodded. 'Wonderful, isn't it? To have it all over and done with. To be going home.'

A whoop of laughter went up from the carriage behind them, as though to confirm it was. Five girls were crushed together on a seat meant for four. Opposite them were four soldiers. War had broken down the old barriers; people were much friendlier these days. There was something of a party atmosphere on the train. Like her, other passengers were elated at the thought of going back to their families.

Beside her, her neighbour sank down on his case too. 'Might as well sit. It'll take hours to get to Liverpool. Are you going all the way?'

'To Birkenhead, actually.'

'So am I.' His smile was warmer.

'What part?'

'Rock Ferry.'

She laughed. 'So am I.'

There was no restaurant car and Lottie had had nothing to eat since breakfast. It had been a long morning handing in her kit and getting signatures on the documents that discharged her from the QAs.

She'd brought a couple of apples and a packet of four ginger biscuits with her. She was hungry now but felt she had to offer her companion a share. He bit into her biscuits gratefully and chatted on, telling her his name was Martin Carruthers. She told him about herself.

At Northampton, the soldiers got out and half the occupants of the corridor made a rush for their seats. Her companion was nearest and took Lottie's suitcase in too, heaving it up on the rack beside his own.

She sank on to the seat thankfully and stretched her legs out. She'd brought a copy of *Forever Amber* to read on the journey and opened it now on her knee. But she couldn't settle to read; she felt too excited and her companion wanted to talk.

It seemed to take an age to get to Crewe. When the train pulled into the station, he got up.

'I'm starving. I'll see if I can get something to eat. The train usually waits here for a while. Keep my seat for me.'

Lottie watched him rush up the train towards the engine.

She wanted to phone Waldo, but was afraid to get out in case it went without her.

Lots of people were getting on and wanted to use his seat. She pulled his mackintosh down from the rack to make it look occupied. The carriage was cold and shabby, the wartime warnings were still displayed above the seats. 'Is your journey really necessary?' 'Careless talk costs lives.'

Just when she thought the train was about to pull away without him, she saw him weaving through the crowd on the platform. She opened the door for him and he jumped on grinning triumphantly.

'I've got us some sandwiches. Only cheese, I'm afraid.'

'I like cheese.'

'Bread's a bit dry.'

Lottie was grateful for anything. The train started off again. She ate her sandwich and felt better.

'It's going to be late when we arrive.'

Lottie was a bit concerned about that. 'I told Waldo not to try to meet me. I didn't know which train I'd be able to catch and he has a business to run.'

'What sort of business?' Martin took another hungry bite.

'A garage.'

'He wasn't in the services?'

'Failed his medical. They wouldn't have him.'

'I don't suppose it's easy, running a garage in wartime. With so little petrol to sell and so few cars on the road.'

'I've only seen it once and that was before he bought it. He mends cars too, and sells them.' She thought of their stay in London, and the expensive restaurants he'd taken her to. 'I think he's doing all right.'

'There's been no petrol ration for the private motorist for

years. Whereabouts in Rock Ferry? I know the district well.'

'He said I was to come out of the station, walk down the hill and turn right into New Chester Road.'

'I know the place.'

When they reached Liverpool, Martin insisted on carrying her case for her as they set off down Lime Street towards Central Station and the underground.

She took deep breaths. 'Smells like home.'

'Smells of smoke,' he retorted. 'From the factories.'

It had been a dark and overcast day, and nightfall had come early. A light drizzle was falling and the shops were all closed now.

'The lights!' For Lottie it was a delight to see the street lamps reflecting on the wet pavements, after years of blackout.

He said: 'If I can see a phone box . . .'

'There used to be some in the station.'

'I'll ring home and let Dad know I'm getting close. He told me to, so he could meet me. Almost impossible to get a cab these days and the buses won't take me close.'

'I thought you said there was no petrol ration for the ordinary motorist?'

'My dad gets it for his job. He can spare a bit for me when I've been away for four years. Here we are.'

Martin put down the suitcases and went into the phone box. Lottie burrowed in her handbag for four pennies and her book of phone numbers. She'd be able to ring Waldo too.

There were broken panes of glass in the box and she could hear what Martin was saying. There was a lift in his voice now.

'Hello, Dad. Yes, I've got as far as Liverpool Central. Another half hour at the most. Right, thanks. See you.'

Lottie eased her way in as he came out, and dialled the number at Waldo's garage. She could feel her stomach knotting. Any second now he'd lift the phone and she'd hear his voice.

But the phone went on ringing. Waldo wasn't picking up the receiver at the other end. If he wasn't there, how was she to contact him? Suddenly there was a ball the size of an orange in her throat. Of course he was there – he'd said he'd wait for her there. In her excitement she'd misdialled. She put the receiver down and did it again more carefully. It began to ring once more and she began to count, keeping her eyes on Martin's back. Ten rings. Give it twenty – that would be plenty of time to cross any forecourt.

It didn't stop. She was worried now. It was gone seven o'clock; the garage could be locked up for the night. Quickly she dialled his home number but it was unanswered there too. She saw Martin look at his watch.

Lottie pressed button B and slid the pennies that returned into her pocket. She'd try again later. She'd made this arrangement with Waldo only last night. She didn't know Oxton at all, and she'd never been to the new house.

'I'll wait for you at the garage. You can come through to Rock Ferry station by train,' he'd said. 'It's only a short walk from there.'

He'd sounded keyed up, almost feverish with excitement that she was coming home at last. The directions he gave sounded somewhat muddled, but having been once Lottie thought she could find it.

'I can't wait to see you, Waldo.'

'I've been waiting for this for years. Till tomorrow then.'

Martin's manner was bracing. 'Perhaps he was busy at the

back, mending a car or something.'

It was all right for him. He'd made contact with his family. Martin picked up the cases and headed down the stairs.

'There's a train in now. It's going to Rock Ferry.' He quickened his step, but Lottie ran faster and opened a door for him. There were plenty of empty seats here.

'Wonderful,' he smiled and they flopped down, side by side, and laughed.

The train started almost immediately. Quietly, too, because the line had been electrified here. Within seconds they were in a black tunnel and the windows were like mirrors. She saw Martin yawn. She was tired as well. Odd to think the waters of the River Mersey were above them now. Lottie closed her eyes.

'Next stop,' Martin murmured. 'Nearly home now.'

The train was above ground, rain gusting against the windows.

'Doesn't seem much like home to me,' Lottie said as she got out on the rainswept platform. 'I've never been here before.'

Martin took up both cases again and she followed him. 'You'd better let me carry my own,' she began, and then Martin dropped both of them to greet an older man.

'I'd better go,' she said.

'This is Lottie, Dad. She's kept me company all the way from Euston.'

Lottie was reaching for her own case. 'I'll be on my way. You'll have a lot to talk about.'

'Dad'll drop you off. Do you know Padley's Garage, Dad? Would you mind?'

'Of course not. I know the place – get my petrol ration there.'

'I'll be taking you out of your way. I'll manage fine.'

'It's raining hard – you'll get wet.'

Despite her protests, Lottie found herself on the back seat of their car. It was only moments before they were pulling on to the forecourt of a garage. With relief, she saw that the lights were still on inside. An old man appeared.

'Thank you, Martin,' she said. 'You've been very kind. Goodbye and good luck.'

She watched the car pull off and turn back the way it had come. Martin waved to her. When there was nothing to see but the rear lights she shivered. Where was Waldo? Surely he'd be anxious about her? Watching for her by now? She was much later than she'd expected to be. She went towards the old man.

'Is Waldo about? Waldo Padley?'

'No.' He was rubbing greasy hands on a dirty rag. 'Called out to a breakdown, he's been.'

'Oh!'

'You Mrs Padley? Said to tell you he'd be back as soon as he could.'

Lottie lowered her case and surveyed the ancient hand pumps for delivering petrol. The place looked generally run down. The cold rain was blowing in her face.

'Boss said to tell you to wait in the office.'

She followed him, carrying her own case through the garage, past the car he'd been working on. Past several other cars, none of them smart. High up on a shelf an old wireless blared out laughter and merriment. The distorted sounds of Itma – It's That Man Again – echoed round the building. The stench of oil caught in her throat.

She was shown to a small office at the back, where an old

315

dressing table with the mirror removed was doing duty as a desk. It was piled high with papers and books. There were two hard chairs and a side table with a gas ring and a battered kettle on top.

'Boss said to tell you to make a cup of tea. If you want it.'

Lottie was parched. She surveyed the milk bottle with two inches of milk left in it and the half-washed mugs. Today's paper was neatly folded in a prominent place. She picked up the empty kettle.

'Where can I get water?'

The old man led her outside again and round the back to a shack. Inside was a dirty lavatory and a cracked washbowl with one cold water tap. She used both and went back with a full kettle, stepping over the oil patches on the concrete floor.

This wasn't at all what she'd expected. Lottie sank down on a chair feeling deflated. She'd set out this morning in such high spirits, with such high expectations. Now she was afraid she'd been looking at her new life through rose-tinted spectacles. Waldo had spoken of his garage with pride. The reality shocked her.

There was a phone on the wall. She dialled his home number but nobody answered. When she put the receiver back on its hook, there were oily marks on her fingers. She scrubbed at them with her handkerchief. Waldo was a person who appreciated the good things in life. He liked expensive clothes, fine food, luxury goods of all sorts. For him, this garage seemed out of character.

Even Martin had asked whether running such a business could be a paying proposition with the present shortages. At the time she'd been sure it paid well, but now, looking at it, she didn't think it could.

She brewed tea in the dented aluminium pot and then pulled one of the account books towards her. She found she couldn't make head or tail of the items listed in it. She drank several mugs of tea and tried to look at another of the books. Impossible to make sense of it; she was too tired now.

She searched her bag for the copy of *Forever Amber* she'd brought with her, but she couldn't find it. She'd only read a few pages on the train, but here by herself it would have helped pass the time. She wished Waldo would come.

It worried her that he wasn't here. The old man had told her he'd been called out to a breakdown, but couldn't Waldo have sent the old man instead? This was Waldo's business, an important part of his life, and she knew nothing about it. It seemed quite alien and made him seem almost a stranger.

She'd imagined her homecoming a thousand times, but never like this. She'd been excited all day expecting the warmest of welcomes. She'd thought he was as eager to have her home as she was to come. This was her new life, and here she was alone in strange and shabby surroundings.

She was so tired she wanted to cry. She folded her arms on his desk and put her head down on them.

Chapter Eighteen

'Lottie! Lottie darling!'

Feeling bleary-eyed, she lifted her head. She knew she'd slept.

'Sweetheart. I waited all afternoon for you to arrive. Expected you every moment, and then when I was called out I prayed you'd be so late I'd be back here before you were.'

Lottie still felt half asleep. Waldo's plump cheeks were close against her own. He was talking fast, his eyes sliding away as he lifted her closer.

'I didn't want you to have to wait like this.' His lips, warm and searching, met hers. 'I wanted everything to be just right for you after all this time. Come on, you're tired out. Let's get you home.'

Lottie managed a smile. Waldo was nervous and really trying to make amends. Everything was going to be all right after all.

'It's lovely to be with you again.'

His car was not at all like the others in the garage. It was a well cared for Rover with a wooden dashboard and leather seats. Lottie couldn't take her eyes from him as he drove.

He still reminded her of her teddy bear. Two years had not changed his smile, but he looked pale.

'You look tired,' she said.

'I am, I could drop. Been on the go all day. But so have you.'

He was more smartly dressed than he used to be and his manner wasn't as relaxed. In fact he seemed nervous, but as though he was trying to hide it. As if it was an effort to be natural after all this time. He knew she was looking at him and turned momentarily.

'I'm so sorry it happened like this. A terrible homecoming for you.'

'It's all right now,' she told him.

She sensed the effort he was making. 'I'm dying to show you the house. I've spent so much energy and time chasing bits of furniture to make it as nice as possible.'

'It's all utility now, isn't it?'

'That stuff won't do. I don't like it. No, I've been going round sale rooms looking for nice pieces, but of course so much furniture was lost in the Blitz. I do hope you'll like it.'

When Waldo pulled up on the drive, Lottie strained her eyes into the darkness trying to see her new home. The wrought-iron gates were wide open, and she saw a brick column on each side. White gravel crunched under her feet when she got out. There was a little light from the street lamp, enough to make out the polished red brick of a large building.

'It looks very grand,' she said as she followed him to the substantial front door.

'Edwardian semi,' he said. 'Nothing extra special, though it's got a bit of space inside.'

'It's wonderful.' The wide hall stretched before her. It had a polished parquet floor with white rugs, and a gentle flight of stairs wound elegantly upwards. 'I'm very impressed.' He flung open the sitting room door for her inspection. 'It's beautiful.'

There was nothing shabby here. It had all been freshly painted.

'The furniture's a bit of a hotch-potch,' Waldo said. 'A mixture of Victorian and older, but the best I could get.'

'I love it. I didn't expect anything half as good as this.'

The kitchen seemed vast, and mouthwatering scents were coming from a large cooker. She looked uneasily at the shelves laden with pans and cooking utensils, hoping the meal was under control. She couldn't do anything tonight – she was too tired to cook.

'Is that supper I can smell?'

'A casserole. You must be starving.'

'I am.'

'I have a woman who comes in and helps. I told her tonight was special and I wanted a hot meal left ready for us.'

Lottie looked round. The place was spotless, everything neat and tidy.

'I don't have time to do much here myself.'

'No, but now I'm home . . .'

'We'll keep her on. I don't want you to scrub floors or anything like that.' He leaned over and kissed her cheek, then reached over for a bottle of sherry and poured two glasses. 'We've something to celebrate tonight.'

'It's all much smarter . . . grander than I expected.'

By Lottie's standards, the casserole was exotic. It contained plenty of lean beef and mushrooms, and there was a salad and floury baked potatoes to go with it. Waldo urged her to put lashings of butter on the potatoes and mayonnaise on the salad. She couldn't remember ever tasting real mayonnaise before. Throughout the war, they'd put plain vinegar on their lettuce; just occasionally, when in luck, there'd been a vinegary salad cream.

Eating in hospitals, she'd always had enough food but it hadn't been elegantly served. Tonight, there was a starched damask tablecloth still showing its creases, and good quality silverware and china. There was a fruit bowl with grapes and tangerines as well as a large piece of Brie and some Bath Olivers. Before the war, food like this must have been around, but her family hadn't had it.

'How do you manage to put on such a feast? I thought everything was scarce?'

'With difficulty. I've been planning this reunion for ages. Hoarding things up.'

'The Brie?' she laughed.

'The Bath Olivers anyway. If you've finished, come and see the rest of the house.'

When Waldo carried her case upstairs, the main bedroom seemed airy and spacious. There was a double bed under a fat blue eiderdown and a huge mahogany wardrobe to put her clothes in.

'You've got good taste in furnishings.' She hadn't known that. There was probably a lot she didn't know about him.

'Come on,' he said, taking her into his arms. 'Let's have a look at you. You're beautiful.' He was undoing the buttons on her dress. 'It's been a long long time . . .'

The doorbell rang through the house.

Waldo barely lifted his lips from hers, ignoring the bell. He was feeling for her zip. Moments later, it rang again. This time, the finger was kept on the bell push for longer.

'For heaven's sake.' There was no mistaking Waldo's

irritability at the interruption. He strode to the big bay window and lifted the curtains. 'Who is it?'

Lottie followed him. 'I think it's Connie. Yes, and her husband.'

'Not tonight, surely?'

Lottie's sentiments exactly. She was tired and she hadn't seen her husband for a long time. She wanted to be alone with him, give her full attention to him, even though she wasn't as eager for his lovemaking as she'd once been. She sensed he didn't have the old urgency either. Things had changed so much. Waldo had changed.

'Hell!' Waldo swore. 'I suppose we'll have to let them in.' He buttoned his shirt and reached for his pullover before running downstairs. Connie Montague was frowning at being kept waiting on the step.

'Is Lottie home yet? I've been expecting to hear all day.'

'Yes. I brought her home barely an hour ago. She's very tired.'

'She isn't going to bed? The light was on upstairs.'

'No, no, just unpacking a few things. You'd better come in,' he said, and received such a look of dislike that it startled him.

He'd damned himself in Connie's eyes and she wasn't going to forgive him. He'd wished many times that things hadn't happened the way they had. It had started them all off on the wrong foot.

'Hello, Clovis.' Her misery of a husband trailed silently behind her. He looked ridiculous in that beret, like a caricature of a Frenchman.

Waldo led the way to the sitting room, then went to fetch

the bottle of sherry he'd opened earlier. The very last thing he needed was visitors tonight. He'd been trying to keep his mind on Lottie but he was worried about Phyllis. Afraid she was dropping him in the mire. Afraid she wasn't coping.

'What a lovely room!' Connie was staring round with envy on her face. 'You are lucky, to find a house like this.'

'Where did you get this sherry? Very nice.' Clovis sipped appreciatively.

Waldo hated questions like that. It was poking and prying. He mentioned a wine merchant in central Liverpool. It was the only way to shut some people up.

Lottie had fastened up her dress and now came running down to kiss her sister. 'Connie! How are you?' She threw her arms round her in a warm hug. 'You don't look well.'

'I'm pregnant again.' Connie sniffed and her dark eyes filled with tears.

Lottie was taken aback. All Connie had ever wanted was to be married and have babies, now it seemed another baby wasn't welcome.

'That's wonderful news.' Lottie made herself sound cheerful. 'I wish I was.'

That wasn't entirely true. Not right now. She had wanted it. She and Waldo had talked about it; it was what they'd planned to do once she was home. But now she was here, she thought they needed time to settle down together again first.

'Do you? Give yourself time,' was all Connie said.

Her hair looked straight and lank, and there were stains down the front of her shabby blouse. Lottie was shocked at the change in her. Connie's hair straight? She used to spend so much time crimping it up, making it go just the way she wanted. She'd always been buxom, but now she was thinner in the face and had dark shadows under her eyes. She looked tired out. So did Clovis. She hadn't seen him since his wedding day. Then, she'd thought he looked sensitive and gentle. Now he looked listless and grey-faced. He pecked half-heartedly at her cheek and then sat down again with his sherry.

'How's little Jimmy?'

'Fine. In bed.'

'At least you've got resident babysitters. It's lovely to see you, Con. Good of you to come straight round.'

She caught Waldo's look of disagreement at that but Connie seemed to recover.

'I've walked past this house many times and often wondered what it was like inside.'

'Come and see it then. I'll show you round.' Lottie wasn't sure of the layout herself yet. 'I'm pleased with what Waldo's done.'

'Pleased! I should say so.'

Lottie caught sight of Connie's face and stopped. There was such twisting envy there. She was almost ashamed to show her the debris of their meal on the dining room table. The grapes were still there and the cheese. The aroma of the casserole still hung in the air. She was afraid Connie would have even more to feel envious about.

Waldo wanted to go to bed. He wished Connie and Clovis would go home. Connie was sitting back listlessly on the settee, one leg crossed over the other, looking as though nothing was going to budge her for hours.

She had developed deep lines running down from her nose to the corners of her mouth. It gave a droop to her chin, a look of dissatisfaction with everything. The sisters looked uncomfortable with each other; he knew they'd only met once since Connie's marriage. He'd hardly seen Connie in all that time either. Hadn't wanted to. It was just unfortunate that he'd met Lottie through her.

Connie had been his girlfriend for eight months and he'd tried hard to get her into his bed. He'd failed, and he'd found that hard to accept. Hard to believe even. She dressed to attract; everything about her seemed to be giving him the come-on. But he hadn't had enough money to suit Connie. She was the sort who went to the highest bidder. She chose her friends with her head and not with her heart. Looking after number one was her first priority. There was no warmth about her.

He'd told Lottie his affair with Connie had never been really serious. He'd played it down. It might have blossomed if Connie had been as warm and loving as Lottie. He knew Connie felt he'd betrayed her by switching his affections to her sister.

Waldo switched off from the chatter, all the questions and the answers that didn't concern him. He felt as though a noose was tightening round his throat. He wanted to know how Phyllis had coped when her husband had walked in on her, and what she'd done with the evidence she wanted to hide. He knew only that she'd asked for his help and he hadn't given it. And that if she was in trouble, he could be too. He was desperately worried about Phyllis.

When Phyllis let herself into her house at ten minutes to seven she was still feeling fluttery. She hadn't been thinking straight, but the drive out to the works at Ellesmere Port had soothed her because she'd been doing something about making things safer for herself.

She'd done what Waldo had suggested and brought everything that could possibly incriminate her away. It was all in the boot of her car; the ink she'd used and the special paper. She'd had to get the closest possible match of both to those used to print official coupons. She'd put her car in the garage and poured herself a gin and orange. She was feeling a little safer.

Not that she was quite safe yet. She'd be glad when Waldo came and they'd got all this stuff into secure hiding places. He knew about such things. He'd been keeping things hidden for years and had survived several searches.

She took her drink and wandered into the sitting room. It felt cold tonight; there'd been no fire here all day. She flopped down on the blue velvet settee and let her eyes go round the room looking for the absolutely safe place.

In the chimney? There was a sort of ledge within reach. Something to do with the dampers that created a draught to draw the fire. Who would think of looking there?

Phyllis knelt down on the hearthrug to see if the ledge was visible, then lifted the brass poker and felt for it. Not a good place to put her large envelope of bank notes. What if Cecil were to light the fire? But perhaps the metal printing plates?

She was smiling at the thought when she heard Waldo arrive. She paused to listen – she hadn't expected him to bring his van into her drive. A key scraped in the front door. This wasn't Waldo! In a blind second, she was on her feet and rushing out to the hall.

'Cecil!' Phyllis had to hold on to the hall table. 'What are you doing here?' She felt awash with panic. Waldo would be coming quietly through the back door at any moment.

'Did I frighten you, dear?' He was blinking in the bright light she'd switched on.

'Yes. I wasn't expecting . . .'

'Of course you weren't. I'm sorry. I couldn't stand the hotel bedroom for another night.'

It was the agonised half-sob that drew Phyllis's attention. He was as nervous as she was, his normally placid face white and twitchy. He put his overnight case down and dropped his coat and bowler hat on top. She saw his hand shake.

'You aren't feeling well? That's why you've come back? What can I get you?'

She took his coat and hung it up. Cecil was usually all brisk competent movements, but now he seemed slow and clumsy.

'Come and sit down.' She pulled him down beside her on the settee. 'Shall I get you a drink? Whisky?' She had to stop Waldo coming in. Lock the back door.

Cecil was nodding. She leapt to her feet with such eagerness that he would have guessed she was up to something if he'd been himself.

Her own head was swimming and she spilled some of the water she brought back to put in his drink, but with the key turned in the back door she felt better.

She put the glass down beside him. 'What is it, love?'

'I felt terrible driving away and leaving you to handle everything. Those inspectors . . . enforcement officers.' She could see he was really churned up. 'I decided to come home because . . .' He stopped and looked up at her.

'You got both the orders? They were in the bag so you thought you might as well come back?'

'I got one. I was to see Middleton about the other tomorrow

morning. Just couldn't put my mind to it. I cancelled my appointment, told them I wasn't well and I'd have to come home, but . . .'

She could see he could hardly bring himself to tell her the real reason. He jumped to his feet to close the curtains. She didn't want that. It was one of her joys to leave them open with the light streaming out after all the years of blackout. Besides, Waldo would be able to see in. He'd see Cecil here and not ring the bell or anything like that, thinking she'd forgotten to leave the back door unlocked for him. Should she try to phone him? But no, he'd be on his way by now.

Cecil was feeling for her hand. She asked: 'You're worried?'

'Out of my mind. I'm sorry. What will you think of me?'

'What's happened?'

'Nothing yet. It's what I'm afraid will happen.'

Me too, Phyllis thought, but said nothing.

'The day after tomorrow,' Cecil said. 'The enforcement officers are coming back . . .'

Phyllis could hardly breathe under the pall of guilt. Had he seen her cache of . . . ?

'I've got a confession to make,' he said and his voice wobbled. 'I've been taking advantage of my situation. Printing illicit petrol coupons.'

Phyllis felt the room begin to eddy round her. 'You have?'

She couldn't believe what she was hearing. Not upright staid Cecil, who liked to think he was part of the establishment? It had crossed her mind when she'd seen how nervous he was, but she'd dismissed it.

'And it's not just petrol. I've been doing favours for Bill Hampton.'

Bill Hampton was a friend who owned five grocery shops. He was a plump dapper man with very white fingers.

'What d'you mean, favours?'

'I've printed a few sheets of points for him. You know, for tinned food and biscuits. Bill added them to those he took over the counter. It allowed him to stock his shelves properly and sell stuff without points to those prepared to pay.'

Phyllis gasped out loud.

'I know,' he muttered. 'I'm ashamed of what I've done.'

She'd thought Cecil above this sort of thing. Relief, blessed relief was flooding through her. She was not alone in this.

'But you're such a law-abiding person.' She wanted to laugh. Share the joke. But Waldo had taught her to look at things in his way. With both of them doing it, surely the chance of leaving some clue behind must be doubled?

'I wish I was. I've never been so worried in my life. It isn't worth it. It's like having a sword hanging over my head. I could go to prison if . . .' He gave another choking sob and dropped his head in his hands. 'I've let you down, haven't I?'

'No, don't say that.' Phyllis understood exactly what he was going through. She put a comforting arm round his shoulders.

'Do I admit it? They're going to ask questions about everything, aren't they? My good character will be gone. And I believe they can confiscate . . . What if they take my business? I could lose everything.'

She wondered just how many petrol coupons he had printed. 'Is it likely to come to that?'

She'd not noticed him doing anything out of the ordinary, but then she didn't spend all day looking over his shoulder.

He looked up at her, his eyes woebegone. 'What am I going to do, Phyl?'

'Do?' Her head cleared. 'Deny doing anything wrong. Tell them nothing.'

'But what if they find . . . ?'

'What can they find?'

'The plates for one thing. And I had to get the right paper, exactly the right ink, that sort of thing. I don't want them asking questions about what I've used it for, do I?'

Phyllis understood that worry too. 'Clear everything out. Leave nothing for them to find.' That was what Waldo advised. 'You've done that?'

'Some of the ink I used is still there, in my office,' he gulped.

'I wouldn't worry too much about them finding ink in your office. We both know we haven't had a legitimate job for it but they won't. To them it's just black ink. Anyway, we could put it in the store tomorrow with all the other bits and pieces left over from doing jobs. Some of it dates back years.'

'Everything else is in my wardrobe. What if they want to look round our house? If they have reason to suspect, they can call on the police and get a search warrant.' He was doubling up with guilt.

'We don't have to leave it in your wardrobe,' she told him. She was getting a grip on herself now. Seeing his panic had a calming effect on her. 'I've never noticed anything there, though. Whereabouts is it?'

'In my hat box.'

It was a long time since she'd opened that. Recently, when he'd worn his best hat, he'd put it away himself. 'Not a bad place.'

'Too obvious. I'm having nightmares – that they'll find everything.'

'We can hide it where it won't be found.'

'But where? Don't think this hasn't been going round in my head. Where would be safe?'

'What about taking out one or two stones in the rockery and burying things underneath? As long as we're careful to make it look as though it hasn't been disturbed, who would think of looking there? I'll do it now while it's dark. So the neighbours won't be able to see me.'

Cecil lifted his head, hope in his eyes. 'The plates – just the place for them. You're so much stronger than I am, Phyl. You can keep your head.'

She wasn't strong at all. She'd been splitting at the seams half an hour ago when she thought she might be going to prison.

'You shouldn't keep these things from me. I'm your wife. You know I'll always help you.'

'Yes,' he sniffed. 'But I want you to be proud of me.'

'I am proud of you. Come on, let's see exactly what you've got.' She stood up and pulled him to his feet. He followed her heavily upstairs. Phyllis knew his incriminating evidence would be the same as hers. With two lots, would there be too much to bury in the rockery? She brought his hat box out and opened it on the bed.

'We'll burn this paper,' she said. 'It's very distinctive, easy to recognise.' She'd already decided it was the safest thing to do with hers. They couldn't afford to have that found here in their home. 'I'll light the fire and do it now.'

'I've got these sheets ready printed.' He pulled out another large envelope. 'Get rid of them first. They're dangerous.'

'I'll see to everything,' she said. 'Leave it to me.'

'I can't let you . . .'

If she was to get rid of her own evidence without him knowing, she had to keep him upstairs.

'There's more ink there. I mixed different inks,' he gulped. 'To get the right shade of black.'

Phyllis's stomach turned over. She'd done the same.

'If they start asking why it's here in the house . . .'

'I could put it down the lavatory.'

'But what about the tin?'

Phyllis lifted it up. It wasn't very big. 'There's some old paint tins in the garage. Been there too long anyway – the paint's all dried up. I could put this inside one and get rid of it with the household rubbish.' It was what Waldo had suggested. She was going to do that with hers. 'You go and have a hot bath. You'll have to unwind before you'll be able to sleep, you poor sweet.'

'It's not getting to sleep that's bothering me. I'll come and help.'

'No, just help me carry all this downstairs.'

She left Cecil twisting his special paper into the sitting room grate and went out to the garage without putting a light on to get two suitable paint tins. She had to use a torch to find them, but hers was still half blanked out as required for the blackout.

She found a tool to lever off the lids, but found that wasn't easy. She took the stiffest one into the kitchen and asked Cecil to help, then sent him upstairs saying she didn't want the neighbours to see a lot of activity at this time of night. Usually they stayed in the sitting room after supper.

Phyllis went out to the garage. The lights were going on

upstairs in the houses all round. The neighbours would only have to twitch up a curtain to see her if she used her torch outside. And what could be more suspicious than digging in the garden after dark on a wet night? She knew she mustn't move the rockery stones now.

She unlocked the boot of her car and dealt with the two lots of ink, tipping it carefully into the water and making sure the pan showed no trace of stain by tipping down plenty of bleach after it. Back in the kitchen she tipped the last two biscuits out of a tin, took it to the garage and stuffed all the money she'd received from Waldo into it. Then taking that and all their printing plates she crept down to the end of the garden, keeping in the shadows as much as she could. She buried everything in the mound of garden rubbish that was being mulched down for manure. It was soft and easy to lift. Easy to manage without using a light. The rain was pelting down. By morning, there'd be no sign that it had recently been disturbed.

On the next fine day, she'd tidy up the garden and find a more permanent resting place for the plates in the rockery. She wasn't sure yet what she'd do about the money.

Cecil was still upstairs when she carried her paper into the sitting room. The grate was full of black ash; some had overflowed on to the hearth. She slashed at it with the poker to break it down, carefully gathered it up into the grate, piled her paper on top and relit the fire. She watched it burn up for a moment and then fetched a few sticks to put on top with some coal. She had to get rid of these black flimsy bits that were flying everywhere. She swept up the hearth – it mustn't be obvious they'd been burning paper.

When she went upstairs again, Cecil was just climbing into bed.

'Shall I bring you some malted milk? I've done all that's needed. It's all under control now.'

'You are clever, Phyllis. A real brick. Come to bed, you must be tired.'

'I'll stay down for a bit to make sure there's no remnant of paper left in the grate. Tomorrow, I'll get up early and re-set the fire. Perhaps even light it, if there's anything left.'

'You think I'll be safe now?'

'Safe as houses,' she smiled. Certainly she was as safe as houses. If the enforcement officers ever did find the printing plates, Cecil would believe he was the guilty person. He'd admit to it. Whatever happened, she wouldn't be going to prison.

She'd done what Waldo had advised. Kept her mouth shut about him and about what she'd been up to. Waldo had said that was the only really safe way. He'd be proud of her, handling it the way she had.

Chapter Nineteen

20–21 February, 1946

Lottie's eyes were prickling. She could hardly keep them open. It was getting late and Connie was keeping up a steady stream of complaint about the difficulties facing housewives.

'The rations are to be cut again. We're going to get an ounce less of butter, margarine and lard. And they're going to stop importing rice.'

'Why are things getting worse?' Lottie wanted to know.

'Asia needs the rice. It's their staple diet.'

'What, the Japanese?'

'Yes,' Clovis said. 'And the Germans have to be fed too, so there's less food for us.'

Waldo seemed to be dozing in his armchair. Now he stirred and grunted: 'Hard to know who won the war. Bet they wouldn't be going short to feed us if it was the other way round.'

'The wheat content of bread is to be cut too. Back to the 1942 level.' Clovis smiled at Lottie. 'My dad isn't happy about that, and I don't suppose yours is either. It'll make the loaf darker still.'

'Victory bread, they call it,' Connie exploded. 'What a cheek!'

'I read that there were riots in France,' Lottie said. 'About the shortage of bread.'

'President Truman has promised a million tons of wheat a month for Europe and Asia.'

It was midnight when at last Clovis and Connie made a move.

'Thank God they've gone,' Waldo said as he shot the bolts on the front door behind them. Lottie pulled herself upstairs to bed. She found her suitcase unopened still and had to rifle through her belongings to find her toothbrush and nightdress.

Waldo was exhausted too, grunting slightly as he undressed.

'Good night,' she said as the light went out.

He heaved himself across the bed towards her and placed a heavy arm round her waist. Lottie lay there waiting. She had never spent even one night with him when he hadn't wanted to make love to her. Always, it had seemed he couldn't get enough of her. Yet, seconds later, she was relieved to hear a soft and gentle snore.

She wished she could go to sleep, but now sleep seemed miles away. She slid from under his arm. Waldo was restless too. He was tossing and turning, not sleeping deeply.

This was going to take as much getting used to as joining the QAs had done. She felt her return to married life had not got off to a good start.

She was woken in the morning by Waldo nuzzling up to her. He'd never wanted to get up early. To Lottie that seemed the only familiar thing about him.

'What will you think of me? Hardly the ardent husband, am I? To fall asleep like that when you've been away so long.'

'We were tired last night.'

He made love to her then but he did it without joy. As

though he thought she expected it of him. Two years ago, he'd only to touch her to send her up in flames. Now all that had died. She couldn't believe their passion had gone.

For all the months of their separation she'd thought of him with love. The time they'd spent together in London had shown up a few cracks, and she'd not expected their relationship to be where it had when she'd first gone away, but she'd had high hopes of this homecoming. She couldn't understand why her feelings for him had changed when she'd only been home a few hours. They were further apart than ever. Was it that Waldo had changed so much?

They stayed in bed until nearly nine o'clock, when he had to go downstairs to let his daily help in. Lottie could hear her clearing the dining table and washing up. She couldn't believe he could afford help in the house like this. She was bursting with questions but he didn't want to answer any of them. He kept kissing her to keep her quiet.

The luxury of her new home bothered her, just as the supper table groaning with good food had last night. Surely these things couldn't have been come by lawfully in these times of austerity?

'You must be doing very well,' she'd said more than once.

In the old days Waldo had told her exactly how much he'd earned. Now all he said was: 'I'm a good businessman.'

She asked him more pointed questions about the garage. She even said it didn't look as though it was earning much. Hadn't Martin questioned the possibility of making a living from it? After all, there was no petrol ration for ordinary motorists.

'It's doing all right,' Waldo said stubbornly.

She asked about the other businesses he owned, like the

greengrocery round, but he didn't reply. Instead he said: 'I've been thinking. Would you like your own nursing home? A business of your own?'

That surprised her. She'd never even considered the possibility.

'You could run one?'

'Yes, I suppose so.'

'Wouldn't you like that? To run your own show?'

'We're going to have a National Health Service. Free for everybody. Who's going to pay for a nursing home now?'

'Maternity cases are the thing. Husbands want their wives to have a little extra comfort then. They'll still be happy to pay for it. You could have separate rooms and furnish them nicely, up to hotel standard. Think about it, Lottie.'

'It sounds as though you already have.'

'Yes, why not? I can see where there's a good opportunity going.'

'Maternity cases are off.'

'What d'you mean? I'm told that's where money can be made.'

'Not by me. I've never done any midwifery. I'm not qualified. If I was in charge of a nursing home it couldn't take maternity cases.'

'Oh!'

'Not unless I hired midwives to run it and sat back in the office. I suppose it could be done that way, but how could I feel in control? Anyway, I don't want a nursing home.' She felt a rush of irritation.

'You said you'd be looking for another job. I just thought—'

'Not a nursing home.' She wasn't sure what her plans were

yet. For months she'd been able to think no further than coming home to Waldo.

'What, then?'

'I told Father . . . He asked me to work for him, but I don't know whether he still wants it.'

'You've never said.'

'Too many other things had to happen first. It was too far into the future.'

The silence dragged out. Waldo frowned. 'We talked of having a family.'

'That's far into the future too. I'd want to stay home to take care of my children. I wouldn't have the energy to work as well.'

Lottie wanted time to think, time to make up her mind, not be rushed into something she didn't want.

Breakfast was eaten in some style. Silver egg cups for the boiled eggs, with tea and toast made by Mrs Gully. She was glad when Waldo said he'd have to leave her to go to work. Racked with doubts and suspicions, Lottie stood at the dining room window and watched him go.

That morning, Phyllis rose before it was quite daylight to check on what she'd done. It was still raining; the trees in the garden were dripping miserably, and there was a puddle on the lawn. She stood looking at the pile of garden rubbish. It had been battered by the downpour until there was no sign that it had been disturbed. The downstairs lavatory sparkled with cleanliness and smelled of bleach. She flushed it.

The sitting room grate was filled with burnt paper again. She'd read somewhere that forensic scientists now needed only one scrap to prove what had been burned. She crumbled the pieces with her hands, wanting to turn it to ash. She relit the fire and added as much of the ash as she could before banking it high with coal. Then she took Cecil a cup of tea. He'd tossed and turned for much of the night before falling into a heavy sleep in the early hours.

'What's the time? I'm going to be late.' He was struggling to pull himself up the bed. He had to be at work early to open up for the compositors. Phyllis didn't usually go in with him; she preferred to lie a little longer in bed and then tidy the house before setting out. Today, she'd been expecting to go in to open up.

She frowned. 'Cecil, nobody's expecting to see you in work. You told everybody you were going to Sheffield, and you told people there you didn't feel well enough to stay. Not even to negotiate another contract.'

'You don't think I should go in?'

It wasn't like Cecil to ask her opinion. He was still jumpy. She'd been through it and was sympathetic.

'Keep to your story, and stay here. Just in case.' Waldo was obsessional about such things. 'You can always come in this afternoon.'

'I knew it was wrong,' he'd muttered as he held her close in the night. 'I wanted more money for you. You deserve a better life than I've been giving you. I know you want to get out and about more. Go to dances and dinners and have a good time. I suppose I haven't the energy any more. That's the problem when you're an old man's darling.'

'You're not old, Cecil,' she'd whispered.

'Fifty-four isn't young. Sixteen years older than you. We're at different stages in life. I do try, but I wish I could make life more exciting for you.'

She set off to the printing works. There was little traffic on the roads at this hour apart from the buses taking people to work. She liked to drive; it soothed her. As she pulled into her parking lot in front of the main door, she saw another car already there.

'Oh my God!' she said aloud, as she realised that, in addition to their staff waiting on the doorstep, the three inspectors had returned. Phyllis took deep breaths to steady her nerves. Did they know Cecil had come home last night? Had they been watching him?

She got out slowly, trying to pull herself together. They'd find nothing. They wouldn't recognise the significance of that ink in Cecil's office. There was nothing else here for them to find.

She struggled to smile at them. That's what Waldo advised: smile, don't let them see you're put out.

'You said you'd postpone your visit until tomorrow. So my husband could be here to show you round.'

'We found we had another appointment tomorrow,' one of them said smoothly as she opened up. 'Thought we'd have a quick look round today instead. Where is your husband, Mrs Rogan? We understand business didn't keep him in Sheffield as long as he'd expected it to.'

Phyllis went weak at the knees. So they were keeping tabs on him.

'He wasn't well, and had to come home. Upset stomach.'

'Sorry to hear that. How is he now?'

'Still got cramps. He stayed in bed.' Thank goodness she'd persuaded him to do so. 'But he's feeling a bit better.'

'Good. We might need to talk to him.'

That made her stiffen; she didn't want them to have an

excuse to visit Cecil at home. She'd done her best there but what if they poked round in the garden rubbish?

She tossed back her blonde hair. 'He said he might come in later. I'll ring him and let him know you've jumped the gun. Ask him if he feels up to coming in now. He'll want to help.'

Then, in case the phrase 'jumped the gun' had upset them, she offered cups of tea before they started work. That seemed to please them but they stayed in her office to hear what she said to Cecil. Then, while they drank tea, they asked her to explain how the business functioned. They were firing questions at her. She answered them fully, but she volunteered nothing.

'Have you got the keys to the safe this morning?'

'Yes,' she said, though she hated showing them what was in there. It was private business, but it was better to go along with what they wanted. That's what Waldo said: 'Once you've made sure there's nothing incriminating for them to find, let them burrow and delve as much as they want.'

Phyllis held herself firmly in check and let the inspectors look where they wished. Her teeth were clenched and she was wound up tight as a drum, but she tried not to show it. There was one consolation. Cecil would be taking the rap if things didn't go well.

Waldo got into the car and drove as fast as he could round to Phyllis's house. He was glad to get away from Lottie. He'd done his best; he'd made love to her and sat and talked through a leisurely breakfast, but inside he'd been seething with worry and foreboding about Phyllis.

All night, he'd been wondering what had happened when

her husband had walked in, and worried about what she was saying to him. He'd broken his first rule for his own safety: he'd been too closely tied up with her.

He knew Phyllis's routine. If her husband was around to open up the works, she'd stay at home for an hour or so. He wanted to catch her; he had to find out what was happening. He'd go out of his mind if he didn't.

It surprised him to find her husband's Rover parked in the drive. Phyllis had told him that if they went into Ellesmere Port together they went in his car, not hers. With his still in front of the house, it must mean Cecil was still at home.

There was smoke coming out of the chimney, and a light left on in the hall. Somebody was inside, but he daren't ring the bell and risk bringing her husband to the door.

He drove instead to a phone box and dialled the printing works. A telephonist managed their small switchboard, and he asked to be put through to Phyllis's office.

'Can I have your name?' the girl asked.

'Mr Caldwell, Eric Caldwell.' It was the name he always used. Phyllis would know it was him. He waited.

Phyllis's voice when it came had a nervous quiver. 'Mr Caldwell, good morning.'

He said urgently: 'Is everything all right?'

'No. No, I'm afraid not.' She sounded scared.

'Are you alone?'

'Not at the moment.'

'Your husband?'

'Not at the moment.'

'Not the snoopers?'

'Yes.'

'Oh my God! I thought you said tomorrow?'

'I did. That's what they told me.'

Waldo felt the sweat break out on his face. 'What about your husband? I've been worried stiff. I saw him come home last night. I couldn't come in.'

'No, I'm glad you didn't.'

'What happened? You didn't say anything?'

'Nothing. He's not in yet, but he's on his way. Won't be long.'

'He's coming to deal with the snoopers?'

'That's right.'

'Don't tell them anything, Phyllis. You'll be all right.'

'Yes, he's not very well, but I told him he'd have to come in and help.'

'Let me know how things go. Ring me as soon as you get rid of them and you're on your own. I'll be at the garage.'

'All right, Mr Caldwell.'

Waldo put the phone down feeling terrible. He drove to the garage where he sat in his office looking at the phone, willing it to ring. When it did, he leapt up to grab the receiver but it was never Phyllis.

He hadn't meant to come here today. His customers were expecting him to make his regular greengrocery round. He should be out doing that but he didn't want to leave the telephone. Until he knew, he couldn't get down to doing anything. He felt he was falling apart.

Phyllis made herself switch off from what was happening in the works. She thought about clothes, pushed the whole problem of inspectors to one side.

Cecil seemed calm enough when he came, though he didn't look well. His face was paler than usual and his movements sluggish. The snoopers shouldn't doubt his sickness story. She let him take over, and he took them round the print shop.

The company account books were spread out on Cecil's desk for most of the day. The inspectors questioned their foreman for ages, went on to speak to most of their workers and watch the work in progress.

Twice more before lunch, Waldo rang up to see if there was any news.

'Nothing so far,' she reported. 'They're with Cecil, poking into everything.'

Phyllis could feel Waldo's tension. Serve him right, she thought. Let him sweat it out. He was more worried about his own skin than hers. He'd have shoved off except that he was tangled up in her affairs. He had no further use for her now his wife was back home.

'Good girl. Ring me the minute they leave. Looks as though you might survive this.'

She was sure she would, but said: 'I don't know. They're very suspicious. There's one poring over the books and another up in the store room now.'

But the inspectors found nothing wrong. The illicit ink in the office had no significance for them and there was no other proof in the building. Cecil wouldn't be summoned for illegally printing coupons for rationed goods.

She stood beside him, seeing them off the premises. The inspectors were very polite, shaking hands before they left. Phyllis felt on top of the world as she saw them get into their car. She looked at Cecil, who was triumphant too. He groped for her hand.

'Later,' she whispered. 'I'm going home now.' It was what

she usually did, leave an hour or so before Cecil, in order to get a meal ready.

As she drove home she felt euphoric. She deliberately avoided ringing Waldo. No point in letting him off the hook too soon. Better if he sweated a bit more.

When Cecil came home later that evening, he looked like a wet rag. Phyllis knew his nerves had taken a battering.

'We're in the clear,' she told him as she mixed his usual whisky and water. He threw himself down in an easy chair.

'Yes, but it's given me a nasty shock. I won't take such a risk again. Not worth it. We're lucky to have escaped.'

'Did somebody tip them off? That wasn't just routine.'

Cecil gulped at his drink. 'A printing business like ours does offer opportunities. They were checking our operators. Asking me if they ever did foreigners. I told them it was impossible. That we keep too tight a check on everything – have to, because we're security printers. Theatres don't want extra tickets printed for their shows. They don't want an audience that doesn't pay.'

'They found nothing. And thank goodness, they didn't come here.'

'I saw the bin men come this morning. The bin was empty when I left. I felt reasonably confident that even if they had come, they'd have found nothing. Thanks to you.'

Phyllis felt close to him. The last couple of days had been a nightmare but at least she knew now where she stood.

Waldo was no good for her. He was nothing but a wide boy. He'd used her as much as she'd used him; there'd been little love on either side. She had no future with him. He wasn't worth worrying about. It would be better to end it here.

She'd learned a lot from Waldo, and not only how to keep

herself safe. She'd learned it was no bad thing to be an old man's darling. At least to Cecil, she'd always seem young. He'd come home with a small box for her.

'What is it?'

'An early birthday present. To show my appreciation.'

Phyllis opened it. A diamond eternity ring sparkled up at her.

'It's lovely,' she said. Cecil rarely gave her extravagant gifts.

'I'll take you out to dinner too. Meant to do it tonight but I'm whacked. Tomorrow, I've decided I must make more effort. We don't want to get stuck in a rut, do we?'

Waldo was pacing up and down his office. He was still waiting to hear from Phyllis. Not knowing what was happening was making this the longest day he'd ever lived through. He was more than nervous – he felt he was coming to the end of his tether.

He slid out the bottom drawer of his desk and looked at the petrol coupons Phyllis had given him, a far greater number than he'd asked for. At the rate at which he used them these would last for months. He kept them under the drawer not in it, hidden inside the casing of the old dressing table that served as his desk. He needed to count them carefully; they had to tally with the amount of money the business was taking.

He should be out in his van, not hanging about in here. He had to do something, to keep busy, so he started to count the coupons. The phone rang and he leapt at it, only to find it was a customer wanting to know if he had oil in stock. Waldo collapsed back on his chair, beginning to expect the worst.

He had to be ready for what might happen next. Most likely a surprise visit from the snoopers, having got a few facts out of Phyllis.

He tried to keep his mind on Lottie. She was even more beautiful than he remembered. Her skin was tight and firm and fresh even when the morning light shone directly on it. But she'd changed. She wasn't as ready to throw her arms round him as she used to be. He didn't feel close to her any more. He didn't want her to know what he was doing – he was afraid she'd despise him.

His best idea had been to get her a business of her own, where she'd be so busy she wouldn't have time to think about what he was up to. But she wouldn't hear of that. She wasn't going to be easy to handle.

Through the dirty window of his office, he saw a car turn on to the forecourt of his garage, and felt himself come out in a cold sweat. He recognised the driver. It was Edwin Carruthers, who'd recently searched his stable and store, one of the more active enforcement officers in the area.

He didn't take his car to the pumps, but parked it round the back. Waldo's heart was thumping wildly as he watched the inspector get out of his car, take something from the seat beside him and go to speak to Bill. He hadn't come to buy petrol then.

Waldo dropped to his knees, suddenly afraid he'd be seen watching through the window. He told himself he was being silly – the window was too small and it was dark in here. But he was wasting time.

Galvanised to action, he threw Phyllis's coupons back into their hiding place and slid the drawer on its runners to cover them. Pulled it out again so the innocent contents were visible and within reach. Sometimes it could jam with the paper beneath and he couldn't afford that to happen.

Then he snatched his account books from the desk and hid them under a loose floorboard. He had to keep two sets of accounts, one for his own information and one for official inspection. These he opened up on top and picked up a pen. He could see Carruthers heading this way. He needed to be seen working rather than watching.

He felt he was panicking too now. Phyllis must have said something to the snoopers at the printing works, and they'd tipped off this fellow and sent him round here. He wouldn't put it past her. If it would save her own skin she'd throw him to the wolves. He'd never completely trusted Phyllis.

Bill was bringing him in. He heard the door hinge creak and told himself he had to look calm.

'Good morning, Mr Padley.' The man sounded affable. Waldo got slowly to his feet.

'I was able to give your wife a lift from the station yesterday.'

'What?'

Waldo felt knocked sideways. Lottie had something to do with this visit? Surely they must hear his racing heart?

'She left this book in my car, on the back seat. My son travelled up from London with her. Terrible journey, I believe. Very slow.'

Waldo looked at the dog-eared paperback. 'Very kind of you to bring it.'

'Not at all. I should visit from time to time. Now I'm here, I might as well take a look round. Check things over.'

Waldo froze. The inspector was smiling at him. As though he'd established good relations and this investigation was a formality. Waldo didn't trust the steely glint in his eye. This fellow would pounce on him if he found anything.

'Of course,' he agreed. 'You want to count my coupons? Bring the tin in here, Bill, would you?'

The snooper followed him out. 'I just need to make a note of what's in the till right now.'

Waldo took deep breaths. There'd be no problems in that direction. He was worried about the coupons under his desk drawer. He wished they were anywhere but in his garage.

Carruthers was coming back with the tin box in which they kept their legitimate coupons.

Waldo said: 'Here, have a seat. I'll get you a cup of tea.'

'What about your books?'

He nudged them across the desk.

'How many gallons did you sell last month?'

Chapter Twenty

As soon as Waldo had gone to work, Lottie lifted the phone in the hall and asked the operator to put her through to the bread factory in Old Swan. Cliff picked up the phone.

'It's Lottie,' she told him. 'I'm back home for good.'

She could hear the joy in his voice as he welcomed her. 'Come over and have supper with us tonight. We'll want to hear all your news. Father's dying to have you back.'

Lottie hesitated. 'There's Waldo . . .'

'Bring him. Of course he must come.'

'He's gone to work. He's expecting a quiet evening, you know, just the two of us.'

She had to get closer to Waldo. They needed to talk. He wouldn't be pleased if she rushed him over to Brightland Street. Lottie could hear Mrs Gully clattering dishes in the kitchen.

She said: 'What about lunch? Connie came round to see me last night. We thought we'd come together.'

'Today? We've got a business lunch, I'm afraid. What about tomorrow? That would suit us better.'

'Tomorrow it is, then,' Lottie agreed. 'I'll take Connie and Jimmy out instead.'

She rang the number Connie had given her. Connie's mother-in-law answered and introduced herself. Lottie thought she sounded very pleasant and very French. It took an age for Connie to come down to speak to her. When she did she sounded apathetic, as though she was still half asleep after her late night. Lottie told her the trip they'd proposed to Old Swan was put off until tomorrow.

'But let's go out, Connie. See what's in the shops. Have a bite of lunch out. It's what we always used to do.'

She met Connie at the top of Grange Road when it was almost time to eat. Lottie had thought that once the war was won they'd all be living happily ever after. But Connie was not as happy as she'd supposed. Nothing was as she'd expected it to be.

'You haven't brought little Jimmy?'

'Mother-in-law offered to look after him. It's no joke pushing him round the shops.' She'd done nothing to improve her hair. 'He's a bit grizzly this morning, out of sorts. He wouldn't be good company.'

Connie had been right: the shops were almost empty. Lottie wanted to find Jimmy a toy but they saw little to interest a toddler of his age.

'Toys can't be bought any more,' Connie told her. 'His grandfather's made him some building blocks. Painted them all different colours – they're lovely. He's trying to carve an engine for him now. Jimmy's not short of toys. He loves the woolly rabbit I knitted for him before he was born. Takes it to bed every night, and of course there's a lot of things Clovis had as a boy. He'll grow into them.'

The lunch proved disappointing. Lottie couldn't talk about her own problems, not yet, but she wanted to hear about Connie's. She said: 'Last night I was so tired. Coming home after two years, it sort of overwhelmed me. I was quite shocked to see you so unhappy. I'm sorry if I wasn't . . . you know, more sympathetic. Can I help? You know, sort things out.'

'There's nothing to sort.' Connie was in a dour mood and didn't want to confide in her either. Lottie wanted to invite her home to have a cup of tea but she was half afraid she'd unleash more envy. When Connie asked her to her flat, she went there instead.

'After all, I haven't seen Jimmy yet.'

But Jimmy was having his afternoon nap on his grandmother's bed by the time they got there. All Lottie saw of her nephew was a small head half concealed by blankets in a darkened room.

Connie's mother-in-law took over, making the tea; showing Lottie round her own bomb-damaged downstairs rooms. Ornate ceilings with cornices of leaves and flowers had been brought down by the blast, and replaced with plain ones under the government's repair scheme. The paint was so thin on them that the join in the plaster boards could be seen through it. In the dining room, half of the plaster cornice remained.

'They told me it was sound so they could leave it,' Mrs Montague complained. 'And doesn't it look silly with half of it missing?'

Lottie had her cup of tea and escaped as soon as she could. It hadn't been a jolly outing.

'I'll call for you tomorrow morning,' she told Connie. 'Lunch with Cliff and Father.'

She was letting herself into her new home by mid-afternoon. All was silent now Mrs Gully had gone. She sniffed at the scent of furniture polish. Everywhere was neat and well cared for. The original plaster ceilings were intact here.

Nothing too fancy, just a thick ridged cornice round the downstairs rooms.

She hardly knew what was here. She looked round slowly, marvelling at the amount of kitchen equipment waiting to be used. She opened the refrigerator – to own one was every housewife's dream. It was stacked with food. She opened the cupboards to find a selection of tinned foods such as she hadn't seen for years.

Tinned asparagus? She couldn't remember ever seeing such a thing before. Nor had she ever tasted it. She felt shocked; her mouth was dry. Surely Waldo hadn't come by these as his rightful ration? There was far too much and it was exotic.

She shivered. She'd read often enough in the papers about black marketeers, people who broke the laws on rationing. They were fined and sometimes sent to prison. Waldo could get into terrible trouble. She rammed the asparagus out of sight at the back of the shelf, but it wasn't only that.

There were five lamb chops for dinner tonight. Mrs Gully had shown them to her before she'd gone out. Lottie was going to cook them.

She opened a cupboard in the hall. There were several expensive-looking overcoats and a whole collection of trilbies. Some golf clubs, too. She hadn't known Waldo played. She couldn't help but compare his standard of living here with that in his basement flat. And that frightened her even more.

There was a handsome carved wooden chest in the hall. It looked Oriental. Lottie tried to lift the lid but could not. There was an engraved brass lock set into it. It made her wonder what he kept inside.

She carried on looking round, opening everything she

could. It made her feel guilty, as though she was spying on Waldo. She told herself not to be silly, she needed to know what was in her home. Doing this ought to be fun. It hadn't bothered her in his flat.

She went out to look at the garden. There was a large sycamore tree in the lawn behind the house, and beds of shrubs and flowers. It was all neatly kept. There was a good lawnmower in the shed and every other imaginable tool needed to keep it that way.

At the bottom end a few vegetables had been planted. She found a vigorous bed of mint and picked a bunch. She was making mint sauce to go with the chops when she heard Waldo's car pull up on the drive.

Pleased that he'd come home early, she opened the back door. He was striding towards her, his face like thunder. He pushed her roughly back inside and kicked the door shut behind him.

'Is this yours?' He slammed down her copy of *Forever Amber* on the kitchen cabinet with enough force to make her jump.

'Yes. Where did you get it?'

'You had a lift in a car last night?' She could see trickles of sweat on his forehead. She thought he looked scared.

'I missed it . . . Did I leave it on the back seat?'

He was shouting. 'Do you know whose car that was?'

'I travelled up on the train with him. Martin, his name was . . . yes, Martin.'

'Martin Carruthers?'

'I think so. His father met him at the station. They were kind enough to—'

'He's an enforcement officer, that's who he is. And you

gave him a reason to come round and spy out my garage. He was there for hours. Giving me a hard time.' She could see from the wild look in his eyes just how hard he'd found it. 'You stay away from them. D'you hear?'

Lottie's heart was thumping hard. She knew for certain now that Waldo was a black marketeer. It seemed he was in business in a big way.

She said coldly: 'And did he see something he shouldn't? Something you wanted to hide?'

Waldo's brown eyes glared back at her. 'It's no thanks to you he didn't. He took me by surprise.'

A flush was running up his round teddy bear cheeks. She knew he realised he'd as good as admitted he was breaking the law.

'I didn't know who he was, Waldo.'

'You mustn't let yourself be picked up by strangers. You have to be very careful, these days.'

Lottie felt he was turning on her and she'd done nothing to justify it. 'Waldo, I didn't know there was a reason to be careful. Not about things like that. I didn't know what you were up to. You didn't tell me.'

The prickly silence lengthened. She felt a spurt of anger. 'You're dealing on the black market, you have to be. You've a huge store of tinned and dried foods in this house.'

He tried to brush it aside as he'd brushed off the questions Connie's husband had put to him last night. He put an arm round her and tried to kiss her.

'Don't do that! You're not going to sidestep me.' Lottie lost her cool and whirled round the kitchen, throwing open his cupboard doors. 'Just take a look at this.' She groped for the tin of asparagus, piling the tins out on the floor. 'Don't try to deny it. You've got to be dealing on the black market.'

'All right, just a little.' He was supporting himself on the kitchen table. 'Everybody does. We couldn't live otherwise.'

He'd admitted it! Actually admitted it. It flattened her.

'It doesn't seem so little. I'm scared you'll get caught.'

'No,' he said grimly. 'I won't. Provided you stop making friends of enforcement officers.'

Lottie fumed at the injustice. 'If you'd answered the phone when I rang from Liverpool last night, you could have met me yourself.'

'I'd just been called out to a breakdown. I told Bill to tell you.'

'I rang half an hour earlier. You weren't there then.'

'We don't always hear the phone. A garage is a noisy place and I can't spend all my time in the office.'

Lottie felt hurt and upset. She hadn't expected Waldo to attack her like this. She'd never seen him in a black mood before.

'Don't let's fight about it,' she choked. 'Surely we can discuss it without losing our tempers?'

There was another prickly silence. Then she saw Waldo pouring out two glasses of his sherry. She saw this as a peace offering. As she accepted the glass she saw his hand shake and realised he was afraid. That really made her heart race. If Waldo was afraid, he probably had good reason to be.

She had to do something. She leapt up to set the table for their supper. Up until now, they'd enjoyed cooking and eating a meal together. She lit the gas and got the dinner started, but Waldo seemed miles away, his mind no longer on her.

She started to tell him about her day, but he didn't want to talk about Connie either. He never did. Any mention of her brought a guilty look to his face.

Lottie knew if she was to heal the rift with Waldo she mustn't say any more about his black market dealings. She very much wanted to close the rift but she couldn't leave things as they were. She needed to know exactly what he was doing, how deeply involved he was, and it seemed he didn't want to tell her anything more.

She couldn't help questioning him, though she could see he hated it.

To deflect her, he asked: 'Have you thought any more about a job? About what you're going to do?' But nothing could take her mind off his affairs. She didn't give the chops the attention they deserved. The meal wasn't a success.

She kept firing questions at him, and then had to try to make sense of his evasive answers. Waldo seemed as slippery as an eel. She found he could talk himself out of almost everything.

'I did it for you, Lottie,' he said.

That infuriated her. 'It's the last thing I wanted you to do. And you know it.'

'Don't you like this house?'

'Of course I do, but I don't like to think of how you paid for it. You've got to stop.'

'You've got a holier than thou attitude. I didn't realise you were so straitlaced. A bit of a prig really.'

'Perhaps I am. I'm frightened you'll be caught and sent to prison.'

'I won't,' he told her. 'I've managed to evade the snoopers yet again. Even though you set them on to me.'

'Waldo, I want you to promise—'

'I'm careful. I keep one step ahead. I'm better at this game than they are. More experienced. They won't catch me.'

'I want you to promise to stop now. Before it's too late.'

Lottie went to bed early, feeling tired out, but she couldn't get to sleep. She'd had a terrible fight with Waldo and it left her mind on fire. What had she done? It had seemed so right to marry him back in 1943, but she'd barely known him, nor he her. For the first time, she wondered if she'd made a mistake.

She'd been so busy that month, her first in the QAs. Marry in haste, repent at leisure. Had she been stupid enough to do exactly that? She could hardly believe it. All these months, she'd thought she could come home and she and Waldo would take up exactly where they'd left off. With hindsight, she didn't think anybody could.

Waldo stayed downstairs for another hour. When he came to bed she hung on to the edge of the mattress and pretended to be asleep. She didn't want to start up the same argument again. He undressed in silence and when he climbed into bed he stayed on his side, leaving a wide gap between them.

It made Lottie feel cold inside. This was a Waldo she didn't know and she didn't like.

When the alarm went off the next morning Waldo scrambled out of bed. He'd been lying awake for ages, worrying about Phyllis. It was driving him mad, not knowing what had happened. He put on the light and Lottie's doubting eyes blinked at him over the edge of the sheet.

Ever since he'd married her, he'd longed to have her home with him. He'd never loved anybody else with half the passion he'd felt for her, but it was all falling flat. After all these months of separation, she seemed a stranger.

It was no treat having her at home. He hadn't expected her to nag like this and look at him with such suspicion. She was poking her nose into things he wanted her to leave alone. The less she knew about what he was doing the better. She was letting him know she didn't like any of it, though it had all been done for her.

He'd had to teach himself to keep a firm check on his tongue and he was afraid she'd babble out what she knew to other people. It was making him feel a nervous wreck.

Lottie got up too. They got dressed in virtual silence and went down together to the dining room for breakfast. Mrs Gully had cooked egg and bacon for them. For once, Waldo had no appetite.

He had to get away from Lottie. She kept asking questions, trying to pin him down. He'd had to remind her that Mrs Gully might hear. Out in the hall, the phone rang. He got up to answer it.

'Waldo?'

He knew immediately it was Phyllis.

He said: 'I'll be at the garage in half an hour.' That was to let Lottie know it was a business call. He was very conscious that she was within earshot.

Phyllis asked, 'Isn't it convenient to talk?'

'No. I expected you to ring yesterday. You said you would.'

'I couldn't get away from Cecil. Sorry.'

'Go on, then. What happened? All went well?' He guessed from her calm voice that it had and was soothed.

'I think so, but I've had enough, Waldo. I'm not printing any more. Not ever. This is the end.'

'Look, if you've come through this you'll be fine. They'll leave you alone for months; won't even think of you.'

'No, it's over for me. I can't go through that again. I'm not printing another coupon.'

Waldo was not too concerned. She'd given him so many yesterday.

'About those I gave you . . .'

He'd been about to offer her a lump sum for the lot, at a much reduced rate.

'I'd like you to burn them.'

He croaked: 'Can't do that.'

'Why not?'

'Waste not, want not.'

'I don't want you to use them. I don't want anything to get back to me.'

'It won't.'

'Well . . .'

There was no way she could know whether he burned them or used them. She must realise that.

'Right. You can use them on one condition.'

'What's that?'

'If you get caught, you keep your mouth buttoned about me.'

'I would anyway. You don't have to bargain about that. I can't pay for them all at once, though.' Oh, God! He'd forgotten Lottie was here, all ears.

'I don't want your money.'

That mollified him somewhat. He'd be able to make more profit himself.

But her voice was full of aggression. 'I don't want to see you ever again. I don't want you to ring me or have any further connection. We don't know each other from now on, okay? I don't want to be brought down by you.'

Waldo swallowed hard. He'd been telling himself that if Lottie didn't want to play ball there was always Phyllis. Now it seemed he couldn't fall back on her.

'All right,' he said.

The next morning, Connie Montague lay back on her bed taking deep breaths. Waves of morning sickness were threatening to empty her stomach. Experts told expectant mothers to get their husbands to bring tea and toast to them in bed before thinking of rising. That, they advised, would settle it for the day. Connie thought the experts knew nothing about life in the real world.

For one thing, she'd been up in the night at three-hourly intervals with Jimmy. She'd been sick at half past four when she'd given him a bottle of milk instead of trying to pacify him with orange juice.

For another, Clovis had been an officer and was used to being waited on. He wasn't likely to wait on her. If she didn't get up and put breakfast on the table for him and coax him out of bed, he'd never get up and go to work. This morning she'd been sick again as she'd tried to cook his breakfast, and for once he'd taken over and sent her back to bed with some tea. It had gone cold in the cup and the smell of bacon was still heavy in the air. She'd tried to cat nap again after he'd gone to work.

Tears of self-pity squeezed out from under her closed eyelids. She'd expected everything to be wonderful once the war was over. Everybody had. She'd so looked forward to having Clovis home for good. He was the biggest disappointment of all. She thought she'd backed a real winner. He'd trained as a school teacher but at the beginning of the war he'd gone straight from college into the RAF to be a navigator.

She'd believed his qualification would give him a safe and respectable job to come out to. A profession to enter immediately without having to waste time making up his mind and undergoing further training. He'd had no trouble finding a job, either. There was a serious shortage of teachers now. It was just that Clovis wouldn't buckle down and do it.

'I'm not cut out for this,' he'd said after only a few days trying to teach a class of eight-year-olds in the local primary school. 'The kids get on my nerves.'

'Give yourself time,' Connie had said. 'It'll take you a little while to settle down.' But he was getting worse, not better. Kicking against what he saw as a frustrating job.

'It's not the sort of work I want to do.'

'But you've trained for it. Of course it's very different from the RAF. It'll take time—'

'Don't keep telling me it'll take time,' he burst out, enraged. 'This isn't what I want to do with my life.'

Connie had to bite back her reply. It wouldn't make him any happier to know she wasn't enjoying life either. Living with Clovis when he was such a misery was no fun at all.

'I miss the men,' he admitted. 'I miss the life. I was doing a man's job in the RAF.'

'You could have been killed. I was worried the whole time.'

'It made the adrenalin run, of course it did, but it wasn't that risky. It's not as if I'd stayed with Bomber Command. Being sent to India probably saved my life. Flying sorties over Burma and dropping supplies to our ground troops was a piece of cake by comparison. We were shot at from time to time, and finding the exact spot to drop the stuff was quite a challenge – not much to see down below but jungle – but there wasn't much danger.'

Connie had heard this several times already. 'You had a good war,' she told him. That was more than she'd had.

'I enjoyed the social life.' That stung her. Was he telling her he didn't enjoy being at home with her? He preferred life in the mess?

'The war's over, Clovis. You're going to have to live without it.'

Once she'd left work, her life had been boring. Clovis's parents had been kind, but they'd been virtual strangers to her.

'We'd like you to call us Mum and Dad and think of us as parents,' they told her. 'Of course it won't be the same, but since your parents were killed in the Blitz we'd like to try to take their place.'

Connie couldn't do it. Her feelings for her own parents had been very different. It would detract from her memories of them. She understood now why Lottie had made such a fuss about calling Steve Lancelyn 'Father', and why she'd been upset when Cliff was able to do it so quickly. Connie called Clovis's parents Mum-in-law and Dad-in-law, and only rarely shortened it as they'd requested.

Life with them had started off well enough. They'd had water piped up to the attic floor and a sink put in the room that had been turned into her kitchen. A washbowl in the bedroom, too.

Connie sighed. Living in an attic with a baby was anything but convenient. The living room faced north and got little sun, and she had to share the bathroom on the floor below.

The Montagues made a fuss of Jimmy and in some ways

the relationship was better after he was born. But Jimmy wasn't an easy baby. Connie never had an unbroken night's sleep and she'd had to find carpet to put down in the bedroom to absorb some of the noise he made, because he was waking his grandparents too.

It was difficult if she had to use the bathroom in the night. It was next to their bedroom and they asked her to refrain from pulling the chain whenever possible because the flushing water woke them. Connie had to take a bucket of water with her to pour quietly down their loo. It wasn't as though they were her own family, after all.

Connie heard her baby son begin to make soft ticking noises. She knew they'd soon develop into a full blown howl. He wanted his breakfast. She sat up and swung her legs out of bed, groaning as another wave of nausea swept through her. When it passed, she stood up.

Jimmy let out a wail of protest just as she reached his cot. He was wet through as usual. Gown, vest, nappy, sheets, both top and bottom. More to add to the mountain of washing waiting for her to do. Her hands were red with having them in water so much.

Jimmy cried a lot in the day too, giving her little rest. Her time was spent carrying coals up and ashes down, as well as washing napkins. Life hadn't been much fun without Clovis. She'd longed for him to come home but he hadn't been back three months before she was pregnant again.

Connie wanted to cry. She felt terrible and she looked terrible. She had big mauve shadows under her eyes and she didn't know how she would cope with another baby.

But the worst part of all was that Clovis was miserable. He'd been all over Jimmy for the first weeks he was home, but now he didn't go near him if he could help it. Heaven only knew how they'd cope with another. Clovis didn't seem interested in anything. He had a face like wet washing the whole time. He wasn't even interested in her.

Connie knew her morning chores needed to be done quickly today because she was going over to Old Swan with Lottie. She washed and dressed her son and put him in his high chair. She set out two bowls of Weetabix, one for each of them. She had to go down to the front door to fetch the milk, and she could hear Jimmy raising the roof from the front step.

Mother-in-law appeared in a pink satin dressing gown, all sweetness and light.

'The little love! Just listen to him. Doesn't like being kept waiting for breakfast, does he?'

Connie scurried back upstairs as fast as she could. Jimmy was so enraged he'd torn the bib from his neck and thrown it on the floor. Hurriedly she replaced it, tipped milk on to his cereal and spooned it into his open mouth.

Thankfully, his screaming stopped as soon as he started to eat. Connie looked round her living room. It was cold; the grate needed to be cleared out and a new fire laid. The debris of Clovis's breakfast was still on the table. She felt another wave of sickness coming, and pushed her Weetabix aside. She'd make herself a cup of tea when Jimmy was settled. She didn't want anything to eat this morning.

She heard the front door bell ring. She never made any attempt to answer it. The caller usually wanted the Montagues and they were down at ground level where they could answer it more easily.

She paused to listen. Was that Lottie's voice? Connie froze. Surely it couldn't be? She'd said she'd be round at ten o'clock and it wasn't even nine. Connie leapt to her feet to tap the clock on the mantelpiece. It had stopped. She must have forgotten to wind it.

It was Lottie. Just like her to stand chatting to her mother-in-law. Connie swept the worst of the breakfast dishes to the kitchen sink, then dashed to her bedroom to straighten the bed and run a comb through her hair. She didn't want Lottie to see her looking as awful as this. Gall was rising in her throat again. She couldn't possibly go over to see Father. She leaned over the banisters.

'Lottie? Is that you?' She was looking down on the smooth dark head three floors below. She expected her to come running up all bounce and smiles. Instead, she climbed slowly.

'Hello, Con. Not ready yet?'

'I can't come today. I was just going to ring you. I feel awful. It's this morning sickness.'

Lottie's eyes were assessing her. 'You poor thing. You don't look well.'

Jimmy let out a wail at being left alone. 'Is that my nephew, then?'

Lottie went into the living room, swept him up in her arms and took him to the window to see him better.

'He's lovely. Beautiful.' Jimmy smiled widely, showing his first four teeth. She was tickling him, making him giggle.

'He loves attention.' Connie heard the misery in her own voice.

'Why don't you come with me? You'll feel better if you do.'

'No. No, I can't. Jimmy isn't ready either.' He still wore his milk-stained feeder.

'I can change him for you. I bet Father makes a fuss of

369

him. A new addition to the family.'

'He hasn't seen him yet.'

'What? Then you must come, both of you.'

'I don't feel like it, Lottie.'

'What's the matter?' Connie felt her sister's arm go across her shoulders. 'I can see something is.'

'I told you. I feel awful, morning sickness.'

'That'll pass. You must know that better than I do.'

Connie scrubbed at her face with a grubby handkerchief.

'You need to get out more and have a bit of fun. Do come with me. Go and have a quick bath first. Wash your hair and I'll set it for you. Make you look like the Connie I used to know.'

'I haven't got a hair dryer. Anyway, there isn't time if we're going to Old Swan.'

'Loosen up, Con. You're going on as though life wasn't worth living.'

Connie felt tears stinging her eyes. 'What makes you think it is?'

'Course it is. The war's over. Everything's set fair now.'

'It's all right for you. You've got a lovely home.' She couldn't quite keep the envy out of her voice. 'Not like this.'

She didn't dare look round. It was such a mess. It needed a good clean on top of everything else.

'And Waldo – he can't do enough for you. Honestly, Lottie, if you were thrown in a midden you'd come up smelling of roses. Everything comes easily to you.'

'No . . . it doesn't. Doesn't at all.'

'Comes easily to Waldo, then. How does he do it? All that tasty food, a fine car and a lovely house. Nobody else can get these things.'

Connie saw her sister's face stiffen. 'I don't know. I've only just got home. Oh, Con – what is the matter?'

'Clovis is so unhappy. There's nothing worse than being married to a man who's always miserable. Makes me a misery too.'

Lottie's tawny eyes were studying her again. 'He did look a bit browned off that first night. Though he cheered up. Is he depressed? Clinically depressed, I mean? What d'you think?'

Connie felt cold shivers go through her. Why hadn't she thought of that?

'Get him to the doctor, if you think he is. Get him sorted out.'

Chapter Twenty-one

Lottie felt upset as she caught the train over to Old Swan by herself. Connie was so changed. Where were her fancy clothes and expensive make-up? What had happened to her bossy know-it-all manner? Yet she'd achieved what she'd set out to do: she had a child and a husband she'd chosen with great care. It seemed to be a family trait that none of them could be happy with the spouse they'd chosen.

Lottie knew now that love was more complex than she'd first thought. Any quarrel, even a minor domestic difference, ground away at her feelings. Relationships were not formed and set in stone for ever. Absence was supposed to make the heart grow fonder, yet she couldn't relate to Waldo after being parted from him. Absence had slackened their feelings for each other.

When she got off the bus outside the factory and sniffed the scent of baking bread in the air, Lottie felt better. This really was coming home. She went straight up to her father's office.

'Lottie – lovely to see you back.'

It took him longer than it used to to get up and come round his desk to hug her. She thought he looked older, rather stiff and not nearly so robust.

Cliff rushed in, shedding his white coat and hat before he

hugged her too. He seemed even taller than she remembered. Healthier, a man on top of his form.

'I saw you come upstairs. Had to pop up to say hello.'

They were both talking at once. 'We're proud of you, Lottie.'

'You did your bit for the country.'

'Helped to win the war.'

'Was it terrifying?'

'At times, but it gave me a whoosh too.'

'Exhilarating, you mean?'

'Yes. Kept me on my toes. Wouldn't have missed it for anything. I'm glad I went. I made some good friends.'

'Your eyes are shining now, just recalling it.' Her father laughed. 'You must have enjoyed it.'

'Some of it. We're proud of you too, Cliff. A tank commander. A Churchill tank, wasn't it?'

Cliff smiled self-consciously. 'I'd have done better to come straight here from school.'

Father said: 'You wouldn't hear of it. I did my best to persuade you.'

Lottie said: 'So did I.'

'Big sister was doing her bit, I felt I had to do mine. To keep my end up, you know.'

'You must have had some good times?' Lottie laughed.

'Had more bad ones. I loused it up, didn't I? Only fought on the front for five weeks before I was captured.'

'I know that. What happened? How were you caught?'

'In a tank battle. It was mayhem. Guns of all sorts thudding away as well as our own six pounders. Tanks on fire, ammunition exploding inside and spewing clouds of black smoke. I could hardly see anything for smoke and dust. Then my radio conked and I lost contact with the rest of my unit. I tried to keep direction by heading for the sun but there was cloud and with all the smoke . . .

'We ran out of ammunition, but saw a tank that had been knocked out and abandoned, another Churchill. We replenished our supplies from that, and tried to use their radio but it was a gonner too. When we came to start off again, I realised we were on our own.'

'What did you do?'

'I could see a bit of a wood. I wanted to get some cover so we could work on the radio and try to get it going again. I headed there but we got bogged down and couldn't move. That was one of my blackest moments.'

'You got out eventually?'

'No, couldn't budge it. We were in a hopeless quagmire. There seemed no point in staying in the tank – it was a sitting duck for a sniper. When we abandoned it, we were captured.' He sighed. 'Some tank commander. I'd taken them behind the enemy lines. Hardly a useful contribution.'

'I want to hear all about it.'

'Not right now. I'm in the middle of something.' Cliff was putting his white coat on again. 'Must get back.'

'He's acting as production manager,' her father told her as they sipped coffee. She thought he looked weary. 'I don't press him to talk about what happened. He told you more then than he's told me. I think it rocked his self-confidence, being captured so soon.'

'Poor Cliff.'

'He's a great help to me here. He's very involved. I've come to rely on him.'

'It's what you always wanted.'

'I couldn't manage without him now. The factory's working flat out. We all thought shortages would end when the war was won, but things are getting worse. There's talk of bread being rationed. Now, for the first time. Bread rationed, would you believe?'

Lottie shook her head.

'Have you thought any more about coming to work here?'

She'd thought of little else since Waldo had come up with the idea of a nursing home. 'Are you sure you still want me? I mean, you've got Cliff now.'

'Yes, I need you. I was expecting my workforce to come flocking back. You know ex-servicemen are entitled to come back to their jobs? That employers are compelled to take them on again? Well, we are. Some are coming but not the ones I really wanted. You won't remember Dennis Hadley. I thought he might make a good manager but he's decided to work for Bibby's instead. Anyway, I'd rather have you. You know I've always wanted to hand on this business to my heirs.'

Lottie was touched. 'I've already had my inheritance. You've others to provide for.'

He smiled. 'What you've had came from Marion – your mother. Quite different.'

He stopped. Lottie saw his eyes assessing her.

'And I need to talk to you about that. You haven't touched any of it. I opened a bank account in your name. I had to do something with your dividends, so I paid them into that. Half the Brightland Street house belongs to you too. I've paid some rent in . . .'

'You don't have to do that.'

'I do. I'm living there, not you. Half an average rent for that sort of house, it's only fair. You're building up a nice little nest egg for yourself.'

'There you are, then. I don't need anything more.'

'Lottie, this business will provide for all of us, keep us in comfort, but somebody has to run it.'

'Cliff . . .'

'Cliff's doing very well, but he won't be able to manage on his own. Geoffrey Montague's due to retire in less than two years and I'm nearly sixty-seven now.'

'You want to retire too?'

'Exactly. I've known for years I need to train more managers, but with the war I wasn't able to keep the right people. Iris and her girls have no interest in it. If I left it all to them they couldn't run it – they'd have to sell. You know how much I want my own flesh and blood to carry it on. What do you say?'

Lottie had had time to think about it. 'I've been demobbed, so now's a good time to try.'

'You don't want to be a full-time housewife?'

'No! Not yet anyway. How do you know I'd be any good? It's outside my experience. I know nothing about bread making.'

'Lottie! You've been here countless times. I've explained what happens, shown you what we do. That was my way of giving you a bit of insight.'

'But would I be of use to the business?'

'We won't know until you try.'

Lottie drained her cup. This was her family; she was more at ease here than with Waldo. She had to give it a go.

'Right, when shall I start? Monday?'

Her father laughed. 'No rush. You deserve a bit of a rest first.'

'The middle of March, then?'

'I'm delighted, Lottie. Utterly delighted. Cliff will be too.'

Over lunch they talked of more general things. Of Connie.

'It's ages since we've seen her.' Cliff frowned. 'I did call at her flat. To see her and the baby. She seemed at sixes and sevens and worried that it wasn't dusted. Uncomfortable. Not our Connie at all.'

Lottie said: 'I'll persuade her to bring Jimmy over here to see you.'

Sitting on the bus on the way home, she mused that extra consideration from a loved one brought warmer feelings in return. She'd melted towards Father because he'd shown such care and concern to all of them. He wanted only to give. She could understand now why Mam had lived as she had. Perhaps she hadn't been selfish, after all. She'd done her best for poor Dadda. Perhaps Mam had wanted to give, too.

And as for Cliff, he'd given and given.

The next morning at breakfast, Clovis Montague pushed his bacon to one side and stopped eating. 'What d'you mean, see the doctor?'

'You might need medical help.' Connie was trying to be diplomatic.

'What for?' He glowered at her.

'Well, you've been very low recently. Really browned off.'

'You can say that again. So what?'

'You're depressed.' Connie lost her patience. 'You never stop moaning about your job. You're making me miserable.'

He was carefully cutting off the rind. 'You think, if I popped a few pills it would straighten everything out? Make me sing and dance and enjoy the children at work?'

'Well, Lottie thought—'

'Oh, God! Save me from the nurses. You two, you think everything's a medical problem.' He pulled a face. 'So you think I'm going mad?'

Connie pulled herself upright in her chair. 'No, of course not. Doctors can help with depression.'

'Connie, they can't help me. I'm tired of telling you, trying to explain.' He slammed down his knife and fork and jerked to his feet. 'I don't like teaching. I don't like being surrounded with screaming kids all day.'

She flared back. 'Or coming home to another. Not to mention a miserable wife.'

'I didn't say that. Look, I know it isn't easy for you either, stuck here all day in these attic rooms.'

'We're going to be bursting out of them when the new baby comes. Two babies and only one bedroom. If only we could get a prefab. They say they're lovely inside.' Connie was fighting tears. 'We've got to get out, Clovis. Get a house of our own. All these stairs with a baby to carry up and down every time I go out. And soon it'll be two babies.'

'Look for somewhere, Connie. When you find it at a reasonable rent, we'll move.'

'You know I've already tried. You know it's impossible. There's nothing available to rent after the Blitz.'

'Right, and that's why we're here. They'll start building houses again soon.'

'They have started, but they're all for sale and there's a mad rush to buy them.'

Clovis sighed. 'Can't buy just yet. What I really need is to change my job. Get out of teaching. That's the only thing that'll cheer me up.'

Connie felt put down. She wanted a husband who was a professional man. 'You're qualified to teach,' she said plaintively. 'What else could you do?'

'I don't know. The commercial airlines only want pilots and they're overwhelmed with applicants from the RAF anyway. No demand for navigators – all that's done by their second pilot. I'm trapped, Connie. Trapped in a job I don't like and I'm no good at.'

Connie knew he blamed her though he didn't say it. He had to work to support her and their family. He couldn't train for some alternative career. He was compelled to carry on earning their living.

'But you chose it.'

'Years ago. I thought I'd like to teach, but I was wrong. Very wrong.'

'What are you going to do?'

'What can I do? Like I said, I'm trapped.'

Trapped with me, Connie thought. I'm trapped too. Life in an attic with a husband who feels I've trapped him.

She spent a day that was more miserable than usual, but when Clovis came home in the late afternoon he was more cheerful.

'Look, Connie, I'm sorry if I go on a bit. I'm an old misery, I know. Perhaps we'd both be better if we went out more. Mother would love to look after Jimmy. We've got a built-in babysitter – we might as well make use of what benefits we have. I bought a paper. Margaret Lockwood's on at the Ritz in *The Wicked Lady*. How about it?'

Connie mused that Clovis could always get round her.

A day or two later, Waldo knew Lottie's eyes were watching

him as he finished off his evening meal with a nice piece of Stilton.

She said: 'What about going to the pictures tonight? Connie says there's a smashing picture on at the Ritz. Do you feel like it?'

'It'll be too much of a rush. It's seven o'clock now.'

'It's James Mason in *The Wicked Lady*. I'd like to see it.'

'Tomorrow,' he said. 'We'll go tomorrow night. I'll come home earlier.' He heard her sigh.

'Let's go somewhere tonight. Just for a drink or something. I've been in all afternoon on my own.'

Hell! He'd been wondering all day how to break this to her.

'Afraid not.' He knew he sounded abrupt. 'I have to go out tonight. I've arranged to meet somebody. Work.'

The landlord of the Admiral's Arms had been buying what he thought were black market spirits from him for the last year or so. He could sell them on to his customers at a good profit. His pub was always full, the only one that didn't run out of liquor.

Waldo did not consider himself a thief, but he knew he was handling stolen goods when he delivered to the pubs. He saw himself as a middleman.

Lottie was smiling at him across the table. 'Can't I come with you? Just for the ride? A car is such a novelty for—'

'No.' He didn't want her watching him across the lounge bar. Taking it all in. It would make him uncomfortable. She was nosy; she'd find out far too much.

He saw her face fall. She'd expected him to take her. Damn it, he just couldn't.

* * *

Lottie wondered why she'd been so keen to come home. Waldo was grumpy and on edge. She could feel him mentally pushing her away, as though he couldn't bear her being close. She wondered why she'd once thought he was like a cuddly teddy bear. He wasn't lovable at all.

They were getting up earlier these days. He'd eaten in silence the breakfast she'd cooked for him. Gone off to work after the briefest of kisses, almost as though he'd been doing it for twenty years. As soon as Mrs Gully arrived Lottie got ready to go out. She felt unwanted and unneeded in this house.

She often went to see Connie. Lottie felt they'd almost lost touch with each other; that their friendship had waned. They'd grown apart because they'd had so little contact over recent years. To feel settled, she needed to get closer to Connie as well as Waldo.

She couldn't understand why Connie wasn't happy. After all, she'd always wanted to be married and have children. She'd been so determined to stay home and look after them properly, in the way Mam had failed to look after them. Now she'd got what she wanted, Lottie had expected her to be contented. It had come as a shock to find she wasn't.

Lottie helped her to spring-clean the flat and reduce the mound of washing to manageable proportions, because those were the things Connie said were getting her down. She persuaded her to go to a hairdresser and have her hair cut and set.

Last week, Lottie had played with baby Jimmy on the bed while Connie sorted through her wardrobe. She'd asked Lottie's opinion on each outfit, though she discounted her ideas on fashion. Connie enjoyed fiddling around with her clothes and she was good at sewing. She borrowed a sewing machine and began to make over some of her outfits to give them a more up-to-date look. When they went out, Lottie helped her choose new material for a skirt and a dress. Home dressmaking made clothing coupons stretch much further. They also found dyed parachute silk now surplus to government requirements, available in the market without coupons. Every day, as soon as Jimmy went down for his afternoon nap, Connie said she now settled down to her sewing.

Not only did she look better with more colour in her cheeks, but she said her morning sickness was less troublesome. Lottie felt they were closer. Connie was talking again about the things that really mattered to her. With her head bent over the scarlet parachute silk she was making into a blouse, she confided in her at last.

'It's Clovis,' she said. 'He hates his job. He'd like to give in his notice but there's me and Jimmy and we've all got to eat. So he can't. It keeps him plodding on.'

'He's looking for another job? What sort?'

Connie sighed heavily. 'I wish I knew. Even he hasn't the slightest idea. It's not that easy. He isn't really looking, just talking about it. I think it's all in his mind. School isn't as exciting as the RAF. I expect he'll settle down eventually.'

'We're all expected to do that,' Lottie said. 'But . . . does he talk about it? To his father?'

'No, I don't think so. When he's not at school, he's up here with me, sunk in gloom. Why his dad?'

'He's had a whole career with Lancelyn's. Why shouldn't Clovis do the same?'

'Make bread?' Connie sniffed. 'That would be a bit of a come down for him.'

'Why should it be? Father's looking for managers.'

'He's a schoolmaster.'

'But if he doesn't like that and he's looking for something else? Mr Montague will be retiring soon, so why not?'

'I'm reaching the stage when I'd agree to almost anything.' Connie gave another martyred sigh. 'If it would make Clovis happy.'

Lottie got to her feet. 'That's what it's about, making Clovis happy. Then you'll be happy too. Come on over to Old Swan with me one day soon. We'll talk to Father about it first. He wants to see little Jimmy anyway and so does Cliff.'

A few days later, over lunch in the canteen, Lottie was making a point of telling Father how miserable Clovis was in his teaching job.

'He thinks he's a round peg in a square hole,' Connie added.

'You know I'm always on the look-out for staff,' Father said without any prompting. 'Why don't you bring him over to Brightland Street to see me? How about Sunday afternoon? I'd like to talk to him about it.'

'Do you really want him?' Connie asked. 'Even with Cliff and Lottie?'

'Yes. Lancelyn's a big concern and it could grow bigger. I'm tired – I could do with taking things easier. And I want to retire soon.'

On the way home, Connie sat on the bus nursing Jimmy. 'Didn't Father make a fuss of him?'

'An addition to the family, what did you expect?' Lottie smiled. It widened into a grin. 'Not that much of a fuss. He didn't offer him a job.'

Connie found Clovis was home before her. She told him her

father seemed keen to give him a job. 'I'm surprised you didn't think of the bread factory yourself.'

'Of course I thought of it.' Clovis tossed his head impatiently.

'Don't you want to work there?'

'You didn't want me to. Anyway, how do I know I'd be any better at doing what's required of me there?'

'Your dad likes it. He's been there for years. Father thinks the world of him.'

'Exactly. Dad looks upon it as his home ground. I don't want to mess up on his patch, make him ashamed of me.'

'You won't,' she said. 'Of course you won't.' She couldn't believe his confidence had been so shattered.

When she took Clovis over to Brightland Street on Sunday afternoon, Father was alone. Sandwiches and cake were set out on the tea trolley in the sitting room. Clovis seemed stiff as they seated themselves round the fire.

As Connie went to make the tea, she heard Steve say: 'Look, Clovis, your dad has been my mainstay and prop for the last twenty-five years. I'd be delighted to have you working for me. You must know that.'

'I might not be as good as he is. He might not like me to come.'

'Why don't you ask him? Talk it over. Then come and see how you get on. No hard feelings if you decide it's not for you.'

'That's very kind.'

'Clovis, I've known you all your life, and now you're married to Connie you're one of the family. You know us all here.'

'I'll have to work on at the school until the end of term.'

'Not a bad thing. It'll give Lottie a chance to find her feet first.'

When she started her new job, Lottie found that Father had moved another desk into his office for her.

'So you can see exactly what I do. I can explain things as they come up. You'll be my assistant. Cliff started like this and it worked well.'

Lottie found her duties very different from anything she'd done before. It took her some time to really understand the company accounts, but she quickly learned to collate the necessary figures and to order the factory supplies.

Father was worried. All bakeries had been ordered to reduce the size of their loaves by four ounces, and breweries had had their allocation of grain cut by fifteen per cent because stocks were so low.

'You must be very careful not to run out of any ingredients, Lottie. It would bring the bakery to a full stop. Bread rationing is coming next month.'

She was soon enjoying what she did, and was glad to spend more time with Father and Cliff. It got her out of the house and away from Waldo. She knew Waldo was carrying on with his black market activities even though he'd promised to stop. It took up much of his weekend and many of his evenings. At those times, the last thing he wanted was to have her near him.

'How is your back?' she asked him. She'd never heard him complain of any pain, but she hadn't forgotten that when he'd been working in Hooton his doctor had put him off sick for months.

'It's all right. I manage.'

She guessed now it had been an excuse to allow him to escape from the job to which he'd been directed.

She knew she sounded suspicious. 'Have you ever had a bad back?'

'You know I have.' He grinned. 'That job in the aircraft factory creased me. It's been better since I left.'

'When you bought your own business?'

'The best thing I ever did. It was no fun being conscripted into a job like that.'

Lottie said nothing. She knew lots of men who'd been conscripted into the forces and felt it was their duty to do their best for the country. She didn't know what to do about Waldo now. She'd been very wrong about him.

She tried to talk to her father about it, but without telling him of Waldo's dishonesty. She couldn't bring herself to talk of that. She thought he would understand because of his own marital problems.

He said quite sharply: 'You haven't given him a chance yet, Lottie. You've only been home a few weeks.'

'Three months.'

'Give it a year at least. It could still come all right.'

Lottie thought the longer they were together, the further they seemed to be drawing apart.

'What can I do? To make it come right?'

Father's eyes surveyed her face. 'Spend more time together. Do things together.'

'I've tried, but Waldo doesn't want that. He wants to go out by himself. I can't get close to him. He doesn't want me to.'

'Connie says he can't do enough for you. He's provided you with a good home.'

Lottie said slowly. 'You stayed with your wife even though you had Mam.'

'You're not thinking of leaving him?'

She couldn't think straight about Waldo. 'Don't you think I should?'

'Not yet. Think about it before you do anything.'

Lottie was fighting for self-control. She was determined not to break down and cry.

Her father went on: 'It's a pity you didn't think before you married him. I can't advise you on this, Lottie. It's up to you. My way isn't the only way – it might not be the best. Iris and I didn't share the same interests, but she wouldn't have wanted a divorce even though we had drifted apart, and neither would your mother. Still, things are different for you. You must find your own way to deal with it.'

'I don't know where to begin.'

'Build a life of your own. You've made a good start by coming to work here. If you can't build a life with Waldo, you must do it away from him.'

To Lottie, it didn't seem enough. She'd expected more from life. She asked: 'That's what you did? Built a life of your own?'

'That's about it.'

She tried to talk to Waldo about it.

'All you need is something to settle you down,' he said. 'Let's have a baby – that would do it.'

Lottie was appalled. It seemed absolutely the wrong thing to do. 'We need to sort ourselves out first. A baby needs loving parents.'

'I do love you, Lottie.' He seemed sincere but she couldn't rely on him.

A baby would tie her to Waldo even more securely, and now she didn't trust him not to get her pregnant. He was insisting on what he called his marital rights whether she wanted him or not. She was afraid she would become pregnant sooner or later. She started spending the odd night or two over at Brightland Street. Cliff was always pleased to see her there. It seemed the easiest way round the problem.

Usually Father was with them, but one night she found herself spending a long spring evening alone with Cliff. They'd both eaten a big lunch in the canteen so after a boiled egg each they sat drinking tea in front of the sitting room fire.

That morning, Lottie had received another postcard from Rex. It was the third he'd sent, a picture of Warrington Town Hall with just a few words on the back saying he was now fully recovered and had found a job. He'd be starting work next week. She wanted to know more. What sort of job, and where? Rex had been on her mind all day. She told Cliff about the friends she'd made in the army. Chatted at length about Emily and June, and of course Rex, though she didn't tell him how much he'd meant to her.

'You never talk about what happened to you, Cliff. You were pleased to be assigned to an armoured unit, weren't you?'

He smiled. 'I was at the time. I thought it would be better than the infantry. A ride and some cover instead of slogging it out on foot.'

'It wasn't?'

'It was hell. Five men squashed inside a tiny metal box, being flung about whenever the tank was on the move. It rocked wildly over rough ground. In battle we spent all day in it and sometimes all night as well. No space to lie down. We had to eat biscuits, hard tack like dog biscuits. We used to spread them with marmalade.'

'We had those too. Didn't like them.'

'We often had good rations with us that we couldn't cook because we couldn't get out of the tank. Not for anything.'

'Not anything?'

He laughed. 'If we got out to take a leak we could be killed by a sniper. Often the men peed over the side of the turret. Sometimes even that seemed dangerous, so then they'd use their metal hats and just tip it over. Conditions weren't great inside. When the guns were in action the noise and vibration were unbelievable. Then there was the continual splatter of sound through the earphones, and the smell of cordite, and the fumes from the gun and the dust that got churned up. Often I couldn't see what was happening, and everybody was relying on me to keep the tank on course. My orders were to stay with the other tanks and with the infantry who were protecting us. I had to stand in the turret with my head out to see anything. But at least I had the best chance of getting out if we caught fire. And tanks caught fire very easily, sometimes at the first hit. Those down in the driving compartment would only have seconds to escape because of the live ammunition we had on board, not to mention all the fuel. You could guarantee a tank would blow up in seconds once it caught fire. I tell you, Lottie, in my five weeks I saw plenty of tank crews roasted alive. And I saw plenty more of those who did manage to get out before it belched flames gunned down by the enemy before they could reach cover.'

'How dreadful!'

'I was terrified. I think we all were but we tried not to show it. I count myself very lucky that all five of us lived to tell the tale. When I think back and go over the odds, it seems a miracle.'

Lottie shivered. She understood now what Cliff had been through. She felt closer to him than ever.

'We treated patients with terrible burns in our hospital. They were often tank crew.'

'Lucky to get out alive.'

'None of them spelt out the odds quite like you have, but I heard enough. I was frightened for you.'

Cliff piled more coal on the fire. 'I managed to get another hundredweight yesterday.' The light from the flames flickered across his serious face. 'I couldn't tell Father just how bad it was. He was worried enough.'

'You have to protect his feelings?'

'We all try to protect those we care about, don't we?'

'Father might prefer to know how things really were. I'm sure I would.'

'Would you?' His soft grey eyes were searching into hers.

Lottie had an uneasy feeling that he'd kept something back to protect her. 'What didn't you tell me?'

'Nothing . . .'

In the emotionally charged atmosphere, she felt very close to her younger brother. 'There is. I can feel it, sense it. There's something you haven't told me.'

He shrugged and looked away. 'It all happened a long time ago.'

'I want to know.' The silence hung between them. 'Come on, I don't like secrets. Mam tried to keep too many.'

He gave a wry laugh. 'After all this time, funny you should bring up Mam.'

'It's about her?'

391

'No, it's about Dadda. About the reason . . .' He faltered and his grey eyes fastened on her again.

'The reason for all Mam's secrets? She didn't want Dadda to know she had a lover? Well, I mean, how would he feel?'

'That's how she explained it to me at first. It took me a while to understand that it was you, Lottie, who were the real reason. Dadda knew what was going on. He could hardly not know. Mam had three babies one after the other while he hardly had the breath to speak. He couldn't possibly . . .'

Lottie pushed her hair back from her face. 'You mean Dadda knew about Father? That Mam spent so much time with him? That he was more her husband than Dadda?'

'I'm sure Mam tried to keep it from him. All the lies about her job were set up with that in mind. Dadda found out later, when we arrived.'

'You're saying he accepted it? I can't believe . . .'

'Did he have much choice? For him it wasn't all bad, Lottie. Having us children there gave him a life that seemed normal. And what else was there for him? He couldn't work, couldn't manage on his own. It would have meant staying in an institution or a hospital all the time.'

'But all those secrets . . . I suppose they became a front for the neighbours? And they saved Dadda's face.'

'He didn't want you to know the truth. You thought he was your father and he wanted you to go on believing that. You were his favourite. I heard him and Mam talking one night. He was pleading with her to let things stay as they were. "Don't take Lottie from me," he said. "I don't want to risk losing her."'

Lottie's eyes were damp. 'He said that?'

'You were always taking him out in his wheelchair. Playing

chess with him. He was afraid that if you knew he wasn't your father, it would upset everything. That you wouldn't spend the time with him.'

'Poor Dadda!' Lottie dabbed at her eyes. 'As if that would have made any difference by then. What I felt for him was built up over years and years. I loved Dadda.'

'I know.'

'Such secrets, Cliff. Secrets within secrets. And the whole point of them . . .' In the end, the whole point had been to stop her knowing that Dadda wasn't her biological father.

Chapter Twenty-two

Lottie had written to Rex saying that now she was back home, she'd be sending only a card at Christmas and the occasional postcard, and she wanted him to do the same. Since then she'd had several postcards from him. Each had just a few lines of news, scrawled where all could read it. She knew now that she had more in common with Rex than with Waldo.

His cards tore her in two. Each one kept him to the forefront of her mind for days, made her think how different life would be with him. To have news of him gave her a lift, but it also made her more dissatisfied with Waldo. She couldn't make up her mind what to do.

From time to time, she received letters from June and Emily. They too were finding it difficult to settle down to life in Civvy Street. June wrote from Newcastle that she missed the companionship of the army, and life at home seemed flat and dull. And that she was so fed up she was looking for a job somewhere else. She wanted something more exciting. She wrote: 'It'll be different for you, Lottie. I'm sure you're finding it much easier. After all, you can be with your husband now.'

Emily wrote too from Warrington, about feeling the same restlessness, and then went on:

Guess what? Rex has started work at the same hospital.

He had a job somewhere else for a few months, but like the rest of us, he's finding it hard to settle down. He often comes to sit with me in the dining room, just like he did in the old days. He's even taken me out once or twice to the pictures and to a pub. Not that he shows much interest in me. He talks about you the whole time. He wants to know if you're happy.

I told him you were. I know that's what you'd want me to say. Anyway, you're bound to be now you're with Waldo. It was all you ever wanted. You were looking forward to that from the day we met. Rex wants me to pass on his best wishes.

Lottie felt the tears start to her eyes as she read that. What had she done? She'd leapt at the chance to marry Waldo; couldn't wait for it. But what she'd felt for him was infatuation, not love, and it hadn't lasted. By the time she'd met Rex it was too late.

She put Emily's letter carefully away in a drawer. She didn't want Waldo to come across it and read it. She was afraid he might be the sort who would read other people's letters, and he wouldn't understand about Rex.

One morning, early in the summer of 1946, Lottie slid behind her desk in the office she shared with her father. She was getting out the books she'd been working on the day before when her father came in. He'd walked up from Brightland Street.

'How's Waldo?' he asked, as he opened his own desk.

Lottie was non-committal. 'All right.'

She could see Father was turning something over in his

mind. His face was serious. 'I've been hearing things about him.'

'What sort of things?' She knew what was coming. It was never far from her thoughts.

'That he's dabbling on the black market. No, not dabbling, that's the wrong word. I heard he's in it in a big way.'

Lottie felt her heart jerk into overdrive. 'It frightens me.'

Her father's startled eyes turned on her for a moment. 'Why didn't you tell me? You've known for a long time, haven't you?'

She nodded.

'Get him to stop, Lottie, before it's too late.'

She straightened her lips. 'Don't think I haven't tried. I've done my best.'

'I hear he's got a finger in everything. That he's a tough operator and isn't liked.'

'Who told you that?'

'Geoffrey Montague did yesterday when I went over, but I've heard rumours before. I think Iris was buying stuff from him years ago.'

'Oh my goodness! Iris?'

'It would only take a tip-off and Waldo could be in big trouble: a huge fine, prison even, and confiscation of his assets. The law would come down on him like a landslide. You've got to get him to stop.'

'Nothing I say is likely to do that.'

'It's like that?'

She nodded. Her dread turned to anger. 'I hate him being mixed up in all this. I loathe him saying he does it for me. It's not what I want at all. How can I cope when any minute he could be in trouble?'

'Isn't he worried?'

'He's as nervous as I am.' Lottie blew her nose. 'I don't want him to get caught.'

Her father said nothing.

Lottie implored. 'What can I do?'

Her father was shaking his head. 'You must get him to stop. That's the only thing. If he loves you, he'll stop. Let him know that's what you want.'

Did he still love her? She wasn't sure. She choked out: 'He promises to stop, but he doesn't.'

'You're his wife. You must have some influence. More than anyone else.'

'What I say and what I want . . . has no effect. He takes no notice. It's like banging my head against a brick wall. Yet I can't just wait for the axe to fall. I feel I've got to do something.'

'If he won't stop, then there's nothing more you can do.' Her father's gentle eyes were on her face, full of sympathy. 'You aren't happy with him?'

'How can I be?' she wailed. 'With this hanging over me?'

In the late summer, Connie's second child was born, an eight-pound baby girl she called Marion. Lottie held the baby in her arms and felt the tug of love. Yes, she would like a daughter too, but she wasn't going to jump into motherhood. She'd jumped too quickly into marriage and now she was very wary.

Connie seemed much more her old self. Clovis had been working in the bakery at Old Swan for the last few months. Last week, he'd moved to the Birkenhead bakery and was working with his father.

Lottie and her own father discussed his progress quite often.

He said Clovis had taken to making bread with all the passion of a Frenchman and seemed to be enjoying it.

Connie said Clovis was much happier, a different person. Lottie thought so too. At first he'd seemed rather a dour personality, but working with him every day she'd got to know him well and found he had a good sense of humour.

'Another year before Geoffrey Montague retires,' Father said with satisfaction. 'I was dreading it, but by then Clovis should be ready to take over. He'll be able to run the Birkenhead bakery. Connie will be all right with him. He's a nice lad.'

Lottie noticed he said no such thing about Waldo.

That winter the temperature dropped. There was a big freeze-up that went on for months. There were power cuts; homes were without heat and light. Coal was almost unobtainable, and there was talk of rationing it. Connie, like everybody else, could get only enough fuel to light a fire in the evenings and meanwhile the temperatures stayed below freezing.

She hated to be bundled up in layers of clothing but had to do it. She got into the habit of going to the Birkenhead factory or occasionally over to Old Swan for a canteen lunch and some adult company. It got her out of her cold attic and into the gorgeous heat of the bread factory. There, they couldn't allow the temperature to drop because it would destroy the yeast and the bread wouldn't rise. They had a special allocation of fuel as well as back-up heating.

She always took Jimmy with her, but her mother-in-law did her best to persuade her to leave the new baby at home with her where she could stay warmly tucked up in her cot.

If Clovis and her father-in-law were busy and not ready to

have lunch when she arrived, she'd stay in the office, give Jimmy a toy and try to read the newspaper until they were. The papers were full of pictures of snow drifts and stories about the RAF dropping food, fuel and animal fodder to isolated communities in Scotland and Wales.

Stories, too, about the black market, which was said to be growing. Connie had heard Clovis and his father talk about the rumours they were hearing about Waldo. They'd decided they must be true. The only possible source of the money and the luxuries Waldo had must be the black market. Lottie didn't want to talk about Waldo or his business and they were all careful not to say anything in front of her because they didn't want to upset her.

One very cold day, when the temperature remained below freezing, Steve came over to the Birkenhead bakery, saying, 'I like to get out and leave Cliff and Lottie to get on with things. I think they like it too.'

That morning, they'd all heard on the news about the clampdown on black marketeers. Connie had just been reading of a nationwide sweep. Shops and restaurants were to be raided. Road blocks were to be set up to stop and search lorries and vans for illicit goods.

At lunch, the talk was about the danger of this clampdown to Waldo. Connie was shocked to find they all knew more about Waldo's black market activities than she did. Worse still, she was finding out over the lunch table that Lottie had confided in Father about being deeply unhappy, yet had said nothing at all to her. She saw Lottie often. They talked of Connie's concerns, clothes and babies, but never of Waldo.

Connie sat very still, unable to swallow the food in her

mouth though she'd been hungry ten minutes before. From the first, she'd suspected that Waldo wasn't honest. She could have saved Lottie all this if she'd told her what she feared on the night she'd brought them together.

She kept her head down, busying herself with Jimmy's eating, afraid her guilt was there imprinted on her face for them all to see. Father would blame her; she blamed herself. Lottie had done all she could to help her and what had she done for Lottie? She'd ruined her life.

She couldn't admit to Clovis and Father that all those years ago she'd continued to keep company with Waldo because she wanted somebody to take her out and about. She'd always hung on to her boyfriends like that, long after she'd decided her future would not be with them. She'd wanted Lottie to know she could attract a good-looking man without her help. Wasn't that why she'd introduced them?

Connie couldn't bring herself to say anything now. She wasn't ready to take responsibility for what she'd done to her sister. But she couldn't sleep that night. She seemed to be dragging a dreadful burden round with her. Now it was pointed out, she knew Lottie was living under a strain. She hadn't looked on top form for some time. Connie felt she'd have to say something to her. Apologise.

One Saturday afternoon, when she happened to be alone because Clovis was still at the bakery, Lottie called in to see her. Jimmy was falling asleep in her arms; she'd been about to put him down for his afternoon nap. Lottie stood watching her from the landing. Connie made up her mind as she tiptoed out of the bedroom that she'd get it off her chest now.

'I should have told you about Waldo,' she said in a little rush. 'I'm sorry.'

'Told me what?' She saw the colour drain from Lottie's face. 'What's he done now?'

'Nothing. I don't mean now.' She put a hand on her sister's arm and led her into the sitting room. 'That night, when I introduced you, I knew what Waldo was like. I should have said.'

'Said what?'

'I'd guessed he wasn't honest. I should have told you. It's been on my conscience.'

Lottie smiled sadly. 'It wouldn't have made any difference if you had. I'd have taken no notice. Haven't you heard? Love is blind. I couldn't see any fault with Waldo. Not then.'

Connie felt the blood rush to her cheeks. Lottie didn't blame her! Lottie wasn't the sort to blame anyone but herself when things went wrong. She felt a rush of relief. She could be at peace with herself and at ease with Lottie again.

The freezing weather continued, and by February 1947 Britain was in chaos. Beer production was cut by half because of the shortage of grain. Bread and meat rations were cut again.

Christian Dior's New Look was shown in Paris and his glamorous clothes caused a sensation. The government condemned them as irresponsibly frivolous, and women were asked to avoid them in the national interest.

Instead they took to the New Look in their millions. The new fashion delighted Connie. Clovis had given her a sewing machine of her own for Christmas. Still not a new one; it was a pre-war Singer but still in good working order.

She bought paper patterns of the New Look, and used her clothing coupons to buy material. She revamped her wardrobe yet again, lengthening other dresses with bands of coordinating material, and her winter coat with bands of fur cut from a stole her mother-in-law gave her. She bought a pair of the latest sling-back shoes. Nobody looked smarter than Connie.

She'd taken in her stride the care of a second baby, and even found time to sew little dresses and romper suits for her children. Both were always beautifully turned out.

When the weather improved and summer finally came, Connie and Clovis took their babies to the open air swimming baths at Hoylake. Sometimes they asked Lottie to go with them. Connie made herself one of the latest swimsuits designed to cling to the body with shirr elastic. Lottie admired it so much, Connie made one for her too. Their old pre-war ones were of wool and inclined to sag when wet.

'No decent bathing caps to be had, though,' Lottie said. 'These plastic ones aren't a patch on the old rubber ones we had before the war.'

'Just don't keep your hair dry,' Connie agreed. She had much more hair than Lottie and so suffered more.

One evening, when Waldo told her he wouldn't be home until late, Lottie walked round to the Montague house after work. She found both Connie and Clovis cock-a-hoop; they'd decided they could afford to buy their own house and it was time to set about it.

'It's thanks to you, Lottie,' Clovis said. 'I'm glad you persuaded Connie that the bakery would be a good place for me. I'm doing all right there, and I love it.'

'Not a child in sight,' Connie laughed.

'Not everyone likes spending all day with them. Especially when they're outnumbered thirty to one.'

Estate agents were opening up again for business and

Connie went round all the local ones in the following weeks. Lottie studied the sheaf of particulars she collected, and went with her to look at several of the houses.

Connie took every newspaper that advertised houses for sale. Lottie thought she was going to be as hard to please as she'd been when choosing a husband. But she and Clovis eventually settled on a semi-detached that was still being built.

'It'll be all new and smart,' Connie enthused. 'We're going to have a special grate fitted in the sitting room that gives background heating and there'll be a garden for the kids. Clovis wants to put it all down to vegetables, he says everybody does in France, but I'm insisting on a little lawn with flower beds round it and roses climbing over the fence. It's got three bedrooms. Lovely.'

Lottie heard again from June. She'd applied for a job as a nurse on the passenger liners that were sailing once again from Liverpool to South Africa.

The following month Lottie had another letter saying that she'd got the job and would be setting out on her first trip at the end of July. June wrote: 'I'm coming to Liverpool to join the ship the day before it sails. How about meeting up for a yack about old times? I'm writing to ask Emily to come too. Warrington isn't that far from Liverpool.'

Lottie wrote back by return to say she'd love to see her again.

The time they'd spent together had been fulfilling. They'd all known what they had to do and they'd got on with it. Everything had been clear-cut and straightforward then. And they'd all believed everything would be wonderful once the war was won.

As the day drew nearer, Lottie grew quite excited. She sent a postcard with a view of the Liver Building to Rex to tell him she was meeting up with June and Emily. She bought herself a New Look summer dress in blue cotton. With its long full skirts and tight bodice, it suited her slight figure. She had her hair trimmed specially too.

'See you at the Adelphi,' June wrote. 'It's the only place Emily and I know in Liverpool.'

She couldn't keep such news to herself. She told Waldo she was meeting her old friends.

He frowned. 'It's time you were putting all that behind you. It's no good clinging on to your past. You should never have gone away once we were married. That's what's spoiled things for us. I grew one way and you grew another. We'd have grown together if you'd stayed with me. As a married woman you could have worked something to let you stay at home. I mean, what's the point of being married if you can't be together?'

She choked out: 'I thought getting married was the right thing to do. That it would guarantee we'd be together when I came back.'

'Well, it's done that. You'll find you don't have so much in common with your old friends now. Perhaps it'll make you realise all that's over and done with. Your life's here with me now.'

Lottie was torn in two. She half hoped he was right, but it didn't stop her thinking about Rex and she was looking forward very much to seeing Emily and June.

She didn't go to work that morning. Father told her to take the day off. It was noon when she went over to Liverpool on the underground and crossed the road from Central Station to the Adelphi.

It was a very grand place to meet. Waldo had been impressed that her friends had suggested it. A doorman in full livery swung the door open for her. Just inside, she stopped to look round and the next moment Emily was rushing towards her with arms outstretched and a wide smile on her face.

Emily hadn't changed. Her long blonde hair bounced as she swung her into a bear hug, and only then did Lottie see that Rex was behind her. She let out a shriek of joy and the next moment she felt his arms go round her. Like Emily he kissed her cheek.

She was thrilled. She had hoped against hope for this but hadn't dared suggest it. She was afraid of the strength of her feelings. Afraid of what another meeting could release, both for her and for Rex.

'It's lovely to see you both! Wonderful!' She couldn't take her eyes off him. 'I half hoped you'd come.' That was a porkie – she'd longed for it. Thought of nothing else for the past week.

He couldn't stop smiling. 'I wrote and told June that if she was organising a reunion I wanted to come too.'

'You look so well!'

Lottie couldn't get over that. He had a healthy colour in his cheeks. She looked closely for scars on his face, but they were difficult to see. He knew what she was looking for.

'All faded from my face,' he grinned.

'I keep telling him he's handsome,' Emily laughed.

'Still got a few scars but only in places I keep covered.'

'The scars on his shoulders and chest aren't too bad – better than I expected,' Emily said. 'I made him take me to the beach at Southport.'

Lottie turned to Emily. 'Are you two getting together then?'

'Sort of. We talk about you all the time.'

'She's helping me get over you.' Rex was laughing too. 'It's therapy. Emily reckons I need it.'

June arrived, and soon started to tell them about her new job. They all had new lives. Lottie told them about the bakery, and how different the work was.

'Don't you miss hospital life?'

'Yes, and I miss you lot.'

They asked her about Waldo and she glossed things over, telling them nothing of her disappointment and misery.

They talked non-stop through lunch and several cups of coffee. At four-thirty June stood up.

'I'll have to go. I'm supposed to be on board before five.'

Rex went out to see about a taxi because she had suitcases. He'd kept his distance, but out on the pavement he drew Lottie aside and asked: 'You are happy? You didn't have much to say about married life.' He looked serious. 'I have to know.'

'Yes,' she said. She was afraid that if she told him the truth she'd reawaken his hopes and that wasn't fair. Not until she'd worked out what she was going to do. Seeing him again was helping her to make up her mind. At least she knew now what she wanted to do.

They all piled in the taxi and went down to Princes Dock to see June aboard the *Durban Castle*.

'It's a beautiful ship,' Emily sighed. 'You're making us envious. I wish I was coming with you.'

When June had climbed up the gangway, she turned to wave from the deck before disappearing from view. Emily and Rex walked Lottie to the landing stage to where she could catch the ferry back to Birkenhead.

A boat was on the point of leaving. Lottie gave each a quick hug before hurrying on board. She was the last to do so before the gangway rattled up. She turned at the rail to wave.

Rex smiled back at her, his eyes playing with hers as the oily waters of the Mersey widened between them. When the ferry was a hundred yards out in the river, they gave one last wave and turned away.

It was low tide and their way back to the pierhead was very steep. Lottie watched in silent agony as Rex took Emily's arm. She wondered about their relationship. Was it as Emily had said?

She wished she could see as much of Rex as her friend did, but the only way would be to get a job in the same hospital. That was out of the question now she was working in the bread factory. And there was the insurmountable problem of Waldo.

He'd been wrong about her feeling out of touch with her wartime friends. They'd really enjoyed each other's company, and she knew it wouldn't reconcile her to life with Waldo. Quite the reverse. It would make her even more dissatisfied. She knew now it had been a bad mistake to marry him.

She was more like her mother than she'd realised. Married to one man and thinking she'd rather be with another.

Chapter Twenty-three

Winter had come round again and the afternoons were drawing in. Lottie had been working for her father for over eighteen months and felt she'd mastered her job. She and Cliff worked well together, and were taking more responsibility for running the factory. She liked being at the hub of the bakery and felt at ease there.

At five o'clock, she went home. The bus journey was slow, and Waldo was on her mind. They'd had another row this morning over breakfast. She felt that being married to Waldo put her in a cleft stick. She either had to fall in with his wishes or fight. And if she fought, things between them became more strained when she wanted them to get better. It seemed impossible to keep the peace. She was coming round to the view that they couldn't live happily together.

There were times when she wanted to drum her fists on the table in frustration. Waldo kept telling her all she needed to do was settle down, but he was making that impossible. They needed to talk without losing their tempers and she couldn't get him to do that. They needed to discuss how they could improve things between them, because they couldn't go on like this.

It made Lottie feel sick to think of divorce. It brought feelings of guilt and failure, but she was beginning to see no other way out. She didn't want to spend the rest of her life with a man who thought so little of being underhand about everything. He thought it clever to cheat, to take more than his share of rationed foods, to make money from dealing in them.

She'd wished a thousand times that she hadn't married him in such a rush. And even harder to accept was that she was sure Waldo regretted it too. He thought her ridiculously straight in her dealings.

'Unnecessarily straight,' he called it. She had to face that she couldn't change him and she didn't want to lower her standards to be more like him. It was impasse.

She was afraid the time for adjustment had gone. It was too late. If they tried to talk it became an angry argument. In the end, Waldo would lose his temper and rush off somewhere else, leaving her struggling with tears and not always avoiding them.

They were both in emotional overdrive. She had worked herself up to such a pitch that she couldn't relax at work. It only took an impatient word from anybody to send her slithering out of control. She was a bag of nerves.

Father had put an arm round her shoulders the other day in the office. To call him Father slid easily off her tongue now she knew he cared about her. He'd always done his best for them; was still doing it. Lottie was surprised to find herself clinging to him for support. She'd always thought herself strong and had prided herself on being able to cope alone. But not any longer.

Lottie knew every nook and cranny of her house, and because of her suspicions about what Waldo was doing she'd made a point of finding out exactly what was in every cupboard and drawer.

The Oriental carved chest in the hall intrigued her. Nothing else in the house was locked, but the first time she'd tried to lift the lid she'd found that was.

Then, a week or two later, when she'd been trying to close a drawer in the sideboard that was overfull of table linen, Waldo had taken out a couple of tablecloths and pushed them into the chest in the hall.

'I thought you kept that locked,' she said.

'No,' he smiled. 'Never bother to lock anything up here.'

The next day, when she was alone, Lottie examined the contents of the chest carefully. The tablecloths were there, with a pair of new blankets and some spare sheets. All seemed very ordinary. She'd lowered the lid and thought about it. Clearly, something had been hidden there, but no longer was.

That was ages ago, and now as she let herself into the house she could see a corner of white damask showing against the dark wood. She went to lift the lid to push it inside out of sight, only to find it had been locked again. That shocked her. There could be only one reason: Waldo had hidden something inside that he didn't want her to see.

She was in the kitchen, lighting the gas under pans and fighting down her anger, when she heard a car door slam. From the window she saw Waldo's car parked on the drive. A moment later he let himself in through the back door and put a package down on the kitchen table.

'Steak and kidney,' he said. 'Get Mrs Gully to make us a pie for tomorrow. One of my favourites.'

Lottie unwrapped it. 'There's a whole pound of steak here,' she protested. 'That's more than a week's ration for us.'

'We've got to eat.' Waldo was stony-faced. He was fond of meat and it would take more than rationing to

411

curb his tastes. Lottie bought their rations from the local shops every Saturday afternoon but Waldo always augmented them. She hardly liked to eat her share of the goodies he brought.

She put the meat away in the fridge. Grim-faced, she said: 'You're early tonight.'

'I thought we could go to the pictures. Would you like that?' His weary smile was that of a busy man who has to fit in the needs of a demanding wife. Lottie felt she had to accept any friendly advance. He rarely wanted to take her anywhere.

'I'd like to. *The Jolson Story*'s on. Connie says it's good.'

He went through to the hall and tossed his trilby on top of the ornately carved chest.

'Waldo, what's in that box?'

She watched him slip his keys into his overcoat pocket and spin round to stare at her. He didn't like the question, she could see that.

'You know. Extra blankets and that. A handsome piece of furniture, isn't it? Comes from the Far East, I believe. Looks good there.' He hung his coat on the hall stand.

'There's a corner of tablecloth showing. You've trapped it under the lid. Why have you locked it?'

'Locked?' He made a show of trying to lift the lid. He was a good actor.

'You know it is.'

'I don't remember locking it. Perhaps the catch has fallen down and caught.'

She knew Waldo well enough now not to believe him. His tone sounded too relaxed to be true.

'Don't you want to get cracking with the dinner so we can go out?'

Lottie had already started to cook. 'Where do you keep the key?'

'I don't think there is one. I might have to force it open when we want to use the stuff.' He went towards the stairs. 'I could do with a quick bath before we go out.'

She waited until she heard him start the water running in the bathroom, and then she slid her hand into his coat pocket to look at his keys. He kept them all on a big ring: his car keys and those of the van, this house and no doubt his garage and store. She could see a brass key on the ring with fancy etching round the top of it. Surely it matched the etching round the keyhole of the chest?

She slid it into the lock and it turned with well oiled smoothness. She gasped to find Waldo was such an out and out liar. Why had she ever trusted what he said? The box was lined with sandalwood, and she sniffed at its lovely scent. Nothing seemed to have changed. She folded the edge of tablecloth back into place. The blankets didn't seem to have been touched, but he must have put something in. Something he didn't want her to see. Waldo would have a reason for locking it, she was sure of that.

She stroked a fluffy new blanket. Then lifted it to see what was underneath. It sent her jerking back in horror.

There were guns, four of them, revolvers! The dark steel glinted wickedly. There were a couple of boxes of ammunition too and a shoulder holster. What could Waldo want with them? Lottie had had more than enough of war and of guns, and was angry to have found him out so easily in a lie.

She propped the lid of the chest open and went back to the kitchen to get on with cooking the meal.

* * *

Waldo had had a busy day. He hadn't been sleeping well since Lottie had come home, and he was tired. But he'd be able to rest in the cinema for a few hours and that would seem like normal life to them both.

He felt better after his bath, refreshed. As he crossed the upstairs landing he could smell his dinner cooking; he was ready for it, and came running downstairs. When he saw the lid of the chest standing open with the blanket moved over to display his guns, he had to grab hold of the banisters and fight for his breath. He felt as though he'd been kicked in the belly. He knew he shouldn't have brought the guns home, but neither the garage nor the warehouse seemed safe any more.

Lottie came to the kitchen door, every fibre of her body arched against him.

'I've opened it,' she said. 'Can't see why you found it impossible.'

'Did you find the key?'

He knew it was a stupid thing to say. She must have taken it from his coat pocket. What a fool he'd been to leave his key ring there. He should have kept it in his jacket.

'What do you want with guns? What are you going to use them for? The war's over.'

It cut him to the quick to see her looking at him with such contempt. It sent normal life away over the horizon. He felt a surge of anger. She was always on at him, like a terrier worrying at a bone. She was spying on him. The love he'd felt for her was gone. He didn't like her. He was scared of her now, scared of what she was going to do.

He did his best. 'Of course the war's over. These are souvenirs of it. Everybody wants souvenirs.'

He knew it was hopeless, he could never convince her they

were harmless toys, but he couldn't help trying. It was almost second nature to him.

'The first thing every soldier wants to bring home with him is a German helmet. The second is a Mauser pistol.'

Then they became hard strapped for cash and were willing to sell them. He knew every crook in the district, many from further afield. He was able to buy guns cheaply and sell them on to gangsters. It had proved a very lucrative sideline.

'Don't tell more lies, Waldo.'

'Not lies. They polish them up and set them up on their mantelpieces. Then they can spin a good story to their friends about how they overcame a German soldier with their bare hands and disarmed him. It makes them war heroes. Not everybody's like you, wanting to push what they did in the war behind them.'

'What's the story on the ammunition? Tell me that one too.' She was egging him on, he knew.

'Had to buy it as a job lot. Nobody wants to be left with ammunition if they're selling their gun.'

'You didn't get any German helmets?'

His patience snapped. 'Oh, give over, Lottie.'

'Now you listen to me. I won't give over on this. I've turned a blind eye to things in this house that I shouldn't have. I'm not turning a blind eye to guns. I've seen the damage they do. Too much of it. In the paper this evening. It came through the door not half an hour ago.' She was opening the pages of the *Echo*, folding it to the right place and shoving it into his face. 'Read that.'

He did so, slowly, playing for time. The previous night there'd been a robbery in a cinema in Liverpool. The cashier had been shot and was in hospital fighting for his life. The gang had got away with the evening's takings.

He was shocked. 'I wouldn't use them for anything like that.'

'I'm appalled,' Lottie stormed at him, the flush running up her neck and into her cheeks. 'You're selling them to gangsters to rob banks and things, aren't you?'

It horrified him that she was on to what he did with them. It left him blustering, unable to find words.

'This gang, were they customers of yours?'

'How should I know? Don't be silly.'

'They could be for all you care.'

'Doesn't say they used Mausers.'

'No, but I want these out of this house. I'll not have them where I'm living.'

'All right, calm down. If they frighten you—'

'They do. Most of what you do frightens me. You say you're a businessman. Surely you've got enough legitimate business for us to live on?'

'Yes, of course. I'll stop if that's what you want.'

'You know it is. How many times do I have to tell you? I don't want you selling guns to gangsters, and I don't want you to get caught. How do you manage to sleep at night?'

'With difficulty sometimes.'

'Turn over a new leaf then. We don't have to live like lords. I'd be much happier if you went straight. So would you, I'm sure. Get rid of those guns.'

'If that's what you want, that's what I'll do.' He wanted to placate her. He wanted to be back on the old terms with her. He wanted to feel her arms round him, to see her eyes shine with love. 'Tomorrow, I'll—'

'Tonight,' she insisted, her tawny eyes glistening with

urgency. 'I'd rather you did that than took me to the pictures. We can do that any time.'

He slammed down the lid of the chest. 'Let's eat first then.'

He thought she was going to send him out without his dinner. But she turned back to the kitchen and started dishing up.

'Stop doing all these things, Waldo. It's against the law.'

'All right. I promise.'

'You've promised before. You don't keep your promises.'

The atmosphere was cold and strained. Neither of them ate much. Lottie looked white with determination now.

'You could hand them in to the police.'

'No!' That was the last thing he was going to do. He didn't want a lot of questions from the police. They'd be sure to ask how he'd come by them.

'How are you going to get rid of them then?' She looked grim.

'I'll go over on the ferry and drop them overboard. They'll be no use to anybody when they've been in the Mersey. That's the best way.'

When the meal was finished, he put the guns into a shopping bag. They rattled when he moved it. He was putting on his coat when Lottie said: 'You'd be better wrapping them up in something. People will remember if they rattle like that as you walk. And you'd have to throw them over one by one. One bundle would make one splash. Even if that attracted attention there would be nothing more to be seen.'

He snatched at a kitchen towel.

'Not that. Something dark. You don't want to advertise that you're pitching something into the tide.'

He found an old navy blue pullover and knotted the guns

and ammunition into that. Lottie would be a great help to him if only she were on his side.

'I want to be proud of you, Waldo,' she said. 'Not ashamed, all screwed up inside because of what you do.'

He caught at her arm. 'I am proud of you. It was heroic to join the army when you didn't have to. You did your bit for old England.'

He went out to his car, musing that for one of them to have done so was quite sufficient. He'd looked after his own interests and hers in the meantime.

It was a cold, starlit night. He put the guns on the floor in the passenger well beside him and told himself there was always another way to make money. But to throw them in the river? What a waste that would be!

He drove instead to his garage. It was all locked up at this time of night. He'd have to hide them here or in the warehouse. What Lottie didn't know needn't worry her.

He couldn't stop now. It wouldn't be possible to carry on like this for ever but right now things were scarcer than they'd ever been. There was more austerity. All through the war, he'd done everything he could think of to feather his own nest, dealt in anything in short supply on which he could make a few pounds. Now he was making a fortune. He'd never want in the days ahead and neither would Lottie. All right, arms trafficking with criminals wasn't nice, but you'd think she'd show some gratitude. He was doing it for her too.

He let himself into his office and looked round. Where? The guns were too bulky to fit beneath the drawers in his old dressing table of a desk. The only other possibility was under the loose floorboard. He'd noticed it was starting to creak when people stood on it, drawing attention downwards.

The best thing would be to get rid of them right away. Sell them straight on. He hadn't meant to keep them, anyway; he just hadn't had time to do anything about them.

He had contacts. He lifted his phone. He'd sold one, a month or so back, to a bum called Stanley Crisp who'd said he'd take more when they were available. Waldo didn't like Stanley, didn't trust him either. There was a wild streak in him and he never wanted to pay the market price for anything. Others had paid more for his guns, but they didn't want more. If Stanley would take these four off his hands now, he'd be glad to see the back of them.

Waldo knew nothing about guns. Once, as a teenager, he'd fired an air rifle on a fairground stall, just to see what it felt like. He thought he'd have no trouble winning one of the soft toys. He'd fancied a fluffy yellow duck. He tried three times but failed hopelessly. Guns were not his thing. He'd have made a rotten soldier.

Stanley would be doing the rounds of the pubs at this time of night. Waldo tried the Lighterman's Arms, but though Stanley had been in he wasn't there now. He caught up with him at the Queen's Head.

'I've got more of the same,' he told him. One couldn't be too careful about what one said on the phone. There was no way of knowing if the operator was listening in.

'How many more?' Stanley grunted.

'Four.' Waldo could feel his interest. He'd been selling stuff on for so long he'd learned to judge that.

'Mind you, the ticket will have to be right if I take them all,' Stanley said. 'And I want to see them first.'

'Of course. I'll come down now and show you. I'll park

round the corner in that first side street. Be there in twenty minutes.'

He could see the slim dark shadow waiting as he pulled into the side street and parked well away from the street lamp.

He'd told Stanley his name was Ricky Moon. He liked to give his clients a name they'd remember easily and one which bore no relation to his own. He always drove his battered van. He didn't want Crisp to know anything about him. Certainly not about his garage or warehouse or where he lived. It was all part of the security that Waldo felt was essential.

Stanley got into the passenger seat and used his pencil torch to look at the goods. He opened each one up and played with the firing mechanism. He knew what he was looking for and seemed to think he'd found it.

'Where'd you get them?'

'Our returning ex-servicemen. Brought in as souvenirs on the quiet. Guaranteed not to be hot property.'

Waldo had recently sold him a similar Mauser for sixty-five pounds. 'Two hundred and fifty for the four and I'll throw in the ammunition for nothing.'

'There was ammunition with the last one.' Crisp sighed. 'It's like this. I'm a bit short of the ready at the moment.' It was what he always said. 'At that price I could only take two.'

Waldo wanted to get rid of them all. He wouldn't touch guns again. He hadn't liked hearing that Lottie was ashamed of him. He wanted her to think he was a decent fellow.

'Two hundred and twenty-five then.'

'You're flooding the market. Two hundred.'

'Two twenty-five's my last price.' He didn't want to give them away to this little runt.

Stanley was twirling one of the Mausers round on his finger.

He was at home with guns, knew how to use them. He shook his head and they argued on.

'I don't have a fortune at my fingertips. Depends on how much I can raise.'

He was always one to drive the price down as far as he could. He was as cunning as a cartload of monkeys but Waldo reckoned he'd pay his price if he had to.

'Tomorrow then?'

'If I can get the money.'

'See you in the car park of the Dog and Gun around four o'clock,' Waldo told him. 'You know the place? Out West Kirby way.'

At that time the pub would be closed and none of the main windows overlooked the car park, which was well shaded from the road by trees. Waldo had spirits to deliver to two pubs out in that direction.

He tied everything back into his pullover. He didn't go into the Queen's with Stanley though he longed for a pint. It wasn't a good idea to be seen drinking with his clients.

He drove back to his garage and put through some more phone calls, trying to find another buyer. Nobody else was biting so he put the guns under the loose floorboard. That would have to do until tomorrow.

He felt he'd earned a couple of beers and called in the Ferry Hotel on the way home. The girl behind the bar was a goodlooker and had a sparky way of capping his anecdotes. He spent an hour chatting her up, doing his best to pull her. She told him her name was Betty. When he was leaving, she said: 'See you again.'

Waldo thought he might do worse than pop in another night.

Lottie was in bed when he got home. As he put on the light

421

she turned away from him and curled up. She didn't even want to speak to him now.

Phyllis had been more fun than Lottie. Betty was too. What had he been thinking of, tying himself to her with so much haste?

At breakfast they were both tetchy. Waldo said a lot of hurtful things. Lottie set off for work and tried to push him to the back of her mind. Her worries about the guns had been going round in her head all night, and now, sitting on the bus on this grey cold morning, she made up her mind at last. She'd move out and go to live in Brightland Street. She had to get away from Waldo or she'd be a nervous wreck. She'd tell him tonight that she was going.

She felt raw and couldn't talk about it, not until she'd had it out with Waldo. Her father was working only two or three days a week now, and wasn't coming in today, so she had the office to herself. Cliff popped in several times and stopped to chat. It was never about anything important.

At lunch time she went down to the canteen as usual though she wasn't hungry. Her father was there. He liked to walk up to the canteen for his lunch even when he wasn't working; he said it stopped him feeling lonely. Lottie pulled out the chair next to his.

'You haven't forgotten about tomorrow?'

All morning she'd kept her mind on tomorrow. She'd arranged to take a day off to have lunch at the Adelphi again with June and Emily. She hoped Rex would be coming too. June had been home for a few days' leave and was rejoining her ship for another voyage.

'Haven't forgotten,' he said, cutting into a sausage. 'A working day for me.'

'I'm very grateful. Good of you to let me take a day off when I want it.'

'One of the perks of joining the family firm. Anyway, you work hard, Lottie. Enjoy yourself tomorrow.'

'I'm looking forward to it,' she smiled. 'Very much.' By then she'd have told Waldo. She was screwing up inside about doing that, but at least it would be over by tomorrow.

As soon as he reached his garage that morning, Waldo tried again to find another customer for his guns. He'd had enquiries; there was a good market for them. Several people showed interest but said they hadn't the cash at the moment.

He carried the guns round all day in his van, though he knew it was dangerous. He just had to hope he wouldn't be stopped and searched.

Stanley Crisp kept him waiting twenty minutes in the car park of the Dog and Gun. Waiting always made him nervous but he'd turned his van round and parked facing the exit so he could make a quick getaway if he had to.

It was a bitterly cold afternoon, and sitting in the stationary van was like sitting in an ice box. He got out and stamped about until he had some feeling in his feet again. Then he opened up the back of the van and took the bundle from the tool box where he'd hidden it. Untying his pullover, he spread the guns out in a row on top and put the ammunition and holster alongside.

Waldo was uneasy. He was a bit nervous of Stanley, and hanging about like this was making him worse. Stanley was reputed to be a dirty fighter, who could sometimes turn nasty.

On the spur of the moment, he loaded one gun and placed it carefully at the end of the row where it would be close to his hand when he opened the van doors. He closed them up again and stamped his feet some more. The winter afternoon was drawing in.

He heard the powerful car coming down the road and moments later Stanley drove round in a big circle and pulled up beside his van. This was it. Waldo watched him get out. He wasn't the sort anybody could trust. There was the look of a weasel about his thin face. He was small and slight and light on his feet. Waldo had seen him move with the speed of a panther. It made him feel slow and clumsy and filled him with shivery repugnance.

He opened the back of his van and asked: 'Have you brought the cash?'

'Could only raise two hundred. It's the best I could do. Come on, man, it's a fair price.' Stanley unzipped the Rexine bag he'd brought and showed him the money.

Waldo had half expected this. 'Two twenty-five is my last price. If you can't meet it, you'll have to take three for one seventy.'

'Look, Mr Moon. I got this two hundred from the bank in used notes, just as you want.' Crisp laid them out on the floor of the van. 'Count them,' he invited, keeping his eyes fixed on the cold steel of the guns. 'Come on, see reason. Two hundred's a good price. Let's do the deal.'

Waldo was jumpy now. Stanley was trying it on. But he felt certain the other had more money on him and would eventually give in and pay what he asked. If he got that, he'd be making a hundred per cent on this deal. He wasn't going to let this parasite get the better of him.

Stanley fingered the nearest gun.

Waldo felt himself twitch. 'You heard what I said. Two twenty-five.'

'Stop mucking about. Let's get it done and get out of here.'

Waldo stood wavering while weasel eyes stared back at him. He wanted to get rid of the guns. Had to. Perhaps after all . . . Better take what was offered?

'For God's sake! Come on, man.' Suddenly, Stanley yanked at the sweater and tried to scoop the guns into his bag. 'I'm having them anyway.'

Waldo boiled up with rage. He was just quick enough to grab for and retain the gun he'd loaded. His heart was racing but his mind was made up.

'You're not having any. Not unless you pay my price.'

He'd known Stanley was a twister, a spiv of the worst sort, but he hadn't expected this. Then he saw him trying to sweep the money he'd brought back into his bag too. That took his breath away.

'You little pimp! Don't try anything like that on me.' Waldo's left hand shot out to grab at the Rexine bag. Crisp's hold was stronger; Waldo felt it pull through his shaking fingers.

Stanley was laughing at him. 'I'm taking everything. You're just mucking me about.'

Waldo was trembling and in a frenzy. Better to have pitched them over the side of the ferry than to make a gift of them to Crisp. He wasn't going to be robbed and cheated like this. He raised the gun, took aim and pressed the trigger. The noise almost burst his eardrums, the unexpected recoil knocking him off balance.

He couldn't believe his eyes. Stanley was still pushing

money into his bag. He'd missed! He'd missed him at point blank range!

He saw the wild and ugly look in Stanley's eyes as he twisted the Mauser out of his grasp and turned it on him. Blistering terror closed in on him. He heard the shattering noise as the gun fired again. Everything was going black as he felt himself slide to the cold ground.

Chapter Twenty-four

On the bus going home, Lottie made up her mind to tell Waldo over dinner. They wouldn't be going to the pictures, not after she'd had her say. He wasn't going to like it. If he turned nasty, she'd pack a few clothes and leave. Go over to Brightland Street tonight. Though perhaps not. Connie and Clovis were going over for a meal. She couldn't face the whole family yet.

When she let herself into the house, the kitchen was warm and filled with savoury scents. She opened the oven and took out the enamel dish of steak and kidney that Mrs Gully had put in to casserole. The pastry was made and rolled out, waiting between two damp tea towels. Lottie was grateful now for all the preparations Mrs Gully made.

She lit the gas under the potatoes and covered the casserole with the pastry. It was easy to burn her fingers on the enamel dish, but there was no point in letting it cool. Waldo would be home early. He thought they were going out.

Once dinner was cooking, she went upstairs to find her suitcase. She'd expected Waldo to be home before now. She looked at her watch. Where was he? She tried a few sentences over in her mind. This wasn't going to be easy.

She was half packed when the scent of baking pastry made her run downstairs. The pie was done to a golden brown.

Where was Waldo? She turned out the oven; dinner was ready. She wasn't sure what to do about the sprouts. They'd taste too strong whatever she did to keep them hot.

It surprised her when the doorbell rang. She hadn't heard Waldo's car, and anyway he had a key. When she opened the door and saw a policeman on the step, her heart missed a beat.

'Mrs Padley?'

Her heart skipped again. 'Yes.'

Her first thought was that Waldo had been caught. She cringed with dread at what she imagined was coming.

'Can I come in? I'm afraid I have some bad news for you.'

She led him to the dining room. 'Have a seat.'

'You too.'

Lottie hovered, then pulled out the carver at the head of the table. Two places had been set for their dinner at the other end. She faced the policeman across a wide expanse of starched damask.

'Where is my husband? I expected him home before now.'

'I'm very sorry – I have to tell you he's been shot.'

'Shot?' Lottie clutched the arms of the chair so tightly that her fingernails went white. All the horror she'd felt when she'd seen the guns in the blanket chest rushed back at her.

'He's hurt badly?' She knew by the serious expression on the policeman's face that he must be.

'I'm afraid he was dead when the ambulance reached him. I'm sorry.'

She felt numb. 'Dead?'

'Yes, I'm afraid so.'

Shock was followed by a feeling of overwhelming guilt. They'd argued all last night and parted this morning on bad terms. She'd been on the point of telling him she was leaving him for good. She felt sick, tears of guilt blinding her.

'Can I put the kettle on?' The policeman was being kind. 'A cup of tea?'

He came back from the kitchen to look at her. She hadn't moved, she couldn't.

'Is there someone who can come to stay with you? A relative or a friend? Someone I can ask?'

'My sister,' she choked. 'No, she has small children.' Cliff was at Brightland Street, half across Liverpool, a long way away. 'My father – he has a car. He'll come.'

'Does he have a telephone? What's his number?'

Lottie couldn't remember. She tried but it wouldn't come. She didn't often ring Brightland Street. She gave his name and address and the policeman looked up the number in the book.

He made a cup of tea and set it in front of her. She sipped it then put the cup back on its saucer. 'I don't take sugar. Haven't since the war.'

'Sugar's good for you. You've had a shock.'

He was clearly very relieved when at last her father's car drew up on the drive. He went to let him in.

The next moment Father's arms went round her. 'A terrible shock for you, Lottie. Awful.'

'I'll go now, sir.' The policeman reached across the table for his helmet.

'But what's happened?' her father wanted to know. 'Who has shot Waldo Padley?'

'We don't know yet. We found him and his van in the car park of a public house. We've taken his van down to the yard. People nearby heard several shots around half past four, but they thought it was a farmer shooting rabbits. Then just before dark the publican's wife went out to her yard to bring in her washing and saw the van in the car park. The rear doors had been left open and she thought something had fallen out.

'But he was shot?' Steve asked again.

'Yes. There's not much else I can tell you yet. We're making enquiries. We'd like to ask you a few questions, Mrs Padley, to see if you can throw any light on it. Could you come down to the station in the morning?'

'I'll bring my daughter,' Steve said. 'What time?'

'When you're ready. Any time in the morning. What was your husband's business, Mrs Padley?'

'Garage owner,' Steve said for her.

'Do you know what he'd be doing in the Dog and Gun car park?'

Lottie could see the policeman's eyes fixed on her. 'He says he's called out quite a lot,' she choked. 'To cars that have broken down. To fix them, tow them in, that sort of thing.'

'I see. Thank you. Tomorrow morning, then?'

Steve closed the front door behind him, and turned back to her. 'Is there any brandy in the house?'

'In the sideboard.' She was shivering.

He came back to the dining room and poured out two tots.

'Come on, drink up, Lottie. You've had one hell of a shock. You'll never need it more.'

It burned her throat, made her cough. 'Medicinal,' he said.

'I was hateful to him this morning, and now . . .' Lottie let the tears come.

'I expect he was hateful to you in return,' Steve said. 'We ought to eat. All we had at lunch time was a sandwich.'

'I can't eat . . .'

430

'Well, I'll have to. Something here is making my mouth water.'

'Steak and kidney pie.'

'My favourite.'

'Waldo's too.'

'You'll feel better with something inside you.'

He was dishing up two platefuls. He set them on the table and she moved down and began to eat. Slowly, between mouthfuls, she told him about finding the guns in the blanket chest; about how she'd told Waldo to get them out of the house.

'Was he shot with one of those, do you think?'

'He promised to take the ferry over to Liverpool and drop them in the Mersey. Get rid of them. But . . . he wasn't one for keeping promises. He wouldn't like throwing them away. It would be like throwing money away to Waldo. He could have kept them.'

'Then it's his own fault if he got shot. No need for you to feel guilty.'

Lottie sniffed. 'I should have had the sense not to marry him in the first place. I was going to tell him tonight . . . that I was going to leave him. The guns and everything . . .'

'You're not the first to feel like that, Lottie.'

'It was one battle after another. There's cheese to follow if you're still hungry. Or cake.'

'Waldo did himself well.'

'Too well.'

Lottie made a pot of tea when they'd finished eating and took it into the sitting room. Father sat beside her on the big settee and put an arm round her shoulders.

'You've hurt each other quite enough. He's gone now,

Lottie. It's over. You don't have to fight him ever again. You don't have to tell him you're leaving him. It'll take a bit of getting over, but you're out of the wood. If you pack a bag, you can come back to Brightland Street with me now.'

'Cliff's asked Connie and Clovis over.'

'They were there when I left.'

She'd planned to go if Waldo turned awkward. Now she said: 'I'd rather stay here, I just want to be quiet, tonight. Anyway, I have to go down to the police station in the morning.'

She could see her father frowning. 'I don't like leaving you by yourself. Not after this. Is the bed made up in the spare room? I'll sleep in there tonight, in case you want anything.'

As she took a cup of cocoa up to her room, she thought of Steven Lancelyn and his place in her family. He was a kind and generous man. She'd made the same mistake that he had, married the wrong person. She couldn't blame him for the way things had turned out and she no longer thought badly of her mother. Waldo had taught her tolerance if nothing else. And yet she hadn't been able to show tolerance to him.

When he was driving Lottie to the police station the next morning, Steve said: 'They might ask about Waldo's black market activities.'

She hadn't thought of that. She hadn't got further than thinking that Waldo was no more. It shook her out of her lethargy, alarmed her. 'What am I going to tell them?'

'Don't talk about your suspicions.'

Lottie frowned. 'I'm not the sort to hide things. I can't.'

'Stick to facts. The hard facts about what he was doing and how he was doing it.'

'I don't know. Well, not exactly. Nothing concrete. He wouldn't talk about it. I know he reached his black market customers through his garage and his vegetable round but not who they were or anything like that.'

'Just answer their questions. You don't have to tell them what you thought, only what you know.'

Lottie sighed. 'I don't think it matters. Nothing can hurt Waldo now. They can't convict him.'

'It's you I'm thinking of, Lottie.'

'I don't care about myself. Waldo's been shot dead. Murdered. I'd like them to catch the person who did that. I want to help as much as I can.'

His hand covered hers in a gesture of comfort.

When a police officer led her to a small bare room for the interview, she said: 'I'd like my father to be with me.' He sat in the chair next to her but said little. He covered her hand with his, and the warmth helped.

The first questions were about Waldo's businesses. The police already had the keys to the garage and the warehouse because he'd had them with him.

'We're searching the premises.'

Lottie was asked about his friends but was unable to give them even one name. He never spoke of friends or acquaintances.

'Enemies then?'

Lottie had to shake her head. He'd kept her well apart from all that.

'Was he planning to meet somebody in that car park? Do you know if he met his killer by appointment?'

She shook her head.

'What was his state of mind yesterday morning? When you last spoke to him?'

'He was upset. So was I. We'd had a . . .'

'A row? An argument?'

'A difference of opinion.'

'What about?'

Lottie told them about finding the guns in the blanket chest and what had happened then.

'He should have brought them straight round here. He might be still alive if he'd done that.'

Lottie thought so too. There were dozens of questions about the guns. She told them what she knew and what Waldo had said about them.

The police officer could tell her little more about Waldo's death. He said: 'We're treating it as murder.'

Both were asked about their whereabouts during yesterday afternoon. Lottie had been in her office and Steve had gone over to the Birkenhead factory, so both had been seen by countless other people.

When at last they came out to the street, Lottie felt exhausted.

'What now?' her father asked. 'Do you still want to go to the Adelphi to see your friends? I could leave a message for them, if you'd rather not.'

Lottie pushed her fringe off her forehead. 'I don't know. Can't think.'

'You could come to work with me, sit quietly in the office or go to Brightland Street. Or stay at home. What d'you feel like doing?'

'Going to the Adelphi. Seeing June and Emily.'

She needed them, but it was Rex she really wanted to see. Waldo's death had changed everything. It was him she needed now. Suddenly she was sure he'd be there.

She opened the door of the car. 'After lunch with them, I'd like to go to Brightland Street. To be with you and Cliff. I can't stay at home by myself.'

'You'd better run back and give the police the Brightland Street phone number. They said they'd let you know if they had any news.'

Lottie did so. When she joined him again, her father said: 'Right, I'll take you home now to get your bag. It can come over in the car with me. I'll drop you outside the Adelphi on my way. Time's going on.'

'I'd like to change.' Connie had lengthened her winter coat with fur strips for the occasion. Lottie pulled a mirror from her handbag and looked at her reflection. She looked drawn and heavy-eyed.

She felt a little better when she'd washed her face and changed. The skirts of her coat swung heavily round her legs, reaching to the new length of three inches above her ankles. It was very fashionable.

June was waiting for her in the hotel reception area. It wasn't more than a minute or two before Lottie was telling her about Waldo's death and the circumstances surrounding it. They sat facing the door, watching for Rex and Emily.

When Emily came in, looking petite and pretty, June got up and waved to attract her attention. Lottie felt a black cloud of disappointment descend on her. Emily had come alone. Today, when she really needed Rex, he hadn't come. She felt close to tears.

'Rex? He couldn't get the day off,' Emily laughed. 'Too

many staff off sick. Flu or something. He hopes to come next time. He told me to be sure to remember all your news so he doesn't miss out.'

Lottie tried to pull herself together, and began the whole story of Waldo over again for Emily's benefit.

'A cruise on the *Durban Castle* is what you need. Do you good,' June suggested.

'Come back to Warrington with me,' Emily pressed. 'Have a few days' rest.'

Lottie was tempted. She knew she'd see Rex if she did, but she didn't know whether it was too soon to be thinking of him again, or, from Rex's point of view, whether she'd left it too late. To think of that was very painful.

'Perhaps a weekend later on,' she said. 'When I've got over the first knock. I'm going back to work tomorrow, that'll help. It's worlds away from anything to do with Waldo. I'll move in with Father and Cliff at Brightland Street. There's nothing to remind me of Waldo there and I won't be alone.'

Lottie knew her news had cast something of a blight over their reunion. It was impossible to talk of such a cataclysmic happening and expect a party atmosphere and light-hearted chatter afterwards. Even so, the time passed so quickly that June had to rush for a taxi to get to the ship on time.

As they watched it merge with the Liverpool traffic, Lottie said: 'I'll walk you to the train.'

She was loath to let Emily go. Emily was in close contact with Rex and she wanted news of him. She asked how he was.

'He's fine, Lottie. Settled down now. He's making new friends and getting out and about with them. Enjoying life.'

Lottie wasn't sure that this was what she wanted to hear.

Emily smiled. 'He said he'd been using me as a crutch but he didn't need me in that way any more. D'you know, he thanked me? Said he could go under his own steam from now on. Though most days he still comes to talk to me in the dining room. He's a lovely person, Lottie. I'm glad he's recovered.'

On the bus going to Brightland Street, Lottie told herself she should be pleased Rex was back to normal but it sounded as though he'd got over her too. She couldn't expect otherwise. Nobody could keep on loving without some encouragement and she'd told Rex to forget about her many times.

It was gone five o'clock and dark when she put her key into the front door. The house seemed empty and cold. There was a note on the table from Father to say that he and Cliff would be working until about seven this evening and then he'd take them both out for a meal, so she was not to bother cooking anything. Lottie wasn't hungry, she'd eaten a fairly substantial lunch.

She lit the fire and for the first time missed Mrs Gully. She'd have had something prepared, so they wouldn't have to go out again. She felt she'd made a mess of her life. She wished Cliff would come home.

To Lottie, the following days crawled at a leaden pace. She was dreading Waldo's funeral, she wanted to shut her mind to it. It came round and she had to face it. The memory of that walk from the church door out to the newly dug grave would stay with her for the rest of her life. She couldn't have made it if she hadn't had Father to cling to on one side and Cliff on the other.

She'd wanted to rush back to work the next day and throw

herself into life at the factory, but Father insisted she took things easy for a week or so.

'You need to give yourself time to unwind and get over all this,' he told her. 'At least two weeks' rest before you think of coming back.'

So she stayed in the house, doing a little dusting and cooking an evening meal for them all. The days dragged, she wasn't used to so much leisure. She felt she ought to be doing more, but couldn't summon the energy. She felt slothful and lazy, spending her afternoons in idleness staring into the fire, turning things over in her mind. If only Waldo had been honest with her, how different things might have been. She thought of Rex too. Emily would surely have told him what had happened and she wondered for the hundredth time what the future would hold for her now.

It was the last day of her enforced rest and she felt ready to go back to work. She was thinking of Rex again when the front doorbell shrilled through the house jerking her out of her reverie. It surprised her because Cliff and Father both had keys, and it wasn't quite time for them to come home anyway.

She found Rex standing on the doorstep, his face a mixture of sympathy and hope.

'I had to come.' The light glinted on his pale hair. 'I hope it's all right?'

'Of course it's all right! Come in,' she pulled him across the threshold out of the cold.

'I was afraid it was too soon.'

'Emily told you what happened to Waldo?'

He nodded. 'The day after you met at the Adelphi.'

'I hoped you might come,' her spirits were lifting.

'I wanted to come straight away, but I didn't want to

intrude. I knew you'd need time . . . Such a terrible thing to happen.'

His arms were round her. 'I couldn't stay away any longer.' Lottie clung to him.

He whispered: 'I always had this gut feeling . . . always knew . . . the time would come when I could be with you.'

Lottie knew, then, that the timing was neither too early for her, nor too late for Rex.

A Mersey Duet

Anne Baker

When Elsa Gripper dies in childbirth on Christmas Eve, 1912, her grief-stricken husband is unable to cope with his two newborn daughters, Lucy and Patsy, so the twins are separated.

Elsa's parents, who run a highly successful business, Mersey Antiques, take Lucy home and she grows up spoiled and pampered with no interest in the family firm. Patsy has a more down-to-earth upbringing, living with their father and other grandmother above the Railway Hotel. And through further tragedy she learns to be responsible from an early age. Then Patsy is invited to work at Mersey Antiques, which she hopes will bring her closer to Lucy. But it is to take a series of dramatic events before they are drawn together . . .

'A stirring tale of romance and passion, poverty and ambition . . . everything from seduction to murder, from forbidden love to revenge' *Liverpool Echo*

'Highly observant writing style . . . a compelling book that you just don't want to put down' *Southport Visitor*

0 7472 5320 X

HEADLINE

Merseyside Girls

Anne Baker

Nancy, Amy and Katie Siddons are three of the prettiest nurses south of the Mersey. They've been brought up to respect their elders and uphold family honour at all times. Then sweet, naïve Katie falls pregnant, bringing shame upon the family's name.

Alec Siddons, a local police constable, cannot and will not forgive his daughter for her immoral behaviour. But Katie isn't the only one with troubles ahead. Amy is in love with her cousin Paul, but owing to a family feud the mere mention of his name is forbidden in her father's presence; and Nancy is eager to wed her fiancé Stan before the Second World War takes him away.

With the outbreak of war, the three sisters offer each other comfort and support. Their mother, meanwhile, is battling with painful memories of the past, and their father lives in dread that his own dark secrets will be revealed. As the war takes its toll on the Merseyside girls they learn that few things in life are more precious than honesty, love and forgiveness.

0 7472 5040 5

HEADLINE

If you enjoyed this book here is a selection of other bestselling titles from Headline

Headline books are available at your local bookshop or newsagent. Alternatively, books can be ordered direct from the publisher. Just tick the titles you want and fill in the form below. Prices and availability subject to change without notice.

Buy four books from the selection above and get free postage and packaging and delivery within 48 hours. Just send a cheque or postal order made payable to Bookpoint Ltd to the value of the total cover price of the four books. Alternatively, if you wish to buy fewer than four books the following postage and packaging applies:

UK and BFPO £4.30 for one book; £6.30 for two books; £8.30 for three books.

Overseas and Eire: £4.80 for one book; £7.10 for 2 or 3 books (surface mail).

Please enclose a cheque or postal order made payable to *Bookpoint Limited*, and send to: Headline Publishing Ltd, 39 Milton Park, Abingdon, OXON OX14 4TD, UK.
Email Address: orders@bookpoint.co.uk

If you would prefer to pay by credit card, our call team would be delighted to take your order by telephone. Our direct line is 01235 400 414 (lines open 9.00 am–6.00 pm Monday to Saturday 24 hour message answering service). Alternatively you can send a fax on 01235 400 454.

Name ....

Address ....

....

....

If you would prefer to pay by credit card, please complete:
Please debit my Visa/Access/Diner's Card/American Express (delete as applicable) card number:

Signature .... Expiry Date ....